REUNION

The blinking light on Graham's private line indicated three messages. The first two were hang-ups. The third contained his secretary's honey-rich voice, which he had come to expect every morning.

"Hi, sweetheart," Jeannie said. "I'm lying here in a bubble bath, thinking of you. I wish you were here with me, but I guess I'll just have to pretend you are until I can get the real thing . . ."

She went on, describing in great detail the pleasures that awaited him. Finally, he breathed deeply and shut off the machine. The mental picture she had painted had aroused him.

"Ooooh," he heard a voice behind him say, then the sound of a door shutting. "The real thing . . ."

"You can't keep leaving messages like that," he said, without turning around. "Someone's bound to hear them."

From behind, she slipped her arms around him, pressing her body against his back, already thinking of new ways to satisfy him . . .

PRIVATE VIEWING
Darcy Lockhart

ZEBRA BOOKS
KENSINGTON PUBLISHING CORP.

ZEBRA BOOKS

are published by

Kensington Publishing Corp.
475 Park Avenue South
New York, NY 10016

First printing: October, 1989

Printed in the United States of America

For Toby and Dakotah

Chapter 1

The '72 Coupe de Ville could eat up the road. He'd often made Las Vegas in three hours. The car didn't have that tight European handling, but he really didn't give a damn because it worked perfectly on American highways. Its eight-cylinder engine hummed softly like a demon possessed with a secret, and its suspension flexed underneath like the legs of an Olympic skier, giving a motionless ride to the occupant. This was the third car of the identical vintage he had owned. He could have afforded new cars each year to fill the six-car garage in his Mulholland Drive home. His wife wouldn't be caught dead in anything but her brand-new, big pearl-white Mercedes.

But the de Ville suited him. It was huge, powerful, and people got out of its way when they saw he meant business. He couldn't stand slow, half-awake drivers; it seemed there were more than his fair share of them in Los Angeles. He often waited in the right turn lane at a stop signal, only to gun the accelerator and race ahead of the other cars when the light turned green.

Why should he, Graham Maddox, wait? He was a busy man. Several dozen projects were continually crowding his brain, demanding that he spend some time to figure them out. Each had its own voice and he didn't feel the need to write any of them down. His wife would have written them down. Would have written down every project and every detail ever mentioned. Her attention to detail drove him crazy.

Had it always? He didn't know. He was vaguely aware of a vast impatience now within him. It moved like a dark pool with its own vortical tidal pull, surging and resting, surging and resting, surging . . . and surging.

"Come *on*, you bastard," he shouted at the Chevette in front of him. The damn thing had a crumpled left fender that would never be fixed. The driver's head was bent down to the side, looking for street numbers shrouded in thick, ever-present ivy.

The canyon was narrow, but the traffic was light. Even though a weak turn signal was flashing through the mangled fender, he floored the de Ville and winged past the Chevette. An approaching van appeared from around the corner, leaning way over on bad shocks. The driver hit his brakes and threw his steering wheel in the opposite direction to avoid hitting the de Ville.

"You fuckin' idiot" followed the tail of the de Ville up the canyon. Three more bends in the road, a quick dip, and the right turn up the street to his house. He'd insisted on this house, up where they could get a view and a little quiet. It was unique, therefore he didn't care that it was smaller. His wife had wanted to stay in Beverly Hills, where the driving was flat and easy and her friends abounded.

He contended that it was only a five,—at the most ten-minute drive down to her beloved B.H. For two weeks she had argued and then suddenly, she had grown quiet. When he had asked what was wrong, she had merely replied that she guessed she was tired of entertaining.

She was the "entertaining queen." What was she talking about?

After twenty-four years of a pretty good marriage, she had decided she wanted to work. She was "just as creative as he," or she could be "if given the chance." He didn't know if she was bored homemaking and entertaining, or if it was her revenge for moving up to the top of the "Fire Gulch" as she referred to it.

The house had had one initial face-lift. She had insisted that *he* make decisions about how his pet project should look. It was comfortable, elegant though not flashy, with a pool and tennis court no one had time for. It might have been ostentatious, except that it equalled the neighbors'.

Now she asked for simple things. "*Producer,* please, Graham. *Executive producer* lacks action."

Glory Bell edged the nose of her '65 Impala carefully into her assigned parking place beneath the apartment building. The car was very wide, and she had to get it between a metal pole and the cement block wall that was not much wider than the broad hood. She cursed softly as she had to back up, turn the wheel, go forward, turn the wheel, back up again, and gradually maneuver in the crowded area so she could go straight into her place.

The manager had reassigned Glory's parking place after she had slightly dented three cars she had been parked next to. (Okay, one was a scrape the length of a brand-new Toyota.) She hadn't meant to do it. She was fine when driving in the street. Honest she was. It was hard to see over the tip of the hood in the parking area and know *exactly* where she was putting the car.

Why didn't she get the seat fixed and the stuffing put back in? asked the manager. It costs a lot to get it reupholstered. I'll take you to Tijuana one day, if you'd like. You can get it done there. Cheap.

The manager was nice, but Glory knew the old woman was shrugging her fat shoulders, realizing that reupholstering was not going to solve the problem.

On one side of the Impala was the cement wall; on the other, a most dilapidated pickup truck used to retrieve supermarket shopping carts. *They* didn't care if her car door hit theirs . . . though everyone *else* in California cared. She had never seen such crazy, possessive people in her whole life. People who yelled at her if she accidentally *touched* their cars with her hand in a parking lot. People in Minnesota had never treated cars like gods. Of course, there, she had to admit, most cars were half devoured by winter's eroding salt when they were just three years old.

She opened her car door the maximum two-foot width

between herself and the pickup, and squeezed out three sacks. Two had groceries and one had goodies from her little shopping spree. Not exactly a *spree.* She couldn't afford one of those. She had picked up a few essential items.

She struggled around the corner to the elevator, her arms loaded with bags, hoping that the elevator had finally been fixed. Why did she always hope for this? It hadn't been fixed in the five months she'd lived in the building. Or, she'd heard, for years before that. She struggled through the heavy door and began to slowly climb the stairs. She lived three flights up.

At the top of the second flight, one of the plastic grocery bags split from the weight and fifteen tins of cat food fell out on the concrete steps. The cans had nowhere to go but down, and she stood there listening to them gathering speed as they rolled.

"I'll come back and get them," she said out loud, not feeling embarrassed, just tired. Why were things like this always happening to her? The cat wasn't even hers. Not officially. A friend had asked Glory to take care of the feline for a week. Glory tried to overlook the fact that that had been four months ago.

Maybe she'd get to like cats.

The girl hadn't really been a *friend* friend. Just a *sorta* friend she had met at the laundromat down the block. Glory wouldn't have been there at all except the manager had neglected to get the washers in the apartment building fixed for a long time. Glory had been in Los Angeles only a month and MariJayne (Glory loved the way she spelled her name) had been there four years trying to make it as an actress.

MariJayne said her boyfriend, who she *said* was a director, was paying for her to go home so she could visit her mom. Glory liked to think the director had also paid for them to go skiing in New Zealand and had married her on a mountain slope. She didn't like to think that the truth was MariJayne had probably never left L.A., but had just moved to another part of the city and didn't want to own a cat anymore.

Glory did not believe she was a sucker. She just had a kind

heart and wanted to help people.

"That's being a sucker out here," said the manager.

The manager was a fat woman who wore cotton print shifts all year round. They came down to her knees and exposed legs on which the hair was always long nubs—never shaved and never fully grown out. She had beady eyes, black hairs above her upper lip, and a tough voice. She always had a cigarette dangling beneath the black whiskers. Her hair was gray and permed and never quite clean. She liked Glory well enough, though she thought the girl "ignernt" about life in general.

Glory hated having to go to the manager's apartment to ask for anything. The place reeked of cigarette smoke, and the manager always talked and talked about pointless stuff for ages on end and Glory never knew how to get away. She hated looking around the apartment at the unwashed dishes and the stacks of newspapers on the floor. The manager, constantly ingratiating herself, went out of her way to help Glory.

Glory was slowly learning how to solve her own problems in her apartment.

Her apartment was a "single." (The manager had referred to it as a "deluxe studio.") Hardly deluxe. The main front area, which served as both living room and bedroom, was a rectangle covered with stained mustard-yellow carpet. The kitchen was a separate nook large enough for a postage-stamp table, a lone chair, an ancient shuddering icebox, a four-burner (with only two working) gas range, a chipped off-gray (should have been white) sink, and a counter that was consumed by a toaster oven and a glass canister of Cheerios. In the bathroom, which occupied the fourth corner of the flat, the tiles had recently been relaid. The manager said Glory was lucky that the rent hadn't been increased. The teensy tub was luxury compared to the rest of the apartment. Glory could sink under a pile of suds and forget her meager surroundings.

Everyone told her to expect roaches, creatures she had never encountered in Minnesota. Though the manager assured her that the place had been "blasted by the eggstermnaters," Glory's heart still pounded whenever she turned on a light in the middle of the night in anticipation of scuttling brown-shelled bodies covering the walls.

The tiny red light on her answering machine was blinking, which meant she had at least one call. "Don't forget the cat food," she reminded herself as she opened the front door and shut it again quickly so she wouldn't lose the coolness in the room. Though Glory couldn't *afford* to run the air conditioner all day, the late September heat would have been unbearable for the poor cat without it. She had visions of coming home to a suffocated cat lying near the turned-off air conditioner with rigor mortis stiffening its joints, sure that its last moments on earth were spent cursing her for ever having taken it into her custody.

She couldn't bear the thought of any creature suffering. She cringed every time she spotted a dark hump ahead on the road and hoped it wouldn't be a pancaked animal.

She went back to the staircase, keeping a wary eye out for the manager who had a sixth sense about when Glory came home and would yell from below that the girl should come down and "visit a spell."

Glory returned to her apartment undetected. The cat came running to her and butted its head and shoulder against her calf. "All right, all right," she told it, setting down her packages on the kitchen table and opening a can of the stinky cat food before putting her few groceries away. She filled the counter canister with Cheerios and stared at it a moment, her mind going way back to a time when she was a little girl and her mother had said, "Just like Daddy, aren't you? Your father loved Cheerios." And her mother's eyes had become very sad as she placed a gentle hand on her small daughter's head.

Glory had not thought of that for a long time. She ate Cheerios every morning for breakfast. She didn't have to think about them. And she didn't think about her job on the set of *Motive.* She didn't think about living without much money. That freed her mind to be creative.

She let her thoughts go and she dreamed up ideas for films. Small films to start with, ones she could produce and direct. That's why she'd gone to film school. That's why she was in Hollywood now, so she could get her foot in the door. That's why she bit her lip on the set when they all thought she was dumb. She wasn't dumb; she was inexperienced. And sometimes she was a little absentminded. That didn't make her a bad person. It's just that sometimes her mind took off and started thinking on its own about film ideas, and she'd be pulled miles away from what she was supposed to be doing (which was usually writing down notes for Richard, the director). Her ideas were much loftier than this commercial prime-time stuff and, she had to admit after facing the daily grind of the work world, perhaps too idealistic.

But Richard tolerated her—she thought he even liked her. He had hired her as a favor to her cinema—school teacher, a Minnesota college pal of his. Though quick-tempered on the set, he often took a moment backstage to tell her she was doing fine. "Learn to relax a little. Just a little. That's all," he'd say.

She took the contents from the third bag and put them on the table. She had bought a few things that she thought might change her image and make her look more Californian. There were a pair of very dark sunglasses with thick red frames, a huge lightweight canvas handbag ("White will get dirty so fast," she could hear her mother say), a pair of red heels higher than anything she had ever walked on in her life, long fake fingernails that she was going to have to figure out how to apply, nail polish that was called "Blushing Fire Engine Red," and a home frost kit for her hair.

She already had all the natural fluff that was needed but could only call her hair color "sorta blond." Bleaching the tips of her hair and the whisps around her face would make her look like a year-round beach bunny. Glory didn't admire beach bunnies, honeys, or hunks, but she realized they were automatically accepted wherever they went. Which was something she rarely felt. She had an evening of work ahead of her.

She remembered her message machine. It was an old cheap relic she had picked up at a garage sale for five bucks.

It didn't have separate tapes for incoming and outgoing messages, so she had had to record her incoming message over and over twenty times,—and that was ridiculous because, she had to admit, she would never be getting twenty messages at one time.

To listen to the calls she had received, she first had to listen to her own voice. When she had first recorded the message, she had tried to make each one sound the same so that no one would know she had only a cheap machine, but then her creativity had taken over and she made each one different.

"Glory, it's Sondra. Richard asked me to remind you to be on the set thirty minutes early tomorrow. *Please* try to make it on time."

"Gloria, it's your old mother. I hate this machine. It costs me money every time I can't get ahold of you. I'll be up till midnight. I love you. Bye, dear."

"Glory, it's me, Sondra, again. I just talked to Richard again. He needs you here an hour early. Try to make sure your cat doesn't get out tonight so that you don't have to find it in the morning. We're going to have some tricky location stuff coming up."

"Hi. Bet you thought I wouldn't call. But I am. I told you I would if you gave me your number. I'm out having a drink and was hoping you could join me. Sorry you're not there. Let's make it another time. Yeah, definitely. See ya tomorrow. Guess ya heard we're all in early. Sleep good, toots."

A huge smile broke out over her face. But why, oh why, hadn't she been there when he called? She was out dolling herself up so he'd pay more attention to her, and here he was calling her. Her heart fluttered and sang. She looked at the bleak apartment and didn't even give the mustard-colored carpet her usual derogatory remark: "French's reject."

Heavy September haze hung thickly over the Hollywood Hills. Ruby Maddox, on her way to pick up the revised draft of a script at the screenwriter's house, stopped her Mercedes at a traffic light. The car satisfied her with its glossy mother-of-pearl paint and its gold trim and gold wire-spoked hubs. Even the hood ornament glinted gold in the afternoon sun.

Sunlight shone densely yellow on an old mansion and Ruby suddenly recognized the street as one she had driven up her first evening in Hollywood. She had been as excited as the kids when they leaned out the open windows of the ancient Nash and asked her if this was where the movie stars lived. Could it really have been twenty-seven years ago?

It was her first time on that street since that arrival day so many years before. She never drove into Hollywood any-more. With only a few respectable neighborhoods left, it was no longer the glamorous area known in the heyday of 1920's movie-making. It barely existed outside the radius of her affluent Beverly Hills and the West Side.

Her memory stung. When she had finally driven into Hollywood, she had promised herself she would celebrate the day of arrival for all the happy years that were to come. Her own day. *Her* day of independence.

And yet the events of the following two weeks had erased that promised anniversary date from her mind. She had forgotten the anniversary, but she could never forget the events.

Ordinarily, she wouldn't have picked up a screenplay, but the writer lived between the studio and her house. She was the producer of *Motive,* the prime-time television series about a down-to-earth detective who travels in a time ma-chine and solves crimes throughout the centuries. It was quickly climbing to number one in the ratings. Though she held the title of producer, her husband Graham was never-theless executive producer and had the final okay on the scripts. The show was on deadline and she wanted him to see the revisions that evening.

When she left the writer's house, she drove west along Mulholland Drive. She enjoyed driving the ridge and rarely got a chance to do it. The freeway was generally faster than the curving road along the rim that divided the San Fernando Valley from the Los Angeles Basin. As the road wound along, she saw views or both sides of the far-reaching city way below. The Mercedes hung closely on the corners, a feather-light touch all that was needed on the steering wheel. Its air-conditioned interior was a restful interlude from the traffic and heat outside. She thought of the old Nash and doubted if she could remember how to drive a standard transmission.

She was spoiled now. Could she even take the hot air? She pushed the button, lowered her window, and leaned forward to shut off the air-conditioning. The breeze was minimal. She lowered the passenger side window, and the breath of the San Fernando Valley aspirated over the leather interior, ruffling the strawberry blond hair on her shoulders and drying the eyelids, cheeks, and neck she so carefully moisturized twice a day and had had lifted only once.

The air was gritty, but she left the windows down. The wind burned her eyes and tugged at her false eyelashes. She felt sweat prick through her skin under her dress and on her forehead under her bangs. She turned left off Mulholland and dropped into the canyon before making another left up the street to her house.

The massive red Cadillac blocked the driveway and garage. Why the heck couldn't that man learn how to drive? But he never had. For the first few years of their marriage, she had bitched about it and he had made an effort. However, now she refused to ride anywhere with him because he was too crazy behind the wheel. He was extremely intense when involved with his projects and didn't have the patience to slow down at all.

She would have one of the kids move the car out of the way. Then she remembered and grinned to herself. The last, Sarah, had moved out three months ago to share an apartment with a friend in Brentwood. The only people around the house were the Garcias, a man and his wife who worked as gardener and housekeeper. But even they had left for the day. Ruby would have preferred to have them live in, but since moving up to the "gulch" (as she had affectionately named it), Graham had insisted on more privacy, which he claimed they couldn't get "with all this damned hired help around."

She honked her horn and moments later Graham came out of the house, wearing shorts and a polo shirt, waving at her with the Cadillac's keys in his hand. He was five feet ten and of medium build. If she had a choice, she might have wished him taller but not any more muscular. Fifty push-ups and sit-ups, as essential to his morning routine as a shower and shave, kept him in shape.

Through his thick black hair, naturally growing gray hairs looked so even that they might have been the work of a clever hairdresser. A heavy crease on his upper nose bridged the intelligent eyes that were the same dark gray color as his hair. The lines on his wide brow reflected intense concentration and rare smiles. Deeply cut grooves, starting on either side of his nose, outlined his mouth and thinned as they disappeared in his strong chin.

She rarely mused on his looks. He wasn't as handsome as he used to be but, as she watched him get in his car, she thought there was something distinguished about him. Even in shorts and bare feet, he had a presence that denoted success and self-assurance.

He backed his car to the side of the driveway, barely missing the prize rose bushes, and turned off his engine. He watched her pull her Mercedes into the garage and walk steadily out to meet him as the automatic door was closing over her head. He liked her well-shaped legs and the way her white dress clung to her waist and rear end.

"Did your air conditioner break?" he asked her, noting her open windows. She greeted him with a polite kiss on the lips.

"No," she smiled, "I was just . . . just . . . I was . . . I guess I was seeing how hot it really was. I don't know."

He waited for her to go in the door first. She handed him the *Motive* script and he padded off across the cool flagstones of the entry hall, back to the living room with the view of the rugged canyon he so loved. He was drinking a Scotch and water, and had freeze-framed the large videocassette recorder.

He explained to her, as she set down her purse and attaché case and kicked off her shoes, "I'm going over the re-edit on *Medical Alert* for the episode that's supposed to air in two weeks. I don't like it. I want your opinion. There's some footage they should have used, because the story's not clear in one place. How many times do I have to explain it to them?"

He amazed her. He executive-produced five shows and was continually on top of all of them. The pre-production, the shooting, the post-production. They all had to have his approval. Her sole show, *Motive,* took all her time and she didn't know where he found the energy or the organization to perpetually track five shows. On top of that, he produced TV movie-of-the-weeks, specials, and theatrical releases.

Through all the years of their marriage, he had been used to her input and did not consider that all her energies were now concentrated on *Motive,* the show he had assigned her to produce four months before. She shifted her thoughts off the next day's shoot and the problems with the *Motive* script she had just handed him, and watched the sequence from *Medical Alert.*

"I may be wrong, Graham," she said gently when he again froze the frame at the scene's end and shook his head in exasperation, "but I think we should see the face, not the back of the head. We assume he's happy, when he really isn't. We need a reverse angle so we understand how he's reacting. The camera needs to be one hundred eighty degrees from where it is here, so we get a behind-the-scenes look at his thoughts. Can you check to see if any footage showing his face has been shot?"

"You're right, baby, you're right. Damn, you're getting smart. I'm calling Jimmy. Telling him to look for a shot like that and then recut that sequence. I'll be right back." He kissed her on the lips again, for that was where they always kissed even if the kisses had grown short and dry. He briefly admired her slight overbite and went in search of his remote phone.

Ruby got up to change her clothes and to heat the dinner Mrs. Garcia, the housekeeper, had left in the refrigerator ready to be microwaved. They always used formal names with each other. The South American woman insisted on calling Ruby Mrs. Maddox, and Ruby, respecting the wishes of the housekeeper, called her Mrs. Garcia. The easy-to-heat dinners were a good system. Even Graham had figured out how to use the microwave. He had an appetite and became quite grouchy when he didn't get his food.

Like all men, thought Ruby.

She listened to the answering machine which, naturally, Graham hadn't bothered to do. Two messages from Martin, one of their children. He needed money again. Guess one of them would have to call him later.

At dinner, over freshly made vegetarian lasagna, Ruby brought up the subject. "Martin called . . . twice. Would you please call him back? I'm afraid my patience is wearing thin with him."

"Heck, Ruby, the kid's just growing up." Graham didn't want to bother.

"He's twenty-five. You let him get by like he's in high school."

"*I* let him get by?" Graham snapped at her.

"*I* sure as hell don't," she replied tersely, putting a forkful of ricotta and pasta in her mouth and chewing deliberately. "Well and fine, then neither of us will call him back."

Ruby's temper delighted him. Normally, she seemed so calm and easy to get along with. That was on the surface. He was one of the few who ever saw her bristle.

"Okay," he replied.

"He's your son," she barked. "Don't you care?"

"He's your son, too."

He didn't feel like fighting over Martin. He couldn't see how Martin's lack of ambition was either of their faults. None of their children showed much interest in show business. He was all for letting them make their own decisions and run their own lives. After all, Julia was doing a fine job of supporting herself in London, and Sarah was contentedly enrolled at UCLA, where she was pursuing an unspecified major.

"I don't know what to do. It pisses me off to even talk about him," said Ruby.

"I don't know what to do, either. Let's change the subject."

"Always avoiding the subject, Graham, is not going to solve the problem."

"I have other problems to solve that are much more immediate and important." He finished off a swallow of wine. "Let me go over that script now."

"Are you coming to the meeting with Garrett and his agent tomorrow?"

"I hadn't planned on it. Is he already asking for more money?"

"I don't think so. They want to discuss next season, since the network's picked us up again. Garrett's just about the most agreeable actor I've ever met."

"Success hasn't spoiled him yet," said Graham, clearing his dishes from the table and putting them in the kitchen sink.

"I'll bet it doesn't," said Ruby, following him into the kitchen. "I'm still in awe of our ratings."

"I wouldn't let my wife produce a show that didn't have all the components of being a hit." Graham opened the refrigerator and poured himself a glass of nonfat milk. "A big hit."

She knew he meant it.

"I'd like to put in a girl. Garrett's character needs a partner, a love interest." Graham said this in a tone that sounded as if he were only making a suggestion. However, Ruby suspected he had already made up his mind.

"It's going so well as it is, Graham, I don't want to spoil the pattern of success."

"It's only aired twice, plus the pilot. There is no established pattern."

"It's *my* show, Graham, and I don't want a female co-star. *Motive* doesn't need a woman. I should be able to make the essential decisions. You told me from the beginning I could make the decisions. *My* decision is *no*."

Graham ignored her, opened the script, and put all his concentration on the dialogue. He didn't say another word. Ruby fumed but, as usual, it was futile to provoke him by continuing the discussion.

She knew one thing. Graham was not going to railroad her and add any role to the show without her approval. Ever.

Margi didn't mind meeting Bob at a motel, but why did he have to choose one so far out? Pomona. Okay she didn't know much about Pomona. She had the address in her purse, on the scrap of paper he had slipped into her hand.

No one had seen him do it. But when he had stepped close to her, she had smelled his sweat mixed with cigarette smoke. She didn't mind that he smoked. When he finished a cigarette, he flipped the butt with his finger, a gesture she had admired in boys she had known in high school. He could aim the glowing end of a cigarette and drop it exactly where he wanted to. Of course, he hadn't been in high school for twenty-eight years, and she for almost that long. It was just an action that was tough, and she admired tough men.

He handed her the note with the address. The only person who had been close by had been that pesky Glory (what a stupid name) that air-head production assistant who talked in a squeaky high voice that drove almost everyone on the set crazy. *She* might have seen the note slip between them, but she was almost certainly too dumb to realize anything.

Then Garrett, the star (he wasn't too stuck up as far as actors went) had come off the set needing his hair fixed, and Margi had quickly shoved the address inside her bra, winked at Bob, and whispered, "I'll see ya later."

I-10 took her straight to Pomona. Still a long way for a married lady to have to go. But, if she thought about it, he was worth it. Yeah, he was definitely worth it.

She could feel the inside of her bare thighs touching under her soft red dress. She wore what he wanted her to wear—silky stockings hooked to a garter belt and no panties. He would be waiting for her, ready to take her into his strong arms and press her against him. He would be lying on cool sheets with a single candle burning in the room, the curtains drawn against any final traces of daylight.

She was lucky she had a job with long, irregular hours. Nobody ever expected her home at an exact time. If she had gone home this evening, she would be cooking dinner for anyone who was there, running a load of wash, and picking cat hairs off her favorite chair while she tried to watch TV. Sometimes she needed the boredom of home. But not often.

Her job hairdressing on the set each day should have exhausted her instead of giving her extra energy. Denny, the makeup artist, always complained about how tired he was. She put up with his whining. She'd known him fifteen years, and for all his complaining, he did a remarkable job with actresses' puffy faces first thing in the morning. He was a good friend, though her husband was skeptical about any friendship with "a queer."

"You wouldn't know he was gay if you just met him," she often said. "He doesn't flaunt it."

"I think they're weird, that's all. I don't want a thing to do with him, all right?" Her husband wasn't angry about homosexuals, he just preferred to pretend they didn't exist.

She had the radio turned on an "oldies but goodies" station, fifties and sixties rock 'n' roll. She sang as she drove, never missing a word to the lyrics she knew by heart, her loud voice remarkably in tune, though husky from the cigarettes she smoked.

Her high school dream had been to be a singer. She and three other girls had formed a short-lived group they called "Bobbi and the Sockettes." She had been Bobbi, the lead singer, and had worn sexy, brightly-colored silk stockings instead of their namesake ankle apparel. Unfortunately, she had been years ahead of her time. Though record companies didn't say a word outright, she knew the Sockettes had been turned down for being too provocative.

Margi wasn't a girl to give in to depression. She was a fighter and knew she had to make a living. She put her dream of being a singer on the back burner and went to school. Hairdressing was a respectable profession. People would always spend money to make themselves more beautiful.

Daylight was thinning. She noted the pack of headlights behind her. She pulled on the Pontiac's lights (her husband would have never let her drive a foreign car). She checked her makeup, carefully dabbing at the black smudge below one of her deep brown eyes. She liked wearing a lot of dark, dramatic makeup. It was fun. It made her feel sexy. Her eyes were flashy and beautiful; Bob called them exciting. She smiled, knowing she would be with him in just a few minutes.

When he opened the door, she stood before him in her low-cut red dress, her black hair in soft curls two inches above her shoulders, cut to show off her jawline. He reached out a hand to touch her face, letting the back of it drift across her lips, gently pushing a knuckle against her front tooth.

She thought he was very sexy. He knew how to move. He knew what she needed. He knew how to make her scream in delight. He was six-two, with a little bit of a belly. She didn't mind it and hardly noticed it when they were in bed together. But he was strong and in good shape for a guy in his mid-forties. His dark gray hair had receded halfway back on his scalp and he wore it short. It matched his thick mustache, which revealed only the middle portion of his lower lip.

He smiled at her—he was always smiling at her—his face set with the deep lines of a man who works hard for his living. He pulled her into the room and shut the door behind them. He didn't like her to say a word. He took her purse from her hand and neatly tossed it into a chair without even looking.

He pulled her against him, feeling her small-boned body against his large one. His massive hands surrounded her rear and pressed the dress between her legs till a trace of moisture came through the material. He liked the silence and liked her responsiveness. She stood motionless and waited for him to tell her what he wanted.

He reached under the neckline of the dress to feel her large breasts. They were firm and velvety. He forced one nipple above the edge of the dress, pinching it lightly until it was darkly flushed. He touched his fingertip first to his tongue and then rubbed it lightly on the erect bud. He dropped that one below the edge of the dress and roughly brought its twin into the open air, pinching harder and hearing Margi's breath quicken.

Her hand slipped to his stomach, undoing two shirt buttons and feeling the warm skin underneath. She reached around his waist and hugged him, luxuriating in a feeling of abandon. She thought of nothing else but the man there with her.

He let her touch his upper body but liked teasing himself, so he stopped her from pushing her hands under the waist of his pants. She was so petite that he loved enfolding her in his arms and burying his face against hers, devouring her mouth, pushing his lips against her teeth, invading her mouth with the whole of his tongue, conquering her tongue and knowing she was submissive and waiting for his wishes.

He decided he wanted her in her red dress. With his mouth still over hers, he clawed at the bottom hemline of the dress, pulling it high enough to get his hand underneath. He lightly snapped the elastic of the garter against her thigh and ran his fingertips along the silky tops of the stockings. His taunting caress was the center of her attention, of her body, of her being. His fingers moved by millimeters, climbing steadily upward, touching every tiny nerve ending on her inner thigh so agonizingly slowly that by the time he reached her velvety warm folds, she went limp for a moment.

He moaned as he supported the weakened body and gently moved her to the bed, supporting her with one great arm and unfastening his restrictive pants with the other. He tugged down on his zipper and pulled himself free. He stood rigid over her quivering body, and as she reached to touch him, he stopped her and flattened her against the bed with his body. She couldn't move under him.

He knew the look in her eyes. She was trying to spread her knees beneath him, but he held her and wouldn't let her. She wriggled and softly cried, "Please, now, please," but his hand went over her mouth and silenced her. The hot breath from her nostrils blew over the back of his hand as her head twisted and turned trying to free itself.

She was ready for him now. He had made her wait, and now she was ready. Still pressed beneath him, he pulled her dress to her waist and roughly pushed one of her knees to the side, pressing his heated cock on top of her, letting it linger for a long moment before he entered her. She pushed up to meet his thrust and cried against his hand, as she did every time he entered her for with his size, the pain was greater than the pleasure for a short instant before she relaxed and moved in rhythm with him.

His shirt, smelling of his sweat and laundry soap, was against her chest and face as he slid slowly in and out, and she shut her eyes and gave in to the sensations that were overtaking her. She struggled against him, her breath caught in his shirt, her knees caught by his legs that anchored them apart. But he didn't change his steady pattern and finally she could stand it no more. The heat surged through her, blinding all her other senses and exploding in her center like a rose blooming in time-lapse photography; the bloom expanding and expanding and then, when full to its maximum, its intensity coming in waves and waves like the soft multilayered petals.

He gave her a second to catch her breath and strengthen her muscles so she could hold his rigidity inside her. The friction burned him ever so slightly as he pushed harder and harder, bound by a velvet glove that held him tightly, refusing to yield its grasp. He couldn't escape, drawn deeper and deeper, his fluid center being pulled through him like a trail of liquid fire, the sensation so strong that he yelled one final animal cry and felt the molten flame burst from him.

Later, when she had taken off her clothes and cooled on the bed, she arose to draw water for a bubble bath. It was her second favorite thing to do with him. She lured him to the tub, where they sat together in relaxing warmth and talked.

Margi blew a handful of suds from her hand and watched the tiny bubbles float in the air. "I wonder if I should call the kids."

"Heck, let 'em be. They're teenagers and can take care of themselves. You always worry too much."

"That's not true," she chuckled. "I hardly ever worry, but that's because they're good kids."

"They're *my* kids. What do you expect?"

"What an ego you've got, my darling," she said, softly

jesting. "As if *I* wasn't there at all."

He rubbed her shoulders and let his hands slip around to caress the breasts he knew so well. His lips nibbled her neck. "You were there. I could *never* forget you were there. Why don't you turn around, Mrs. Owens, and give me a kiss."

She smiled and flopped over in the suds. "I'll give *you* a kiss if you give *me* a kiss, Mr. Owens," she said, her mouth finding his and tasting a trace of soap on his lips.

Hole 14 was an engineering marvel.

It was clearly the most well-designed setup Denny had ever seen. With the correct amount of force, the golf ball would glide up a three-inch-wide ramp, over the camouflage carpet (which is very hard to judge distance upon) and, if timed perfectly, fall between shooting gallery ducks, down a spiral, and roll out on the lowest level, heading right into the hole.

There was the chance, however, that the ball could make it up the ramp but then get knocked around by one of the ducks. If that happened, the ball would fall down another hole and end up a dog's leg downhill from the hole.

Two Saturdays ago, before playing the Southern Gold Cup Tournament, Denny had sat for almost an hour near Hole 14, counting the seconds it took for a ball to go up the ramp and the seconds the ducks were apart. Though he had made a hole-in-one during the tournament, he wasn't convinced that skill, rather than luck, had guided the ball between the ducks.

Hole 14 was the ideal. When he built his chain of miniature golf courses, all the holes would be like this: perfectly engineered, creatively thought out; an interesting challenge to the player. Tournament stuff.

Not like the boring, mundane routine mini-golf courses you saw spread across midwest America, located on highways leading out of town, next to drive-ins that still sold malts and homemade onion rings, in the part of America where you found bugs squashed all over the front of your car. Unlike Southern California, the rest of America yielded swarms of mosquitoes on any given summer evening. He'd have to remember to get those purple lights that zapped bugs.

He had never had to scrape bugs off his Alfa Romeo. He'd had it painted the #3 medium blue shade of eyeshadow from his most reliable makeup source. The shadows were wonderful. They never got oily or flaked under one-hundred-footcandles. He loved the #3 medium blue—rich, light luxurious. It reminded him of the sky he had seen once—probably as he sat with a malt in hand—watching the sun set over the Midwest.

He was wending his way home from the studio on the side streets. He never drove the freeways. The side streets were slower, but they always moved. The Alfa was the right size and had enough acceleration to get through yellow lights. He needed to stop for groceries and at Royce Beauty Supply. He was in no hurry. Jeff was taking out a client for dinner and wouldn't be home until later.

When driving, he usually thought about miniature golf. He refused to spend his spare time thinking about his job. Puffy-faced actresses and bloodshot-eyed actors were to be faced first thing in the morning and not to be dwelled on at any other time. He'd been in the business too long to worry that he wouldn't apply the makeup correctly for the lighting conditions. He was a pro. He never got it wrong. Sometimes the director asked him to make a change. But he never got it wrong.

Denny was just under six feet and quite thin. He had been a vegetarian for twelve years, not because he felt sorry for animals, but because his body felt healthier when limited to beans, tofu, fruits, and vegetables. Though his hair had turned prematurely white while he was still in his twenties, Jeff thought Denny looked only thirty-one, ten years younger than his actual age. His neatly trimmed mustache was salt-and-pepper gray, a contrast to his snowy head. His eyes twinkled a blue that matched the #3 eyeshadow.

Easy-listening music floated around him in the car. He had neglected to buy a tape deck, since numerous L.A. stations, with tremendously powerful signals, sent waves of the velvety music far out over the desert and along the coast. As he wasn't big on driving, the farthest he ever took the Alfa was to mini-golf tournaments around southern California. Then he was never out of radio range of his favorite stations.

He lived up Beachwood Canyon, an area of old-Hollywood architecture. Cream-colored stucco, red-roofed houses, crowded along hillsides and in furrows, were reminiscent of Italian villages. He rented a one-bedroom apartment in a building that housed four units. It was built against the hill, so that each apartment was on a different level and had its own patio and small garden. Lush tropical foliage, planted in the thirties when the place was built, neatly landscaped the walls, stairways, and corners. There were no rough edges. They were hidden by the intense green, jungly quality of the growth.

Jeff, who had moved in with Denny three years before, had brought his twice-per-week Mexican maid who waxed the hardwood floors until they shone richly and polished the wavy old glass in the windows so sunlight could fall across the tawny floors.

Jeff was the perfect roommate—and lover. Five years older than Denny, he was discreet, loyal, and handsome in his own way. He and Denny enjoyed many of the same things: evenings at the Hollywood Bowl, equity-waiver theatres, jazz clubs along the Strip, their great gray mama cat who had borne three litters of kittens, their Sunday brunches at the Marina.

They had met on the set of *Warning Sign,* a TV movie produced by Graham Maddox. Jeff, an agent, had come to watch a young, virile actor for whom he had contracted a costarring role. Bringing the stud to the makeup table before the day's shooting, he had been on the verge of suggesting how the young face might be contoured, when he noted Denny's skill and self-confidence. Jeff stayed near the makeup table most of the morning talking to Denny, practically forgetting to watch the performance of the youthful stud who was stripped to only his unzipped jeans and luring a buxom actress down upon a soundstage beach.

After the day's shoot, the stud forgotten, Jeff had followed Denny home to take-out Chinese food. They had a lot to talk about. They had so much in common.

This was a relief to Denny, after all the excruciatingly boring time he had spent with Art. Art had been rooted to sex. Art wanted a relationship at the same time that he wanted lots of lovers. Denny had scarcely been able to get an intelligent word out of him even about as simple a thing as an international news event.

But Jeff was different. He had recently joined a new agency. A dynamic firm with leads, pull, real power. They had actors under contract who commanded the best deals in town. Jeff never sat still. He was always on the phone. Always friendly. Polite. Talking, talking. Always lots of ideas.

Jeff was interested in Denny's job, and read the scripts his roommate brought home in case there was a spot for one of the agency's minor players. He rarely accompanied the champ to mini-golf tournaments, though he had expressed interest in investing in Denny's chain of golf courses.

Denny's gut glowed rich and happy when he thought of Jeff and their life together. They were the best of friends, truly the best of friends. Denny didn't need or desire anyone but Jeff.

Denny pulled up their narrow dead-end street. He was surprised to see Jeff's car in the carport, its tail end blocked by a dilapidated Volkswagen Bug with Kansas license plates. Denny pulled in front of his neighbor's garage, with its "No Parking Violators Towed" sign reigning at eye level.

Denny placed the small cardboard box with his three-hundred-dollar makeup purchase under one arm, a sack of groceries under the other, and went down the curving flight of stairs to his apartment. He hummed "New York, New York" (with the drum beats) to himself as he unlocked the door and pushed it open. He expected to see Jeff in the living room, but the apartment was silent. He put the makeup on the dining table and the groceries in the kitchen.

He stood in the dining room and listened. The cat brushed against his leg, and all seemed quiet as the evening glow, reflecting off west-facing windows across the canyon, spread orange light throughout the apartment.

Then he heard a moan from the bedroom, through its closed door.

His heart stopped. What if Jeff had been injured? He was always digging things out of the high closets. Always standing on shaky chairs to do it.

Denny opened the door carefully, fully expecting to see Jeff on the floor with a broken leg. What he saw was even more surprising.

There was the bed, with the knotted top sheet fallen to the floor and the bottom sheet rubbed off so half the mattress was showing. And there was Jeff, his dark hair curling on his thin arms and legs, lying with a boy of about sixteen. The boy's blond bangs had fallen across his forehead and his flushed, soft lips were opened in surprise as Jeff's arm held him around his firm, taut waist.

Denny didn't move. He could barely react.

Will leaned back in the wooden chair and looked out the grimy plate glass window of the bar to his scooter parked in front. It, too, was dirty, the black Harley tank devoid of luster. Its whole appearance was that of a beetle, resigned to death, whose shiny shell has dulled in summer's heat and dust. Beer neon blinked smudged pinks, blues, and whites at the far edges of the window. He avoided looking at the reflection—the inside of the joint and his own face. Instead, his gaze was concentrated on the line of bikes outside, his mind as far away as he could get from Spud's, the "best damn biker bar in L.A."

His chair creaked as he balanced on its back legs, the rhythmic rocking sound reminding him of a gentle night wind blowing a screen door on a porch back and forth. Was it a particular porch? Oh, yes, he could see it, broadly lapping two sides of the farmhouse. And he could see her sitting there, singing in the soft darkness of starlight, unaware that he had stopped to take in the breath of the night and inhale the pure air her sweet notes hung on.

She was forever in that night, just out of his reach, waiting patiently for him. She knew a lot of songs. She made up a lot of songs.

The beer bottle in his hand had grown warm. He glanced at the bar to see Joe nervously talking to a girl and keeping a wary eye on his friend who preferred to sit alone at a table. The tabletop was tattooed with gouged-out names and symbols, many a drunk biker having tried to copy the vein-green artistry on his skin to the wood. Few had succeeded. The tabletop was a mess, with barely a flat place left to set down a beer.

Joe moved quickly from the bar with a cold beer in his hand. "Here ya go, Will."

"Thanks, Joe," said Will, finishing the warm beer with a long swallow and handing his friend the empty bottle.

Joe went back to the bar and tried to explain to the girl why his friend sat alone. In fact, Will had been doing that for the past three weeks since he'd come to L.A. He'd sit and stare out the window and never socialize with anyone else in the bar. Joe realized Will's unfriendliness was wearing thin the edges of a few erratic personalities around the place, but his friend was not in a smiling mood and nothing could induce him to pay much attention to the regular customers.

Will was a lean six feet three, his upper body broad and his hips narrow. His chest was wide and strong, the muscle not thickly meaty but sinewy. The arms under his faded denim shirt were hard to the touch even when relaxed, and his hands, though large, had refined fingers, and, therefore, were not awkward. His thighs were long and thin, almost as long as his lower legs.

His hair waved roguishly on his shoulders. It was the same golden brown as the eyes of a sheepdog he'd once owned. His own eyes were a deeper brown, set wide above his high cheekbones. He wore a long and sweeping mustache, the same color as his hair. He kept it neatly trimmed, and it curved over the edges of his jawbone and accentuated his strong, square chin. There was a time when it had curved around a smile as well, but now his face was set in a hard look, an angry look at the world around him.

He couldn't seem to move, to motivate himself.

Joe had come to Oregon and begged that Will ride back to California. Joe cared. Hard to believe that a nervous, punky personality that most people chose to ignore worshipped Will so much. He had been lost without Will. He was so proud of his friend—logger, biker, part-time stuntman—and bragged about him relentlessly. Will had had more than one scrap because Joe believed there was no one in the world tougher than his buddy. A thin smile crept across Will's face as he mused on how people end up with friends they never thought they'd have. Joe had so desperately needed a friend that Will could have never hardened his heart and ignored the little guy.

The rustic tavern, situated in an uninhabited canyon north of the city, had a worn wooden floor, a half-dozen of the mutilated tables, a bar running the length of the room along the back, and a low ceiling. The jukebox and cigarette machine, partnered between the door and the bar, emitted the only whitish light in an otherwise dusky blend of reds and ambers. The front door had had a glass panel at one time but was now patched with several pieces of plywood. The mirror behind the bar had been broken so many times that the largest fragments were all that were still tacked behind the liquor bottles. It was amazing that the huge plate glass window in front was still intact. Three bullet holes could be found near a vertical crack on its surface.

On the wall by the jukebox was a bulletin board, plastered with photos of the regulars, their ol' ladies, their bikes, their parties, their friends, their escapades. On the ceiling were nailed mangled beer cans from the insiders' personal contest, competing to see who could totally—and perhaps creatively—destroy a beer can with only one hand and, if desired, the teeth. The bar was going through its second generation of clientele and some of the cans dated back to the days when they were opened with church keys. The cans all hung like bats affixed to the roof of their cave, suspended indefinitely over the guano below.

The noise of a beer can about to join its tribe above sounded six inches from Will's right ear. He had not been paying attention to the crowd, but his mind quickly focused on the crushing metal. He continued to stare straight ahead, depending on his peripheral vision to catch any quick movements. He wasn't afraid. He was annoyed. They could have just left him alone. But no, they always have to hassle. Always.

He turned his head slowly to see a two-hundred-sixty-pound mammoth, in a dirty T-shirt that didn't cover his breaching belly, wadding the aluminum into a little ball. Shit, the guy outweighed Will by seventy pounds.

Will's only movement was to squint his eyes at the growling mass before him. "Somethin' the matter?"

"I don't like you, you son of a bitch."

Will turned his gaze toward the window again. "Lots of folks don't like me," he replied.

Without being obvious about it, Will was keeping an eye on the reflection now. Joe had slid off his bar stool and slipped in between the quickly gathered crowd. The mammoth threw the beer can ball onto the table in front of Will, where it bounced off onto the floor. Will was aware that it was the only sound in the entire bar, except for the jukebox changing a record. He waited for the song that never came on. The bartender must have shut off the machine.

Will felt like being left alone. He didn't feel like being challenged. But he was being pushed into it.

"Is there something you want?" he asked the fat biker.

"I want you outta here."

"I ain't causing no trouble. Just trying to drink a beer in peace. You don't look like a manager to me."

"You think you can hang your face out here and act like an asshole and everybody's going to like you?"

"*They* should leave me alone, because I'm leaving them alone, and everything'll stay real peaceable." Will felt the energy of the crowd behind him. He knew they wanted to see a fight, wanted to watch the biggest bully of the place knock someone over the head.

"I think you need to have some manners taught you," said the giant, doing his damnedest to provoke the unprovokable stranger.

"Why don't you let me buy you a beer?" asked Will, trying to remain relaxed-looking while steeling his muscles for swift maneuvers if he needed them.

"I wouldn't let a scum-bag like you buy me a beer if it was the last beer on earth," replied the mammoth, wobbling unsteadily on drunken legs.

This guy sure had something bothering the hell out of him, thought Will, but he felt too apathetic to let some jerk he didn't know draw him into a fight. He didn't feel like fighting. He didn't feel one ounce of anger move through him. The guy was like a huge horsefly buzzing around your wet legs and back when you've just gotten out of swimming in a lake and you're trying to dry off in the sun. It moves in to bite you, you keep waving it away, but you feel too relaxed to get up and move.

The biker stepped closer, his hairy, sweaty belly inches from Will's nose. "I heard tell you come down from Oregon," said the growling voice.

The hair on Will's neck bristled. "What about it?" he replied.

"Heard you was involved in a mighty ugly accident there."

Will clenched his teeth. "I don't think it's any of your business."

"I don't give a shit what you think. Why're you here? They run you outta Oregon?"

The anger that had been nonexistent seconds before snarled like a boiling, capped geyser deep in Will's gut. He slowly rose to his feet, keeping one hand on the neck of his beer bottle.

"Listen, you fat slime, *nobody* mentions Oregon and *nobody* mentions what happened there. You understand?" As he said those last words, his voice low and menacing, he cracked the beer bottle against the edge of the table and brandished the formidable jagged glass in the monster's face.

The biker's jaw dropped as he saw rage storm across Will's face, darkening the eyes, hardening every muscle. Will swiped the bottle as the massive belly and the biker took one quick step backward.

"You fucking slob, I don't even know you and here you are thinking you're somebody by bringing up what ain't any of your business."

The biker's concentration was on the ragged beer bottle. Will brought his fist up and nailed the biker in the groin. As he doubled over, Will kicked him in the side of the head and the hulk fell to the floor. Will kicked him again in the stomach, a solid blow with his black leather steel-toed boots. The biker gasped for air and tried to grab the leg of Will's pants.

But Will was quick, and he stepped out of the man's grasp. The crowd was around them in a large semicircle, and Will held them at bay with the broken bottle. It was not the jagged glass but rather the possessed look of a madman that made them keep their distance. He backed away from the prostrate biker, his lips curling, the adrenaline urging him to pulverize the blubber on the floor.

Then he vaguely heard Joe near him, "Will, Will, it's all right, buddy. Come back over here. Come back over and sit down. He won't bother you no more." Joe touched the shoulder of the arm that was not attached to the bottle. He tugged gently on the shirt and Will backed up, staring straight into the eyes of all the onlookers, warning them not to fuck with him anymore.

The scroungy crowd had violence in their faces, the jean-and-T-shirt-clad men ready to mangle the stranger who fought swiftly and precisely.

It was a tense moment, for Will was in their territory and establishing his dominance.

"I'll take on anyone who wants to fight," he told them, "one at a time. Who wants to knock the shit out of me?" It was a reverse challenge, their tough idol already fallen before them. Will was confident. His .38 was tucked in the back of his pants and he felt no reservations about using it.

But they didn't make a move toward him.

Will shot them a grin and said, "If nobody wants to knock the shit outta me, then maybe someone'll buy me a beer?"

"I will," said the bartender, thankful that he hadn't had to call the police. The bar could be shut down if violence summoned the law too many times.

Will sat at a table with his back to the wall, where he could watch the bar and look out the window. The jukebox had started up again and the crowd filled the bar and a few tables, their voices raucous as they casually glanced at Will. The fat biker sat alone at a table across the room and coldly stared at Will. Joe was suggesting they leave when the bartender brought Will the promised cold beer.

"I'll buy *him* one," said Will, nodding at the beaten biker and digging a couple of crumpled dollar bills out of his pocket. "Thanks for the beer and I'm sorry about the trouble."

The bartender smiled slyly. "Can't say I've ever seen Mad Dog get the crap knocked out of him before he even got a swing in."

Will drank his beer quickly, the coolness flowing into his gut, easing the burn of the anger that was always centered in him. It never quite left, though he tried hard to ignore it. He wanted to get on his bike and race through the night. The air outside would be hot and smoggy, but he didn't care. He just wanted the vibration of the bike on the road; the loud, intense hum filling him and driving away the bitterness that ran through his veins.

He stopped at Mad Dog's table on his way out. "See ya tomorrow night," he said, and walked steadily from the bar, Joe at his heels.

Chapter 2

The camellia half shrouded the window, its shiny leaves a shadowy green, the delicate flowers soft pink, their texture like crepe paper. A tall sycamore stood ten feet from the camellia, its shade luxuriously cooling the lawn beneath it. The lawn covered a small, well-kept courtyard within the wall of the single-story studio bungalows. Neatly trimmed bushes edged the oval of even, tender-bladed grass, and brightly-colored flowers crowded the brown dirt of their curved beds.

Ruby's desk stood kitty-corner in her office so she could look out at the garden. In the two months since they'd been filming *Motive,* she had hardly gotten a chance to do much decorating of her quarters. Longtime employees had been nervous when Mrs. Maddox had become a fixture rather than a wife passing through whom they all had to scrape and bow to. Now they did it all the time, and she had slowly become aware of how cautious they were around her. She knew she had to make them more comfortable when near her, but she wasn't sure how to go about it.

A thick pile, richly-hued Persian carpet took up ninety percent of the floor space. The chairs she had chosen were thin-legged mahogany with caned seats. She had a mahogany bookcase as well, but it contained only a few volumes because she couldn't decide which ones to bring from home. The walls were white, and she liked their simplicity. Only one painting hung on the wall, and she was beginning to think she might not bother getting more. It was a Texas landscape she had painted many years before. Southern prairie. She needed it because it reminded her of where she had come from, of how long ago that had been.

Graham resented the painting, so for many years it had been locked in the duel of a storage closet. She had learned that when Graham didn't like something, it was a lot easier not to argue with him about it. He never really *said* anything; he just sneered silently and shrugged his shoulders with shivering disgust.

But how that painting had freed her when she'd hung it in her new office.

The morning sun slanted in at an angle through the courtyard, under the sycamore, and washed the canvas in its glow. She enjoyed watching the painting as much as she enjoyed gazing at the garden. Graham rarely came into her office, but when he did, he made a point of standing with his back to the painting. There had been another time in her life, and it was funny to think that Graham, after all these years, was still jealous of that fact.

She glanced at her watch. She had five minutes before the ever-punctual Dillon Hughes came in for their meeting. Dillon was meticulous in a lot of ways. Graham had hired him because Dillon could be relied on—without fail.

Dillon was the production controller who kept track of the finances, making sure the productions stayed within budget. Graham said Dillon was honest, a rarity in Hollywood, especially after the greased palm his predecessor, Bert Levy, had become too evident. Graham was no fool. He realistically expected someone to take advantage of him . . . up to a point. After that, it became stealing.

So here was Dillon. Young and smart and too conscientious to ever take a cent under the table or to write off dinner with his girlfriend on his expense account. Reliable and uncorrupted at thirty years old.

Ruby didn't *dislike* Dillon. She just didn't *like* him. He seemed like too much of a kiss-ass to her. He was pleasant. He was courteous. He was on top of all their productions and knew the current standing of each project, whether it was in story conferences or rehearsal or on location or being edited. He didn't seem to have many ideas of his own. He just did his job to perfection Graham's specifications.

Dillon walked into Ruby's office, the two buttons of his lightweight sports coat closed over his muted rose shirt. His slacks were soft gray, as were his shoes. He was always the perfect dresser. He stood smiling, his teeth a flashing white line of enamel, his face clean-shaven and looking very, very smooth, as though he had shaved only minutes before. His hair was dark brown and fashionably trimmed to an in-between length, which reflected his conservative taste. His face was broad through the cheekbones upon which there was always a healthy flush, and his large, intelligent eyes glistened with enthusiasm.

He was "on," always on. How did he do it?

"Good morning, Dillon," said Ruby, watching him draw a chair up close to the front of her desk.

He put a pile of papers before her on the desk, sat back, and gleamed his smile. His eyes danced off hers and took in the room in a sweep, pausing to contemplate the camellia's pink, which was like the inside of a lip, through the Glass-Plus panes.

"Good morning, Mrs. Maddox," he replied. "How are you today? May I get you anything? Coffee?"

"Thank you, no," she said. "I had one cup at home and I've almost cut it out altogether."

"I know what you mean," he said, producing a gold pen from his jacket pocket. "I haven't drunk caffeine in five years and I feel just great."

"Well, there's something about the taste of fresh-brewed coffee in the morning that I can't resist. It's one of those things that it's hard to say no to. Let's see what you brought in. How much more will it cost us to put another lead in *Motive?*"

He held out the top page of his report. She read it thoroughly, double-checking figures that Graham would have known without looking. Settle down, she told herself, you just got into the business. Sure, Graham can guess at things, but he's been doing it for years. She could see that there was easily enough money in the budget for another actor or actress. Graham was really pressing for a female character. It was strange, though; so unlike him to go back on a previous decision. After all, when the show was in development, he had said that a woman character was totally unnecessary.

"If we talk with Garrett about it," said Ruby, "what do you think his reaction will be?"

"As you know, the ratings have been remarkable. I don't know Garrett very well, but if he's like other actors, especially those with meteoric rises, he'll be unhappy about sharing the camera—and the residuals—with anyone else."

"I'm meeting with him and his agent in an hour. Graham wants me to tell them that we're putting in an episode which will introduce a woman."

"There's not much Garrett can do. He's under contract for the season. He should be happy he's acting. He's damned lucky to have landed the role of Frank Harrison."

Ruby looked up at him, her eyes narrowing for a moment and then widening again. "Are you telling me you don't like Garrett Gage?" Her tone was almost one of insult. After all, it was she who had pushed hardest to get the unknown actor onto the show.

Dillon hesitated. "It's just that Frank . . . well, I think Frank's a lot smarter than Garrett."

Ruby had to admit to herself there was nothing kiss-ass about that comment. Inwardly, she smiled. Dillon was becoming more palatable. "Have you ever mentioned that to Graham?" she asked him.

"Would it make any difference if I did? Does my opinion amount to something with him?"

She smiled and shook her head in empathetic acknowledgment of what he was saying. She was learning with firsthand experience what she had only vaguely been aware of before: Graham was lord and master of all his productions. She held out her hand for the rest of the papers. "What else have you brought?"

"I need you to approve these other budgets. A couple of revised ones. For the episode we're shooting in two weeks. The writers have added a lot more stunts."

They worked together for forty-five minutes before she excused herself for her meeting with *Motive*'s star. Dillon sat in her chair going over her signatures and gazed out the window. Mrs. Maddox was awfully businesslike around him—around everyone on the set, for that matter—as if she were afraid to let her guard down. Dillon could see she had gotten herself into a more competitive situation with her husband than she'd ever imagined. It had been easy for Graham Maddox to give his wife an office and a producer's title; it had not been so easy for him to accept her success.

Dillon had kindly explained many things he would not have had to clarify to someone who had been producing longer. Yet he admired Ruby. You only had to tell her something *once* and she remembered it.

Ruby had lucked out being related to someone in the industry. If he, likewise, had kinfolk in the business, a few phone calls might have put him near the top in a short time. But he had moved to Hollywood at the age of twenty-four, without knowing a soul, and the past six years had been a long, uphill struggle. He had learned a lot, had made contacts, and had quickly realized never to burn bridges behind him. He was a careful politician and, at times, wondered at his own self-control around the bullshit he put up with.

Dillon was playing the game right. He was "paying his dues," that old Hollywood term that people constantly threw in his face. There was one thing he prided himself on and that was that he'd never worked on a loser. He had shrewdly picked money-makers, or at least efforts worthy of hefty critical acclaim. He had had chances to produce some low-budget pictures, but had turned down the deals in favor of staying with Maddox Productions and being promoted from within.

Dillon never made up his own rules. He followed those that were established. He figured people, far wiser and tougher than he, had made the rules. He was certain, however, that if he hung in there long enough, the big deals would happen. He would be recognized for his efforts, his precision, his loyalty. He knew Hollywood was hardfisted and that many people were beaten to a pulp before they gave up. Those that were themselves pulpy cynically told him that faithfulness would only get him treated like a dog.

He thought that Ruby sort of treated him like a dog, but he didn't think she did it intentionally. She was uptight. Trying to do her job well and under extreme pressure. She hardly knew Dillon existed and she didn't yet know that she could rely on him one hundred percent.

He stood up to look at her painting of Texas, a stark realistic portrait done in grays and browns and tans that was a million miles from the desert-concealing, superficial greenery embodied in the palm trees and lush ground cover throughout Los Angeles.

He'd once asked her why she'd painted Texas.

"Because I used to live there," she had replied.

Dillon was collecting the papers from the desk when he heard a footstep behind him. He turned to see a blond kid with up-moussed short hair, a slew of bland freckles, a surly mouth, and arrogant eyes. The kid would have been cute, Dillon supposed, if it weren't for his insolent countenance.

"You seen my mom?" the kid asked rudely.

Dillon blinked once—slowly—and said, "Who is your mom?"

"Come on, man, you must know who I am. I'm Martin Maddox. Ruby is my mom. Are you her new secretary or something? Where is she? I'm kinda in a hurry."

The kid, who Dillon was reevaluating quickly as more like twenty-five rather than the seventeen he was dressed as, shifted on restless, well-tanned legs. He wore Hawaiian print shorts and a white cotton shirt that was unbuttoned and hanging loosely. The open shirt revealed that the sunshine which had so graced his legs had not been denied to the upper portion of his body. The smooth chest was toasted marshmallow, a color that is rarely obtained by people who work all week long. Dillon could see the kid had reached his maximum growth potential. He would never be five-ten, though he would probably claim it. His muscles were smooth and semi-tough, a result, no doubt, of all the beach activity he had been getting.

"Ruby's in a meeting and won't be back for a couple of

hours," stated Dillon.

"Shit," said Martin, spitting the word from his mouth. He slammed the palm of his hand against the doorjamb in an angry gesture. "I just needed to get a few bucks. Shit."

The kid blocked the doorway, looking at his feet in their worn canvas shoes, shaking his head as if he didn't know what to do. He slowly lifted his eyes and surveyed Dillon.

"Say, man, you don't have a few bucks you could loan me, do you?" he asked, his left hand twitching nervously.

Dillon had fifty dollars in his pocket, but he was damned if this impertinent brat was going to get it. "Sorry, I'm real short right now."

The kid glowered at the floor. Dillon rescinded his hard line. "I've got ten bucks. How 'bout ten? I haven't made it to the bank for a few days."

"Ten's better than nothing," said Martin, holding out his hand. "Just ask my mom to pay you back." He grinned at the green bill in his hand, turned abruptly, and walked away without a word of thanks.

The little shit, thought Dillon.

So this was Martin, the ingrate who'd had everything given to him all his life, the troublemaker everyone in the company rumored about. Dillon could never go up to Mr. or Mrs. Maddox and ask them to pay him back. He wouldn't embarrass himself like that. He vowed never to "loan" Martin another cent. Dillon wished he could have slugged that impudent expression off the kid's face.

The intercom on Ruby's phone buzzed. "Mr. Hughes," said the voice of the receptionist, "you have a call on sixty-one."

He picked up the receiver. "Hello?" he said. "How are you, sweetheart? The meeting with Mrs. Maddox was okay, but I just ran into one of those people who'll piss you off. No, I'm not mad now. I was. What should we do tonight? But I *want* to pick you up." His voice was emphatic.

"I don't know why I can't come to your house. Why shouldn't I? Never mind. Just tell me where to meet you. Okay. That sounds okay. I love you. I love you with all my heart."

Located on a major studio lot, a group of bungalow-style offices housed Graham Maddox's entire production company. It was a convenient site, which provided easy access to the production and post-production facilities a major had to offer. To accommodate his private suite, Graham Maddox had built a second floor over a wing of the one-story buildings. At the top of a sweeping staircase, his secretary, Jeannie Hansen, sat in a large waiting area and received visitors to the huge office where Graham stabled himself daily. Inside were doors at opposite ends of the room: One led to a plush fifteen-seat screening room; and the other led to a small private bath and sleeping quarters for the times when Graham was caught in an all-night editing session and couldn't make it home.

This entire upper floor was covered in a pile carpet that was colored three parts vanilla ice cream mixed with one part crème de menthe. The furniture was walnut. Plants hung from the ceiling and stood guard in corners, so the atmosphere was not unlike that of a greenhouse. Large stills from Graham's hit shows had been carefully spaced along white walls—the photographs not the usual publicity shots, but rather extraordinary insights into the actors and their characters.

Inside the office, Graham's desk, open underneath except for a single thin drawer, was a vast surface of finely finished wood grain. Along two walls were white duck-covered couches, each ten feet in length. There were several walnut chairs which, though straight-backed, were comfortable during long meetings, and a wall unit that contained a stereo, television, and video playback equipment.

From the long window behind his desk, he looked out to the thick foliage of massive dual sycamores. His view was private, the office being higher than the other bungalows and the sycamores secluding the interior.

Graham had hired Jeannie Hansen only two months before as his secretary—"guardian of the gate," as other members of his staff referred to her. She saw Martin Maddox step onto the stairs below.

"He's in a meeting," she called down to the insolent youth in a crisp and loud tone so he could not mistake that she was talking to him. Her voice warned him that she would be exceedingly unfriendly if he continued up the steps. "I'll tell him you came by," she added with finality.

Martin waved, mouthing *bitch* as he turned away.

She knocked on Graham's door—a soft, quick one-two-three that he recognized—and entered, closing the door behind her. He smiled at her, noting the shapely calves beneath her suit skirt. Most thin women had thin straight legs—which looked good on film and a little wanting in reality—but Jeannie had a pleasing smooth muscular curve to her calves. That same angle of curve bowed around her hips and narrowed into a very small waist.

Though she wore excellently tailored business suits every day, she rarely wore her hair up. The chestnut mane fell halfway down her back—combed, shiny, and conditioned—and gave her a bit of a wild look.

But then the wild look might have come from the way her full lips were always parted just slightly, an unconscious gesture that gave her face a look of incredible innocence. Her dark green eyes also carried that aura of innocence, while digesting every detail they observed.

"Excuse me, Graham," she said in her professional, calm, flowing voice, "but they just buzzed me from downstairs and Garrett is waiting."

"Good," said Graham, standing and straightening his shirt along his taut stomach. "Am I taking a folder with me?"

"No, Mrs. Maddox has the material."

"Good," he said, reaching for a pen and putting it in his pocket.

"I enjoyed dinner the other night," she said.

"I did, too," he said, thinking she had already mentioned it. He picked up the leather-bound notebook. It had been a Christmas present from his staff one year and, although he never wrote any notes down, he didn't want to insult them by never using it. So he carried it with him.

He looked at Jeannie's face. She was about to say something else but seemed momentarily suspended.

Though she could see his mind was on his meeting, she stepped forward and put a hand on his arm. "I'd like to do it again," she said simply.

He could see the tips of her teeth beyond those parted lips and could not avoid looking straight into her eyes. "Okay, soon," he agreed, politely waiting for her to release her grasp on his arm.

But she stepped closer, placing her other hand against his chest and moving it downward under his tie, along the buttons of his shirt, reaching the waist of his trousers and continuing down. Her touch caught him by surprise and, for an instant, his mind switched off his meeting, off his deadlines, and onto the hand that was burning through his pants. He felt himself harden.

"How soon?" she smiled.

"Soon. I promise." He pulled away from her but paused at the door and looked back. He'd have to wait a minute before going down the stairs.

Tony Keene—"camera operator," his credit read—preferred the Golden Time Lounge to any other bar close to the studio where they could unwind after work. Twelve-hour days were strenuous, especially when the director was never satisfied with the takes. After you got off the set, one part of your brain was saying you were dog-tired, while another was hyped on adrenaline and needed a few beers to cool down.

The Golden Time was perfect. It was a block's walk from the lot. The owner, who frequently worked behind the bar, remembered all his steady customers. He knew the names of the shows and the stars, knew how they were doing in the ratings, and was up on more of the inside politics than the crews.

There were tall, icy mugs of beer on the bar, drawn in the time it took Tony and fellow crew member, Roy Scott, to walk from the door to the bar stools. They chuckled and clinked the mugs, nodding at the bartender and looking to see the six other technicians from the *Motive* set nod and swallow as well.

Tony wiped beer foam from his graying mustache with the

back of his hand. "Boy, that's good," he said, lifting the mug to his lips again and reaching into his shirt pocket for a pack of cigarettes. The deep lines in his face made him look like he had spent twenty years with a job in the sun rather than on a soundstage behind a camera. Callused fingers withdrew an unfiltered cigarette and struck a flame on the butane lighter.

"You want one?" he asked, pushing the pack to Roy.

Roy shook his head no, pulling feather-weight, low-tar smokes from his own shirt.

"Those things are like suckin' air," Tony said to Roy, smiling, "but I'm glad to see you're staying with them. Wish I didn't like these so much." He rolled the cigarette between his thumb and forefingers, exhaling thick smoke from his nose. He picked a piece of loose tobacco from the end of his tongue.

"When you get married again," said Roy, "I'm sure you'll cut down."

"Married? I ain't been in that state of affairs for seventeen years and that suits me just fine," said Tony, running his hand through his thick hair, which was a deep nut-brown and showing the same gray strands that had overtaken his mustache.

"It was a bitch of a day, wasn't it?" said Roy.

"Yeah," replied Tony. "Richard ain't too bad at getting the performances he wants out of the actors, but *technically,* his directing sucks. We had to do that one scene in the barn *six* times because he wouldn't listen to Don."

"Richard's got to learn that Don's been a director of photography for a lotta years, and he knows what he's doing."

"Don was pissed at Richard. There's no doubt about that," said Tony, squishing out the half-inch butt and pulling a toothpick from his pocket.

"I thought Don was gonna deck him," said Roy, scratching a chin that hadn't been shaved in two days.

"Or quit," said Tony, pulverizing the point of the wooden pick between his molars.

Roy tapped on the bar to order a couple more beers and

asked the other men in their crew if any of them wanted refills. Two declined and four said yes. "I don't blame you boys. Working with Richard can cause a powerful thirst," Roy told them.

"I wonder how many *Motive* episodes he's going to direct this season?" mused Tony.

"He's Maddox's favorite director," said Roy. "I'll bet he's scheduled to do half."

"Damn." Tony leaned closer to Roy. "I can direct better than him. Wish I could get them to let me direct one episode."

"You always get like this when a director pisses you off."

"But they always hire these assholes that don't know a damned thing!" cried Tony. "It's all politics and who they know. And the crew's got to carry them through the shoot because they don't know what they want or how to get it." He swallowed the last of his beer. "It's frustrating, fuckin' frustrating."

"Why don't you apply with Maddox and tell him you want to direct one," said Roy. "He's a jerk of sorts, but if he likes you, I'll bet he'd let you try."

"Maddox wants directors with credits or else someone jacking him off telling him what a great guy he is. I asked him two years ago and he said he'd think about it. I guess he's still thinking about it." Tony spat out ground toothpick slivers and took another cigarette.

"Oh, shit, look who's here," said Roy, glancing at the door.

Turning to look, the unlit cigarette dangling from his lower lip, Tony said, "It's the dyke. Wonder what the fuck she wants?"

A tall, skinny woman in her late twenties had paused to look around the bar with a haughty, hostile glance. Straight white-blond hair hung to her shoulders, framing a severe Nordic face with high, protruding cheekbones, heavy eyebrows, and a prominent chin. Her mouth was broad and her lips full and downturned. She might have been pretty if her expression were less harsh. She squinted in the darkness before spotting the crew on the far side of the bar, then strode over to where they sat.

Her bony legs, clothed in blue jeans, gapped a triangle between her thighs. Her loose-fitting shirt hung limply over an uninspired chest.

"Excuse me," she said roughly. "I needed to give you the revised time schedule for the morning. Don said I might find you over here." She was the first assistant director, Richard's right-hand helper.

"Sure, sure," said Roy, standing and gesturing that she take his bar stool. The other crew members were leaning back on their own seats, silent and waiting for her to speak.

"How 'bout a beer, Sondra?" Tony asked her.

"I don't really have time," she said, motioning for Roy to sit again. "But thanks. Another time," she added, her eyes glancing uncomfortably at Tony and then at the rest of the crew.

She was very self-conscious with them all staring at her, their eyes hot on her hips and nonexistent breasts. "The message is just for Tony," she said, seeing relief flood through their eyes as they turned back to their beers. "Richard wants to go over some setups with you and Don in the morning. Will you please come in an hour earlier than the time on the call sheet?"

"Fine," said Tony, feeling his resentment of Richard's sloppy direction rise as a bad taste in his mouth.

"I'm sorry," she said, in a voice that didn't sound like she was a bit sorry. "See you tomorrow."

She turned from them and, as she walked toward the door, they watched her flat butt barely rock under stiff hips. She moved more up and down than from side to side.

"Ain't she something," said Roy. "That is one of the all-time nastiest bitches I ever met."

"She's a strange thing, all right," said Tony, only now remembering to light his smoke. "I'm not sure I'd call her a bitch. I'd call her real unfriendly."

"What the hell's the difference?" Roy scratched his beer belly.

"Them dykes is different. When they don't like men, they just prefer to say as little to 'em as they have to."

"That's a bitch in my book," said Roy, taking a long

swallow that dropped his mug down to three-quarters empty.

"But bitches act nasty on purpose," argued Tony. "Bitches are women that want something out of you or want to cause you grief. This Sondra just simply don't want contact. She don't act nasty on purpose. It's just part of her character."

"Still sounds like a bitch to me, and here you are getting off on your professor yakking, being the social worker."

"Sociologist."

"Whatever." Roy grinned at Tony's musings. Tony often started analyzing subjects and would go on and on, and Roy would listen politely for as long as his attention held, which was generally not more than five minutes. "Listen, ol' buddy, it's your turn to buy a round," reminded Roy.

"Sure is," said Tony. "Order 'em up. I gotta make a quick phone call."

When he returned from the dark alcove near the restrooms, which housed the phone, he was grinning.

"Jeez," said Roy, "what you been doing to yourself in there?"

"It figures a depraved mind like yours is always thinking about sex," said Tony, trying to hide a smile.

"What did she say?" asked Roy.

"Who? What did who say?"

"I know who you were calling. Is she gonna put out?"

"Don't talk about her like that."

"Sorry, sorry," said Roy with mock concern. "What did she say?"

Tony looked over at Roy, a shit-eating grin covering his face. He didn't say a word.

"Are you gonna tell me, man?" pressed Roy.

"Okay. You deserve a tidbit about the life of a single guy. She said—" He paused.

"What?" Roy sat with his beer mug poised halfway to his mouth.

"She said I should come over."

"That's it? That's all?"

"I thought that was a good offer." He stood up and shoved a bill at Roy. "Here, pay for the beers and drink mine for me."

"You aren't staying to have one more with us?"
"Shit, no. She said she can't hardly wait."
"She didn't say that."
But Tony was moving toward the exit, his short, stocky body passing behind the line of regulars. He winked at the barmaid and was gone.

"I don't know what to do. I don't know what to do," sobbed Denny on Margi's doorstep, trembling from his inner agony. The fingers on each hand were spread taut, the palms turned in toward his thighs. The rims of his eyes were red, his cheeks blanched from the stress.
Moments before she had been lying on the couch in the den, her head resting in her husband's lap as they watched TV. When the doorbell had rung, they had waited for one of the kids to answer it. The kids always had friends coming over, so it was a surprise when it was announced that Mom had a visitor.
"Who is it?" asked Margi.
"That guy you work with," said the disinterested kid, stuffing the final gooey corner of a peanut butter sandwich into his mouth. "You know, the *one*." The kid disappeared into the kitchen.
"Oh, my God," said Margi in a panic, jumping to her feet. "It must be Denny."
"Ah, shit, the fag?" said Bob with exasperation, sitting up and sighing miserably.
"Shhhh," said Margi, placing a hand across his mouth. "Stay in here. I'll talk to him in the living room."
"Why does that fruitcake have to show up over here?" complained the man who was just trying to have a quiet evening watching the tube with the old lady.
Margi was stern, her voice concerned. "I told you he's got some troubles. He won't stay long."
She took Denny's hand and led him into the living room, pushing him down into a corner of the sofa. "I'm going to get you a Coke," she said, solidly believing that a glass of the cold, black, bubbling liquid would cure half of anyone's

problems. She'd been drinking it for years. It worked. It always worked.

She cut back through the den and glanced at Bob, who glared at her. "I hope he ain't staying long," said her husband, his tone unnecessarily bullish.

Bob's rudeness raised her hackles. "It's my house, too. He's my friend. He can stay as long as he wants," she retorted, and blew a hot, defiant breath from her nostrils.

In the living room, Denny couldn't make out the words, but he could hear the tone of voice. He didn't know whom else he could talk to. Margi had been his friend for fifteen years. She had been in on his relationship with Jeff from the beginning. He had told her about how he had first met Jeff, and he had introduced her to him when his roommate had first started coming around the set. She had heard a lot about how one man could love another. Yet the tone in Bob's voice reminded Denny that Margi had another life, a life with a short-tempered, redneck stagehand.

She returned and slipped an icy glass into Denny's hand. He sipped at the syrupy coldness. He couldn't bring himself to look her in the face, so he stared at the carpet beneath his feet. Margi let him sit, and she watched and waited for him to talk.

He wanted to talk and yet could not open his mouth to speak of the details.

He remembered standing in the doorway, looking at his bed. Upon it was a faun, a delicate young boy who had enough masculine characteristics to one day be a leading man. Judging from the naivete in his eyes, the actor was probably a kid from rural America trying to "make it big in Hollywood"—whom Jeff was taking advantage of.

Jeff had been led into temptation, and here was the proof.

A sick feeling turned Denny's stomach at the thought that he couldn't trust Jeff. He had always trusted Jeff, and now he had been betrayed. How often had Jeff done this to him? At how many dinners and parties and over weekends, when Denny hadn't been with him, had he cavorted like this? Denny felt a fool for having trusted Jeff, for having put a high price on their relationship when obviously Jeff didn't think any more of it than to screw some doe-eyed, blond-headed kid with a smooth white ass.

Denny had leaned against the doorjamb, unable to leave the room, unable to go any farther into it. He had visions of screaming and running toward the bed with his fists and fury, and yet he was stopped cold. He had never reacted to anything with hot-blooded anger. It just wasn't his way.

The sick feeling had turned over in his stomach again as he watched the boy disentangle himself from Jeff's hold and scramble for cover under the sheets. Jeff rolled over, his nudity sticky-sweaty all down his front, and looked at Denny. His look was not quite insolence, but it wasn't guilt, either. He did not look sorry for what he had done.

Hot tears pushed into Denny's eyes and clouded the room for a second. Jeff was holding out his hand to Denny, crooking his fingers, beckoning him to the bed, asking him to join them there in the damp sheets and pungent male odor.

But Denny had never believed in promiscuity and having sex with just anyone who came along. Sex was an intimate, private time between two people, a time they could share exclusively, a time that was a secret from all the other people in the world.

That belief evidently meant shit to Jeff, who had had the gall to bring someone to *their* home in the middle of the day. Jeff had known Denny would be coming home. Why had he done this? Jeff wasn't even supposed to be home, but out for the evening. Why? Why? He knew Denny would be home after work, bringing groceries. Denny had told him so on the phone from the set that morning. . . . Why was he here now with the boy?

The boy was on his feet, edging past Denny to get to the bathroom. He caught Denny's eyes for a moment, and Denny could tell that the boy had been duped as well. There was an uncomprehending hurt in the boy's eyes, a fear at being caught in the middle of a lovers' quarrel, a look that told Denny the boy was regretful about the situation.

Jeff jumped from the bed to take Denny's hand, but Denny jerked it back and stood rigid.

"Den, come *on,* forgive me," said Jeff, trying to touch Denny's smooth neck.

"Don't touch me," replied Denny, not sure if he could stay in control of his emotions and not become a raging maniac screaming out "Why? Why? WHY? Why did you do this to me?" at the top of an hysterical voice.

The words boiled inside him, exploding and subsiding, the nausea more than he could bear. He shoved Jeff's shoulders hard with the palms of his hands. Jeff staggered backward from the blow, surprised because he had always esteemed Denny's gentleness.

"Denny, we need to talk about this," said Jeff, unaware of his nakedness, concerned that Denny would do something irrational.

The tears welled into Denny's eyes again, but he was determined that Jeff wouldn't see them rolling down his cheeks. He blinked and sniffled and spoke with a strong, stern voice.

"I want you out of here," said Denny.

"It's a misunderstanding. I don't want to go anyplace. It's *you* I want."

"No, it isn't. I'm sure this isn't the first time you've done this. I want you out of here tomorrow when I come back. OUT!! Don't ever try calling me. Take all your crap, and those sheets," Denny yelled, pointing at them like they were diseased and should be burned, "and your young stud, and get the fuck out of my apartment. Out of my life. By tomorrow."

Denny turned from the bedroom and strode evenly into the kitchen where he shook out some dry food for the cat. Then he left by the front door, emotion pushing up, up inside him, swelling, pressing, strangling. When he got into his car, he hid his face against the steering wheel and cried out the agonizing question, "Why? Why? Why?"

"Gosh, Den, can you say anything at all?" Margi asked him. "I want to help, but I can't if you won't talk to me?"

"It's so—so awkward. I don't know what I'm doing here. I can tell I've pissed off Bob."

"To hell with Bob," said Margi. "I want you to talk to me.

Where is Jeff now?"

Wretched tears fell silently down Denny's cheeks. "I don't know," he muttered forlornly. "I told him to get out, and he got out. I don't know where he is."

"Well, you better stay here tonight. I'll fix the couch for you."

He urgently grabbed her arm. "No, no. I can't do that. I can't stay here. Bob won't like it."

"To hell with Bob," said Margi. "What's wrong with you men? I live here, too. I pay my half of the bills. And I say you are going to stay."

Denny couldn't argue and she wasn't about to give him any choice. "That's better," she said, seeing that he had acquiesced. "You can use the small guest bath over there. I'll get some sheets."

"Thanks, Margi, thanks ever so much for being my friend."

As he said these last words, they heard the back door slam. Margi ran to the den to see if Bob was still there. He wasn't.

He didn't come home all night.

Tanya lay on the bed, feeling the yacht's gentle rocking over the swells, hearing the Caribbean water softly rush against the other side of the hull near her. It was early morning. Long, blushing rays of the sun lighted the curtains that covered the portholes. She had awakened alone and lay with her eyes shut, wishing she could fall asleep again. Though she was allowed to sleep as long as she desired, she didn't want to get up and face the day.

She preferred sleeping in the nude, free of nightgowns that twisted around her as she slept. But now that she was married to Norman, she always wore a nightgown. She just couldn't bear the thought of sleeping with his old, loose flesh touching hers. She stretched her long, firm legs across the sheets, loving the silky feel of the material against her skin.

Her waist-length blond hair was worked into a single braid so it wouldn't tangle when she slept. A beam of sunshine fell through a crack in the curtains and lit the rich Rapunzel's rope to its full brightness. The hairs were many different shades, ranging from pale straw to fawn brown, thanks to patient hours at the beauty salon getting it woven. She particularly liked those that wound brilliantly through the heavy braid like gold thread.

She missed sleeping naked. She missed spreading her hair fanlike about her head, as she had before she met Norman. Not that Norman would have objected in the slightest to a leggy vixen with untamed hair in his bed. But, around him, she just couldn't let herself go with that much wantonness.

This morning she was lucky. Norman had already gotten up and left the cabin. She wanted to feel her hair loose about her.

She slid off the soft nightshirt and unbound the braid. It fell in waves around her, soft upon her breasts and shoulders and back; a feather touch that started bringing back all kinds of emotions. She sprawled on the sheets, totally alone, reveling in a moment of freedom where she cast herself adrift from her everyday worries and remembered.

Remembered a touch. Whose? Norman's?

No, no, not his. She didn't know what Norman's touch was like, because she blocked him out of her reality every time he laid a hand on her.

It was Russell's touch she remembered. Always Russell's touch. The one thing that would never leave her. The exquisite understanding in his hands of what she needed. His hands beginning to lightly massage the skin under her collarbone, gradually working down to her upper breasts and then around each handful in such a relaxed, nonsexual way that the fire inside her built slowly, the flame always catching her unawares. His hands moving over her stomach, her hips, her thighs, her knees, deeply relaxing, letting her release all tension, giving all of herself to him without really knowing she had done so.

What turned her on was the way he began—nonsexual and yet exciting. And Russell had known how to do it every time. He had "trained" her—to use her expression when they would talk about it—so that after a while anywhere he touched her made her body respond. They could be going into a restaurant and he would hold her arm as they walked to the table, gently flexing his fingers against her bicep. This caused heat to gorge her loins and race through her body. He would make her wait through the entire meal—smiling, talking, eating, acting normal—all the while telling her in hundreds of nonverbal ways that he knew she was excited.

Her excitement had been all it took to arouse him. Sometimes their eye contact over several hours of being in a public place, like at a party or out shopping, became so intense that she had to look away from his commanding gaze. When they finally coupled in a private place, the pent-up energy burst from them both, unleashing a hunger that took hours to satisfy.

Now, she tried not to think of Russell, tried not to let him cross her mind, because inevitably the memory of his touch led her to recall how she had left him. How she had broken his heart. How she had discarded him in the cruelest of ways, backing over his ego like a loaded cement mixer and destroying all the trust he had ever placed in any person. Not just in women, but in all people.

She lay on the bed remembering the luxury of his loving touch, her own fingers tracing the courses his once had, the sensation pushing the tears she had grown accustomed to crying out the door, pushing the guilt under the bed, pushing the terror at her ability to manipulate people out the sunny portholes.

She realized now—now when it was too late—that she had really loved Russell. At the time, he wasn't good enough for her because he wasn't making enough money. His dream was to be an actor, just as her dream was to be an actress. She had pictured herself in a soap opera; he had seen himself on the Broadway stage. But she had had little faith in Fate, and she had a low tolerance of crummy apartments and cars that were forever breaking down and clothes that had to be worn every single week because that was all you owned.

When she had married Norman, she had gotten everything she deserved: several glorious mansions around the world to choose from; limos, yachts and private jets at her beck and call; ashamedly expensive clothes that could be tossed aside after a single wearing; and a husband whom she couldn't bear laying a hand on her.

At first, it had been all right. She had been so in need of the material things she craved that she hardly noticed his nightly ravaging of her body. It was a fair trade. She had seen it as such. So had Norman.

She had been only one of many women contending to be Norman's "lady." None of Norman's friends ever thought he would actually marry her. He could have kept her as a mistress and companion, and no one would have given it a second thought. Many women had passed through Norman's life in that capacity.

But he became possessive of Tanya. He desperately needed to own her body and her soul. He knew she had walked out on the man she loved. Just walked away cold. He knew it would take more than love to hold her.

What would keep a woman like that?

Control.

So he controlled her.

Sometimes she felt like she was choking from the close watch he kept on her. He took her with him everywhere. He hated to let her out of his sight, and when he had to, made sure there was someone observing her. She didn't like to be "accompanied." But she didn't have any choice.

It wasn't like her whole life with Norman was miserable. She was treated with the utmost respect at every turn. People inquired into her opinion, and she had learned to have one ready to give. She had fun with Norman—just as long as he didn't want to have sex. But how long could she turn him away? She knew it wouldn't be forever. She wished she could have Russell and his perfectly shaped, perfectly kissable lips instead of Norman, with his barely perceptible thin line of grayed pink and his obnoxious, hard-pointed tongue.

"My darling," she heard his voice behind her, "I didn't know you had awakened."

She moaned as if she were dozing and he were disturbing

her, but he did not notice.

His Venus lay naked and ready before him, more tantalizing and available than she had been in months. He shut and locked the door behind him, the deal he had been about to phone in to his New York broker forgotten. He focused on the soft, coiffed triangle of hair that had been trimmed to a very risqué bikini line.

His hands fell upon the taut skin of her golden thighs, pushing them apart to drop his face into her honey nectar and delicately taste all that he loved. The forbidden fruit was as easy to be had as cherries in a cherry pie.

He caught her by surprise. Wet from her fantasy of Russell, Norman thought she was ready for him. His white pants were unzipped and off in record time, followed by a carelessly tossed polo shirt.

Before she'd met Norman, Tanya would have never guessed that a man of sixty-two could be so hard and ready at any time. He didn't need coaxing. Though he liked her willing tongue and squeezing hand, he didn't require it.

He had a paunch. It was squishy to the touch and reminded her of loose, room-warmed rind fat on a cheap cut of pork. He dove against her, the repelling squishiness resounding against the front of her body. His face was unshaven and rough and, careful as he was not to kiss her satin face, his movements carried him away. His chin slipped against the hollow of her neck, grating like a sandy pestle in a petal-soft mortar.

Grunts came steadily from his opened lips. Tanya was afraid to open her eyes lest she have to look into his.

He was barely aware of the sound at first, but a terrifying low moan had started beneath him, a wail like a ghost wind through a cavern, building and building in volume until it reached a high-pitched scream.

He looked at Tanya's face. Tears streamed down under the clenched lids of her eyes. The noise that emanated from her throat raped him of his pleasure. He stopped moving and braced himself on sturdy forearms. He couldn't believe she was doing it again.

"Darling. My darling. Open your eyes. Whatever is

wrong?"

Tanya didn't stir. Her body lay quietly as a forgotten rose, cut and dropped in a garden. Her lips spread tightly over her teeth, revealing ivory-capped tips. She gasped for air between her violent sobs.

Norman withdrew and took her into his arms, hushing her and holding her tightly against his chest. "There, there. Please tell me what's the matter," he coaxed her, his voice tender. He lightly stroked her head while she continued to sob against him.

"Tanya, for God's sake, you have to tell me what's wrong," he pleaded. Her sobs grew quiet, but she still could not look him in the face.

Finally, she spoke. "Norman . . . Norman . . . I'm just so . . . so miserable."

"Unhappy?" His voice was crisp. She had caught him by surprise. "Are you unhappy with me?"

She didn't answer for the moment it took to align her words just right. "No, not with you. Of course, not with you. With me. *I'm* unhappy."

"But why, darling? Tanya, you're the most beautiful woman on earth and I shall give you anything you want. Whatever it takes to keep you from being so unhappy."

She bit her bottom lip and finally looked at him. Her eyelashes were wet and her high, fragile cheekbones tear-stained. Her fair, round, ingenuous-looking eyes clouded with more tears. She blinked them back and said, "I'm not sure what's wrong."

"You must have an idea." If she had not seemed so helpless and in need of him, his mind might have turned back to his investments. But her fingers dug so urgently into his arms that he gave her all his attention.

"I feel so useless, Norman. You do important things every day, and I feel like another of your toys."

The thought horrified him. As beautiful as the woman was, he had never thought of her as inanimate. He had tried to give her everything she had ever wanted. Including all his love. He felt a little impatient.

"That's ridiculous, Tanya. You aren't one of my *toys,* as

you call them. You're my wife. I hate to see you so unhappy. What would amuse you?"

Her mind raced to think of something she could ask for. She knew his tone of voice. He was on the verge of getting angry. "I want to act, Norman. You promised me when we first met that you would help me get into acting. I want to try it. I really do. I won't be happy unless I can."

Norman kissed her forehead and laid her back down on the bed. He stood up with determination and got his terry-cloth robe from behind the door.

"I'm calling Graham Maddox right now," said Norman tying the robe's belt. His and Maddox's relationship went back many, many years, and his investments in Maddox Productions had been numerous. Graham owed him more than one favor. "I've discussed it with him before and he thinks he may have a part that's right for you. A show his wife is producing. We shall go back to Los Angeles immediately so they can go through the formality of auditioning you. Additionally, I need to talk to Graham about our deal on that feature film he wants to make, *Fool's Gold*."

Tanya started to open her mouth, but Norman held a finger to his lips. "Whatever it takes to make you happy, my dear," he said, hand upon the doorknob. "We can't have you crying, poor thing, every time we make love. Please pack. We shall put in at the nearest island today. I will arrange to have the jet pick us up."

He left the bedroom in a hurry, neglecting to shut the door all the way. She pulled the sheet up to her neck and stared at the ceiling. Tanya could make out traces of his conversation with Graham. It sounded like she was going to get the part whether she wanted it or not.

Chapter 3

"I don't want that air-brained twit on the show," said Ruby, her voice caught between laughter (for surely Graham was joking) and anger (because he sounded so serious about it).

"I think Tanya would be the perfect actress to offset Garrett's handsome, dark looks. She's blond and tall and soft."

"And Norman's wife."

"*That* has nothing to do with it. We need a girl. We'll screen-test Tanya. She may not work out for the part."

Ruby stood up and looked at Graham. He seemed more and more like a stranger to her. Here in his office, he was in an ultimate position of power behind his desk. In back of him, the sycamore leaves were still, some lit by the sun, some dark. Her mind blanked out for a moment, and she was aware only of the abstract forms made by the patterns of shadowed leaves. *Motive* was her show. He had said so. Yet now he was trying to take away her right to make decisions.

"Obviously, my opinion doesn't mean diddly to you. You've forced me to put in a female lead whether or not I want to. Now you're telling me whom to cast. I certainly wouldn't choose that half-baked floozy Norman's hormones couldn't help but marry."

Graham leaned back in his chair, shutting his eyes and wondering why he had ever allowed his wife to come into his domain. "You can't deny that Tanya's a good-looking girl. But it's more than that. My instincts tell me that we need to put a woman into the show. It will draw a larger more male audience. Come on. Where's your business sense?"

Ruby's hands balled into fists without her realizing it. She placed them on the edge of Graham's desk and leaned forward so that her face was a foot from his face. His eyes were cool; hers fiery.

"Business sense tells me that there are a whole lot of actresses in this town much more qualified for the role. You told me from the beginning it was my show. *My* show. Therefore, I should make the decisions. And my decision is no."

"My dear, try not to be so emotional about it. We'll screen-test Tanya. Then we'll make the decision. We can't afford to jeopardize our ratings."

His tone of voice was distant. She might as well have been standing in another room. His mind was made up. She knew that look. That was the way he was when he decided not to go to a social function, or not to visit relatives, or not to live in Beverly Hills any longer. When his mind was made up, there was no changing him.

Graham looked at the script on his desk, his concentration totally absorbed in the pages. He had dismissed her like she was just another flunky working for him.

She fumed. She felt impotent. She felt like calling Norman and crying on *his* shoulder (which she had done a number of times over the years when Graham had infuriated her). Norman always sided with her. However, he wouldn't in this case. His spoiled brat wife wanted to act, and Norman was going to see to it that she did.

If Graham was able to insist that a female role be added to the show, he was going to have his hands full with screen tests. Ruby made up her mind that the whiny blond Tanya would not get the part. She would call a half-dozen agents and audition a slew of women.

Graham was not going to act toward her the way he did the others working for him. "You could have the decency and courtesy to finish the conversation," she said coldly, "without treating me like I'm so much shit you have to contend with."

Graham sighed heavily, glanced up from the script, and

gave her a condescending look. "I'm sorry," he said, a false smile coming to his lips. "I thought we had settled the matter."

"We have *not* settled the matter. If you want a woman on *Motive,* then I'm holding auditions for the part. You are not simply giving it away," she told him, her voice getting louder and louder. "You are not going to ruin my show with that stupid, stupid blonde." She spat out the last words, turned abruptly and walked to the door.

Graham's secretary was looking down at her desk, pretending she hadn't been listening to every word. Ruby glared at the sultry face until it was forced to meet her stare. This secretary—Jeannie was her name—was not as sharp as some he had had. Ruby knew instinctively that she couldn't trust her. The face backed down from Ruby's hard eyes.

Why was it that a secretary had to know all of a man's business?

Ruby marched down the middle of the staircase, neglecting to take hold of the railing, forgetting, in her anger, her fear of catching a heel on the thick carpet and falling. At the bottom of the stairs, she shot one more superior glance up at the secretary but saw that the woman had already gone into Graham's office.

Graham was rubbing his eyes with one hand and looking embarrassed at his wife's outburst. Jeannie came into his office, softly shutting the door. She stood there with her mouth slightly open. It was a look that reminded him of a mouth that had just been kissed.

"Don't let her get to you," Jeannie said, sitting in a chair by the side of his desk. She wriggled on the seat in her tight gray skirt, adjusting it around her rear end. She ran a hand over her silk-stockinged leg. Graham watched unbelievingly as she pulled the slack in the stocking up, moving the hem of her skirt aside and revealing the scarlet garter belt that clasped the top. She smoothed the skirt over her leg again.

"Did you want me to make you a reservation for lunch today?" she asked him.

"Who am I supposed to meet?"

"Norman."

"Shit," said Graham, continuing to stare at her thigh. "If it were anyone but him, I'd cancel."

All eyes in Spud's biker bar turned to look out the huge plate glass window at the blinding headlights glaring inward. Someone was parking a brand new Volvo. It was obviously not someone who was a regular, for regulars knew that only bikes are parked in front of the window and that you kill your beam before it can shine into the bar.

The car's driver, fumbling to turn the lights off, accidentally hit the brights. "Ahhhh, fuck," said a half-dozen cursing voices as everyone scowled out the window.

The headlights finally died, and they saw an incredibly skinny blond chick get out of the passenger's side and stand in front of the car with her arms crossed in mock patience waiting for the driver to emerge. He was just about six feet in height, had smooth brown hair, and was wearing a well-tailored sports coat that deceptively covered his musculature so you couldn't really tell if he had any substance or if the lack of it was seductively hidden.

"This joint was your idea, Dillon," said Sondra outside. "It's way the fuck and gone out of the city."

He carefully put the car keys into his front trouser pocket. "This is what the script called for," he replied, eyeing the establishment skeptically.

"I don't mind location scouting, but I don't get paid for hazardous duty," she told him in a low, terse voice that sounded more pissed off than she was actually feeling. She could see he was worried and trying not to show it.

They stood inside the door, getting their bearings. The smell of smoke and dank soured beer staggered both of them. They moved to the end of the bar, aware they were being watched.

The bartender spoke to them from the center of the bar. "What can I get you?" he loudly called to them.

"We'd like to talk to the owner," said Dillon.

"Oh, yeah?" said the bartender, his tone of voice getting a few deep laughs from the people sitting down at the bar. "Is he expecting you?"

"Yes," said Dillon, to the bartender's surprise. "My office spoke with him on the phone this afternoon."

"I'll get him," said the bartender with more respect.

A few minutes later the bartender returned. He was followed by a grizzled man of sixty, whose eyes were bleary and bloodshot. His face was unshaven and his thinning hair combed with his fingertips.

"You the movie people?" he asked them.

"Television," said Dillon, pulling out a business card and presenting it to the man.

The man ignored it. He stood his ground, wavering on unsteady feet, crafty eyes sizing them up. "I'm Spud," he said. "How are ya?" He stuck out a strong, thickly-jointed hand to Dillon.

"I'm Dillon Hughes," said Dillon, shaking the man's hand. "And this is Sondra Prescott, our assistant director."

"How do you do?" said Sondra, extending her hand.

Spud had not expected to have to shake it. Her hand was soft, but her grip firm. "Are you beer drinkers?" Spud asked them.

Before Dillon could answer, Sondra said, "Yes, as a matter of fact, we are. We were just saying how good a cold beer would taste, right when we were parking, weren't we, Dillon?"

"Right, Sondra," said Dillon, with about as much enthusiasm as a bug stuck in a porcelain bathtub. He hated beer.

"Good!" said Spud with growing confidence. "Bring us three," he ordered the bartender. "Let's go over here and talk." They followed him to one of the engraved tables, unaware that they were safe in the owner's presence.

They discussed the terms and the shooting schedule with Spud, telling him parts of the storyline so he could see how his place would fit into the immortality of the networks. Spud was pleased. Both he and Dillon thought they were getting a deal; Spud because he was getting so much money for his crummy joint without having to do any work, and Dillon because he had only offered one third of the normal price they paid for renting locations.

"We'll be needing some extras, you know, to add color to the scene," said Sondra. "Maybe some of these people would be interested in a little work."

Spud rose to his feet and cleared his throat. "Everyone listen up here. This little lady has an announcement." When he sat down and looked at Sondra, at her stern face that wore no makeup, he wondered if he'd carried the "little lady" line too far.

Remarkably, the voices quieted down so she could speak. She smiled gingerly, looking at the rough, dirty clothes, hair, and beards, and raised her voice so they could all hear her.

"We're from the show *Motive.* We're going to be shooting an episode out here at Spud's in a couple weeks. We'll be needing some extras, some people in the background drinking beer and doing what you're doing right now." She paused, hoping to see their faces lighten up. "If any of you are interested in getting in a couple days' work, you can put your names on this sign-up sheet, which I'll pass on to my casting director."

They all stared silently at her. "Are there any questions?" she asked, looking at Dillon and then at Spud for some reassurance.

"What do we get paid?" asked a tough petite woman who sat on a man's lap.

When Sondra told them, there were several approving whistles. "And we feed you lunch besides," she added.

She sat down again and drank straight from her beer bottle without thinking about it. Dillon, who was still using his glass, looked at her with astonishment. Spud laughed and thought she might be all right after all.

On the other side of the bar, Will and Joe looked on with interest. The pained look on the blonde's face almost pulled at Will's heart. He knew what it was to be in this bar and not have a friend. But he had a piss-poor attitude about movie people. He'd never seen people in his life that were so willing to trample down other people to get what they wanted. It was one of the most ruthless businesses in the world.

"Shit, Will," Joe was saying, "we could get a few hundred

bucks together just working a few days for them. Come on, man. Let's sign up."

"You sign up if you want to."

Will continued to stare at Dillon and Sondra as they sat with Spud. The bar owner rarely made an appearance. His son-in-law was the bartender and the place generally ran itself. Spud only showed up to make trips to the bank. His son-in-law was now basically honest, having once been caught with his hand in the till and finding a butcher knife an inch from his jugular. Spud didn't put up with any shit from anybody. Rumor had it that he had dumped more than one body out in the desert. When he started talking about "coyote bait," people knew he wasn't joking.

Yet there he was, nice as could be, talking to Dillon and Sondra and ordering them more beers. After a while, Spud disappeared out the back of the bar. The deal-making was completed.

"Will," nudged Joe, "you need some money, too. Your mom's been helping you out, but she won't do that forever."

Joe had gone one step too far. Will glared at him. "Since when is it any of your fucking business?"

"Jesus, relax, man," said Joe, getting to his feet and moving a step back from the table. "I'm your friend. We need some money. We've just been stringing along on practically nothing. Come on, man, these are easy bucks."

Joe looked ready to dance away from the table. "You're right," Will assented. "You go first. I'll be over in a minute."

Twenty people had signed Sondra's list. Will took the pen to add his name. Joe, who had just signed up before, had an unsteady nervous handwriting. He stood at Will's side, proud of his friend, nodding at the list. Will looked at Sondra Prescott. She had a hard face that was trying to smile. She wore no makeup, but he thought her long blond lashes were pretty as they brushed over her eyes.

"Say," he said, his shoulder-length mane framing his rugged face, "are there any stunts involved? Are you looking for any stuntmen?"

"There are some stunts, aren't there, Dillon?" asked Sondra.

Dillon looked from Sondra to the tall, handsome biker. "Yes, there are. Some dangerous ones, in fact. With a motorcycle."

"I do stunts," said Will.

"I can, too," joined in Joe.

"You can't," said Will. Then, noting the hurt on his partner's face, he said, "You have to be—"

Dillon interrupted him. "You need to be a member of the Screen Actors Guild to do stunts."

"Oh," said Joe, "whatever that is."

"I've got a card," said Will deliberately.

"Oh," said Sondra and Joe simultaneously, in awe.

"You need to talk to our stunt coordinator," said Dillon.

"I'll need to get his name, sweetheart," Will said to Sondra.

She bristled at the word *sweetheart,* but looking at Will's eyes, she could see he wasn't trying to be an asshole. She wrote down the information for him.

"I didn't know. . . ." said Joe, but a sideways glance from Will silenced any further comment.

"Can I buy you a beer?" Will asked Dillon and Sondra.

Dillon had drunk only half of his first beer and half of his second. He couldn't face having another brought to the table. "No thanks," he said. "I have to get going soon."

"Come on, Dillon," said Sondra. "Where's your sense of adventure? At least finish the one you've got."

"I've got to be somewhere," he said, feeling her alliance imperceptibly drift over to Will's side.

"Hot date?" teased Sondra, a warm laugh following the question. "The little girl?"

Dillon flushed. "I need to make a phone call."

"Out in front, man," said Joe, pointing through the plate glass window to a phone booth under a streetlight.

"I'll be back in a minute," said Dillon. "Let's get ready to clear out of here."

"Please sit down," Sondra invited Will and Joe. Before they could ask her about the television business, she asked them about their motorcycles. They were impressed with her knowledge of bikes, though her experience had been with off-road vehicles.

Dillon came back from the phone booth. He had pulled off his tie and opened the collar of his shirt. "Are you ready to go?" he asked her.

"Don't you want to finish your beer?" she asked him.

"No," he said impatiently. "I have to go."

"Dillon, you are just too uptight sometimes," she said. "I'm having fun talking with these gentlemen, and you're in a hurry. He's always in a hurry," she added, to Will.

"That's not true," said Dillon defensively. "I just happen to have plans and don't want to put my life on hold all the time for the sake of this damned show."

Sondra gave him a cool look. "Are you saying that all there is to *my* life is the show?" she asked, her voice sharp.

Dillon looked embarrassed about the confrontation. Joe stared at his beer bottle. Will watched Dillon, then Sondra, then Dillon again.

"Sondra," pleaded Dillon, "don't get pissed. I'm just trying to tell you I have a date, and you can have a little courtesy because I'm driving and I need to take you to your car."

"Finish your beer," she said, unyielding.

"Shit," said Dillon, taking the beer bottle and turning it upside down against his mouth. He finished the liquid before placing the bottle back on the table.

Dillon was being an ass. "Sorry," apologized Sondra to Will and Joe.

Joe couldn't believe the next words he heard.

"I'll give you a ride home on the back of my scooter," offered Will.

"Thanks," said Sondra, extending a rare smile to a face that was not used to receiving many smiles.

"For Christ's sake, Sondra," said Dillon, exasperated. "I'm not going to leave you here."

"Why not?"

"I just won't. I can't. Please come with me."

"I'll be just fine," she said. "This gentleman will see me home."

Dillon didn't understand why she was being so difficult. Maybe she was drunk, though she didn't seem so. For some reason, she had resolved to hold her ground. The angrier he got, the more she would resist him. Her stubbornness infuriated him. However, he decided it would be smarter not to fight her.

"I'll buy us all another round," said Dillon. "I'm not leaving you."

"Don't you think you can trust me?" said Will, his voice on edge, challenging.

Shit, thought Dillon, two of them. "Look, I trust you, buddy. I never said I didn't trust you. Would you go off and leave a woman you knew at a dump like this with people you didn't know?"

Will agreed it was a dump. "No, I wouldn't," he answered. He turned to Sondra. "It was presumptuous of me to ask if you wanted a ride. I'll see you when you come out to film," he told her. "Nice talking with the two of you. Come on, Joe," he said to his small friend.

Joe followed Will out the door, where they climbed aboard their motorcycles and drove off onto the dark highway.

Sondra, still pissed off, followed Dillon to his Volvo. "I can open my own door!" she snapped when he unlocked it for her.

He didn't say a word. He didn't know why she had acted the way she had. He pulled on his headlights before backing out of the parking space.

"Turn them off until you're out of the parking lot," she reprimanded. "Are you so damn dumb you can't see your lights blind everyone inside?"

They drove back toward town: she angry; he anxious that he would miss his rendezvous.

They didn't know that Will had doubled back and watched them pull away, to make sure that the blonde had safely left the bar.

"No way, man, no fuckin' way," laughed Martin, rolling over on the couch, his hip deep and comfortable between the cushions, the eyes above his freckled cheeks concentrated on the television.

"Yes," said James, one of his two roommates, gleefully. "It's your turn to pay up. You had to lose some time, you know."

Martin extended his arm with the remote control channel changer affixed to the end and flipped through the many stations hooked to the satellite dish. "I haven't lost yet," he smirked. "There's still tonight."

"Technically, only till midnight. But you'd have to do *three* to win."

"Three hides aren't so many," said Martin, plumping a throw pillow under his head and staring at a Michigan pool tournament.

"But you don't feel like it, do you?" said his roommate, squatting his body builder's frame next to the couch, taking the remote control from Martin's hand and turning to stock car racing in Alabama. "You haven't been off that couch all day. You've been partying too hardy."

"I'll call Tina. She'll bring her sisters. That'll make three," he said, sniffing at a glass of room-temperature orange juice. Dried flecks of the pulp were stuck to the inside.

"You're dreaming," said his roommate, retreating to an armchair, locating a Tennessee evangelist whose heavy shock of slicked-back hair had fallen into his eyes as his treacherous, low voice bespoke of the evils of sex outside marriage. "Tina's grandmother is visiting," he continued, "and those girls haven't been seen in public for a week."

Martin shut his eyes as his headache swelled in his head, pounding out the inside of his ears. "How 'bout Carmen? She's so big and fat, couldn't she count as three?" A dry laugh crackled from his throat.

"Even *she* isn't desperate enough to want to do it with you," said James, blinking to the local news with its beach and surf report. The screen focused on steady, broad-sweeping gray breakers crashing against the beach south of Newport. "God," he exclaimed, "it's almost past the season, but will you look at those waves? Let's get our wet suits and boards and head down there tomorrow morning."

"I won't be able to afford it," said Martin wearily. He was trying to think of a way to approach his father for money, since he'd just borrowed enough to make his car payment.

"Too bad," said his roommate, switching to a game show and concentrating on the question the host was asking the contestants. "The Rolling Stones," he blurted out. "God, who doesn't know the answer to that?"

The contestant gave the wrong answer and James leapt from his chair in exasperation. "What a fool! Can you believe they didn't know that answer? That stupid son of a bitch!"

Martin had been about to mention that he didn't know if he could get the money, but James's mood would not have taken the news.

"Nice of you to pay the rent, old boy," said James. "I'm calling in sick tomorrow and hitting those waves."

When Martin didn't reply, James looked at the prone figure and eyed him carefully. "You *do* have the funds, right, man?" he asked.

Martin lay without saying a word, the game show breaking to a commercial.

"A bet's a bet, right, man?" said James, pushing the "mute" button and hovering over Martin.

They shared a Redondo Beach house, a block from the sand. It was an older two-story building, covered in faded green ship-lap siding, with top floor windows that looked out to sea. There were three bedrooms, the third made by converting the garage. Martin occupied this. It was the largest, though coldest bedroom, with its cement floor covered by thin indoor/outdoor carpeting. The biggest inconvenience was that the house's only bathroom was upstairs.

Martin's roommates, James and Stan, were old friends from high school with whom he had lost touch until a few months before, when he had run into them at a Fourth of July party on the beach. They told him they needed a third roommate; he told them he had a great idea about paying rent.

"A bet," Martin taunted them.

They had laughed over their beers and asked him if he could top the bet made the summer after high school, when they had gone down to the Baja peninsula in Mexico to find the lost tequila factory of Juan Mesqualito.

"This is serious," Martin told them, spinning a volleyball in his hand.

"Sure," they laughed again, never taking him seriously.

"Listen . . . if you guys don't want to do it . . . or even hear about it." He scratched at a sand flea.

"Okay, okay, what is it?" James dropped his mirrored sunglasses down onto the tip of his nose and looked over the lenses.

"It has to do with ladies."

"We're listening, ol' buddy," said Stan, picking at a hangnail on his big toe.

"We'll see who can screw the most chicks a month. The one who gets the most doesn't have to pay rent. The other two split it in half."

"Does each girl count as one, or can you screw the same girl several nights?"

"The *most* girls a month means *different* girls. Shit, you could screw the same girl five times in one night, but it still only counts as one."

James and Stan laughed and said it sounded like something that Martin would dream up. But they took him up on the bet, saying they were all going to end up with sore pricks and horrible diseases.

"Nah," said Martin. "We'll only go after nice girls."

The bet had worked out well—in Martin's favor. He knew what a lot of girls liked, and it wasn't sex. It was the vial of white powder he kept in his shirt pocket.

In a nightclub, talking to a girl, he'd tap his pocket after a while and ask her if she wanted to go out to the parking lot for a "refresher." The girl usually said yes, and he generally didn't have to take her back into the bar and buy her more drinks. She would be willing to "go down to his place on the beach and party."

It had been an easy summer rent-wise. His part-time job waiting tables had paid for the loose ends that he couldn't get his father to cough up. He knew how to approach Graham, when the producer was busy and didn't have time to do anything but sign a check and whisk the kid out of his office.

Martin lay there on the couch, staring at the television. James still stood over him, a pissed-off look on his face.

"A bet's a bet, right, Martin?" He turned off the power to the set, his stare so intense that he forced Martin to look up. The pressure was on. The good humor had vanished. James tightened the muscle in his massive arm, then relaxed it.

"All right, man," replied Martin sulkily. "I'll pay."

The girl sat on Garrett's lap hugging him. She murmured contentedly, her eyes closed against his shoulder while he observed his living room.

The furniture was used-used; he had picked up a lot of it off curbs and refinished it. (He could be handy around the house when he had to be.) Four tall windows were set in stucco arches. The ceiling was ten feet high. One doorway was the front entrance, another led to the kitchen, and the third passed to the spacious bedroom and bath.

It was a large crummy apartment on a crummy street in an old run-down Hollywood neighborhood. He had lived there for the past five years, while seeking fame and fortune. It had been slow in coming. Now that it was upon him, it was still overwhelming and unbelievable.

Against the opposite wall leaned a chunk of cloudy mirror. He could see his bare feet, calves, and knees; legs attached to a body that was insured for a million bucks. In less than two months, his value had increased considerably.

When he sat in his apartment, he was the same guy he had always been. When he looked in the mirror, he saw Garrett Gage, the realization of his dreams,—still vaporous, as yet more intangible than solid,—but becoming increasingly tactile.

Part of him had become Frank Harrison, the detective with the boy-next-door personality and the *Gentlemen's Quarterly* face, the bumbling, intelligent, winsome sleuth who solved crimes throughout the centuries by going anywhere he wanted in a time machine. Frank was continually knocking over the girls with his handsomeness and, at the same time, was unaware of his looks.

Garrett had been contemptuous of the character when he had first read for the part. However, when it was awarded him, he had been responsible for creating Frank.

Now, he had grown fond of Frank. Of course, the producers, writers, and directors were continually filling him in on *their* version of Frank. He listened to them politely (Lord knows politely) because if there was one thing he had learned over the tough years in Hollywood, it was to support every ego that could help you get to the top. He would discuss Frank with them if that's what they wanted. What Frank would or would not do in a certain circumstance. In the end, he portrayed Frank exactly as he wanted, meanwhile letting them all think they had helped greatly.

The girl snuggled against his chest. "Where are we going for dinner tonight?" It had become the nightly question when he came home from the set.

"I don't know," he sighed, not wishing to make a decision. He would have preferred to let her sit on his lap most of the evening, while he held her and thought. Brenda was comfortable and safe, reminding him of what he had so recently been and, if luck turned against him, what he could so quickly be again.

"You're so quiet," she said. "Do you want to talk?"

"It's the same stuff we've been talking about for a month. I feel like I'm living in a dream world."

She sat up, looked in his face, and rubbed his temples. "You should talk about it as much as you need to. You know I'll listen."

He let her rub his entire head. It released the stress. Brenda believed in him. She had paid the rent and bills many times during the lean months. He was grateful for her steadfastness and felt loyal toward her. Though he had never fallen in love with her, he cared for her very much. There was a tight bond of friendship between them. He had sworn to her that he would always take care of her if he made it big.

Now was a time of unaccustomed luxury. They ate out every evening, and laughed and drank expensive bottles of wine, and still felt incredibly guilty for spending the money.

Because she felt she was losing her control in the relationship, Brenda had adapted much differently than he to the change in their lifestyle.

He had recently come home from the studio and found her crying. She explained that a woman had appeared on their doorstep looking for Frank Harrison; a woman who had looked sane but had insisted she would wait forever until he returned. Brenda had asked her to leave. She wouldn't budge. Finally, Brenda had had to call the police to have them haul the woman away. That was the first rabid fan to throw herself before Garrett.

Garrett was frequently recognized now. He took it good-naturedly and signed autographs with a smile. Brenda looked on with growing dismay. He was the most gorgeous man she had ever met, had ever been to bed with. Many times, she was content just to look at him because he was so handsome.

He had shiny dark hair and bright blue eyes. Thick dark eyebrows made his eyes even brighter. He was always being asked if he wore colored contacts, and he would cheerfully respond, "No, they're really *that* blue." He had an all-American smile, a happy triumphant row of teeth to be found in any copy of *Sports Illustrated.* He was six feet one and thin, and he didn't think it was a problem since the camera always added bulk. They were talking now about having him work out with a trainer an hour a day, just so he could do more scenes with his shirt off.

He figured one of the benefits of appearing on a series like *Motive* was that women all over America would fall in love with him. "Fans," he explained to Brenda, "are what makes the ratings. You gotta be nice to your fans." And, boy oh boy, could he do a good job of charming them off their feet. There had been a couple of evenings when no one had acknowledged him and he had become depressed. Brenda tried not to think about it.

Garrett's eye caught a dark spot moving on the wall above the mirror. It was a big roach.

"Goddamn it," he said through clenched teeth, dumping Brenda into the chair and striding to the bug that was scurrying rapidly up the wall.

About to smack it with the palm of his hand, he stopped himself and looked for something to hit it with. It had gained a foot and was moving up. He kicked a bare foot, his heel crushing the crusted body, flattening it into a dark spot. His face was full of rage.

But it amused Brenda. She laughed, watching him totter on one leg, finally lose his balance, and fall to the floor.

"That does it," he said, his anger settling into humor. "We're looking for a new place to live. Come here, woman," he said, grabbing for her leg.

She got down on her hands and knees and crawled to him, kissing the chin with its single day's growth of beard—the shaving neglected by Frank and not by a meticulous dresser like Garrett.

The gray cat bumped Denny's leg as he stood in the kitchen tearing lettuce for a salad. He had sliced sweet red onion, zucchini, tomato, a hard-boiled egg, and grated some cheese to mix in it. The tender lettuce reminded him of rose petals—soft, delicate, smooth. Like a cheek. A young boy's cheek. A sweet, smooth face of a sixteen-year-old.

The knot he couldn't swallow welled in his throat. He was determined not to cry. His eyes were red and burning. If he showed up at work again looking like that, they would all have another good laugh. He put the lettuce down on the sideboard, wiped his hands on his apron, and sat down on the floor in front of the sink.

His mama cat was unusually perceptive and crawled into his lap. She knew he was in distress. She kneaded his chest with her paws. He held her closely and wished that Jeff would walk through the front door. He'd take Jeff back. He didn't care what Jeff had done to him. He couldn't live with the separation.

But then the face of the duped kid came back to him and he saw Jeff's finger crooking to invite Denny to join them. Oh, it hurt. The anger burned. Rumbled. Roiled inside him. Jeff had been unfaithful many times, and Denny felt the fool for never having guessed it.

Denny had subjected himself to one AIDS test and had fearfully awaited the results. They had, fortunately, been negative. It was ironic that he found himself hoping Jeff had chosen only young virgins from the Midwest for his sexual ventures instead of Hollywood boys who had made the rounds.

The silence of the apartment overwhelmed him. It was too quiet. He used to like the quiet after being on a crowded set all day. He had liked coming home and not talking for an hour. He had needed time to be by himself.

Now he had it. He had given himself as much time alone as he could use. He needed to talk to someone.

He carried the cat to the bedroom to retrieve the phone. He sat on the edge of the bed to dial, but a clamminess crawled over the back of his neck—it was *that* bed—and he retreated to the living room.

"Is Margi there?" he asked when the phone answered.

"Just a sec," said a voice he recognized as the teenage daughter. He heard her yell to her mother, adding, "It's Denny . . . agaaaaaiiiin" in a singsongy voice.

"Can you talk?" he asked Margi.

"Sure," she replied. "For a few minutes. Bob's gone out for some cigarettes." She had been hand washing lingerie and was wiping her sudsy hands on the back of her sweatpants. "What did you eat for supper?" she asked.

"I made a salad but I don't feel like eating," he said.

"Denny, you're too skinny as it is. Would you please eat? You're not doing anybody any good if you don't eat."

"Do you know what I want more than anything else right now? I want to find Jeff and tell him to come back." The cat pushed the top of her hard, softly furred head up under his chin.

"Denny, he'll do the same thing to you, over and over."

"I don't care. I've never been so devastated in my whole life. You saw how I was today. Impossible, just impossible. Garrett was nervous in the scene with the murderer, and he was sweating and I couldn't get his powder to look right. It was awful. Richard, our cheerful director, chewed the eraser off his pencil when he asked me to re-powder for the fourth time. And there was that smug jerk of a cameraman, Tony, chuckling to what's-his-name on the sound boom. Then I trip over the fucking cable and every grip on the set starts laughing out loud."

"It didn't help to flip them all off, Denny."

"I know that. They only laughed harder. I suppose everyone knows what's wrong with me."

"I haven't told anyone but Richard," said Margi, not quite truthfully. "I think he's being very understanding. You know how pissed he can get when the close-ups are hard to take."

"How did everyone find out? Richard wouldn't talk. You wouldn't tell a soul."

"Have you ever been on a set where anybody on the crew has privacy? Everybody knows what's happening with everyone else."

"Men are so callous. They don't care. Women are so much more gentle and understanding. I am not going to get near a man for months. No way. There are a lot of women I'm friends with. I'll spend time with them."

"Denny, are you trying to tell me you're going to *date* women?"

"I didn't say that. . . ."

"Oh, shit," she said suddenly. "Hold on." She paused, listening to a car pull up in the driveway. "Bob's back. I got to go," she said. "I can't get into another fight with him over this. You'll be fine. I wish you'd eat. I'll see you in the morning." She hung up quickly.

He shook his head. He'd been dealing with the Bob Owenses of the world most of his life—the macho rednecks who hated homosexuals. Poor Margi, married to such a boor. He pulled out the cast and crew sheet and phoned another number.

"Hello," answered a female voice.

"Is this Jeannie?" he asked.

"Yes," she said, her tone brightening at the sound of a man.

"This is Denny. We met on the set of *Motive* last week when you brought some papers by for Mr. M?"

"Denny?" she said softly, unable to place him.

"Remember, we talked about using peach on your upper lids and trying a lighter foundation and less powder?"

She swallowed hard. "The makeup artist?"

"Yes," he said. "I thought maybe you'd like to meet me for a drink later this evening."

There was a long, long pause before she answered. Her tone was cool. Her words revealed that she was probably shocked. "I . . . I don't think it's a good idea for me to go out with people that I work with."

"We don't really work *together.* Not on the same show or anything."

"Mr. Maddox wouldn't like it," she said firmly. "I just couldn't do it. I just couldn't."

"Okay. If that's the way it is."

"That's the way it is." She was insulted he had offered. "Thanks anyway," she added, a flat stone falling dully on a rocky beach.

Not all women are gentle, he thought. Nor are they approachable. He kissed the mama cat on her head and lay back on the couch. He meant to fall asleep and forget his troubles. But thoughts of Jeff swam through his mind like huge schools of silvery slippery fish; he was unable to stop them, catch them, or rise to the surface above them.

The fog began rolling in. Dillon waited for her in his Volvo, near the point where Sunset Boulevard joined the Pacific Coast Highway. She had wanted to walk up the beach, but now undetectable wisps fuzzed the clear crescent of lights along Malibu and gradually thickened like the inside of a pudding.

Presently, he was alone, except for the clear radio strain of Long Beach jazz cutting through the soupy sky and his orange parking lights glowing against the smothering clouds. He had met her here only twice before. She was late. Was she lost? Had her evening class run overtime? Had she been stopped by those that forbade her to see him?

Notes tumbled from a piano: acrobats doing floor exercises; smooth, square-shouldered, never losing a beat, lightly skipping and somersaulting. He began to enjoy the wait. He relaxed against the sounds and chuckled to himself at his situation—alone, blanketed by fog that pushed clammy hands against the windshield, waiting for a girl he had to meet in secret.

He wondered at his patience—for meeting her clandestinely, as she insisted; at his reasoning—for allowing it to go on month after month without bringing it out into the open; and at his sanity—for being so much in love with her he couldn't stop himself.

The thought of her made butterflies start inside his stomach. His sense of logic laughed at this feeling, at the out-of-control mushiness whose origin he could not explain. It was ridiculous—everything that was logical within the man said it was ridiculous—yet, when it came over him, he let it happen. It fluttered strong wings inside his gut, which spread to his chest and loudly thumped his heart. It was a marvelous warm-caramel sweetness that he had never felt before.

The jazz played harder; a complicated percussion below, a simple horn in the middle, a schizoid violin on top. It waylaid the oozy syrup inside him and brought him up short on the edge of reality.

He thought of Graham Maddox, his employer, and how the man had never warmed to him. Maddox trusted him, but it was a trust that was expected not respected. Maddox never joked with Dillon. He had been good friends with Dillon's predecessor, and that friendship had scalded him. Now, Maddox would let nothing interfere with a straight-line employer-employee relationship. It bothered Dillon. There was a tension in the air between them that he would have preferred to work without, a lurking doubt that undermined his self-confidence. Graham knew how to play him. As Dillon became more worried, he worked harder and made fewer mistakes. The young exec had no reason to fear losing his job, yet he succumbed to the stress, the worry that Maddox might irrationally fire him.

Now that Mrs. Maddox had appeared on the scene, she

eased some of that anxiety. Ruby relied heavily on Dillon's knowledge, expertise, and sense of humor. She seemed to like him now more than she had at first. She teased him, and they both laughed. She had found a friend in him.

Everyone was afraid of letting themselves go around her because she was Graham Maddox's wife. But she wanted to be liked. Dillon truly believed that she would never sabotage anyone's adequacy the way her husband did. She wanted to be accepted on the same terms as everyone else on the production team.

Headlights flashed through his car. A small BMW parked next to him. Penny got out and came toward his door. As he rolled down his window, she pressed her nose against the glass, smiling playfully and clutching her coat around her neck, then pushed her head in and kissed him happily. Her lips were sugary and giving against his, her breath warm, her laughter and energy delightful. She clung to him, coming halfway through the window, kissing and kissing like she hadn't seen him for years.

After ten minutes, she finally let him breathe. She had slid in the window and was sitting on his lap, lodged between the steering wheel and his chest. Her warm wool hat had fallen off, her bobbed hair was mussed, and her eyes shone with love. Her nose was pert, a little bit of a thing, and her small mouth kept whispering, "I love you, love you, love you," against his face, her lips touching his eyes and cheeks and forehead.

To him, she was a earthly beauty. Not an unreachable, untouchable icon of popular dictates, but a real, sensitive, loving girl that was so open to him. She was eighteen. She trusted him. Had told him everything about herself. Had cried when she had explained her family, their values, and what they expected from her. He wanted nothing more than to hold her in his arms and protect her.

Yet, this was precisely what they must keep secret.

"Where shall we go?" he asked her. "It's too cold and foggy to walk on the beach."

"I have an idea," she said, asking him to drive up the coast road toward Malibu.

He pulled on yellow fog lights and moved cautiously out onto Pacific Coast Highway. Dillon had opted for a solid front seat in the Volvo rather than bucket seats. Penny moved close to him, her arms entwined around his, her chin resting on his shoulder. He drove carefully. Often, taillights loomed suddenly out of the cloudy denseness, intense red and very close. His attention was so concentrated on his driving that he was barely aware of the girl sitting next to him.

Before they reached Zuma Beach, she pointed to the right and bade him take the small road that led into the mountains. It was winding and narrow, the pavement wide enough for only two cars, with no white line to mark the center of its black surface. Though there were houses, they were too far off to the side for their lights to cut through the fog.

"Where are we going?" he asked, nervous that he might miss the road on the next curve and they would plunge over the edge and roll hundreds of yards into the manzanita-ensnarled gully below.

The incline was so steep that they climbed a thousand feet in just a few minutes. Before Penny could reply, the vapors thinned and in another moment they were free of the coastal fog bank. They still climbed, up, up, as the road went deeper into the mountains. The night sky was starry and an old moon hung a shimmering spoon lip of light across the wild, dry ridges.

Penny was warm and alive next to him. Every sense in his body was attuned to hers. He found a lane that wound out of sight a hundred feet from the road. Huge, silent live oak trees partially shadowed the Volvo as Dillon parked. He cracked his window and a thin stream of the cold outside air moved slowly into the car.

As the sound of the engine died, her mouth was upon his, urgently pressing, ravenously craving his touch. She clawed at his jacket and, underneath, his shirt, her hands touching the smooth skin of his chest, sliding over thick supple muscle that the conservative business clothing concealed.

She was knotted into her coat, and he had to push her

back and let her unbutton it herself. She wore a cotton dress that smelled faintly of the dry cleaners. Its hemline flounce was worked over her knees. He felt her bare legs. They were damply cold and he guessed she had not expected the night to be so chilly. He tried to put his coat over them, to warm them, but she pushed it away.

"I want to feel you," she murmured. "I just want to feel you."

He tugged at the zipper of his pants. She put both hands around him, each circling the opposite way, and squeezed gently, feeling the pulse surge through him. He had already been stiff, but he felt himself swell in her grasp and the rush of fire ripple through each sensitive nerve ending. He wanted to place his hand beneath her dress, but she was just out of his reach and he was unable to move under her molten contact.

He sat in the middle of the seat and she moved to straddle him, pulling the dress to her waist, pulling aside the crotch of her panties so he could enter her. She sat carefully, a little dry, her skin tugged apart sweetly and painfully as he strained into her. She gave up control to him, and he pulled her hips against him, forcing himself all the way in her, feeling her quiver, searching to kiss her mouth.

Their passion was quickly loosed; a frantic flight of two wild birds escaping captivity, hearts pounding, wings beating a blind path into the infinite, climbing higher and higher with only the physical as real.

Then they trembled against each other, their arms fiercely gripping the other who could give them so much satisfaction, so much love, unstopped and flowing between the two of them. Penny buried her head against Dillon's neck, reluctant to open her eyes, content to feel the warm wetness uniting them. He felt the whole of the girl who clung to him. Nothing in the world mattered but the two of them, alone and interlocked, at this moment.

As his head cleared, he felt the familiar gnawing start through him, the anguish he lived with every time he thought of Penny. A bolt of anger jolted him, and she felt the change in his mood. She silently slipped from him, the cold air chilling her skin that had been touching his, the dampness not confined to one spot, but here and there in her clothing.

"I'm sorry, I'm sorry," she whispered, reading his mind, the tears coming fast into her voice. "Oh, Dillon, what are we going to do?"

Stand up to them, thought Dillon. Tell them you love me and you don't care what they say. But the words were mute within him. Her family, "old money" people, didn't think Dillon was good enough for their daughter. They wanted her to be involved with someone from her own social strata—someone with lineage, East Coast education, world travel, a promising career, and parents just like themselves. They despised men like Dillon, who had clawed their way up the dirty sides of a vertically-walled lower-class grave; men who relied more on instinct, luck, and determination than on intellect; men who were on the verge of gaining affluent status with no heritage to support that acquisition. They were threatened by men like Dillon. They would never associate with them if given a chance, and they didn't condone—or even allow—their well-bred daughters becoming emotionally attached to one.

Penny was caught in the middle. She was angry with her parents for their snobbery, infuriated because they thought she was too young, but could not desert them simply because their views differed from hers. They had done her no harm; they had simply expressed opinion.

Dillon, on the other side, drew her sweetly to him, her heart helplessly caught as he reeled her in. She didn't know what to do, so she let the relationship continue with as little upheaval as she could manage. Dillon had been patient so far, meeting where she wanted, glad for the few minutes he could be with her.

He dreamed of the time when she would be with him. He tried to understand why she wouldn't do it now, why she wouldn't make a hundred-percent commitment to him. Her parents knew of Dillon, and they had told her to stop seeing him. She had pleaded with them to accept him. But they had laughed like it never could be. Dillon was tempted to spit in their faces, but wouldn't it be a much sweeter victory if he continued to climb to their strata where they would have to accept him as an equal?

So he hung on. The more difficult it was to see Penny, the weaker his insides felt at the thought of her. His love for her hurt him and consumed him.

He pulled the girl close and kissed her head, knowing he would have to descend into the fog again and return her to her car by midnight.

Chapter 4

Glory looked around her apartment one more time. Was everything perfect? Was everything clean? Had she disguised her bed to look like a couch? Would he care that she just lived in this inexpensive studio apartment? Surely, he must know she was the lowest paid member of the crew. He'd been around long enough; probably nothing surprised him.

A hum of excitement hit her throat like the vibration of a mosquito trapped in a small space. Tony had been around for a while. She didn't know his age for sure, but she believed he was at least twenty years older than she. Maybe twenty-five. Her mother had called from Minnesota with prying questions, but Glory had been evasive. Glory's mother would have been horror-stricken to think her daughter was going out with a man the same age as she.

But Glory didn't see him that way. He certainly didn't act fatherly toward her. On the set, between takes, she'd catch him looking at her from his position behind the camera with sexual, not paternal glances. They embarrassed her deep down and she hoped, because a set is a very busy place, that no one else noticed. She'd glance over and there he would be—looking and grinning. They had gone to lunch a few times at the commissary. He had always insisted on paying. She would have bought her own lunch, but he had insisted. So he must have known she didn't have much money.

Cameramen were in a high income bracket. He probably drove a real cool car. Something fast and luxurious. She pictured something sleek and black with a tan interior. Leather. She could smell the leather. And she imagined the valet parking attendant at an expensive restaurant opening the door and Tony waiting for her to take his arm so they could go inside.

Tony was so good-looking, with his heavy brown mustache and graying head. His hair was thick. She wondered what it would be like to catch her fingers in a thatch like that and hold on. He wasn't much taller than she. Oh, what if her new high heels made her too tall? That worry instantly went to her toes, and when she turned to look in her hallway mirror, she smacked her shin against the coffee table.

"Hell," she said out loud, knowing a great purple bruise would rise in that spot.

Tony had no trouble finding the building. He waited a couple of minutes for the elevator before a tenant informed him, "You could wait there all night, mister. The thing ain't worked in four years." So he climbed the stairs.

Glory's curtains were drawn. He inspected his reflection in the glass, hoping he didn't look too old, hoping she wouldn't be repelled by it. He knocked.

"I'll be right there," called out Glory's squeaky voice.

He smiled to himself. He thought her voice was cute. He ignored those crew members from *Motive* who jestingly put their fingers in their ears at the sound of it.

Glory opened the door and looked so good it took the breath right out of him. She wore a ruffly white blouse and turquoise slacks, which were especially tight around her full rear end. Oh, it looked good. He didn't like small or flat-assed girls. She rocked on red high heels and motioned for him to come in.

It was an average apartment. He wondered how many people in L.A. could afford to live alone. He immediately went to the two old movie posters, framed and covering one entire wall.

"Two of my favorites," he commented. "These are the original one-sheets, aren't they?"

"Yes. When I lived in Minnesota, I wrote to some movie memorabilia shops on Hollywood Boulevard. Those posters weren't cheap, but it meant so much to get them."

Glory stepped close to Tony, her finger touching the glass over the poster and outlining the movie face. Her eyes shone. "He's very handsome," she said softly about the actor. She smelled something and realized there was a hint of alcohol on Tony's breath. He'd probably had a couple before coming over. It surprised her that he as well, might be nervous about the date.

With white sweater and purse, she followed Tony out to the front of the building. There she saw the hefty manager in an orange-and-green print cotton dress writing the license number of a very shabby, oxidized green older Toyota parked on the curb.

With fleshy hand on hip, the manager eyed Tony and asked, "Is this yours?"

"Yeah, it is," he replied.

Glory's heart sank. This old car?

"You parked in the red zone," continued the manager, "and I was about to get a wrecker out here to tow it off." There was not a trace of kindness in her voice.

Tony hesitated a moment, deciding whether to be brusque or kind. It was hard to imagine being gentlemanly with this wreck of a human. "I'm sorry," he said. "I didn't realize it was a red curb. I thought it was a loading zone. I was only gone for a couple of minutes to retrieve Ms. Bell."

The manager harrumphed and said, "It's not a loading zone unless you stay in your car. It will be impounded if you do it again."

As Tony and Glory drove off, he laughed when he caught a glimpse of the manager's pasty face in his rearview mirror. "My God!" he exclaimed. "Do you have to see much of her?"

Glory groaned, "More than I like. She's always putting her nose in my business. Can you imagine what she's going to think now? She'll probably be all over me tomorrow to find out who you are, what we did, and everything else in between."

"Don't tell her."

Glory grinned. "I'll try not to."

When he pulled out his pack of unfiltered cigarettes, she rolled her window down. The smoke plus the odor of liquor would have been too much for her. Her other dates were generally with boys her own age, and if they smoked, she usually had the courage to ask them to wait until they were out of the car.

Tony didn't notice her discomfort. He held the glowing car lighter to his cigarette, speaking between puffs. "Good idea of yours to go to the movies at the county art museum," he said. "I haven't been to classic films in years."

Glory blushed. "I thought it might be a good idea, since the art museum gets good prints. Sometimes they have guest speakers. I've heard directors talk there before. Famous directors." Her eyes lit up as she said that and then, suddenly, she felt foolish. She knew he had worked with a lot of famous directors.

The night was still warm, though it would drop to the low fifties by sunrise. After Glory's years of Minnesota snow, the upcoming Southern California winter did not seem like it would get very cold. All she knew was that it had to be more comfortable than the summer months—those hot, smoggy desert days—they had just passed through.

She leaned back and looked out the window. He drove through one of the canyons that connected the San Fernando Valley to the Los Angeles Basin. A line of traffic wove up the hill, a steady stream of cars whipping around curves, their brakes applied only at the last possible second.

Streetlights illuminated the road, both sides of which were overgrown by heavy foliage. For long stretches there was no sidewalk, only a curb and dirt. Houses were built treacherously close to the speeding roadway. If she lived there and had children, she felt sure she would be in a constant state of anxiety that they would be hit. She would have been worried sick over a dog or cat.

Cat? Cat? Suddenly she remembered with a pang of guilt that her cat had not come home before she left with Tony.

They crested Mulholland Drive and began winding down the south side of the canyon. The houses were packed side by side and the occupants' parked cars crowded next to the curbs. Glory wondered how many of these cars were crashed into. There was barely enough room for the traffic. Nervous, she sat upright, her hands folded in her lap. Her pointy right shoe pinched her toes, but she gritted her teeth and resolved not to do much walking.

Disappointment crept into thoughts as she sat in the small, loudly humming car. She felt silly for having imagined Tony in a luxury car. But surely he made good money. Why was he driving this piece of junk? She hoped there would be no valet parking. She couldn't have endured the look on a parking attendant's face.

At the bottom of the hill, they sped through the flat residential streets toward the museum. The air smelled of cut grass, eucalyptus, and exhaust fumes. They had to park a block away and walk. Glory, who could barely maintain her balance in the heels, unconsciously grabbed Tony's arm for support.

After the two movies, Tony suggested a cafe. "It will make you think you're in Europe," he told her.

"Okay," she said.

"It's an artists' hangout."

"I've never been to Europe, but I adore creative people." She thought of her aching feet. "We don't have to walk, do we?"

"No," he replied.

The cafe was large, lit with low golden lights and candles on each table. There was a lot of wood in the place—the floor, beams on the ceiling, tables, chairs, bar, the walls. Glory's eyes darted back and forth as she tried to recognize celebrities who might be lifting a forkful of quiche to their mouth.

Tony ordered a carafe of rose wine and lit a cigarette. Glory's hair glimmered in the candlelight. "Have you done something with your hair?" he asked.

She blushed. "I lightened the ends. Do you like it?"

He nodded his approval and smiled. "What would you like to eat?"

She ordered an omelette with the whole garden thrown

in, and he, Hungarian goulash. She had had only a couple sips of her wine when Tony nervously finished his and refilled his glass.

"Where did you go to college?" she asked him.

"U.C.L.A. I was a film major. In those days, I had all kinds of inspirations about making movies. I should have kept at it. I started making a thesis film but couldn't get enough money to finish it. Then I got married. I thought my wife was behind me a hundred percent. I thought she wanted me to be a director. But, damn . . . I got to working for the studios, got in the union, bought a house, and got roped into all kinds of payments.

"Do you know how much work it is to be an actor or a director? How much socializing you have to do? Keep your name and your face out there in front of all those people? I could have played their games, played executive, politician. It's a bunch of shit, but that's the way Hollywood works.

"But the wife kept wanting this and that. I lost sight of my goals. Should have kept at it. Finished that student film. It was a good one. I've got it half shot. All the footage is developed."

"I'd love to see it," said Glory, who had created a couple of her own ten-minute student films.

"I'd have to dig it out from storage."

"I was a film major, too," said Glory. "In Minnesota."

"Were you?" said Tony with little interest. "The only place you can attend film school and hope to *get* somewhere is in Los Angeles or New York.

He pushed his half-eaten plate of goulash to the side and lit a cigarette. "You know, I get so fucking frustrated with the directors they hire to shoot the show. Especially Richard the Great. I could do better than him. He thinks he's hot shit. He'll probably go some place with that attitude. *He* gets out there to all those parties. That's what it's all about. *Who* you know. It doesn't do much good to bitch about a situation. I just sit behind my camera and let him make all those mistakes. Just pisses me off, that's all. He's got a career and I could do it so much better."

Tony had drunk half of their second carafe of wine and

was smiling warmly at Glory. She realized he was getting quite drunk, and she wondered why. Was he unhappy? Did he need to forget?

He certainly didn't give a damn about her. He hadn't asked her a single question about herself and didn't act like he had even heard her when she made a comment. But maybe he needed to talk to someone. She would be his friend. She would listen. It sure bothered the hell out of him that he was only a camera operator.

Only? She thought his job seemed so interesting. But he thought it was below his potential. Whatever potential he had had, he had let slip away years ago. Bitterness showed in his eyes, through every word he spoke, in every swallow of wine that rolled down his throat. He needed someone to believe in him.

"Tony," she said, spearing a last piece of bell pepper and cheese with her fork, "I think you and I should work on a project together."

"Sure, sugar, let's do that. You're a smart girl. What should we do?"

"I don't know yet," she said, her eyes smiling. At last . . . at last here was someone with whom she could share her passion for film. "First thing . . . promise me you'll show me your student film footage."

"Oh, you don't really want to see that old stuff," he said, coughing a smoker's hack as he squished out a cigarette butt.

"Yes, I do," she insisted. "Promise you'll show it to me."

"Do you really want to see it?"

"Absolutely."

Her voice had dropped to a low timbre, a sweet honey note of positivity. It was sexy. It was encouraging. He forgot the scatterbrained, squeaky-voiced production assistant that stumbled over the cable on the set. This girl looked at him with keen eyes and an inspiring smile.

"Tony," she said, "you're talented. You can't let that go to waste."

"Thank you, my dear. Let's toast to that." He lifted the wine to his lips and winked at her over the rim of his glass.

Hers was the warmest smile he'd seen in many, many months. He squeezed her hand. The contact with her soft, warm fingers made him feel very horny. (On top of everything, she made him horny.) He often joked with the guys on the crew about being horny, but he had to admit to himself that he hardly ever was anymore. Not horny enough to do something about it. And then . . . here was this girl. Her face seemed so eager. She wanted to be with him. He could tell.

When they got back to his car, he leaned her up against the side to kiss her. She turned her head to one side, but he gently pulled her chin around and pressed his mouth on hers. She gave in sweetly, reaching her arms around his neck, tentatively touching his hair with her fingertips.

She asked if she could drive. It was a hell of a time to learn how to drive a standard transmission, but he was too drunk to get behind the wheel. She wasn't quite sure how she got him up the stairs of her building, for he kept stopping and insisting on kissing her. She laid him on her bed and went to the kitchen for a glass of water.

Tony called her. "Come here, baby."

She did what he asked.

It seemed only a few short minutes later that she rolled away from the snoring man. She was wide awake. Not a bit sleepy. Her blouse clung damply to her. Her slacks were around her ankles. She slipped out of her clothes and into her old robe. She sat in her armchair and drank her glass of water.

He had said sweet things to her, about how she was the only woman in a long time that had turned him on. She didn't know if she could believe him. It seemed too incredible, especially from a man like Tony, who was so handsome and so easy to want to run after. But he had said he needed *her.*

She had only been to bed with a half-dozen men in her life, and she wasn't sure why she had succumbed so quickly to Tony. If only he hadn't said he *needed* her so much . . .

She had thought sex with him would be more rewarding, for she was pretty sure she knew what an orgasm was and she knew she hadn't had one this evening. He had quickly spent himself and was now lying so haphazardly upon the bed that she couldn't have lain there herself if she'd tried.

She heard a scratch at the door and looked out to find her cat waiting. She let it in and opened a can of "kidney stew in heavy gravy."

She sat down in the chair again and looked at her fingernails. Darn, but she'd broken one. It must have been on the stick shift of Tony's car. She got her nail file and rounded off the blunted tip. She stared at the snoring, immobile man on her bed. It was going to be a long night.

"The weather today is going to be just like yesterday. Fabulous. Sunny. Haze along the foothills. High temperatures around eighty in L.A., eighty-seven in the San Fernando and San Gabriel Valleys, and seventy along the beaches. Chance of precipitation is ten percent. We're broadcasting from Pasadena. Stand by for sports after a word from our sponsors."

A small ditch, built to channel rainwater, called "dip" on the road sign, ran diagonally across the street. Invariably, the Coupe de Ville hit it at too great a speed, throwing the driver's head against the roof and scraping the underside of its rear bumper against the asphalt.

"Damn," said Graham Maddox, recovering the steering wheel and realizing that even the strong suspension of this hulk could only take so much abuse. He paused for a moment at the stop sign on Mulholland and turned east, toward the studio and breaking daylight. The city lights on the valley floor below still shimmered in the predawn darkness.

The gray line of morning crept into the sky unobtrusively, much as the evening's pale left daily—unnoticed. The best time for him to think was when he first awoke. Ideas raced to him. His mind spread hundreds of tentacles onto all his projects. He had only to think about them to know the answers to questions that had plagued him the day before.

The de Ville's headlights glanced off thick knotted wild

shrubs as he rounded every corner. He saw a movement a hundred feet off, which turned out to be a coyote smelling something along the edge of the road. It looked up for a moment, its eyes glowing red in the headlights, then darted behind the bushes.

The coyote reminded him of the way he sometimes got involved with women. He darted behind bushes so he wouldn't be seen. There had been a number in his life and, he chuckled to himself, many bushes.

Just before he rounded another corner, he glanced in his rearview mirror and saw the shadowy shape of the doglike animal back at the edge of the road.

He knew that in Southwestern Native American culture, the coyote was the craftiest, cleverest, and often the most respected animal in their legends. Rangy and with stringy muscles, these beasts adapted to any condition and survived, living in the wild or coexisting with humans.

The coyote deserved a story. Would it be an Indian boy who befriends an orphaned pup? Or an orphaned pup who comes out of the hills near suburbia and is adopted by the children of a neighborhood? Or maybe it is a man—perhaps an Indian—who has too many women in his life? Or maybe it is the name of a junction on old Route 66, where there's a truck stop and the owner's life is wretched? Or maybe it is more of a docudrama about the plight of the sheep ranchers and their battle with the coyotes?

Graham took a small scrap of paper and wrote "coyotes" upon it. From that one word he would remember all his ideas and come up with more.

Waving at the guard who stood by the studio gate, Graham was the first person into his production offices. He entered and pressed in the code on the security alarm pad. He rarely asked employees to come in early, for all his technicians were union members and the union had strict rules about paying large fees for overtime. He was pleased to see Dillon Hughes often coming in an hour or two before he was required. Most of Graham's producers waltzed in as their shows demanded, occasionally early, mostly midmorning.

He had to admit he was impressed with Ruby. She was hanging in there and still enthusiastic. She had a good eye for drama and timing, and she knew how to plan the tense moments in an episode just before a commercial break. That rhythm came naturally to her. He had admired her skill for years and had often asked her advice. She had so willingly and wholeheartedly trusted him and given him her thoughts.

A pang of guilt had welled through his chest that morning as he had eased out from between the sheets. She was used to his running around. She had stopped questioning him years before.

In his office, he saw the blinking light on his private answering machine. His new secretary—Jeannie with the wild hair and slightly parted lips—had suggested he get his own line for ultra-private phone calls that he wished no one to know about. He thought it was a good idea, though he couldn't imagine whom he would give the number to. Business deals. Maybe it would be a good way to do safe business deals.

He pushed the playback switch and smiled when he heard the voice. It was Jeannie's. The girl didn't give up trying.

"Hi, darling," she said. "I thought you might be in early and I just wanted to leave you with a thought."

He glanced around at the sound of her voice, hoping no one else would hear it, then reminded himself he was alone in the building.

"I want you to think about this," the recording went on. "We can have our own private screening upstairs by your office. We'll let the projector roll and lock the doors. I'll come to you in my purple teddy and kneel in front of you while you relax in one of the velvet seats.

"I'll unzip your pants and take out your cock. . . ."

Graham's heart beat fast. What kind of message was this girl leaving? He hit the fast-forward button. The sound of a frenetic mouse voice squiggle. It slowed again.

"And then, I shall sit on your lap, facing the screen, with you deep inside me, and we can both watch the movie together. How does that sound, darling? I'll see you later this morning, and just remember, I'll be wearing my purple teddy under my dress."

Graham shut off the machine and laughed nervously. The girl sure was aggressive. Now to get the tape out of the machine.

His phone rang. It was Jeannie.

"What kind of message is this?" he exploded.

She was taken aback. "You don't like it? I thought you'd like it." She was near tears.

"Good God, girl. What do you think you're doing?" he inquired.

"I just thought," she began to sob, "that . . . af . . . after the other night, y . . . you'd like it."

"You can't phone this in to my office. You don't know who will hear it."

"I'm sorry, I'm sorry," she moaned.

"Get rid of this tape when you come in."

"Yes, Mr. Maddox."

He hung up and thought back a few nights. He had been the old coyote sliding out of sight.

Ruby, ex-Beverly Hills housewife, producer of a hit TV series, liked eating in the studio commissary. It was fun. Where she would have snubbed such an eatery in her former life, she enjoyed the camaraderie of the cast and crew. She didn't tell her husband Graham how much she liked it, for he would have thought she was crazy. He never ate on the lot; if he got too busy to leave, he simply didn't bother with food.

Even more fun than the commissary were the catering trucks that were brought in when the show was on location. Meals were served buffet-style, on lawns, under tents, or in spare rooms on picnic tables. This was a secret delight of hers. Anyone in the business for years would have shrugged his shoulders at the notion that the lone-hour break was *fun.* But Ruby got caught up in the energy and bustle of a busy show, and she watched with excited eyes, like a farm girl on her first trip to the big city.

Motive was shooting on the lot. She had been locked in a story conference the entire morning with a team of two writers. Glory Bell, the production assistant, called from the set and informed her that the show was about to break for lunch. Ruby asked the writers if they wished to join her. They declined, noting they had a lot of rewriting to do.

Ruby rushed to the soundstage. However, she found the red light on outside the door, which indicated that shooting was in progress and no one was to enter. She waited five minutes for it to go off.

Inside, everyone was preparing to head in the direction of the commissary. A few said, "Hello, Ruby," while most still respectfully called her Mrs. Maddox. She found Richard, the director, explaining something to Garrett Gage. Garrett looked as though he were rooted in the exact position he had been standing when "cut" had been called on the last scene.

"You've got to look scared here, Garrett," Richard said. "Frank would be scared. He's human. He's too human. He's still building inner strength."

Garrett nodded at the words. "Richard," he said, "I'll try again. I thought we had it all down in rehearsal."

"What I'm trying to explain to you," said the director, his words distinct, his hands clasped before him, "is that sometimes we have to *change* what we did in rehearsal. We have to revise it if it isn't working. Notice I'm revising the camera angle, as well."

Garrett looked tired. "Okay, boss," he said, "I'll get it right . . . first take after lunch. I promise." He glanced at Ruby, his gaze level, his riveting deep blue eyes so sure of his look, and smiled. He turned toward the edge of the set where Denny was waiting with a towel.

Richard looked at Ruby and rolled his eyes as if to say, "I still don't think he's got it."

Richard sat agitated through lunch, while Ruby discussed three upcoming scripts, locations, guest stars, costumes—for costuming had become a major item in the budget—and what they would need Graham's approval on. Richard had worked for Graham for eight years, directing during the past four, and knew most of the executive producer's patterns.

However, Richard's mind was on the episode he was shooting that day and *its* logistics. Ruby didn't seem to perceive his need to concentrate. "Ruby," he finally said, softly yet sternly, "I can't think too far into the future today. I've got a hundred problems I'm trying to cope with here and now. Next week, I'm scheduled in preproduction. Can some of this wait until then?"

She nodded. He abruptly excused himself.

A wave of anger passed through her. The anger was not at Richard but at herself, for not comprehending his absorption with the current episode. In the past, at parties, when she had spoken to Graham's directors, they hadn't seemed so intense, so single-minded. Perhaps it was Richard's own style. She knew she needed to be more sensitive to the needs of the people she worked with.

She heard a deep-throated "ahem" and looked up to see Garrett holding a cup of coffee. He was alluring, with his unshaven face and blue denim work shirt half unbuttoned. "May I?" he asked, gesturing to a chair to indicate he wished to join her.

"By all means," she said.

"I understand we're having an audition later in the day that I'm to be on hand for?" he said.

Ruby had forgotten about it. This was the day the child bride of Norman's was to make her appearance. "Yes," she told Garrett.

His jaw tightened at the thought. He'd made it clear he didn't desire a co-star. The actress's only saving grace was that apparently she didn't have any acting experience. Therefore, she wouldn't upstage him. If they hired her, maybe she wouldn't last long.

"Garrett," said Ruby, "I want you to know that I'm not wild about the female co-star role, either."

He looked shocked, because she had been reading his thoughts.

"I've agreed with Graham that we'll do the two-hour special. After that, everything is only a *maybe*."

She involuntarily reached out and grasped his wrist, her

hand reacting to a need to make herself understood. Richard's reproval had made her feel more impotent than she cared to admit. They all believed she was only *playing* at being producer. Her fingers pressed intently into Garrett's strong wrist. "I mean it. *I* hired you, you know. And there's no way I'm keeping a woman on *Motive* if I don't think she'll work."

Her voice seemed to reassure him there was nothing to fear or be jealous of. But turmoil shuffled inside him. Ruby could see it in his face. She patted Garrett's arm in a maternal way, which said that she would protect him.

After all, he represented her judgment. So far, the world loved him. He *was* the show. The critics loved him. The fan mail had piled up deeply. Advertisers were asking for his endorsements (which he couldn't give while under contract) therefore they were begging for commercial space. *Motive* was hot. It was making money. Lots of money. Ruby was responsible for that. She was responsible for choosing the star. She was responsible for approving the story lines and for hiring everyone that gave the show life.

Her whole being was immersed in *Motive.* The self-assurance, that minutes before Richard had drowned inside her, once again became strong. She had purpose. She *would* be a success. They would all see that.

The skepticism on Garrett's face turned to respect. She meant what she said. "Can I ask your opinion about something?" he questioned Ruby.

"Sure," she said.

"I'm thinking about buying a house in Studio City. Is that a good area?"

"There are some excellent neighborhoods. And it's close to the studio. Do you know a broker?"

"Not a good one," he told her.

"I have a friend that will find you exactly what you need. He knows all about tax write-offs, too. Call my secretary and ask her for the number."

"Thank you, Ruby," Garrett said, downing the last swallow of coffee.

Sondra, the skinny first assistant director, appeared at

Garrett's elbow and tapped his shoulder. "Come on," she told him. "We need you back on the set. Get back to makeup and hair."

"Okay," he said, standing and smiling at Ruby with eyes that were perhaps a little too flirtatious.

"Sondra," said Ruby, as the blonde was about to follow Garrett back to the set, "you do know that we are auditioning Tanya Thomson this afternoon, don't you?"

"I hope it's at the end of the day," replied Sondra tersely, "because we are supposed to shoot all this." She opened the script and pointed to eight pages.

Sondra's tone of voice irritated Ruby. She might be a very capable assistant director, but that was no attitude to display in front of your producer. "The audition is scheduled for four o'clock. Please have the crew ready," Ruby said with finality.

"I thought preliminary auditions were done over in your offices," sad Sondra, critical eyes boring into Ruby. Mrs. Maddox nettled her with so many questions and delays.

"They are done where I want them to be done," said Ruby.

It was an order. Ruby, who usually spoke in such a calm, clear, nice voice had no more patience. Sondra thought it wise not to challenge the woman any further. "I need to get back to the set, Mrs. Maddox. Will there be anything else?"

"I can't think of anything. However, I will walk back with you."

The two women walked silently side by side: Ruby, medium height and curvy, dressed in an expensive suit, walking on French pumps, her strawberry blond hair bouncing slightly on her shoulders; Sondra, dressed in slacks and baggy shirt, her strong, unsmiling jaw tightly set, her eyes riveted straight ahead, her movement stiff-legged instead of smooth and feminine, her limp white-blond hair like dried summer grass.

When they reached the set and Sondra was about to go round up the actors, Ruby said, "Thanks for your cooperation, Miss Prescott."

Sondra looked at her for a full moment, not able to read

the meaning of the thanks, then said an unsure, "You're welcome."

As the shooting resumed, the crew seemed to forget Ruby was there watching. She sat to one side in a canvas director's chair, knowing she could interject any suggestions she wished.

When she had time to call her old friends—wives of agents, directors, producers, investors, lawyers—they always spoke of *Motive* with admiration. She had reached a new level of status in their eyes. *They* were still content to be protected and kept; wives whose purpose in life was to bolster their husbands. They played the game well. They were well compensated for their efforts, for their lives that they sacrificed. Of course, Ruby realized, they didn't see it as a sacrifice. Being supported was better than working.

Ruby had done it for enough years. It had satisfied her for that long. She had pursued social rosters and had not missed a significant party, benefit, event, or premiere. She had been hungry for status. Hungry that her name should appear in magazines and gossip columns. Shining. Her husband glorious. When she had had a party, those left off the guest list felt like lesser human beings for it. She had applied a fortune of energy toward becoming a name, a status symbol. But not any longer.

One night, from the pinnacle of the entertaining world she had conquered, she felt a void. It was after she had read an article about a husband and wife team of doctors who traveled together to poor countries and did nonprofit operations. It had touched her. It was the most humane thing that had snuck into the artificiality of her world.

She pictured herself and Graham producing motion pictures—husband and wife filmmakers who brought stories of value to the screen. Compassion. Humanity. Real stories about real people. Classic struggles.

She imagined the comments and wonder of her friends if she could pull that off.

It would be a long way to come for a woman who, practically penniless, had fled Texas so many years ago with two small children. A woman in disgrace. A personal disgrace that had left a horrible, bitter taste in her mouth she could not spit out.

Ruby Maddox remembered her first trip to L.A., twenty-seven Septembers before. While the northern parts of the United States were cooling with autumn, the brutal land between Texas and the Pacific Ocean had been baking at one-hundred-plus degrees. She had been alone with her two small children in their 1948 Nash. The car, which was a gray color not unlike that used on battleships, had had a worrisome noise in the right side of the engine. She hadn't known if it would even make it to the coast.

Every time she stopped for gas, she made sure she filled the canvas water bag that was tied to the front bumper. Ruby wasn't sure how to put the water into the car, but she envisioned the canvas container as her and the children's only salvation against slow dehydration in the treacherous Mojave Desert.

She had been warned to drive only at night, when the temperatures were bearable, but wanting to put as many miles as she could between herself and Texas, she drove relentlessly and tried to ignore the children whining in the back seat from the suffocating air. Heat shimmered off the pavement and desert like waving sheet metal, glaring into her eyes in spite of the dark green sunglasses she wore. She had bought the children cheap plastic glasses at a truck stop in eastern Arizona, and they had played at being movie stars for about an hour until the novelty wore off. Then they had worn them because it hurt too much to take them off.

On the third day, she had stopped just past noon in Blythe for gas. She took the children into a fan-cooled cafe for cold drinks. The waitress said it would be all right if they wanted to wait there until sunset to go across the desert.

Ruby had looked into the wide pleading eyes of her children, who were very quiet by now because they had never seen their mother like this—driven and unapproachable. She decided to rest for two hours. She had had very little sleep for the past two days, and while the children played a quiet game between themselves in one side of the booth, she had unexpectedly dropped off to sleep.

When she awoke, the sun's rays were low. She figured she had slept nearly five hours. Her dress was damp with sweat and a slight headache pounded at the top of her head. The children! Her heart jumped into her throat. Where were they? The cook told her they were playing with the waitress's son in her small adobe house behind the cafe.

She was grateful to the waitress. She had had five hours of escape from her exhaustion and her heartache. She scrounged in her purse for three one-dollar bills, not much for a tip and babysitting, but all she could afford.

But the waitress wouldn't take it. "I've got a home, honey. And you're goin' to need all your money when you get to where you're going."

Then there had been the highway again and the hot air rushing in through the Nash's windows and the tires sounding like they were fusing into the melting asphalt. The sun had slipped behind the brown horizon, and the land, so perilous during the day, became mystical and beautiful as the shadows lengthened and purples hung in the folds on the hills.

"When are we going to be there, Mommy?" her son asked.

"Tomorrow. We'll be there tomorrow," she reassured him.

And she vowed to herself, as she drove westward through San Bernadino, Chino, Pomona, Covina, Downtown L.A., and finally into Hollywood, that she would quietly celebrate this day of arrival for all the happy years that were to come. Her own day. Her day of independence.

Yet the tragic events of the next few days had erased that promised anniversary date from her mind.

Ruby started. Sondra was shaking her shoulder. "Could you please move over here, Mrs. Maddox? We need to get the sound boom situated about where you're sitting."

"Can you believe her?" Margi asked incredulously. Garrett sat under her skillful comb, but her comment was directed at Denny, who worked on the face of another actor. "Did you see the mess she made of her hair? She has got to be about the most stupid thing on earth. How can anyone mess up a home frost kit?"

"She should have come to you," replied Denny calmly.

"Like *I* would even do it for her," said Margi with an offhanded laugh.

"She's trying," said Denny with sympathetic urgency.

"She is so stupid," said Margi. "Glory Bell. Who would have a name like Glory Bell?"

Garrett chuckled to himself.

"Well, what's so damn funny?" demanded Margi.

"You are," said Garrett. "I agree with Denny. The poor kid's trying. What's wrong with her name?'

"You men!" said Margi with exasperation. "Always falling for a twit."

Denny cleared his throat and smiled. "Frank Harrison," he said, referring to Garrett's character, "would not want to be compared to an effeminate makeup artist."

"Begging your pardon," said Garrett. "I don't think Frank would even notice. And, Denny . . . you're not so effeminate, you know. I—" he paused, "I didn't even know you were of that persuasion for almost a month after I started the show."

Both Denny's and Margi's jaws dropped open.

"You're a detective, baby," said Margi in a bold, aggressive tone. "You can't tell me you didn't know."

"I didn't know," admitted Garrett. "Damn, I was keeping my nose to the grindstone. Denny, the only thing I'm trying to say is that I appreciate the fact you don't swish into everybody's faces."

"You're welcome, Garrett," said Denny, undisturbed. His sexual preference was his own business. He was glad Garrett regarded him as just another guy.

"Why doesn't Margi give Glory a few pointers about her hair?" queried Garrett.

Margi sprayed a couple of squirts of hair spray on Garrett's dark hair and waved to Sondra that she was finished. She kept her eye on the actor's hair. "She needs more than my advice about her silly hair. Look at her clothes. Listen to her voice. Look at her taste in men. Tony can sit behind a camera, but that's about all he can do."

"Shhh," said Denny. "Keep your voice down. They can hear you."

"Good," said Margi. "He's an old drunk, and he ought to stay away from a pretty and innocent—not to say stupid—thing like Glory."

"Margi," said Garrett, taking her shoulders and kissing her on top of the head, "I love you. You're opinionated as hell, but I love you. Thanks for the great job." He gave himself one more approving look in the mirror.

She watched him walk back to the set. "Bob used to have an ass like that," she told Denny. "I'm not complaining, though. Bob knows how to make a girl real happy."

"I'm glad you're happy with him," said Denny, sitting wearily in a chair. He hadn't slept well since his split with Jeff. The sleepless nights had worn hollows under his cheekbones.

"Me and Bob are lucky," said Margi, sitting and lighting a cigarette. "We've been together a long time and we've had our fights, but we get along. We always mend our troubles."

Denny had heard this little speech many times. Sometimes she sounded like a broken record, but he didn't mind.

"There are a lot of women who wish they could have a man like Bob," she said. As an afterthought, she added, "But they'd better keep their goddamn hands off him."

Denny played the devil's advocate. "Who, for instance?"

"Who? What a crazy question. They're all after him. I mean, they would be if they thought they could get him. Ruby. There's a lady in trouble. She hasn't been satisfied sexually in months. Maybe years. She could use a man like Bob.

"Then there's that secretary of Graham Maddox's, Miss Jeannie Hansen. One night with Bob, and she wouldn't ever give a man like Graham a second look again. I better watch out for that bitch. She'd fuck Bob if she could get away with it. She's just that kind of woman."

"It takes two to tango," said Denny innocently. "I don't think Bob would go for it. Why go for it, while there's a panther on the home front?"

"Panther? Me?"

"Yeah."

"You know," she said, musing, "the only one that's really been keeping her eye on Bob has been Sondra. That skinny-assed bitch."

"Why would Sondra want Bob?" asked Denny.

"Don't tell me you believe that shit about her being a dyke?" asked Margi, the words exiting her mouth as cigarette smoke signals.

"That's the rumor," confirmed Denny.

"Well, them lesbos are the ones who need it most of all," said Margi. "Shit, what time is it, sweetheart?"

"Almost lunch," replied Denny.

"Bob should be by any minute," she said, with a satisfied smile.

"Having lunch together?"

"You could call it that. Bob knows what makes me happy . . . and he knows how to keep me satisfied."

Her husband appeared from a side door at that moment. He walked stealthily in her direction. She rose to meet him, and he swept her into his great, strong arms. She seemed tiny against him. She turned and gave Denny a wink—Bob gave Denny a dirty look—and the two of them departed for the parking lot.

Tanya had redecorated her bedroom four times—once for each year she had been with Norman. Their bedrooms adjoined. He preferred that they sleep together. It was her choice; they could spend the night in his room or hers. She usually opted for his, since she preferred to think of her own room as off-limits and unspoiled by Norman's presence.

The first time her room had been decorated, she had wanted the "little girl look," the bedroom she had never had as a child. There were pink flounces on the bed, lace ruffles at the window, white furniture, and a pink carpet.

Her interest then turned to expensive antiques. Every piece of furniture in the room had to be over one hundred fifty years old, and intricately inlaid with mother-of-pearl or colorful marquetry depicting flowers and animals. But the room became too much of museum and she could not relax there.

The third remodel was exactly the opposite—high tech. A low, sculpted bed and dressers, shiny lacquered lamps and mirror frames, a thick soft carpet, and black, rose, and gray predominating the color scheme.

This fourth time, she had been a lot less enthusiastic. It wasn't as much fun. She looked through a hundred decorator magazines to find the right room to copy, and it was so boring. She settled on a country-estate look, with a massive headboard on the bed, light blue bedspread, long flowing white curtains, and a simple wooden dressing table. The carpet was pale, pale blue, like the sky with a light cloud cover.

She sat in front of the huge dressing table mirror. A mild breeze blew through the window and caressed her bare shoulders. Her waist-length hair was bound in its familiar braid. She was having a hard time deciding on the best way to apply her makeup.

Her phone buzzed and the butler informed her that Mrs. Maddox was calling. "Hello?" she said, pushing the button that connected her to the outside line.

"Tanya, dear, this is Ruby Maddox. How are you?"

"Very well," lied Tanya. "How are you?"

"Fine. I'm confirming our appointment today. We'll meet in my office about two-thirty. Since you have been out of the country and are not familiar with *Motive,* we'll view a couple of episodes on the VCR and you can acquaint yourself with our series. About four o'clock, we'll go over to the set for your audition."

At the word *audition,* Tanya's stomach knotted into a ball. She looked out her second-story window, down to the limousine that stood waiting below, ready to whisk her to the studio. The knot doubled in size.

When the actress failed to answer, Ruby asked, "Is everything all right, dear?"

"Yes, ma'am," said Tanya. "Everything's fine. I'll be there at two-thirty."

"Good," said Ruby. "I will arrange a drive-on for you."

"Thank you for calling," said Tanya. She hung up. Her legs felt weak. Her eyes were fixed on the limo. The driver was probably sitting in the kitchen drinking coffee.

She felt as though she were in a dream world and not in touch with reality. Today was her first "big" audition—at one time, getting an audition such as this had been the only important thing in her life—and she was scared to death. Though Norman had arranged everything, at four o'clock today, *she* would be on the line. *She* would be on the set, in front of the producers, other actors, and an entire crew. She did not want to make a fool of herself. She had been repeating her lines over and over, but they fled from her head like a rabbit bounding across a highway and scooting into dark undergrowth.

When Russell had been in her life, he had promised to go with her and give her confidence in her auditions. But he wasn't around anymore. A disillusioned laugh broke from her throat. The laugh flooded her eyes with the tears that were hiding there. She blinked them back quickly. She couldn't show up on the set with puffy eyes.

She scrutinized her makeup again, dusting her cheeks with powder, setting narrow lines of peach blush along her cheekbones, and painting her lips melon. She couldn't decide what to do with her hair, so she left it in the braid.

Her hands were trembling from anxiety. Her performance would be one hundred percent *her.* Her heart pounded in her chest. She inhaled great gulps of air and told herself to calm down. Why were her nerves on edge? Was it because she didn't really want to act? That she had blurted out the plea not believing Norman would actually follow through with it? She had a fine life; she didn't need to be an actress. . . .

Or was she disquieted because she really *did* want to act? Would her training come back to her? Could she relax like her acting teacher had taught her? Could she let go and allow her subconscious to take over the lines?

She didn't know. She was awfully nervous. The thought of driving to the studio in the limo made her more nervous.

Norman was very firm with the driver, who was not allowed to let Tanya go anywhere by herself. The limo was Norman keeping his ever-present eye on her. Controlling her whole life. Every moment of every day, Norman knew where she was, what she was doing. She had no privacy. He controlled her. Every cent she spent, every friend she met for lunch, every book she read alone in her bedroom. There was no place to escape him and his hold over her.

Usually, she ignored the verdict of her captivity the best she could. Now, she was expected to perform, to do something creative. She couldn't, just couldn't do it from her present confines.

She had to escape. Just for a little while. Just long enough to relax, to think, to get her thoughts together, to program her subconscious.

She couldn't call a cab. All the servants would see it. She could try walking off the three-acre property, but the security gate opening would alert the prying butler and ruthless head housekeeper. They were very haughty and didn't hide their dislike of the young mistress of the house.

She was a prisoner. Goddamn, she was a prisoner. Tears started again. She dabbed them back with the corner of a tissue.

There was only one solution. She had to borrow May's car. May was the English girl who worked as a maid. She was a shy thing, with white skin, dull hair, and a chinless face, who brought breakfast up to Tanya's room daily. Tanya realized she hardly ever thanked the English girl for her efforts. Momentary guilt made her gnaw on the edge of a fingernail.

She stopped herself. "No time to feel guilty now. I've got to get that car."

She had to find May and she had to be secretive about it. She pulled her robe around her shoulders, tightened the belt, and searched the second floor before descending the stairs, hoping to find the girl any place but in the kitchen, where all the servants congregated.

However, when Tanya entered the dining room, she heard May's voice in the kitchen. The driver was teasing her about her British accent. He was from New York, and Tanya was tempted to go in there and tell him a thing or two about accents.

"Damn," said Tanya under her breath, "how am I going to get her out of there?"

Then a better idea occurred to her. She didn't need *May,* only the keys to the girl's car. She hurried back upstairs to finish dressing. Five dresses had been laid out on the bed. She finally chose one that was ruffled at the throat, fully-skirted, and tight-waisted. Piped darts, snug over her rib cage, showed off her firm breasts.

She phoned down to the butler and informed him she would be another half hour. Would he please have the driver wait? She crossed the upper floor to Norman's study and found an extra remote control that would release the electric security gate.

She cautiously went down the stairs. Dressed to go out, anyone who saw her would immediately summon the limo. She slipped out the French doors in the dining room and quickly walked around to the rear entrance, to the back entry hall, a "locker room" of sorts, where the servants hung their coats and where May would leave her purse.

A spaniel started from the back door at the sound of her footstep and barked before it recognized her.

"Shhhh, Sheila," Tanya whispered. The dog wagged its tail and followed her along the gravel to the back door.

This is really stupid, thought Tanya, having to sneak around my own house. But there is no other way. I have to have some time alone to cool out, to think.

May's purse hung on a coat hook under a pink acrylic sweater. She could hear them chatting in the kitchen: the butler, the housekeeper, May, and the driver. The voices were dangerously close, only ten feet on the other side of the door.

"I look just like me ol' dad," May was saying. "I got a photo o' him and me, taken last year when I was 'ome on 'ollies."

" 'ome on 'ollies?' " laughed the New York driver, mimicking her voice.

"All right, smart ass," said May, changing her accent to a flat California sound. "When I was *doing* my vacation with the family. But I've got the picture." Her voice resorted to its accent in its enthusiasm. "You want to see it? It's right in me handbag."

Oh, God, groaned Tanya, fumbling in May's purse. How embarrassing to be caught with a servant's possession.

"I'd rather see a picture of you in a bikini on Malibu Beach last summer," said the driver.

This brought a large guffaw from the butler. The housekeeper said, "You won't see May out in a bikini. This girl don't believe in sunbathing."

"It's the ultraviolet rays, you see," began May apologetically.

Tanya heard no more. The keys were in her hand and she was moving for the crumbling auto. Its color was lemon chiffon gelato dried upon a sidewalk in the July sun. Something about its shape recalled the last car she had owned before marrying Norman. It was a Pinto. Of course she could drive a Pinto.

The engine chugged and turned over. She looked around. No one had seen her. The spaniel stood patiently next to the car, its sad eyes watching her drive off around the side of the house and past the sleek, sparkling limo. Tanya pushed the remote control to release the gate.

Exhilaration at being free charged through her. Her fear of being caught broke loose into wild abandon. A great loud whoop escaped her lungs. She felt victorious. She felt in control of herself once again. She began to say her lines. They balked and then began flowing freely. She was busy listening to the unheard voice of the other character in the dialogue.

"Is anyone here?" he said.

"I am." Tanya replied. "Who are you?"

"Where am I?"

"London. The year is 1557."

She was so intent on this conversation in her head that she failed to hear the grind of the Pinto's decayed transmission.

There was a horrible grating sound—marbles chewed

between cast-iron dentures—and the gear shift refused to respond. Three miles from the studio, third car back at a traffic light, she could only get out and shrug her shoulders at the cars honking behind her.

The asphalt was scorching around her. A stream of fluid ran under the car, like the trickle under the desk of a first-grader who has forgotten to go to the bathroom. The closest service station was six blocks away. Nobody stopped and offered to help. She couldn't push the Pinto. Her high heels were held on only by the skinniest of straps. She began walking, careful not to go too swiftly lest she sweat.

She had only ten dollars in her purse. She handed it to the young gas station attendant, who spoke no English, and pointed to the ruptured Pinto.

"Bring here, bring here," she told him.

All he could do was stare at the tight fit of her dress over her torso. It had never occurred to her that she might not make the audition.

"Get the car," she said, pointing to the yellow auto stranded like a banana fallen upon the grocery floor and kicked near the potato bin.

She called a cab from a phone booth that was so dirty she was afraid of catching a disease from the receiver. Was she sorry she hadn't gone in the limo? No, no, she wasn't sorry.

But the cab took twenty minutes to get there and, he apologized, the air-conditioning had not been repaired. She felt like crying but gritted her teeth and emitted a thin laugh.

The cabdriver looked back in surprise.

"You wouldn't get it," she told him, digging in her purse for her melon-colored lipstick.

Deposited at the door of Maddox Productions, Tanya was whisked inside Ruby's office by a tight-lipped secretary. One look at the blond actress and Ruby could tell she had been through minor hell to make the audition.

"I thought you were coming by limo?" said Ruby. "They've been calling here, worried about you."

It agitated Tanya that she might be yelled at for having done something wrong. All she had wanted was a little time to herself. A flash of young girl crossed her face. "I'm sorry," she said, "but the car broke down."

The phone buzzed on Ruby's desk. Ruby put the phone on the speaker. "Mrs. Maddox?" said a woman's voice.

"Yes, Sondra?" answered Ruby.

"We're ready for the audition. You were supposed to be here five minutes ago. We're holding up shooting the close-ups until we finish this screen test. How soon can we expect you?"

Ruby's voice was cool. "In fifteen minutes. Please have your makeup person ready to do a few touch-ups."

"Okay, Mrs. Maddox," said the crisp, unfriendly voice. "Just remember that this little audition is taking us way over budget today."

"I'll see you in fifteen minutes," said Ruby, disconnecting the call and turning her attention back to Tanya.

"I'm sorry," repeated Tanya. "Really I am."

Tanya seemed dazed and Ruby realized the actress was the same age as her own children. It was hard to believe this girl was Norman's wife. Ruby's motherly voice took over. "Will you be all right, dear?"

"Yes, surely. I just didn't think the car would break down."

"Would you rather do it another time?"

"No," replied Tanya. "I know the lines. I know the lines."

As they walked to the soundstage, Ruby said, "I understand you and Norman have been on the yacht?"

"Yes."

"It's too bad you haven't had a chance to get a feel for the show. *Motive* is very unique in its concept."

"I tried to get here on time to see the tapes."

"I know, dear," said Ruby, wondering if Tanya weren't under too much stress to audition. She guided Tanya to Denny's chair and asked him to take care of her.

"I will, Mrs. Maddox," he said cheerfully. He gently pushed Tanya into a chair.

"We've got to be real quiet because they're shooting a close-up," he told Tanya. "Then you'll go on."

He could tell she was caught between tears and shock. He smoothed her makeup, powdered it, and boldly laid on blusher. He talked to her the entire time, telling her how good she looked and how well she would do in front of the camera. He motioned to the petite, dark-haired hairdresser, who began brushing out the long braid.

"It's beautiful hair, isn't it, Margi?" he asked, not expecting an answer.

"All quiet on the set," snapped a stern female voice, which Tanya recognized as the one that had spoken through Ruby's speaker phone. Out of sight of the set, she heard the action start and the murmur of the actors' voices.

Denny had a calming effect on her. Her state of shock disappeared and her nerve came back. She felt cool again, the burnt asphalt around the stranded Pinto forgotten.

"You'll do fine," whispered Denny.

"Do you think so?" she asked him.

"Of course, sweetheart, of course. You're star material. I can tell. I've been in the business a long time. I know a star when I meet one."

His words brought the blood pounding through her heart.

"Are you ready?" a voice demanded.

Tanya turned and saw a skinny blond woman with harsh eyes. "Yes, I am," she said. She told her subconscious to take over and guide her through the scene.

"You enter over there," said the skinny woman, pointing to a gap in the back of the flat. Through it, reddish light poured from the set.

"Okay," said Tanya.

The skinny woman called to the actor on the set, out of Tanya's sight, "Garrett, ready please."

"Break a leg," said Denny, touching Tanya's shoulder.

"Thank you," she said. "You've been so kind."

She stood quietly behind the flat, out of sight from the set. The skinny woman said, "Garrett, ready please," and then called for silence. The cameraman confirmed they were rolling, the clapper sounded, and the skinny woman called, "Action."

Garrett spoke the fist line. "Is anyone here?" he asked. How familiar it sounded. The words? Or was it the voice?

Tanya stepped from around the edge of the flat and entered the set. The reddish light was in her eyes. The actor's back was turned toward her.

The next line was hers. "I am. Who are you?" she asked.

He turned and she knew. It was Russell.

Chapter 5

Both Graham and Norman despised California nouvelle cuisine. They preferred a simple, quiet place like Le Chat, with its white tablecloths, good food, formal waiters, and male atmosphere. The maitre d' knew them both. Either could have walked in sans reservation during the lunch or dinner peak and have gotten an excellent table coupled by excellent service.

As Graham followed Norman's portliness between the tables, he hoped he wouldn't see someone he'd have to stop and devote a couple of minutes to. His mind was not yet disengaged from his prelunch meeting with the writers of *Medical Alert.* His brain was still trying to figure out a better ending for the episode.

When he sat, he stared blankly across the table.

"You all right, Graham?" asked Norman.

"Sorry," said Graham, his mind locking onto lunch and the man sitting across the table from him. "I guess I'm going to have to fire those two writers. They burned out faster than I expected them to."

They ordered lunch and talked business.

"I've got an idea," said Graham, "for a nice homey Christmas picture I'd like to get on the air a year from now, during the holidays. I was thinking an oil company might put up a chunk for development. Good for their image and all. Who do you know at American Oil?"

"Stewart Reynolds," said Norman, a carrot clenched between his fingers in the same manner he held his ever-present cigars. "You want me to talk to him first? He's been disappointed a couple of times on the quality of the final product. This guy wants Public Television caliber."

"You don't make any money on PBS. You've got to go to the networks," said Graham. "Talk to him. Tell him I'd like to talk to him."

"I'll go ahead and set up a meeting. Next week? My offices?"

"Sounds good."

Lunch was served and they nodded approvingly at each other, as if to say, "We pick 'em right every time." Graham enjoyed lunches with Norman. They were good friends, and he could relax and enjoy the taste of his food. Often meals were not for eating; they merely provided an atmosphere in which to conduct business deals. On the outside, he would look at ease, while on the inside he was churning and strategically planning. He would be so mentally on edge that he wouldn't notice the passage of food down his gullet. It was an illusion that was both singular and vital to L.A.—everything *seemed* casual when in truth it wasn't.

"Tanya seems quite happy with her work," said Norman of his young wife.

"Good," said Graham. "We're airing the two-hour special next week. It's a dynamite script. I'm sure the ratings will be excellent."

"May I see it before?"

"I'll have my secretary send a cassette copy over."

"I think Tanya is very beautiful," said Norman. "Don't you?"

Graham eyed Norman. What did that question mean? He replied cautiously, "She has a definite *look,* a style about her. Her blondness perfectly complements Garrett Gage's dark hair."

Norman wiped his thin lips with his napkin. "I feel very lucky to have found her . . . and married her. She is a woman many men would want to have for their own. Especially after she has been on the air." He leaned forward intently, looking Graham directly in the eye. "But I intend to keep her for myself."

Certainly Norman, the jealous husband, wasn't implying that Graham was interested in bedding the blonde. Graham was far too prudent to do a thing like that. His reply was neutral.

"To tell you the truth, Norman," he said with a chuckle, "I *hope* she has adoring fans. It will boost the ratings. Ruby is very enthusiastic about her."

"Then why has Tanya been crying about Ruby being so impersonal toward her?"

Graham sighed. Had it been another actress, he would be angry. He couldn't stand prima-donna behavior. Since Tanya was Norman's wife and Norman could rock the Maddox Production boat in a big way if he chose, Graham decided it best to be political. "Tanya is overreacting. She's never been on a set before. There's a lot of work involved. A lot of concentration. Ruby can't worry about hurting someone's feelings. If she was abrupt with Tanya, you can rest assured it wasn't on purpose. Come on, you've known Ruby for years. She's the sweetest person alive."

"You're right," apologized Norman. "I didn't mean to imply anything. I know Ruby will take good care of my wife. It's just that I worry about Tanya. She's so young, so vulnerable. . . ."

"Are you worried someone will take advantage of her?"

"There are a lot of men who will tell a woman like her anything to get her favors."

"You think she would have an affair?"

"She'd better not," said Norman, his voice that of an owner expressing his proprietorship. "Let me know, will you, if any of her behavior is suspicious."

So that was it. Norman wanted Graham to stop Tanya from screwing around. Graham was not about to make any promises. "I'm not a very good watchdog, Norman. I've got five casts. I can't keep track of the personal lives of all those people."

"You, if anybody, know how an affair can mess up a life. It can potentially hurt the innocent people. Tanya is a hot woman. I don't want a story about my wife showing up in supermarket tabloids. I won't be able to concentrate on my own business if I have to worry about her."

"Okay, okay," said Graham. "I'll talk to Ruby about it. She sees more of Tanya than I do."

"Thank you. I'm glad you understand."

Understand? Graham understood well enough. If Norman caught Tanya with another man, he might not only pull her from the series, but redirect his investments into other projects. Norman's lawyers were very good. Into every contract, there was always an extenuating-circumstances escape clause.

The gate was made of thick, dark lumber bolted so tightly together that not a thread of light passed through it. Heavy metal braces made an X across the massive obstruction, which was set into a ten-foot-high, cement wall. The stucco-covered wall was anchored by tall, solid, square cement posts every fifteen feet. Lush ivy curled at its base. Carriage lamps, set on top of the posts on either side of the impenetrable gate, gave off a soft, yet sufficient glow to illuminate the quiet street.

Dillon, in his Volvo, looked at the gate. Behind it was the house in which Penny lived. He had followed her home one night—to make sure she made it safely—and had glimpsed the stately residence, with its narrow front lawn and great, protective trees. It was white and California colonial, meaning it was recognizably colonial, but was embellished by some California architect's idea of style. Then the gate had closed smoothly behind Penny's car, obliterating the respectable home, in the very respectable neighborhood, from his sight.

Dillon had often driven by the gate. He now thought about trying to locate a crack through which to peek, except there were observation cameras concealed in the bushes.

As he looked at the gate, his longing grew stronger. He felt like a criminal barred from what he wanted most. The girl that set his heart on fire. He could not be free unless he had her. Yet, he was no criminal, unless his crime was his love for her.

He pushed the button on the access speaker in front of the gate. A couple of minutes passed and a cool voice asked, "Yes?"

"Dillon Hughes to see Penny," he said, without a hitch in his voice.

There was another pause—it felt like three minutes to Dillon—before the huge gate rolled open. The driveway circled the front of the house.

He parked next to the front walk. It was made of flat white stones and bordered by pink flowers, each set separately in the bed of brown earth. He didn't think a leaf on a single plant was touching a leaf of another. The front lawn was smooth as a putting green, imperceptibly inclined so rainwater would wash down the drive. Tall, narrow windows on either side of the front door, made of clear beveled pane set in lead molding, were covered inside by a delicate, yet opaque curtain.

Penny's father opened the door. He was a fit man, with iron-gray hair, in his early sixties. He stood six feet tall and had a manner about him as though he were looking down at whomever he was addressing, no matter what the person's height.

"How do you do?" he said. "I'm Mr. Huntington."

"Dillon Hughes," said Dillon with his disarming smile, extending his hand and giving the man a robust handshake.

Dillon felt intimidated. But, he told himself, this was because the man was Penny's father. If he had met Huntington in business, he wouldn't have flinched.

"Penny didn't tell us she was expecting a visitor," said Mr. Huntington.

The night before, when Dillon had told Penny he was picking her up, he presumed she would inform her parents. Perhaps she had, and Mr. Huntington was playing a little game with him. "We made the date last week," said Dillon, exaggerating the truth.

"Please come in," said Mr. Huntington.

To the right was the formal living room, with its pastel colors and elegant furniture. "Would you care to wait in here?" asked Mr. Huntington, leading the way to the left, to a room that looked like a den.

"Thank you," said Dillon politely.

"Would you care to watch television?" inquired Mr. Huntington, walking toward the set and reaching to turn it on.

Dillon was surprised. "No!" he blurted out. "Certainly not."

Mr. Huntington turned slowly and looked at him. "I'm sure Penny heard the doorbell, but I shall tell her you are here, anyway."

He hadn't asked Dillon to sit down or if he'd like a drink, or hadn't extended any other hospitable gesture. In other words, he hadn't hidden his dislike of Dillon.

Dillon heard someone running down the staircase, and a second later, Penny put her arms around his waist. She lightly kissed his cheek and quickly jumped back, so that no one would see her affection. She wore a pink quilted dressing gown and had four rollers in her short hair. Dillon's face broke into a smile. He had never seen her semi-dressed before, getting ready to go out. She looked like what he envisioned a wife to be, and he loved her all the more for it.

"I'm not ready yet," she giggled.

"I can see," he said.

"Make yourself at home," she said.

He was about to say, "That's hard to do around here," but Mr. Huntington reappeared and walked toward them.

"I'll be back in a few minutes," said Penny. "Daddy, please give Dillon a drink," she added before running up the stairs again.

Dillon sat in a wooden-armed chair. The touch of the girl had brought a flush to his skin—a hot, rushing glow that gurgled happily within. Nothing in the world could bring him down when he had a feeling like that inside to propel him. He tried to make conversation with Penny's father, but the man replied with only three or four words at a time. He preferred, instead, to scrutinize his daughter's guest.

Finally, he said, "You're the young man in the television business?"

"Yes," replied Dillon, thankful for any question to break the stillness.

"Where did you go to school."

"Harvard. I graduated with an MBA."

"Harvard?" Mr. Huntington said, contemplating the word as one would the taste of a brandy. "Old family connections?"

"No, sir, a lot of hard work." Dillon saw that Huntington meant to play hardball with him.

Huntington nodded. Obviously, nothing about Dillon's life was going to impress him. He smiled coldly. "Penny tells us that you are involved with one of the top television shows we might currently see," he said, pausing a moment before adding, ". . . if we watched television."

"*Motive*," replied Dillon. "The name of the series is *Motive*. I work for Graham Maddox, the executive producer. Perhaps you've heard of him? He's a well-respected producer. He's been the genius behind many shows you would recognize the names of . . . of course, only if you watched TV."

Mr. Huntington went to the mahogany bar to make himself a drink. He held a lead crystal glass in his hand and said to Dillon, "You probably don't want one of these if you're driving, do you?"

The man was insufferable. Dillon fumed. Had the girl been anyone but Penny, he would have told Huntington what he thought of him and his snobbery, and told him where to shove it. Dillon's mind flashed to Graham Maddox. Huntington would never have dared speak to the producer in that manner. Dillon wondered if anyone had ever treated Graham Maddox, aged thirty, in such a demeaning way, or if Maddox had always commanded respect when he walked into a room. Dillon rapidly sifted through his thoughts—like a video cassette recorder on "search mode"—to assess what Graham would do that would bring instantaneous high regard.

He didn't know. Maddox's power was more of an enigma than Huntington's. So Dillon smiled cheerfully and pretended that Penny's father was having absolutely no effect on him. He was relieved to hear Penny's happy, bubbling voice.

"Mother, come on, you've got to meet Dillon."

Penny led her mother into the room. Mrs. Huntington

was a petite woman, with smooth, shiny, dark blond hair pulled into a knot at the back of her neck. She extended a feather-light hand to Dillon and nodded graciously when he said, "I'm pleased to meet you."

Penny was dressed in slacks and a pale apricot angora sweater. It complemented her hair and complexion perfectly. Dillon found it difficult to keep from staring at her.

"Are you going out dressed like that?" criticized her mother, looking from Penny to Dillon's tweed sports coat. Her comment implied that she did not think her daughter to be dressed well enough.

"Mother, *please*," said Penny, irritated. "We're only going to a movie and late dinner."

As Penny put her hand on Dillon's shoulder, signaling they should leave, the phone rang. Her mother rose in one fluid movement, disappeared into the hallway, and picked up the telephone before the third ring.

She returned with the news that Mallory was calling for Penny.

"Couldn't you have told him I was out?" snapped Penny. "Dillon and I are trying to get out of here."

"He said it was very important," feinted her mother.

Penny left a daring kiss on Dillon's lips and went to take the phone call.

Mrs. Huntington, seeming to ignore Dillon's presence, said to her husband, "I think Mallory's calling to ask Penny to the ballet next week."

"I trust she'll say yes," replied Huntington. "The Burtons have a season box."

"I'm afraid our little Penny is keeping a lot of men on tenterhooks, darling," said the contriving mother. She turned to Dillon and offered the explanation, "Mallory and Penny have been friends since they were very little. His father is a partner in the same firm as Penny's father. His parents are good friends of ours. *They* have been hoping beyond hope that our Penny will someday marry Mallory." (The emphasis was on the *they,* as though the Huntingtons hadn't thought of it themselves.)

The words rankled Dillon. Penny had never mentioned

this Mallory. How often did she see him? Had Mallory, in fact, already proposed? Could Penny be pushed into such a wedding by family pressure?

"Mallory is proving himself an outstanding attorney," said Huntington. "He is the type of stable, conscientious provider a girl like Penny should marry."

Penny returned to the room. She was clearly exasperated. "Mallory is such a *bore*," she exclaimed. "Next time he calls, Mother, please, please, *please,* tell him I'm not here. He wanted me to go to some ballet with him. The ballet might not be so bad, but if I had to sit in the same box as Mallory, I would *die*."

"Did you tell him no?" asked her father.

"Naturally," replied Penny, having no hint of her parents' conversation with Dillon during the past few minutes.

"I'm sure he's a very disappointed young man," commented Mrs. Huntington. "I do wish you'd reconsider."

Penny rolled her eyes and sucked in a deep breath. "Come on," she said to Dillon as she marched toward the door.

Dillon stood to follow her. He spoke to her parents in the most sincere tone he could muster. "It was so nice to have met both of you." He nodded curtly and tailed Penny to the Volvo. She had already gotten inside and shut her door.

"I'm sorry," she said earnestly, the tears brimming in her eyes. "I'm so sorry. I didn't know they would treat you like that. The boors. The insensitive, self-suffering boors."

Penny wrestled with a devil inside her. Her parents made it so hard for her to be a good girl. She was going to college. She was getting straight A's. To her maximum capabilities, she was doing what they wanted her to do. They didn't want her to make her own choices. She didn't want to have to decide: her parents or Dillon. She wanted both. Why shouldn't she have both? Because of the old values and inexplicable expectations her parents made of her?

"I'm sick of them. I'm so sick of them," she cried, "I could scream!"

"Okay with me," said Dillon. "Scream."

As the massive gate rolled open and the Volvo exited the Huntington premises, an ear-piercing scream filled the car.

Dillon clapped a palm to his ear. The scream died off dramatically and Penny grabbed the wheel, turning it in the opposite direction. Where did she want to go? A block down the street, she made him stop along a shadowed wall.

Then she was against him, her mouth hungrily reaching his, deeply inhaling everything that was him: his breath, his smell, his essence. She clung to him more tightly than she ever had before, her arm muscles so rigid, it was as though she didn't want to let him go.

He let her hold on, let her mouth kiss and kiss and kiss, the only escape for the passion that burned in her.

"Dillon, I love you. I love you," she gasped. "Don't take me to a movie. Please take me to your apartment. Or a motel. I don't care. I don't care. I just want to spend the night with you. I've never spent the whole night with any man. I want to spend it with you. Please . . . *please*."

Her voice was so desperate, so pleading, her body so urgent against his, he could only respond with a long kiss and a quiet, masterful, "All right."

Heavy traffic boxed in Tanya. Five lanes of freeway in each direction and she was in the middle lane. Southern California was a wilderness of cars. There were hundreds of thousands of them. Even if you commuted over the same route every single day, you'd probably never see the same car twice.

After the incident with the auto of her English maid, her husband had relented and let her drive her own car. Norman bought her a Jaguar sedan, equipped with phone, all-leather interior, an extraordinary stereo and an innovative alarm system. He had denied her a convertible top.

After a few weeks of working together on the set, Garrett Gage had finally consented to meeting her. She had a vital need to be alone with him. He had said very little to her, behaving so professionally that he had raised angry uncertainty within her. But when she was next to him, her body drawn magnetically to his, she constantly found herself on the verge of reaching out to touch him. It took all her willpower to control that behavior. There were many eyes on the set.

The traffic was drastic. She would be late. Tanya hoped he would wait. She edged toward the far right lane to exit. Side streets had to be quicker. He had chosen to meet at a remote restaurant that was in neither of their home territories. They couldn't go to his house, because of his girlfriend. He refused to meet her at a hotel, using the excuse that his face was too recognizable.

Questions flooded her mind. Did he still care? Did he hate her for the way she had left him? Over the past few months, her regret at leaving him had grown acute. It never left her alone. And the guilt was worse, chipping at her like bitten nails, gnawing closer and closer to the quick.

She felt stupid for having shown up to screen-test without having seen one single episode of *Motive.* She would not have gone had she known Garrett had the starring role. During the past two weeks, she had to train herself to call him Garrett . . . and only Garrett. She must never slip up and use his real name, Russell.

At home, Norman came to her every night and asked if she was happy now. She was exhausted—truly exhausted—but telling him so did not daunt his advances. His sexual appetite seemed stimulated by her refusals. The harder she fought him off, the more turned on he became. The tears she had used as a deterrent for so long refused to come to her eyes. She had no other weapon.

In the dark (for it was only in blackness that she could do it) she bent over Norman and mechanically worked on him. Just like a whore, she thought bitterly.

Norman was not entirely selfish. "What can I do for you, my beautiful wife? I want to please you."

"No, no, that's all right," she would mutter. "I don't feel like it."

He would nudge her, but her body remained slack. She could not fantasize any longer. Not even with the lights out. With Norman, her sexual desire abandoned her.

"You don't want me, do you?" he asked.

"That's not true," she replied. "I do."

"Then show me."

"I'm so tired, darling. Don't you understand how exhausted I am? I've been putting in long hours on the set."

"Then I insist a driver take you to the studio." His hand would move up her side, under her silky nightshirt, his fingers reaching to the softness under her arms that gave way to her breasts.

"No," she would panic, "I must have the time to myself."

He had boxed her in worse than any traffic. Not only did he expect her to give him sexual satisfaction but also that she, in turn, be satisfied by him. She was a mouse caught in a steel box that had very high walls. How much more could he want from her? How much more could he take from her?

A mile from the restaurant, she waited at a traffic light and observed an ugly tan car in her rearview mirror. She thought it funny. She was almost sure it was the same car she had seen when she pulled onto the freeway. But surely it couldn't be the same one? The color was so putrid. That's the only reason she had noticed it in the first place. With so many pretty colors to choose from, why drive a car that was painted tan? It couldn't be the same one, could it?

A feeling went through her like lead shot sinking into a cold lake. Norman was having her followed. She made a quick right turn. The tan car followed. She made a left and another right to get back to the main street. The tan car stayed with her, back some distance, but there nevertheless.

She had to get ahold of Garrett. She picked up her car phone. But what if Norman had bugged it? She was scraping at the sides of the box with frenzied claws, unable to climb up. She was racing around the bottom with nowhere to go.

She passed the restaurant, not wanting to slow too much and give away the location, but looking for Garrett's car. She drove by too fast. The tan car filled her rearview mirror. She needed to call Garrett. Tell him she was being followed and that they would have to make other plans.

She had to find a phone booth. She was three blocks beyond the restaurant and traveling away from it. On the other side of the street, she saw a phone booth at a convenience store and made a quick left turn. There was a terrible lurch and a grinding sound. She'd hit a high curb and the bottom of her car was stuck.

She quickly climbed out and saw black oil leak its own slick onto the street. Oh, shit! Her bad luck with cars! She reached into her car for her purse. She would call Garrett before she called a tow truck.

There was a step behind her. "May I help you, miss?" asked a man. It was the driver of the tan car. "Are you all right?"

"Yes, yes, I'll be all right. I'll call the Auto Club. Please don't worry about me."

"Miss, I couldn't leave knowing you might not be all right. I'll stay until help arrives."

When Garrett stepped out of the restaurant, he looked up the street and saw the flashing yellow beacons of a tow truck several blocks away. It must have been routine; there were no ambulances. He waited for the valet to bring his black Porsche around. How stupid he was to have believed Tanya. Same old Tanya.

He hadn't lied to Brenda. He had been honest and told her he was meeting Tanya. It was perfectly natural the two of them should rehearse, discuss the script. How stupid he was. He had really thought the actress would show up this time.

The attendant brought the car around. "You're Frank, aren't you?" he asked. "Frank from *Motive?* I know you are, man. I love that show. You're Frank Harrison. Frank's the best guy that ever hit the earth!"

Garrett handed him a big tip. He smiled as he drove away. He liked being famous. He liked being liked. To hell with Tanya.

At daybreak, Spud's Bar was barely discernible. Low and dark, it was built against the west-facing hillside of the canyon. When daylight colored the edges of the sky and night's darkness slid west, the place was usually deserted.

Will roared his motorcycle into the dirt parking lot,

backed it into its accustomed place in front of the plate glass window, and killed the engine. He straddled the bike and observed the activity of the film crew unloading equipment from a half-dozen trucks. He figured close to fifty people were actively engaged, their busy noise filling the silence.

" 'Scuse me, buddy," said a narrow-hipped, down-vested man who held a roll of black cloth, "could you park that thing over there? We gotta move a bunch of cable through here, plus we gotta tack this black-out material over the window."

It was a decently put request. Will said, "Sure."

He started the engine, gunned it so the tires spit a little gravel, then parked his motorcycle at the end of the trailer of portable dressing rooms. Each room was a narrow cell with its own door to the outside and a window on the opposite wall. Will smelled coffee in the clean, cold air, and he pointed his nose in the direction of a catering truck that had set up, out of the way, and was offering sweet rolls as well. He helped himself to both.

A trickle of excitement moved through him. He hadn't been on a film set in several years. The energy and bustle sharpened his senses. The crew would be shooting at Spud's for two days. When he had signed up as an extra, he told them he could do stunts. They had told him to contact the stunt coordinator.

Will asked around for Arnold and was pointed toward a lean, hard man of nearly sixty, who stood in the roadway with a couple of assistants and a long tape measure. They were calculating the logistics of a fall. Will respectfully watched them for five minutes before introducing himself to Arnold, who asked him about his experience.

Sufficiently impressed with Will's background and credentials, Arnold eyed him and said, "Okay, son, you look like you know what you're talking about. I had Petey-boy scheduled to slide a hundred feet down this here highway, but he fucked up his knee yesterday when we was rehearsin'."

"Sorry to hear that," said Will.

"Yeah, me too. I got a call in to the association for someone who can take this fall. They want to shoot it today."

"You got the bike here?" asked Will.

Arnold jerked his thumb over his shoulder at an equipment truck. "I got six over there."

Will didn't bother to look at the truck. "I'll do it," he said, his instinct telling him he could trust the judgment and planning of the veteran stunt coordinator.

"Let me see your card," said Arnold, adding, "Just a technicality, you know. Then I want to see you ride. They're shooting inside all morning. That'll give us plenty of time to get this sucker ready. And sign up with the production secretaries. I don't want to get into trouble for failing to report you to SAG. I'll get my ass kicked all the way to hell and back if you don't."

"I'll do that right away," said Will, who knew the Screen Actors Guild had extremely strict rules.

"Okay, son. Good. Then get back out here, so we can pace this out. I'll try to get the director for ten minutes worth of his valuable consultation."

When Will turned in the direction of the trailer that housed the production secretaries, Arnold asked, "Say, son, you seem kinda familiar. Have I seen you working before?"

"Maybe," replied Will, "but it would have been a few years back." Though beams of sunlight were working their way down the opposite canyon wall, it was still chilly where he stood. Another cup of coffee would be mighty good.

Graham awoke at five A.M. when Ruby slipped out of bed. *Motive* was on location and she needed an early start. He lay in bed and watched her pad through the room in slip, bra, and pantyhose, then sit at her dressing table located in the alcove between the bedroom and her bath. She pushed her hair out of her face with an elastic headband. Her profile had changed little since they were married.

She exuded energy, yet it was calm energy. She was not frenetic, just eager. Her face had a satisfied glow that he could not recall ever seeing. He wasn't sure why this change had come over her. She had been family-centered for years;

nothing outside of her husband, children, home, and good standing in the community had swayed her devotion. Now she was her "own woman." It was frustrating to feel like she might be slipping from his grasp.

Ready to leave, she sat on the edge of the bed, tousled his hair, made a comment about adult breath, stroked his rough chin with the back of her fingers, and then leaned over and laid her head against his chest. Her hug was brief. But she shut her eyes and breathed deeply, as though trying to regain something that had been irretrievably lost before she had even realized it was missing.

The seat of the Coupe de Ville was cold. Graham drove with the windows down. The wispy morning mists hung suspended over lawns and streets, gradually rising as daylight strengthened. He enjoyed driving in the morning. It was easier on his back than jogging and he could think just as effectively.

A favorite donut shop, situated on the Glendale-Burbank border, loomed out of the mist. Parked outside were two police cars, a station wagon full of ladders and paint cans, a pickup truck towing a mini-cement mixer, and a cream-colored Porsche. Inside was a man's world, filled with the aroma of brewed coffee, fresh-baked donuts, and cigarette smoke.

"Hi there," said Graham to the man behind the counter.

"How are you today, Mr. Maddox?" answered the pleasant-faced fellow with a Slavic accent. "Two of those?" He pointed at a tray of Long Johns smothered in maple icing.

"Are they fresh?" asked Graham with a smile.

"What a question! What a question! Are they fresh? I wouldn't have them on the shelf if I did not bake them this morning. Right here, right here, I bake them." He pointed to the stainless steel ovens and poured Graham a cup of coffee.

It surprised Graham that this donut shop was nowadays the only place that didn't fill him with a restlessness, an urgency he couldn't explain nor get rid of. Here, he could sit in the corner, read the entire *L.A. Times,* and become so absorbed in it that he didn't even realize time was passing. Everywhere else, he couldn't forget the relentlessness of time.

Here, they only knew him by his face. His name and reputation would mean nothing to them. He doubted they would care he had the number-one-rated show, *Motive,* and four others that were not far behind. Once, when he had first come into the place, he had chatted about show business with a retired postal worker, who ended up asking him if he had known a cousin who had been an electrician on the old *Jack Benny Show.* Graham had had to shake his head apologetically and say no.

These people didn't care about the complexities of the entertainment industry. They only wanted something to watch on TV when they got home after work. Outside of the fraction addicted to the tabloid lives of celebrities, the rest of the world did not give two hoots about "Hollywood." Only in Hollywood was such reverence paid to such an illusory business.

From his early morning musings came the conclusion that his restlessness came from having mastered the "business"; it was boring, no longer a challenge to him.

However, by the time he got to his office, he was so caught up in the events of the day—schedules, deadlines, sound and editing sessions, meetings with producers, directors, writers, and investors—that he quite forgot the donut shop meditations.

Upon reaching his office, he noticed Jeannie was not at her desk. He had been lucky hiring her. He could rely on her. She caught on quickly and did her assignments without his having to check up on her every two minutes.

Inside his lair, the blinking on his private line answering machine indicated three messages. The first two were hang-ups. The third contained Jeannie's honey-rich voice, which he had come to expect almost every morning.

"Hi, sweetheart," she said. "I'm lying here in a bubble bath, and it's barely covering my nipples. I'm pinching them to get them aroused because I'm thinking of you. Oooh, this water is so warm. I'm sliding my hand down my stomach, down, down between my legs.

"You know what's there, don't you? And oooh, I've got to feel it with just one little finger, just a little ways in, and . . ."

He turned off the machine and breathed deeply. The mental picture she had described aroused him.

"Oooh," he heard a voice behind him say, then the sound of a door shutting. "Just a little ways, that's all I wanted till I got the real thing."

"You can't keep leaving messages like that," he said, without turning around. "Someone's bound to hear them."

"Nobody's going to hear them. I erase them every morning."

From behind, she slipped her arms around him, her deft fingers unbuttoning his pants and moving under his shorts. She touched him gently. Her body pressed against his back. He felt her hard breasts above his kidneys. She pushed his slacks over his hips and took a better grasp of him, so she could better satisfy him.

At lunchtime, most of the cast, crew, and extras ate under a temporary tent set up near the catering truck. Will needed a quiet place in the sun, where he could shut his eyes for a few minutes, undisturbed. He walked around the back of Spud's Bar and was surprised to find someone else had also searched out a little solitude.

"Aren't you the camera man?" Will asked as the man looked up.

"Yeah, hi. I'm Tony," he replied, a cigarette dangling from his mouth, the smoke curling heavily against his face. He extended his hand from where he sat.

Will shook it. "Hi, I'm Will."

"Extra, huh?"

"Stunts. Doin' some stunts this afternoon." Will reached into a pocket and extracted a joint. "Say, I was looking for a place to smoke this. Want some?"

"Sure thing," said Tony, glancing to either side to reassure himself they wouldn't be interrupted. There was no worry.

The back of Spud's was not very hospitable. Shards of broken glass covered the ground and a disreputable rusted dumpster, filled with bullet holes, stood open. Since there was no back porch, a person had to not mind parking his butt on the dirt and a few weeds, and leaning against the wall.

Will sat down and squinted into the sun. It was easier to close his eyes. He lighted the marijuana and drew in deeply, letting the drug relax him. He handed it to Tony.

Tony nodded his thanks and took a hit, gulping in as much of the pungent smoke as he could. He held the home-rolled number between his thumb and forefinger and passed it back to Will.

"Guess we got to move the cameras outside this afternoon," said Tony. "At sunset, they want to get shots of the whole motorcycle gang coming around that bend in the road. You riding in that?"

"I ain't been asked," said Will. "Guess I could. I gotta do a stunt after lunch. They want me to lay one of those babies down in a skid."

"Shit!" exclaimed Tony, "you gotta *fall* with the bike?"

"Yeah, no sweat. I used to ride a lot of stunts."

"But not lately?" asked Tony, retrieving the joint and sucking in more smoke.

"I've been out of state." Tony didn't respond, so Will added, "Up livin' in Oregon."

"I hear that's a real pretty state. A good place to live when you get some money together."

"It's pretty, all right," said Will. "I think of it as home."

"Why the hell you ever come back to Smogville?" asked Tony, slowly releasing a lungful of smoke.

Momentary emotion choked out Will's voice. "No money," he finally said. "Couldn't make enough money there. Was cutting trees . . . lumberjack. But they laid me off."

It was a sufficient answer for Tony. "Sorry to hear that," he said sympathetically.

They had smoked the joint down to roach status. Will produced a clip from his pocket and held the stub to his parted lips. The pot had eased some of the tension from his shoulders. He would have liked to smoke another one, but he knew it was too dangerous if he was expected to do a stunt.

"Say," he asked, "what's the name of the blond chick who's giving everyone orders?"

"Sondra," replied Tony, taking the roach and gently drawing the last traces of smoke. "She's the first AD."

Will nodded. "Does she ever go out with anybody?"

Tony began laughing. "Shit, no, she's a dyke."

Will didn't think that was anything to laugh about. "You sure?"

"Don't even try, man. She is *the* nastiest bitch you ever saw. My God, you know how they say 'if looks could kill'? The whole bunch of us would've been massacred months ago. Besides, what do you want with such a skinny ass?"

Tony, sensing he needed to get back to the set, stood up. Will followed him. They paused at the side of the building and watched the bustling crew.

"That is my idea of an ass," said Tony, pointing to a curly-headed girl with a wide-eyed, open look to her face that almost made her pretty. "Her name's Glory. Look at that ass. It's something a man can hold on to."

Will nodded at the girl's ample padding and said, "If there was ever a cold night in L.A., she might come in handy."

His eyes searched out Sondra. She stood with the director near the edge of the road. She must have sensed someone watching her, for she looked around and finally met Will's eyes. She made no response.

"Bones," said Tony, following Will's glance. "She's all bones. No tits. No ass. Her mouth is so hard, it'd be like kissing a brick."

Will smiled to himself. He didn't agree with the comment.

Denny lit Margi's cigarette. They sat side by side on the narrow steps that led up to the makeup and hair trailer. The sunshine felt good.

"I don't know how you survive on location," teased Denny, "without having Bob for lunch every day."

Margi stretched, her arms reaching up, her firm breasts thrust forward. She laughed throatily. Denny never commented on her sex life, though he would have had to have been blind not to notice it. "It gives me something to look forward to when I go home," she answered.

Denny nodded, opened his mouth to say something, then shut it again.

Margi noticed him holding back. "What is it, Den?"

"I . . . I just wondered . . . well, it's really none of my business . . ."

Her curiosity was piqued. "What? What are you wondering?"

"Do you and Bob have sex *every* day?"

She burst into jubilant laughter, grabbed his neck, and kissed him on the cheek. How long had he been waiting to ask that question? "I've never hid the fact that Bob and I have a great sex life."

"Guess some people are lucky like that," he mused. "I could never have sex every day. I don't crave it that much. If I did, maybe I wouldn't have lost Jeff."

His voice sounded very sad. Though he was outwardly quite cheerful, she knew he continued to harbor a lot of grief about his estranged lover.

"Oh, Den, it wouldn't have mattered how much sex you had with Jeff," she said straightforwardly. "He would have treated you the same way no matter what. It's the way he is. He had no respect for you. He wasn't good enough for you."

Sondra Prescott, clipboard in hand, came by. She wore a man's jacket that was too big over her skinny shoulders. "Denny," she said, "please stand by on the set. We need to even out some complexions under the lights."

"I'll be right there," said Denny. He stood up and went inside for his makeup case.

Margi followed him in and took up her brushes and a can of hair spray.

"You were nice this morning," said Denny, "showing Glory how she should fix her hair so she'll end up with curls instead of frizz."

"She's so stupid," said Margi with exasperation.

"You don't think she's stupid," said Denny as Margi followed him out of the trailer and over to the interior set.

Margi only pretended not to like Glory. That morning, she had been quite solicitous and patient. Richard, the director, had started barking for his assistant and Margi had been forced to snap at him, "For God's sake, Richard, hold your horses. She's over here. Just a minute." When Glory had slid from Margi's chair, Denny patted her on the back. Thirty seconds later she was back, looking embarrassed. She had forgotten to take her notebook and ballpoint pen.

"She's spaced-out. Doesn't use what little brain she has," said Margi.

"You're wrong," said Denny. "She's a girl who's full of ideas."

Margi nodded at the girl standing near the camera operator. "Look at her mooning around that damn Tony. He ain't the right kind of guy for her. She needs some sound advice."

And you're the one to give it to her, thought Denny. He shook his head, realizing that if there was one thing Margi was unable to do, it was to stay out of other peoples' business.

Denny kept a wary eye on Sondra most of the afternoon. He knew what most of the men on the set said about her, how she was unapproachable, a bitch, a dyke. He didn't care what the current opinion was. She never snapped at him, and though he couldn't say she had ever acted truly happy when they chatted, she had been pleasant.

Hers was the most high-pressure job on the set. As first assistant director, she had to know everything that was happening at all times with the cast members, extras, props, sets, scenes to be shot, atmosphere, and special effects. If she made a mistake in judgment, it could cost the production company thousands of dollars. She couldn't afford to have a laid-back attitude.

While the grips were moving the equipment to the roadside, Sondra rested with a cup of coffee in her hand. Denny walked over and stood next to her.

"How are you doing?" he asked. "It's not too hot for you? Did you put some sunblock on your face?"

"I'm tired, Denny," she replied. "But thanks for asking. I forgot all about sunblock. Do you think it makes a difference?"

"Heaven's yes, dear. Here." He pulled a small bottle from his case. "Put some on."

She smoothed some of the lotion into her skin. She was very fair and had only been saved from sunburn that morning because she had been working inside. "Thanks," she said, screwing on the top and handing the bottle back to him.

"You're welcome. Can I ask you something?"

"Why not?" she said, swirling the thick coffee around the bottom of the Styrofoam cup.

"I'd really like to take you out to dinner sometime," he said. "Would you like to go?"

Her face registered complete surprise. "It would be wonderful, Denny, if I ever had any energy. By the end of the day I'm so exhausted, I go straight home. But thanks for asking."

He nodded. It was a put-down. He knew it. At least she wasn't cold about it. He could have taken her out on a weekend, when they weren't working, but he wasn't going to push it. Maybe he could ask her again in another month.

Looking at his disappointed face, she added, "It's nothing personal, Denny, but I prefer not to socialize with the people I work with. I have to give a lot of orders, and people don't like taking orders from friends. It makes things too complicated when we're under a tight schedule. I hope you understand."

A second put-down to clarify the first. He kept his mouth shut and watched her become absorbed in the show again. Her concentration was riveted on Richard's direction. Her eyes hardened, her jaw muscles tightened, and her shoulders hunched, she tapped the end of her pen against her clipboard.

Nice try, anyway, he told himself. Maybe women aren't any softer than men. Maybe, in general, people are assholes.

The motorcycle skidded on its side, pressing its rider against the asphalt and throwing gravel into the eye of the camera.

"Perfect," said Richard, the director, in reference to this third take of the accident.

Will stood up from the fallen cycle and Arnold, the stunt coordinator, ran out to make sure he was all right. Will nodded. He was padded against abrasion. He knew his muscles would feel it for a few days. He'd have a few bruises. But it was worth it. The money would be great. Three falls worth. It gave him a sense of security, even though his body was trembling from the exertion and the adrenaline.

It was late afternoon of the second day's shoot. Richard wanted another shot of the motorcycle gang coming around the bend at sunset. Will didn't feel like riding anymore. However, he had been doubled for the lead, Garrett Gage, and they needed him to ride at the head of the gang.

Arnold clapped him on the back. "We're going to have more work for you, son," he said. "We haven't found anyone else who looks as much like Gage as you. The producer is going to appreciate that."

Will nodded. He hadn't worked in months. Now, he ended up as double for a faggot's dream of a centerfold. He didn't know how he felt about that. Yes, Gage was good-looking and capitalizing on those looks. Will was good on motorcycles, but he didn't know what other stunts would be required. He decided to play it by ear.

Tony came up and said, "Good fall, Will. I thought you were hurt when you did it yesterday, the way the bike twisted and you got smashed in the gravel. I'm glad you're all right."

"Thanks," said Will. "Hope you got it all on film."

"Absolutely," said Tony with a smile. "Richard should have gotten it in one take, but our less-than-talented director doesn't care how much money he wastes by not getting it right the first time. You going to be doing any more work for them?" He gestured toward the producers' trailer.

"Don't know. That Arnold, in charge of stunts, told me I could get more work. I wasn't intendin' on staying in L.A.

that long, but I guess I could use the money."

"Money's the only reason *I* keep doing it," said Tony. He looked in the direction of the sunset and the bend in the road. "We don't have much daylight left, so they better hustle. After this last take, you want to smoke a number before we pack up?"

"No thanks," said Will. "Another time. I've got some business to take care of."

After the take, Will made his way to the producers' trailer. The entrance was blocked by assistants, secretaries, bit players, and miscellaneous crew members. Will hadn't seen the producer up close during the two-day shoot. Mrs. Maddox, as everyone called her, had stayed out of the way and allowed her crew to do their job. Will concluded that most people thought she was nice but not very sensitive to the different temperaments on the set. He wanted to talk to her.

At the trailer door, Sondra blocked his entrance. "Excuse me," he asked the skinny blonde. "Can I talk to Mrs. Maddox?"

"You can't go in there," replied Sondra authoritatively. "You can't just walk in here and bother Mrs. Maddox. She's very busy."

Her nasty tone of voice set his teeth on edge. He was trying to be nice. "It'll only take a couple of minutes."

"I don't think so."

"Come on. Just ask her."

She contemplated Will, the tip of a pencil in her mouth, her clipboard in the crook of her arm, covering her chest. "What's it about?"

This woman was too much. "It's of a personal nature," he said. "All right?"

"It's not all right. I can't let every extra or stuntman just barge in. I'm getting paid to handle the things that Mrs. Maddox shouldn't have to. *You* fall into the category of people that *I* talk to."

Will raised his voice. "Could you please ask her if I can talk to her for a couple of minutes?"

People standing around turned their heads at his loudness. This Sondra was going overboard in her job. "Would you please ask her?" he repeated loudly.

Sondra's eyes blazed in defiance. She was used to bossing people around and her word was final. But here he was, standing up to her, making a scene. Inside, Ruby sat with the director, the director of photography, and her secretary. Sondra climbed in the trailer and said to Ruby, "There's a man who wants to talk to you. He's just an extra. I tried to get rid of him, but he's being real insistent. I'm sorry."

Ruby smiled graciously. "If it's that important," she said softly, "please ask him to come in."

Daylight had almost left the sky. The canyon was cool, but Will's leather pants and jacket kept him warm. Sondra returned to tell him it was all right for him to go in and talk to Ruby.

He stepped up into the trailer and Sondra followed him. She resented wanting to know what was so important that he had to force his way in.

He stood before Ruby, tall and strong, his mustache long and sweeping, his body weary, his eyes devoid of aggression, open and waiting.

Ruby was stunned. All she could manage to say was a very weak, "Will . . ."

He took her arms and pulled her to her feet.

"Will," she repeated unbelievingly, her hand in front of her mouth, her eyes searching his body, his eyes.

"How are you?" he said quietly.

"Will, oh, Will," she said, the voice in her throat thin.

"It's good to see ya, Ma," he said, gently brushing his fingers against her cheek to catch a falling tear.

Chapter 6

Garrett was almost hostile toward Tanya. He had scarcely spoken a word to her offstage since their ill-fated rendezvous. No one on the set noticed, since he was in character. Frank Harrison was polite to stowaway Janet, Tanya's character, yet he wanted her out of his life. Frank hadn't fallen in love with Janet, though Tanya believed the screenwriters were slating a romantic entanglement between the two.

She had acquiesced to Norman's wish that she be chauffeured to the studio. She hoped to hell she had put the man in the tan car out of a job. Never had her nerves been so rattled.

It occurred to Tanya that she had not once been alone with Garrett in a room. Someone always watched their rehearsals, even if it was only the absentminded Glory. Glory was willing to do anything Garrett asked, and when he insisted she stay and give her opinion on the interaction between Frank and Janet, the production assistant was flattered.

Tanya was frustrated. It was ironic she should be so close to Garrett and yet find him so unreachable. She began to realize he was avoiding her—a skillful trick to pull off with a large crew around them all day long. Tanya had to give him credit on his acting ability. He smiled continuously, though not a single smile was directed her way. If his face was pointed in her direction, his eyes never sought hers. They veered off to one side of her head and looked past her.

It was possible that Garrett had learned of Norman's

quirky hold over his young, beautiful wife and had decided to play it safe and leave Tanya alone, but there was no longing for her in the actor's eyes.

Her fantasies became acute and vivid. She was so close to Garrett and yet she was never able to touch him. Wanting him and yet forced to succumb to Norman. In the entire world, there was not a solitary thing that could be purchased that she desired. She only wanted a few hours alone with Garrett, to let her fingers trace the course of her fantasies over his body.

She was dismayed that she hadn't made friends with a soul, yet she trusted no one on the set. Tanya was met with cold respect, but she could not understand the source of their unfriendliness. It did not perplex her long, however; she passed it off as the professional manner in which stars are treated by the crew.

One morning, as her limo dropped her off, she saw Garrett parking his brand-new Porsche. It was black and tricked out. She thought how well it suited him. A plan formed in her mind. Later that afternoon, she asked Glory to make a phone call for her.

Glory complied. "Hello," she said into the phone. "This is Ms. Hansen, Mr. Maddox's secretary. Are you the housekeeper? Very well. Tanya asked me to relay a message to her chauffeur. She is delayed this evening for extra rehearsal. She will call about ten P.M. to arrange for him to pick her up."

Glory nervously hung up the phone. "What if they call Mr. Maddox's office back?" she whispered.

"They won't," said Tanya with false confidence, unsure herself. "I am mistress of the house. I know what they will do."

"Why can't you call yourself?" asked Glory.

Tanya smiled condescendingly. "I usually have Ms. Hansen make the calls for me because I'm so busy. I didn't want to worry my household staff with a phone call from someone they aren't familiar with."

Her answer silenced Glory, but did the assistant know it was a lie? As an afterthought, Tanya gushed, "I appreciate your efforts, I really do. And not just the call today . . . all the little ways you help out."

Glory said a quick "You're welcome," and ducked away.

The day's final take required only Garrett on camera. Afterward, he hurried through the parking lot, his keys jangling in his hand. A voice behind him called softly, "Russell, please wait."

He pretended he didn't hear. But her footsteps dogged him and he turned to face her when he reached the Porsche.

"What are you doing?" he queried.

"I need to talk to you," she said boldly. She was wearing a short dress and a light coat. Her beautiful legs were sturdy beneath her.

"We have nothing to talk about," he said, deactivating the alarm and unlocking his car.

"That's not true," she wailed as he made motions to get in and leave her.

"Where's your limo?" he asked snidely.

"I told him not to pick me up."

Her waist-length hair had been tethered into its manageable braid. With the hair pulled back from her temples, she had a different look; her cheekbones seemed more pronounced, her face more triangular and fragile. She wore almost no makeup.

"I don't think it's a good idea if we talk," he said.

"Why not?" she asked, her voice weak.

He glanced around the parking lot to see what cast and crew members were coming out to their cars. Tanya was recognizable with that massive braid and long legs. Suspicions would flare if the two were seen together.

"Get in," he told her abruptly.

She got in and sat silently while he started the husky-throated engine. Driving past the guard gate, she instinctively slumped down in her seat and turned her head away. Garrett waved at the guard and sped from the studio, his general idea to take her home.

She snatched his hand ferociously and held it against her cheek and lips. The lips were soft and wet and warm. Her kisses came faster and faster upon his hand, on each fingertip, deep into the palm.

"Tanya, don't," he said.

"Why not? Why not?" she asked, clutching his hand.

"It's not right."

"I don't care."

"I'm in love with someone," he said, pulling his hand away to downshift and leaving it on the stick shift.

"That's not true," she said, sitting up on her knees and leaning over, putting her arms around his neck. "*I* love you. *I* need you. You've got to forgive me."

"You, you, you! All you ever think about is what Tanya wants, isn't it? You broke my heart once . . . real bad. I don't need it again."

"Russell, don't say that."

"Don't call me Russell. I'm Garrett now. I've got a good lady. She gives me moral support—something you wouldn't know about. She's interested in *me,* in *my* career."

"Does she know about us?" asked Tanya, still kneeling, her breath soft upon his ear.

"Please sit down," he said.

"Does she know about *me?* About *our* love?"

"Tanya! Sit down!" He pushed her back with his arm, the car jerking in the lane, the car next to them honking furiously.

"You can't love her. You can't. Not as much as you loved me."

"Stop this," he said, realizing she was becoming more and more delirious. He couldn't leave her at the gates to her home in this condition. Who knew what she'd say? He couldn't afford to take a chance with a woman on the verge of hysteria.

"I love you. I can't stand living with Norman," she wailed. "He's horrible. He's old and ugly and I can't stand it when he touches me." Her voice rose higher and higher, her words coming faster and faster, her breathing in short gasps. "He always wants to touch me with his horrid old hands. All over me. It's terrible. All I can think about is you."

She wasn't looking at Garrett, but was looking forward, her eyes dry, wide and white-walled, seeing not the road—

but Norman—in front of her. "I'm trapped. I'm his prisoner," she shrieked. "Something he thinks he can fuck any time he wants to. Do you want someone fucking me like that? Don't you care anymore? Don't you still love me?"

Her breathing was so rapid that Garrett worried she might faint from hyperventilation. He stopped next to a dark park, got out, put on a jean jacket, and came around to her side of the car, where he opened the door and squatted down on the curb. He placed a hand on her forehead, stroking her gently. Gradually, her heavy breathing eased. He felt no pity for her, only worry for himself that he was involved.

"The night I was supposed to meet you," she said, "I was followed. Norman had me followed. This man in a tan car followed me. I was going to phone you at the restaurant, but I wrecked the car. I wanted to see you. I did. I did. Please believe me."

Garrett was not sure if Norman had really had her followed, or if the man in the tan car was a figment of her imagination or, even, a concoction of her cunning. He remembered her scheming.

"You don't believe me," she said, her voice dry.

Garrett took her hand and urged her out of the car. He pushed the door shut and it made a solid thunking sound, the way well-made car doors do. That sound pleased him. It was almost a nightmare that the sound should be accompanied by Tanya before him, wrapping her arms around his waist, clinging close to him.

Garrett knew that Frank Harrison would help the girl. Frank was the nicest, most handsome boy-next-door in the world. Frank would buy her hot chocolate and listen to all her woes. Frank was a humanitarian. They walked down the sidewalk and then out across a softball diamond.

She gripped his arm with a love so desperate it welded itself against him. "I can't stand working with you and not having you," she said, stopping far outfield, in the center territory where four softball fields merged. The immediate radius was dark. The city glowed luminescently three hundred yards away, and sounds of traffic came indistinctly across the cool, dry grass. She turned her mouth up to be kissed.

Long-buried urges flickered through him. They seemed so removed from the here and now. What would Frank do? Lucky Frank managed to be surrounded by women and was never challenged by sexual desire. The writers circumvented sex in the script.

Well . . . Frank might give her a kiss. He wouldn't screw her. At least, not so the audience knew about it. But Frank would kiss her.

His mouth was upon hers, his tongue sliding past her soft lips and smooth teeth, searching her tongue. Wet against wet. Warm against warm. Sparked by the chemical charge that had always existed between them, his old desire devoured him and made him want to devour her. He couldn't get enough of her mouth.

Her hands tugged his shirt upwards and moved underneath, caressing his stomach, rubbing his chest hair, gripping his supple pectoral muscles. Her hands were burning wherever she touched him—it was so much more than she had fantasized. The feel of him made her weak all over; her legs cotton candy, her insides bursting, carbonated bubbles.

Her hands unbuttoned his pants and slid the zipper apart. Her hands cupped around him, one feeling his rigidity, the other his soft pouch. She squeezed gently, perfectly, the memory of what pleased him instinctive in her touch. She pushed the pants from his hips and slid onto her knees, taking him into her mouth as far as she could. The wet warmth, which had pressed against his tongue moments before, now sucked steadily.

He stood, his feet braced apart, his fingertips touching her shoulders, his eyes closed to the night. His anxiety vanished and his concentration focused on the rhythmic movement that fanned fever through his gut. It built terrifically, a pounding force of liquid sweetness that grew in intensity.

Just before it reached the boiling point, he, too, went down on his knees, his mouth sucking her wet chin while he pulled off his jean jacket. He put it on the ground behind her and forced her down upon it. Under her short skirt, sheer pantyhose ran up to her waist. He roughly pulled the elastic waist halfway down her thighs, exposing the tender, voluptuous flower blooming shadowy pink in the dim light.

Three fingers forced their way into her, savagely, not taking time to ease in. She gasped and her muscles clamped tightly.

"That's right, baby," he said to her, pushing even deeper into the rich velvet. "How do you like that?"

"More," she murmured.

He pushed in farther, his knuckles grating against her pubic bone. He withdrew the fingers, placed them against his lips, and moved into her, his swollen head a purple villain in the flushed rose, caving in the petals and beating the tenderness with all that was hard within him.

She struggled to pull one foot free from the stockings that trapped her, so she could wrap her legs around his back. Her backbone curved and brought her ass up in the air. He sunk deeper into her. With hands on his buttocks, she pulled him tight.

"Don't stop, don't stop," she pleaded, her orgasm at arm's length, refusing to come closer. "Don't stop."

Her words spurred him and, in a torrential flash, the burning liquid rushed from him. He plunged into her again and again, laying his seed as deep as he could, her muscles rubbing his oversensitized head.

"Don't stop," she repeated.

With effort between breaths, he moved in her, no longer stretching the inner walls but sliding tactilely. Her legs spread farther apart. She bucked up with her hips, gripping his shoulders. "Don't stop, don't stop." Her breaths came quicker and the elusive pinnacle came closer, until it rolled over her like a hot wave, drenching her in molten delight.

They lay still, together. He, on his elbows, rested protectively over her, keeping her breaths under him as he looked into the blackness of the park. For the first time, it occurred to him that their lovemaking might have been observed. He pushed himself up on his hands, but saw no movement nor heard a voice.

"Not yet," she begged, pulling him back against her. "I don't want to go yet."

He kissed her damp forehead and flexed in her. She smiled at the twitch below her belly button. Oh, how good he felt. Like she had come home after many, many years away on a ceaseless voyage on which she had never rested. He would take care of her.

In Garrett's brain, there was another conversation:

"You didn't think I'd do it, did you?" asked Frank.

"I'm proud of you, boy, real proud," Garrett replied.

"If you want money from me, Martin, you're going to have to do something to earn it."

Graham surprised even himself. Usually, it was so much easier to write the kid a check and forget about him for a couple of weeks. But Graham had had only three hours sleep the night before, the day had been one long, complicated bitch, the front yard of his home looked a mess because the gardener had been sick, and his housekeeper had forgotten to buy a new bottle of Scotch.

Martin leaned against the stone front of the elaborate fireplace in his parents' house and stared at his father. At the mention of working for money, the sly smile on the kid's face turned to surliness.

Martin let out an exasperated sigh, stating, "I suppose that was Mom's idea."

"It's *my* idea," snapped Graham. "You will work as a stand-in on *Medical Alert*."

"A stand-in?" whined Martin. "That the most fuckingest, boringest job in the world. Hanging around while they make sure the lighting is all right."

"It will do for now."

"Don't you have anything on a movie-of-the-week? Second assistant director or something?" Though Martin faced the window which viewed the rugged canyon he was staring into space. There was a blank, disapproving look on his face.

"I'm not paying union dues on your ass," Graham stated bluntly. "I wasted enough money on you when you went to film school. And you didn't even finish. If you want a job that requires the sanction of a union, you'll have to pay the dues yourself."

"Come on, Dad. *Third* assistant director. You can dock the union dues from my paycheck."

Graham thought a minute before answering. "Okay. It's a deal. But you do exactly what they tell you to do," he said, realizing he might be adding a burden to the *Medical Alert* crew, especially to the first and second assistant directors. He would give Martin a few weeks' trial and then evaluate how he was doing.

"Can I get some money now?" asked Martin. "I have rent to pay. They're really pissed I haven't come up with it."

"No," said Graham, getting off the couch and crossing to a cabinet that contained crystal decanters of liquor. The one with the Scotch tag around its neck showed only a quarter inch of the amber liquid in the bottom.

"Damn," he said, resigning himself to the bourbon decanter. The whole damn house was full of bourbon. Nobody ever thought of him. Ruby had promised that Mrs. Garcia could manage the upkeep of the house. Well, there was no Scotch and, damn it, he wanted Scotch after a hard day. He'd never had this problem before Ruby had gone to work.

The room-temperature bourbon burned smoothly. It bit gently into his gut. He thought of asking Martin to run down the canyon and pick up a bottle, but his son was not the kind of kid to do anyone a favor. If he wanted Martin to go to the liquor store, he'd have to pay the kid's rent. If he gave the money to his son before the trip to the store was made, Martin would just take off and not bother returning with the liquor.

Martin could try anybody's patience. He didn't know what was wrong with the kid. Martin had no motivation, no desire, only a willingness to let the world go by while he "partied." Graham shook his head at the California term. "Partying" had not only become a verb, it had become a way of life. And Martin refused to grow out of it. What can you do about a kid like that? Part of you loves him as any parent would love a child; you feel responsible for him, even if he doesn't try. Martin didn't seem able to function in the normal world. Where had the kid strayed?

Martin poured himself a glass from the bourbon decanter, swallowing hard on the first gulp to go down. "Dad, if I don't come up with the money, they're going to kick me out. Then where will I move? Back here?" Then he added with confidence, "Mom would love it."

"Don't be so sure of that," said Graham, leafing through some production reports and wishing Martin would leave, even though he knew the kid would stay through dinner. "Your mother has gotten to be an *independent woman.* Things will never again be the same around here."

"Is that what's eating you?" commented Martin cautiously, realizing that his father's ambivalence about a working wife *might* be the cause of his sour moods. Martin would have to play his hand easy. If he took his dad's side, perhaps Graham would not feel so desolate. On the other hand, there was the chance that Graham was happy to have Ruby gone more often.

"*Nothing* is eating me," chafed Graham. "I've had a long day and I'm not in the mood to shell out money to someone who hasn't done a goddamned thing except hang out at the beach and sniff cocaine."

Martin's face flushed fast, the red running into it as quickly as blood flowing from a wound.

"Don't look so damned surprised," said Graham. "I'm not dumb, you know. You aren't dressed well enough to be spending all your money on clothes. You shouldn't have that trust fund at all. Your grandparents were much too generous."

Martin was indignant. "I don't do any drugs. I don't know where you got that idea. I don't."

"I see the symptoms," said Graham. "When you want to quit, dry up, or whatever they call it, I may see fit to pay for your therapy. Otherwise, let's just say I'm tired of supporting your habit."

"You don't know anything, man," argued Martin, swallowing another gulp of bourbon and inhaling violently to counteract the kick.

Graham suddenly felt very sorry for his son. Martin was not a fighter. He was pushed around by his peer group. He did whatever he thought was "cool." He was a product of the Television Age, of commercials, which made him desire a lot without having to expend anything for it. Perhaps Graham was responsible on a higher level than just being Martin's father.

"Show up for work tomorrow," said Graham. "I'll tell payroll to write you an advance."

The worry left Martin's face. "Okay, Dad," he said. "What time am I supposed to be on the set?"

"Seven A.M.," said Graham. "Report to Paul Wilson. He'll tell you what to do."

Martin nodded. "I'm kinda hungry. When's Mom going to be home?"

"We're on our own tonight," replied Graham. "Your mother said she had something she wanted to do this evening."

"Should I order out for a pizza?"

"Please, no," said Graham. "There should be something in the fridge we can fix up. I guess you haven't heard, have you?"

"Heard what?" asked Martin, making his way to the kitchen, opening the freezer door and staring into the frosty depths.

Graham followed him to the kitchen and leaned against the counter. "Will's in town."

Martin turned and stared at his father in disbelief, while the icy breath of the freezer swirled around him. "Will?"

"Back from Oregon. He's doing some stunts on your mother's show."

"How long will he be around?"

"How the hell should I know?" gnashed Graham. "Your mother is as happy as a pig in shit about it."

"Where's he living?"

"How the hell should I know?" said Graham with increased irritation. "Even your mother doesn't know."

"Shit," said Martin. "Last time I saw him, he beat the crap out of me. I thought we had seen the last of him when he moved to Oregon."

"Well, he's your mother's son, her firstborn, and there will always be a special place in her heart for him." And, thought Graham bitterly, he is Matt Long's son and there will always be a place in her heart for Matt, too.

"How 'bout this?" Martin held up a couple of frozen steaks.

"No, thanks. You make whatever you want. I'm not hungry." Graham retreated to the living room and poured himself three fingers of the bourbon.

The pearl-white Mercedes rolled southward along the freeway. The city, spreading in every direction, was crystal clear. Santa Ana winds had run the smog bank far off the coast where it lay, a fugitive to the weather reporters. On the seat next to Ruby were a map and a scrap of notebook paper with an address on it. Though Graham had become extremely angry—more angry than he had been since six years before when Will, aged twenty-six, had finally given up on L.A. in favor of Oregon—she had to see her son.

She needed to talk to Will, to clarify his absence and manhood in her mind.

When he had phoned her, he hadn't told her much. She knew there had been a girl in Oregon—he called her Candy—but she didn't know if they had ever married or if they had children. Each of Will's infrequent calls had wounded Ruby, like a deer shot during hunting season whose injury is not fatal and who somehow survives to the next season.

When Will was sixteen, Graham had so vehemently run the boy from their lives and Will had responded with like hatred that Ruby could scarcely bear the pain of those memories. She had other children, but Will was her firstborn—from that other time, that other place in her life, before Graham, before California, before experience had wrestled her naivete to the ground and had stood smugly, victoriously enlightened, over the expired innocence.

The day Will had come to her, after working on *Motive* for

two days without her knowledge, he had assured her he was all right, confirmed that she was well, and had ridden off with only a comment that he would be doing more stunt doubling for Garrett Gage. Will wrenched her soul from mute acceptance that she might never again see him to a perception that he had returned—at least to the perimeters of her life. Every time she thought of him, a dark swirling emotion consumed her. That emotion . . . she had first learned to live with, and then to live without. Usually, she repressed it in a steel-walled dungeon and forbade its entrance into the luminescent grand hall of her day-to-day existence.

Ruby had gone to Sondra, hoping the first assistant director would have a list of the extras' addresses in her files. But, among those addresses, Ruby did not find Will's. She next approached Arnold, the stunt coordinator, who smiled approvingly at Will's abilities and said he had not heard the biker was Ruby's son. No, he didn't have Will's address, but he had the phone number of a short guy who seemed to be a good friend.

Ruby tentatively called and asked for Joe. She explained that she was Mrs. Maddox, the producer of *Motive,* and that they wanted to get in touch with Will to discuss more stunts.

Joe was cautious. Perhaps, he instinctively knew producers didn't make calls about such matters. Perhaps he knew who she was. "I could get a message to him," said Joe.

"No, no,"said Ruby. "We're shooting tomorrow." She was trying to think fast, but it wasn't working. "I'll send Ms. Sondra Prescott down to talk to him. We've got to touch base with him tonight."

"Mrs. Maddox, I'll have him call you."

"No," said Ruby abruptly. "This is urgent. I've got to see him."

Joe protested. "He'll kill me if I let his mother know where he is."

So Joe did know.

"Why?" she asked. "Why would he care? Would he be angry?"

There was silence on Joe's end. "No, ma'am, I guess he

wouldn't," said Joe, having thought about the course of Will's anger. "I know what pisses him off. You see, he gets pissed off real easy, but I don't suppose he'd care if you found out where he's staying."

Joe gave Ruby a Venice address and directions about driving through the canal streets. Will was staying at Joe's house, and Joe was staying at a new girlfriend's. Ruby thanked Joe, the address trembling in her hand. What if Will didn't want her to come to see him? He had given no indication that he did. She only knew she had to talk to him. Look at him. Prove to herself that he was real and alive. He owed her a little peace of mind.

In some parts of L.A., great orangish streetlights, placed fifty feet apart, flood block after block. Under their glow, there is no color. Eyes become deceptive, robbed of all color; they register everything in shades of gray, giving credence to the unprovable myth that humans dream in black and white.

Streetlights in Venice are rare, and the black in that district is the black of night. It is an old town, wedged between stylish Santa Monica and high-tech Marina del Rey, a holdout of a former time that has yet to be remodeled into upscale yuppie-dom.

Ruby drove slowly, nearly stopping at each corner to read street signs. Fortunately, cars were infrequent. She found a small, dark wooden house on the edge of a canal. A dirt yard stretched from the potholed asphalt to the door. She discerned a motorcycle parked near the house, in the shadow of the shadowy yard. A worn fence from which white paint peeled bordered the yard. She pulled the Mercedes onto the dirt, its headlamps beaming steady light across the top of the murky, fluid canal, which seemed a gray replication of older, more historic waters.

She killed the lights and engine at the same time. A momentary vacuum—of no light or sound—surrounded her. The idea that the area might be dangerous or that she might be at the wrong house had not occurred to her. A light switched on on the porch. She saw the silhouetted figure of a man looking in her direction. He waited, unmoving, the bare bulb behind him not releasing his identity. She gathered her purse, jacket, and car keys, then got out.

Two steps up on the small porch, Will stood before her, his eyes shadowed, his mustache and long hair his only recognizable features. He turned so the light caught his face. There was no smile.

"Oh, Ma, I hate to have you see me in a dump like this," he implored angrily. "I wish you'd called. I would have met you somewhere."

"It's perfectly all right, Will," she said, still standing below him. "I wasn't sure that you would try to look me up. I didn't know if you wanted any contact with me."

Near the canal, a duck quacked. It was a foreign sound to Ruby's Mulholland Drive ears, a sound that was as distinct as the night. A gust of wind swept across the canal, ruffling her hair, stinging her legs with sand.

Will opened the screen door and waited for her to go in ahead of him. The house was three rooms long. The first, which they had entered, was the linoleum-floored kitchen, the second a living room, and the third, the bedroom, which had been part of the living room until it had been partitioned off. A tiny toilet and shower were off the kitchen.

Will was indecisive about where to sit with his mother. The ancient dirty couches in the middle room sagged pitifully and the wooden spool that served as a coffee table was covered with hardened candle wax, cigarette burns, dust, and dried-on food.

The kitchen wasn't much better, but it was the neater of the two choices. There were three dinette-type chairs, no two matching, at a chrome-legged table, vintage early 1960's. The counter was short, the cabinets wooden, with the same paint effect as the fence outside. Rust and minerals stained a sink, over which a window looked out to the canal.

Ruby guessed the house had originally been built in the teens or twenties as a weekend getaway. It had deteriorated dreadfully from lack of maintenance.

"It's a junk heap," said Will apologetically. "I wish you hadn't come. I don't like you to see places like this."

"It won't kill your old mother, you know," said Ruby. "I

may not frequent such dwellings at this point of my life, but I'm not ignorant of them, either."

Nor was she ignorant of the reasons people lived in hovels like this. The small size could be attributed to lack of money, but the filth . . . it had to be depression. Will didn't care what his surroundings looked like. He smiled at her, but it was a thin facade. She didn't know what his sorrows were, only that he had them.

He moved to the small gas stove and turned on an aluminum saucepan full of water. Methodically, he found two chipped mugs, washed them well in the sink, set them on the short counter, and waited for the water to boil. It didn't take long, and he poured water over tea bags.

"You didn't tell Graham where you were going, did you?" he asked, dunking the tea bags as the water darkened.

"He knows you're in town. He'll assume I want to see you."

"Bet he's pissed off." Will put the dripping bags on the counter and carried the cups to the table. He handed her one. "Sugar?"

"Please, if you have some," she said.

He looked inside a cabinet, producing a small bowl in which rock-hard sugar was packed into one corner. "Guess not," he said. "Sorry."

"That's all right," she said, sipping the hot blackness, expecting an unpleasant taste but pleasantly finding only strong, bitter tea against her palate.

"Does Graham know I worked on *Motive?*"

"Yes, but he didn't say anything . . . I mean, he didn't say you *couldn't* do it."

"Your stunt coordinator, Arnold, said he could get me more work." Will sat across from her, one black-booted foot resting on his opposite knee, a flannel-shirted elbow resting on the table.

"He was very impressed by your fall on that motorcycle. If I had known it was you, I'm not sure I could have watched you go through with it."

He smiled winningly at her, his great love for Ruby showing in his eyes. It made her ache to look at him, but she couldn't take her eyes away. He was a stranger, a grown man with a sorrowful, hardened edge to his face. Yet, he was so familiar, she knew him intimately; as intimately as one family member knows another from years of uninhibited love and behavior in front of everyone, of having the freedom to be oneself.

She asked, "When did you find out that you were doing stunts on one of Graham's shows? And when did you find out I was the producer?"

He pulled the ends of his long mustache. "The end of the first day, I heard someone mention Mrs. Maddox, and I knew there was only one. I guess I was waiting and kinda hoping maybe you'd recognize me. But I shouldn't have thought that. You wouldn't want anyone to know what kind of mess I've made of my life. Why, you could have been embarrassed as hell when I finally came up to you. All those people. What would they think? But you didn't care. Sometimes, I lose track of the way you really are when my mind starts telling me Graham's influence might have changed you."

He paused, smoothing his blue jeans across his ankle. "But you're the same. You're my mom."

She impulsively reached out her hand across the table. She couldn't touch his arm, but her hand waited, palm up, and she said, "I'll always be your mother. And no one will ever change my love for you."

The emotion was too strong for Will. He couldn't look at her. He kept staring at his boot, unable to acknowledge her hand on the table.

After a few minutes, she withdrew it and receded, too, into the protective shell from which she had ventured too quickly, too forthrightly, sure that if she were direct, he would respond by coming to her bosom.

Sometimes when you have been on guard for too long a time and you are suddenly with someone familiar, you let your guard down so fast that it's like you're a stone skipped across mirrorlike water; free for a few bounces, then pulled down. When you are caught, you start fighting for the surface—which is not as safe as the shore, but is safer than being pulled through the mirror.

"I never had anything against Graham," Will said, finally breaking the silence. "He's resented me for as long as I can remember."

"That's not true," replied Ruby, too swiftly.

"Mom, all those fights with Graham seem so long ago. They feel like another life. Another me. I never wanted all those arguments to begin with."

"Graham was good to you when we met."

"I was five. It didn't last long. After a few years, he had his *own* kids."

"It's not going to do us any good to go over these things we've been over so many times before. I love him. I love you. I love all my children. I want it all. And I want everyone to live in peace with each other."

"It's so hard to come back, Mom. So much happened in Oregon."

"Do you want to tell me about it?"

"Not now. Maybe some other time," he said. His tea had cooled to lukewarm. It was bland and bitter, but he didn't notice as he swallowed the last quarter-cup. "It's such a hassle to come back to L.A.," he said. "That's why I haven't bothered. Graham and all his fucking problems. I thought they might have vanished, but I guess I was wrong. In six years, you'd think he would allow his wife to see one of her own kids without having a shit-fit about it."

"I promise you I'll resolve this thing with Graham," she said, tension pulled tight as a winch cord between a tree and a truck stuck in the mud stretching in her. It was a taut, metallic anxiety that worked against her image of the perfect couple and their perfect lives together.

"Have you eaten anything?" she asked him.

He shook his head. He hadn't eaten a good meal since he had been on the set and been fed by the catering truck.

"Let's go out and get something," she offered.

"Like what?" he asked.

"I feel like a hamburger and fries."

He looked surprised. She laughed. "Well, what do you say? A nice double-double cheeseburger?" That had been his favorite his sixteenth summer.

"Okay," he said, standing awkwardly. "I'll change my shirt."

He returned in a few minutes, wearing a clean shirt, jeans, and a pair of sneakers. He held the door for her, and she stepped from the porch onto the dirty yard. The porch bulb shone soft yellow light across her car. She waited for Will to come up next to her and held out her hand.

This time, he held his out to hers. She put the Mercedes key into it.

"You drive," she said.

Glory looked forward to having lunch with Tony. He had come up to her at seven-thirty that morning, when they had just arrived on the set, had slipped his arm around her waist, and had kissed the back of her neck. The sensation of goose bumps down her spine was mixed with the burn of a blush across her face.

"You are delectable," he said softly. "Let's have lunch."

Glory cringed and wriggled out of his grasp. He laughed at the embarrassment on her face, which only made her look more charming and innocent. It was this innocence, in part, that made him feel so horny every time he looked at her. She was sweet to him, her affection involuntarily escaping her fingertips as she touched his arm or lips or stomach. She was a smart girl, though disorganized to a flaw. Her brains kept him interested; her sexuality kept him coming back for more.

He was aware of the talk around the set. He was twenty-five years older than Glory. Men he had known for a long time either winked as if to say, "You've got a fine piece of ass there," or they shook their head, unable to comprehend how anyone could find such a scatterbrained girl appealing.

Tony saw the devotion in her eyes and it worried him. He thought of what they had together as an extended friendship—the physical added to their rapport. But she had fallen in love. It showed in the intense way she watched him, in the reaction of her body every time he touched her, in the awe reflected in her soft blue eyes, in the quiet listening she afforded him every time he needed to talk.

He had talked his heart out. He had been silent for so long that talking about himself was energizing. He realized he was taking advantage of her kindness and love. However, it was so pleasurable to have someone in love with you, so fulfilling to have someone believe in you, that it was hard to turn away from her and tell her she was making a mistake.

After all, how could he be seriously interested in someone so much younger than he? She would meet a younger, more virile man one day and Tony would be out the back door like so many dried leaves that had accidentally blown in.

She didn't hide her love from him. She knew it showed all over her face and she felt the fool for it. The night he had drunkenly passed out on the bed, she had fallen asleep in the armchair. He had wakened her before dawn, kneeling before the chair, his breath heavy with stale wine. He had gently lifted her and carried her to the bed. She had been very sleepy and had barely been aware of his strong arms and soft voice telling her how sorry he was. He had taken her robe off, lain her on the sheets, crawled in next to her, and drawn the covers over the two of them. He had pulled her close, so her head rested in the dip between his shoulder and chest, and had held her tightly. She had fallen into a tranquil, deep sleep, which had freed her from her current life and transported her to a place where she was safe, eternally safe.

Waking in the morning had wrenched her from that safety. But he had been there, holding her, stroking her head soothingly. She hadn't meant to fall in love with him.

For lunch, she wanted to buy sandwiches and find some shady lawn where they could eat. He agreed reluctantly, since he didn't think it acceptable to eat anywhere on the lot except in the commissary. He didn't want anyone to think he was antisocial, for film crews are a communal, gregarious bunch that can quickly snub someone who doesn't fit in. Tony was "one of the boys," and he didn't want that long-held status jeopardized.

Glory picked up on his uncertainty. She led him to a fake, deserted New York street on the back lot and sat on the shady steps of a "brownstone." "No one will see us here," she said.

"I thought you wanted a lawn?" he asked.

"This is better," she reasoned. "We're all alone. I think these sets are eerie, don't you? The buildings look so real, yet they're just a few inches thick. I almost feel ghosts walking here." She smiled.

Tony smiled back, momentarily caught in her fantasy, then shaking his head at how ridiculous the thought was. He wondered if there had been a time, when he had first started working on the lot, that he had felt a set was practically alive.

"I told my mother about you," said Glory.

"Yeah? What did you say?"

"Oh . . . I told her how handsome you were. And how talented. And what you do for a living. And how we're going to write a script together. And that you studied filmmaking in college like I did. And that you take me to all kinds of neat places for lunch."

He gave her a sideways look, a grin turning up the edges of his mouth. She laughed at her teasing and scooted next to him, hugging his neck, kissing him all over one side of his face until he was forced to start laughing from the delight of her affection.

"Did you tell her how old I was?"

Glory couldn't tell if he was serious or mocking. "No," she said, sitting on the step below him, her back to him, her elbows on his knees. She unwrapped the plastic from her sandwich. "She probably wouldn't think that it was *proper*." It was obvious she wasn't concerned what her mother's views on being proper were.

But it bothered him. "She wouldn't like it, would she?"

"I don't know and I don't care," said Glory, her mouth full of sandwich. She did not perceive that their difference in age plagued him with doubt, for there was no doubt in her mind about the way she felt about him.

"Your mom and I must be around the same age," he said. He had put his half-eaten sandwich on the plywood (painted to look like stone) step next to him, and was smoking a cigarette.

Glory turned and looked up at him. "Does it matter?" she asked, suddenly hurt. "Would you rather be with someone your own age? Am I too young for you? You think I'm really too stupid and immature, don't you?"

She moved and sat down on the very bottom step. So this was the explanation for the casual way he treated her. He couldn't take her seriously. Maybe he found her sexy, but he didn't think she had any substance. "You don't really like me, do you?" she cried. You're just filling in the time till someone your own age comes along." Frustrated tears streamed from eyes and she felt even more stupid.

"That's not true," he said. "You're everything I ever wanted." The words sounded false to him, and she didn't believe him, either.

"Don't tell me that kind of shit," she said. "Just be honest. You don't have to be in love with me. Just be honest. I'm too young and I feel so goddamned stupid. Stupid, stupid, stupid! I like you. *I like you too much.* I'm crying. I feel stupid crying."

He sat where he was on the top stair, drawing deeply on his cigarette. He wanted to comfort her, yet he couldn't move. He could only watch her. "You're a fabulous girl," he said. "You're much too good for me."

"That's bullshit," she screamed. "You don't even want to work with me. You don't want to do a project together. It was all just a lie. Why? Why would you lie to me? Not just for sex? Was it? *Was* it?"

The question hung in the air of the quiet street. A couple of shrewd pigeons moved about expectantly, and the sun, in contrast to the shade cast by the flats, was harsh and bright.

Tony tried to summon a little emotion—anger, despair, sadness, love. They were all very far from him. All right, she made him horny. But *was* that the only reason? Maybe she was right. But how could he tell her? Sure, baby, I like your ass and I like fucking you. There were a lot of women he could fuck.

But then, he hadn't been horny for a long time. Glory had brought it out in him. So, he concluded, there had to be more than physical attraction. She was a girl he could talk to . . . and that was a precious commodity in a world where most of the women he met were concerned only with their fingernails, hair, figures, and clothes. Glory had actually stimulated some thinking in him. She believed in him and they shared interests.

He looked at her. Her tears had eased and now her face was stained red from the salty drops, her eyes raccoon-masked by melted mascara, and her nose was running. She grabbed at the crummy paper napkins that had come with the sandwiches and held them to her nose.

She wasn't angry, she was embarrassed. Embarrassed that she could feel this way about him. The pain rocked within her like a twig bobbing on waves that lapped at a lake shore. Oh, you fool, she thought to herself, you are young and so stupid.

"Glory," he said finally, "I'll be honest with you. I like you a lot. I really do. *I'm* insecure about being so much older than you. I'm sorry you took it any other way. I really want to work on a script with you." He lit another cigarette with the butt of the one he had just been smoking. "Okay?"

She nodded. She believed him. Her doubts eased within her and a smile played on her lips. "Okay," she said, reaching for his sandwich, breaking off chunks and throwing it to the pigeons.

"I wonder what's eating him?" Tanya remarked blankly.

She sat in makeup. Denny poised a powder brush over her cheek. Garrett Gage sat next to them and waited for Margi to finish his hair. The three had just observed Bob Owens, Margi's husband, stalk angrily in his wife's direction. One look at Bob's blazing eyes and his tight lips under the bushy mustache, and Margi had shoved brush and spray into Garrett's hand and gone to intercept her huge stage-hand spouse.

"He's a big guy," commented Garrett. "I'd want him on my side." He admired his hair in the mirror and applied the spray himself.

"He was looking at you, Denny," observed Tanya. "Why was he looking at you?"

Denny's face remained unchanged. "I don't know. I've known Bob for years. He's a pretty good guy."

"Let's hope he's thinking the same about you," said Garrett. "Did you see the size of those arms?"

"Did you see the way poor little Margi ran out there when she saw his face?" said Tanya. "I would never put up with a man who got that angry with me."

Garrett thought Tanya's comment stupid; she was putting up with a whole lot more from Norman.

Denny's concentration was on Tanya's face. "Normally, Bob's very easygoing."

Tanya shrugged. It really didn't interest her. She couldn't see devoting too much time to the personal relationship of the hairdresser. It might be of interest to the crew, but not to one of the stars. "Denny, do I look all right?" she asked.

"Beautiful, just beautiful, dear," Denny reassured her. He pointed to her hairline. "See how I put the blusher over here? It adds dimension."

"What do you think?" she asked Garrett.

He nodded and said a neutral, "Denny does a great job." After a further close-up look at his own visage in the mirror, Garrett wandered back to the set.

"He's very handsome, don't you think?" Tanya asked, turning around in her chair, her eyes following the actor.

Denny swallowed and hesitated before answering. It wouldn't do to be misconstrued by the vacant-brained actress and have the crew think the makeup artist had a crush on the lead. "He has a special look about him, all right."

"I never thought I'd see him again," mused Tanya, speaking her thought out loud.

"Never thought you'd see who? Garrett?" queried Denny.

Tanya realized her mistake and covered quickly with, "Nothing . . . uh . . . it's one of Janet's lines." She continued to stare at the dark-haired actor.

"Dear, please turn around so I can finish your makeup," requested Denny.

She obeyed. "You've spoiled me, Denny. I'll never be able

to let anyone but you put on my makeup. I couldn't even do it myself. Promise that if I have a party or have to go to one of Norman's benefits—God forbid—you'll do my makeup."

Denny said nothing. He didn't like to have his time off infringed upon. His time off the set was *his* time.

"Say you will," she begged.

"Maybe," he smiled.

"Maybe's not good enough."

"Let's talk about it when the time comes," he said evasively. "You'll be able to do your own makeup, dear. You always have in the past."

"I've lost confidence," whined Tanya.

"Listen to me," he said intently. "No matter who applies the makeup, it's still your remarkable face that holds all the beauty." The comment satisfied her and she hurried back to the set.

Margi returned, looking apologetic. "I don't know quite how to put this, but Bob told me he doesn't want you coming over for dinner tonight."

Denny was silent. Stopping by her house had become a comfortable ritual with him. It saved him from his empty apartment and the memories of Jeff. He had gotten to like the Owens's teenagers and took special interest in their school projects, their friends, and their fashions.

"Just say hi to the kids for me," Denny said nobly. "Tell them something else came up and I couldn't make it."

"Listen, Den, Bob's attitude pisses me off. I was going to fight with him, but I can't afford to do that on the set. I'm sorry. Sometimes I can't fight with the man." Denny's feelings got hurt so damned easy.

"He doesn't like me anymore. Guess he never did," affirmed Denny.

"I don't want to talk about it anymore," she said, straightening up her table. A few strands of Garrett's hair were stuck in a brush. "Denny," she said, "did you see the way Tanya and Garrett were looking at each other? There's something going on between them."

"There can't be," replied Denny, his voice tremulous from the stricken dinner plans. "She's got that old, rich husband,

and from what I hear, there's a limo here every night to take her home."

Margi extracted a long, slender cigarette and lit it. "She can't keep her hands off of Garrett. Walking over here. Putting her hands in his hair. Asking me if he was using a good conditioner. She doesn't fool me. Her fingers are drawn like magnets to him."

"Now that you mention it, she said something strange. Something like she never thought she'd see him again."

Margi's eyebrows arched with incredulity. "She did?"

"Then she said it was one of Janet's lines. I lose track from one script to the next. Is that a line this week?"

Margi quickly flipped through the current script. "No. That's not in here. They *must* know each other. But from where? When?"

"But," interjected Denny, "*he* only acts professionally toward her."

"Come to think of it," commented Margi, "I've never seen a co-star act quite so coldly as he does."

"You think he's covering up?"

"Of course, he is. And he's not the only one around here."

Denny smiled. Margi was a busybody if ever there was one. Interpersonal intrigue on the set didn't hold much fascination for him. Margi, on the other hand, lived for it. Her eyes and ears were open all the time. She didn't miss a detail.

He acknowledged her desire to tell him. "Okay, who else?"

"Graham Maddox and that secretary of his. The one with all that hair." Margi inhaled the last draw on her cigarette, held it in her lungs, and let it slowly escape her lips.

"Jeannie Hansen?"

"Yes." How did he know who she was?

"How do you know that? They're always in their offices, never on the set."

"I can't reveal my sources," teased Margi. "But it's true. They've been seen having dinner a few times."

"Big deal. Dinner. What's that prove. It's probably business."

"She was wearing *very* revealing outfits," countered Margi.

"Not much to reveal," declared Denny, more as a reaction to Jeannie Hansen's rejection of *his* dinner invitation than a true judgment of her endowments.

"How would you know?" asked Margi, with little sensitivity. "Women aren't your specialty."

"Don't get mad at me," snapped Denny, "just 'cause Bob's pissed you off. You always do that. It isn't fair."

Margi kept her mouth shut. Denny was employing his irritating whine. He can get so bitchy at times, she thought.

Sondra asked for silence. Tony sat behind the camera while two dolly grips moved it smoothly across the length of the set, following Tanya and Garrett. Glory was watching Tony intently.

Margi pointed at Glory and hissed a whisper into Denny's ear. "She's another one who thinks the world doesn't know she's seeing that worthless cameraman."

Margi was so damned opinionated and self-righteous. "If he's so bad, why do you cut his hair?" Denny wasn't about to forgive her for her previous comment.

"What's that got to do with it? He's a friend, of sorts. But he shouldn't be going after a young girl."

"Isn't Tony about the same age as Bob? Is he setting a bad example?" Denny hit the nail on the head.

Margi's eyes glowered, her lips thinned and tightened. "Bob would never go after a young girl," she said caustically. "He doesn't need to."

"Then why don't you shut up about Glory and Tony. It's none of your business."

Margi's jaw dropped. Denny never talked to her like that. "What the hell kinda bug's up your ass?" she demanded.

Suddenly, Sondra's head whipped in the direction of their petty, whispered arguing. Both Margi and Denny bit their tongues and stared at the set. Margi flipped the script over, took one of Denny's brown eyebrow pencils, and scribbled a message to him:

"Guess we're both a couple of bitches."

Denny glared at her a minute before breaking into a smile. Then he took a green pencil and wrote: "Ha, ha."

Martin thought the procedure on the *Medical Alert* set was boring. It seemed to take forever for the crew to get the lighting right, and then there were all the takes—establishing shots, two-shots, close-ups, reverse angles, point-of-view angles—for the same crummy quarter-page of script.

Filmmaking was tedious work. The director of photography worked agonizingly slowly. Between the guy's salary and all the experienced grips, it was ridiculous he couldn't move faster. And, even worse, if the director didn't get *exactly* the performance he wanted out of his actors, he insisted on doing the takes over and over.

They had Martin compiling list after list that had to do with the following day's filming, then checking and rechecking to make sure bits and extras were briefed well in advance of the time they were to appear on camera. He felt little more than a bit or extra himself. And he was afraid any technical job on any set on any show would be equally as boring.

Medical Alert was sitting well in the ratings, though it was nowhere near the smash hit that *Motive* was. Martin decided to wait a week or two, to let his father's temper die down, before asking for another kind of job.

When they had perfected the lighting and were ready to shoot the scene, Martin decided he was due to take a break. He went over to the sidelines, sat in a chair, and picked up his magazine. There was an article about catamaran racing. He had been interested in the sport since winning a just-for-fun race with ten local catamaran owners. He had gained a certain amount of esteem with them and one even suggested he try to find sponsors. Catamaran racing might look like fun, but it also seemed like it would take a tremendous amount of effort.

"Hello, Marty," said a voice behind him.

There was only one person who had that voice who would use the name Marty. He hated being called by his childhood nickname, mainly because it had been half of the despised "Marty-Farty." He turned to see Will, dressed identically to one of the characters on *Medical Alert,* standing behind him.

Will might have been there five minutes, watching. Martin couldn't be sure.

"Dad told me you were back," said Martin, not making any attempt to get up or shake hands.

"I'm doing a stunt on this show today," said Will, squinting at the set where the director was walking through some blocking with the actors.

"Did the Hell's Angels decide they had had enough of you and throw you out of Oregon?" Martin continued to look casually at his magazine.

Will's smile was brittle. If Martin was trying to get his goat, he was going about it the wrong way. "Never was with the Hell's Angels," replied Will. "And why I'm here ain't none of your business."

Will was half again as tall and as heavy as his half brother. Martin noted that not only had Will become better-looking in the six years since they'd last seen each other, but he was also measurably stronger. Will had dynamic forearms, like those of a man who lifts weights, though Martin doubted if his half brother had ever been inside a gym. Will was born strong—a hard, lean power that flexed within him like the steely muscles of a cougar.

"I'd forgotten you were such a little creep," said Will. "Or maybe I'd hoped you had grown up. You're still the baby. Mom and Graham still covering your ass."

"Who do you think *you're* working for?" asked Martin, uncrossing his legs and continuing to stare at the magazine.

"I could work for anyone in town. I just stumbled into this job."

"I heard," said Martin. "Hanging out at some dive. It's probably just an accident that you're working at all."

Will crouched before Martin, tearing the magazine from the younger man's hands and placing a strangling grip around Martin's arm. He kept his voice low, for already a couple of people had begun to notice them.

"You are a shit-head," said Will. "I was hoping we could be civil. But you're the same self-centered fuck-off you always were. I suggest we both stay out of each other's way. But don't—I mean *don't*—say one word against me. If I hear about it, I'll take your head off with one jerk."

The hot, low words beat at Martin's head. He saw a danger in Will's face that had never been there before, a capacity for violence that was not imagined.

"You are worthless, Mart-*ee*," said Will. "Absolutely worthless."

Martin watched him stride over to Arnold, the stunt coordinator. There was a big grin on Will's face, an ease to his body, a friendly air that Martin guessed was only the superficial cover to a time bomb that would someday explode.

Jeannie Hansen, secretary of the executive producer's office at Maddox Productions, had very little to do after she typed two short letters dictated by Graham that morning. He would be out all afternoon at meetings and she was only needed to answer his phones. But she had other plans for the afternoon. She would switch the phone calls to the main receptionist and leave early.

She read the trade papers thoroughly, paid a few personal bills, and waited for Graham to phone in after lunch. He called punctually, in a jolly mood after a few drinks. She gave him his messages. Finally, she had a chance to make her own phone calls without interruptions.

"Hi," she said softly. "No, I can't talk any louder. Of *course* I have my own office, but somebody could hear. He's at lunch right now. The messages on the machine? He loves them. He thinks I'm erasing them.

"Don't worry. I have the situation under control. Don't worry. *Please!* Okay, I've got to go. I'll see you soon. I promise. Real soon. I love you, too."

She hung up, applied a fresh coat of lipstick to her mouth, then rang the receptionist and told her to pick up all calls for the rest of the afternoon. Then Jeannie went down the staircase and slipped quietly out the front door. It would be a good afternoon to spend shopping.

Chapter 7

Ruby had worn a suit that she didn't like very much. She wasn't quite sure why she didn't get rid of it. The fit was excellent, but the color was off. It was a brownish-gray not a true gray, like a mouse or ashes or a horse, but rather a dirty gray that never looked right with any color blouse except a white one.

Leaving her office to drive home, she looked up into the twilight sky. The sun had already disappeared. Straight up, the color was hazy blue; above the eastern horizon, a wide band of smog was the same color as her suit. Where blue and brown met, an almost-full moon was like a hole in the sky patched with mother-of-pearl, and a banking airliner seemed to touch the disc with the tip of its port wing.

Ruby stood transfixed, watching the plane in perfect silhouette move through the motionless sky. She hoped it would gain enough altitude so that the sun below the level of the horizon would gild its wings and underbelly, but it curved east, toward the night. Ruby looked west, where the brown-gray band was losing its sunset tint of orange, like color draining from the lips of a dying man.

At home, she found Graham in the shower. They were supposed to attend a dinner party, yet she was tired and didn't feel like going. Too bad they had RSVP'd "yes." If she told Graham she was tired, she would face more of his hostility. He couldn't understand that she did not have her previous enthusiasm or energy for dinner parties. She no longer had the entire day to pick out a dress and get her hair done. She didn't want to take time in the middle of the week to go to some party, when there was work to do on *Motive.*

"Where have you been?" asked Graham accusingly, towel wrapped around his waist.

"Just came straight from the office," she responded, not turning around from her walk-in closet where she stood in slip and pantyhose, trying to decide what to wear that night. "You must have left early."

"I had two meetings this afternoon," he said, drying himself.

She watched the thick terry cloth absorb beads of water and thought how much she liked his well-formed legs. They were seasoned, muscular, mature. She knew them intimately. Had known them for years. His whole body was that way. The scar on his stomach. The pattern of moles on his back. His small, wide-set nipples. His one foot that was slightly pigeon-toed.

Now, it seemed she knew his body much more than she knew the man. His actions, his tone of voice, alienated her. She didn't know why he acted the way he did. She felt as though he resented her. Yet, how ridiculous that would be. He was so successful, so self-assured. Surely he wasn't resentful.

"We have to leave in a half-hour," he said.

"Not so soon," she protested.

"Yes," he insisted. "You should have come earlier. You know we had to go to this deal."

"Dillon, Sondra, and I were working late. She brought in the breakdown of the script we're shooting in two weeks. There are a lot of details and an army of extras. Dillon wants to cut back on the extras. He's going to talk to you about it tomorrow." She had taken off her clothes and slipped into a robe.

"Then let's wait till tomorrow to discuss it," said Graham. Why were they bugging him with details like this? Either the extras were in the budget or they weren't. Set and special effects were the critical big-money problems, not extras.

Ruby had stopped on her way into the bath. "I'm sorry I even brought it up," she said sarcastically. "Sorry I have problems that I seem to be dumping on you. After all these years, I'm sure you're spoiled, because *I've* never discussed *my* problems with *you*."

Graham sighed and followed her. She turned on the shower, tucked her hair in a shower cap, and stepped under the flow.

"Look," he said as the steam built up on the glass of the shower door. "Remember you're shooting television. You don't need to use masses and masses of people. They don't come off well on the little screen."

There was no response from inside the shower. "They don't," he repeated. She could be such a pouter when she wanted to be.

After her shower, Ruby sat at her dressing table with the serious task of putting on evening makeup. During the day, she wore a very modest amount. The Beverly Hills salon that had given her facials for years had done a "business-woman make-over" on her. She hadn't wanted to look bland and wear no makeup, yet she wanted to be tasteful and not look like a producer's beautiful wife who knew nothing about dressing for the business world.

But for the dinner party, she wanted to be softer, sexier, more like her old self. She thought it would cheer up Graham.

He reappeared with two drinks and set one down for her.

"Thank you, darling," she said, smoothing foundation over her eyelids. "When are you going to New York?" she asked.

"In a couple of days. Can you make it without me?"

She grinned at him. "I suppose I'll have to."

He wasn't smiling back. "When you were so late, I thought maybe you had gone off to see Will again."

"What if I had?" she retorted.

"I want to know what was so damned important the other night that you had to go tracking him down? Driving into a neighborhood like that. Really, Ruby, you are out of your mind."

"I was perfectly safe," she said.

"Mercedes are unheard of in areas like Venice."

Ruby rolled her eyeballs in exasperation.

He continued chewing her out. "Thugs carrying baseball bats will jump your car at red lights, smash in the windows, steal your money, beat the hell out of you. You've got to be more careful."

"Isn't it amazing I lived through the experience?" she commented acidly.

"I was worried."

"Bullshit. You were jealous of me going to talk to Will."

"Jealous?" he laughed raucously. "No, not jealous."

"Then why don't you just drop it? There are some things in life we obviously will never agree on. My son is one of them. Just because you don't like him doesn't mean I can't see him. I love him. Why can't you get that through your head?" Her voice echoed emotionally. Every time they discussed the subject of Will they clashed. She didn't want the tension. She preferred never to mention her son's name.

"You always defend him," stabbed Graham.

"I haven't said anything in his defense. I said I love him. I haven't seen him for years. And here you stand, not a drop of feeling in your heart for *me*." Tears started down her cheeks, streaking through the carefully applied layers of powder and rouge. "Graham, if you can't come to terms with Will in your life, why don't you just drop the subject and leave it alone?"

She had gone through too many years of Graham's brutal, inexplicable anger toward the boy. Martin was Graham's only son, and Graham had continually forced Martin into competition with Will, telling him that he was better than his half brother. But Will had been a natural athlete, and had been intelligent and motivated throughout school. Martin had never matched up to Will, and Graham hated that. Graham could have warmed to Will but never did. More resentment. She had felt it for years. How had she lived with Graham for so long?

"You love Will more than Martin," attacked Graham.

"That's absurd," she countered. "I love all of my children very much. They all have their endearing qualities. They all have their problems. If I can help them with their problems, that's what I'm here for."

"You love Will more than Martin because Will is Matt Long's son." Graham gulped down the final swallow of his Scotch.

Ruby, who had barely touched hers, held out her glass to him, her eyes wide with surprise, her tears retreating like a watering hole in a dry season. Graham clearly did not understand a mother's love for her children. Graham only understood his *own* distress—built-up animosity for a man who had been out of her life for nearly thirty years. Matt Long had been the ultimate bastard. She hated him. And here Graham thought she had loved Matt all these years?

"I haven't even *thought* of Matt in a very long time," she said truthfully.

"You think of him every time you think of Will." Graham's words were venomous.

She finished her makeup and thought she looked pretty good. "Do you really think so?" she replied, quite coolly, in total control. The issue no longer seemed to be Will, but rather Matt.

"Of course. I've watched you for years, looking at the boy, the love and longing in your face for that man who dumped you."

Graham was broadsiding her and she was barely responding. She felt as though she were hardly in the room with him, in a sort of dreamworld. Ever since she had begun producing *Motive,* he had become more and more of a stranger.

"I guess I don't feel like fighting. Sorry, Graham." It was the only thing she could think of to say.

She brought a black, full-length, clinging dress from the closet. It had a single two-inch-wide gold stripe that started at one shoulder and descended diagonally, wrapping around her waist. The neckline was low. She rummaged through a drawer until she found the bra she was searching for. It gave her plenty of cleavage.

"What did you talk to Will about?" he pried.

"I already told you. Mostly the show. The stories. The characters. He was very interested."

"What's he been doing in Oregon?"

"I don't know. I honestly don't know." She slipped the dress over her head and turned so he could zip it up.

"He must have told you something. Why are you keeping secrets from me?"

Ruby touched Graham's cheek, her fingers cool against his anger. "There are no secrets," she said. She tried, in fact, to think of something she knew that he didn't, but nothing came to her. "I've never tried to deceive you, Graham. It hurts me that you think I have."

She took the glass back from him and sipped the ice-weakened liquid. A laugh escaped her lips. "Matt Long. He seems so long ago. Why would you think I still carry a torch for him?"

"Because you loved him so much."

"I've loved you a long time. Over half of my life. Here you stand and you're telling me things I don't understand. I don't know why you're saying them. But I can't figure out the answers to these damn perplexing problems tonight. I want to go to this damn dinner party—now that I'm dolled up—and have a good time."

She walked to the front door, put a few essentials from her purse into her evening bag, and found a fur wrap in the front hall closet. She didn't feel angry, forlorn, or unhappy. The dreamworld effect still hung on. She couldn't tell how he was responding. He would be a maniac behind the wheel when he was feeling like this.

She jingled her keys. "You coming with me, or are you driving your own car?"

The ringing phone wakened Margi. She stirred in bed as she heard Bob answer. It was still very dark outside. She squinted at the clock. It was five-thirty A.M. She scooted closer to the warmth of Bob's vacated sheets and half listened to the conversation. It was his union.

"Yeah," he said, "I requested extra work. My call isn't scheduled till three this afternoon. You want me to go somewhere this morning?"

His words annoyed her. He had worked extra hours for the past two weekends. Here was a regular weekday, and he was still wanted. What the heck was the matter with the union? Didn't they have enough members? Why would he *request* extra work? They didn't need the money. She had hardly laid eyes on him for a couple of weeks.

"I'm fine, Harry," he was saying. "Shit, got home at midnight. No, no. It's a different studio. Just don't tell anyone I didn't have my twelve hours off. Honest man, I don't mind. Bye."

Margi had unwillingly become fully awake. She had been waiting languidly for Bob to come back to bed, but he had gone into the bathroom to take a shower. She got up and stumbled in to pee. She kept her eyes shut against the bright light and said to him, "Why are you going out so early?"

He looked around the edge of the shower curtain. "Didn't you hear them? They need me to go in."

"Is there some reason you've been working so much lately?" she asked sleepily, rubbing her eyes. "Or has it just been my imagination?"

"You don't really want to know, do you?"

She opened her eyes and grabbed a wad of toilet paper. "Are you trying to tell me something that I'm not catching on to, Bob?"

"I don't feel like talking about it."

She could smell his soap. It had a masculine scent. He refused to use any soap that she would use, especially one with cleansing cream. He loved to lather up. It always reminded her of soap commercials. She could never figure out how they got so many suds.

She flushed the toilet and Bob yelped. "Goddamn sonofabitch! What'd you flush the fuckin' toilet for? Trying to burn the hell out of me?"

"I'm sorry, sweetheart," she said. "I wasn't thinking. It's too early in the morning for me."

She pushed aside the curtain and looked at him. His right thigh was bright red from the hot water. His hairy chest had trapped thick, foamy soap. She reached in, drenching her arm, and touched his leg. She reached farther, for his penis, but he pulled back, out of her grasp.

"Come on, sweetie," she said. "Don't you want a little?"

"Not now," he told her. "I'm in a hurry."

"Bob," she whined, "why not? We could have a nice quickie before you leave. Give me that soap."

He dropped the bar into her hand, and she worked it into a lather. She reached for him again, and this time he let her stroke him, the soap slick and slurpy.

"Come closer," she said as the water beat against her neck and shoulder, wetting her hair and nightgown. He groaned at her touch, and she waited expectantly for him to harden. But there was only a slight erection.

She massaged faster, cupping his balls with her other hand. There was little response. It puzzled her. "Rinse off," she said. "I hate the taste of soap."

"Let's try later, Margi," he said, pushing her hand away and turning his back to her, the water rinsing his back.

She retreated from the shower, pulling off her nightgown and toweling her hair and wet skin. She decided to wait for him on the bed. She pulled out their favorite bottle of aphrodisiac massaging oil and set it under the nightstand lamp, while she stretched naked on top of the bed. He would see her and the oil. She would set his mind at peace.

But when he came out of the bathroom, clouds of steam following him, he went straight to the closet. It was as though he didn't even see her. He dressed quickly, not once turning his head to look in her direction.

"I'll see you later," he said. "I'll stop by the *Motive* set." He moved to the bedroom door and was gone before she could protest.

She rushed to the window overlooking the driveway and watched his pickup truck back out. She turned back to her bed, not sure how she should interpret his actions.

The oil thickly beckoned her from the bottle. She had gotten horny touching him in the shower, and even more so waiting for him to come to the bed. She lay back on the sheets and squeezed some of the oil onto her hand. The musky, sexy odor penetrated all her senses.

But she could not touch herself. It wasn't the same if Bob

didn't want her. Inexplicable guilt rose strongly in her gut. Had she done something wrong? What could she have possibly done that was making him act this way? He hadn't made love to her in two weeks. What had she done? He never treated her this way. Was there another woman?

Her gut somersaulted. There was something going on that she didn't know about. She had always trusted him. Panic knocked the breath out of her, and her core felt drained.

She grabbed his pillow and pulled it to her, the oil on her hand absorbing into the pillowcase, her breath coming fast and shallow as her heart beat harder and harder. Her desire for sex disappeared and was replaced by fear. She wretchedly held the pillow, afraid that she was losing her husband.

"What are we going to do? What are we going to do?" cried Ruby, rushing into her office, her secretary and Richard on her tail. She pivoted behind her desk and sharply asked the secretary, "Have you placed that call to Mr. Maddox?"

"Ma'am, I've tried. He hasn't arrived in New York yet. I left a message at his hotel."

Graham's business trip could not have happened at a worse time. Ruby had a real emergency and she needed Graham to take care of it.

"Call the airline!" she told the secretary. "Tell them we've got to speak to him. Get the number. We can call him."

"Ruby," implored Richard, "Graham hates to be bothered on a coast to coast flight."

Ruby sank into her chair, her heart pounding, her palms damp. She glanced up to see her secretary still standing by the door. "Don't stand there like a fool. Call the airline!"

The secretary's face had a blank look for a moment—she had never before seen the coolheaded Mrs. Maddox become panicked—then she darted out of the room.

"Richard, we're doomed," moaned Ruby, who had dragged the director away from the middle of a *Motive* shoot, where he had left the full cast and crew ready. The clock was running, and here he was in Mrs. Maddox's office.

"I wouldn't say *doomed,* Ruby," said Richard.

"If this sponsor pulls out, the network's going to cancel us."

"It's not that easy."

"If one sponsor pulls out, I can see the rest of them losing faith in *Motive.* 'Objectionable content.' What's that supposed to mean?"

"The first thing you've got to do, Ruby, is calm down," said Richard.

"Calm down! Where is everybody? I wanted those lawyers in here fast. Where are they? Why does Graham have to leave today when all hell breaks loose?"

Richard was not a businessman. He was a director, an artist. When he had been summoned to help with the crisis, he had been drawing the tenderest emotions from two characters in a love scene. Of course, he was concerned. *Motive* was his livelihood. It occupied a tremendous amount of his time. If footage in an episode about to air was found questionable, he was prepared to reshoot any sequence immediately or to work with the editors recutting the segment. Just tell him what needed to be done. As far as he was concerned, networks and sponsors were far too high-handed with the creative force of a series. Innovation was too often snuffed out.

Moments later, Dillon Hughes, dressed in a neat brown suit, entered the room. His modest haircut was smooth and shiny, his winning smile displayed perfect teeth.

"What are we going to do?" gasped Ruby, tension straining her face.

"I've got everything under control," said Dillon. "I've spoken with the network. I've got a call in to the sponsor. I believe there has been a misunderstanding."

His manner was so positive, his voice so calm, his confidence so reassuring, that both Ruby and Richard relaxed.

"We don't have to needlessly worry Graham," Dillon went on. "We don't need to blow this thing out of proportion." He said the words, knowing full well that Ruby had already worked herself into a state of alarm. She was as worried about her husband's reaction as she was about the fate of *Motive.* Though more rattled than he had ever seen her, her makeup was still flawless, the beautifully curved false eyelashes darkly accentuating her flashing eyes.

"I thought we were being so careful," she said to Dillon and Richard, as if they were both responsible for the content of the script.

"We have been careful," reassured Dillon. "How could we know that a script which takes Frank back to the Prohibition Era would perturb the beer company sponsor?"

"Where are those writers?" asked Ruby, going to the door of her office and telling the flustered secretary, "Get me those writers. Get me those writers!"

She felt cornered. Somehow, she saw all the blame falling upon her. Why wasn't Graham here to make a decision? He'd taken that gaspy-voiced secretary of his to New York for two days of business. And he thought she hadn't noticed? Ruby had noticed every secretary he ever had. Some accompanied him on business trips, some did not.

Ruby's secretary scurried in. "Mr. Hughes," she said, "Mr. Vandermere, from the network, is on line three for you."

Ruby, her hand on the receiver, said, "I'll take that call."

"No," Dillon replied authoritatively. "Better let me."

Ruby glanced uneasily at Richard, who said, "Let Dillon take the call. He knows what he's doing."

Richard didn't see there was much he could contribute. He was more worried about losing a day's shoot while he babied Mrs. Maddox through this crisis. He realized she had gone straight to him because she had known him the longest of anyone connected with the show. He took Ruby's hand and made her sit in a chair.

Within ten minutes, Dillon had solved the matter. He had spoken to the network, to the sponsor, and to their advertising agency, which created and booked the commercials, and had convinced them there was nothing objectionable about any of the content of the episode. It was historically accurate, and the sponsor should be proud to affiliate with a series that was so well researched.

Not once did Dillon say that Maddox Productions had

made an error. Not once did he apologize. Not once did he lose his temper. He laughed, coaxed, and explained his way out of the entire problem.

Richard excused himself, after first explaining to Dillon that they might have to work overtime that night to make up for the past two hours lost. Dillon nodded.

"Just wanted to clear it with you," said the director, "so you didn't come down on my ass when we go over-budget."

Ruby was so impressed with the way Dillon handled the emergency that she insisted on taking him to dinner that night. Besides, she didn't feel like going home alone, with the knowledge that Graham was spending most of the night awake in New York City. She didn't want to feel lonely when she knew damn well he wasn't. Since the relationship between Jeannie and Graham would never amount to anything, she had learned long ago that it was far more judicious to overlook her husband's flings. She had no great desire to keep jealous talons hooked into him.

"I hope you didn't have plans this evening," Ruby said to Dillon after they were seated in the restaurant.

"No," he lied. He had cancelled his date with Penny, after looking forward to her fingertips massaging the day's calamity from his temples.

Penny had understood, however. "Dillon, my darling, if your boss wants you to go to dinner, please go. I don't mind. I love you madly. If I have to wait to see you, it will only make our meeting so much sweeter."

"Dillon," said Ruby, "tell me about yourself. Have you got a girlfriend?"

He felt himself blush. "Yes," he replied.

"She's very lucky," said Ruby. "You've got a great career ahead of you. You're the most levelheaded man I've met in years. If Graham had to handle that situation today, he would have been screaming into the phone in two seconds."

"That's why he hired me," said Dillon. "So he wouldn't have to yell."

"Graham's used to getting his own way."

"I wouldn't want to piss him off, that's for sure," said Dillon. He expertly ordered a bottle of wine from the waiter.

"Graham trusts you," said Ruby.

"I have my priorities. The company I work for is my number one priority. I'm proud to be working for Graham."

"It'll look good on your resume?" queried Ruby.

He cleared his throat. "I guess that's one way of looking at it."

"What are your aspirations, Dillon?"

She was being so blunt that he could only answer her questions frankly. "I want to produce," he told her. "I'm learning a lot about the business now. I'm trained in accounting. I understand numbers. But I think I'd enjoy doing something more creative."

"What's your girlfriend think about your career?"

"She's behind me one hundred percent."

"It's so important to have that moral support, isn't it?" Ruby cut the lettuce of her salad into very small bites. "Are you planning on marrying her?"

"I wish it were that simple," replied Dillon. "I'm afraid her parents don't care for me."

Ruby was surprised. "What do you mean? You're a wonderful man. I would be proud to have you as a son-in-law. Or even a son, for that matter."

"Thank you, Mrs. Maddox," said Dillon, her warmth totally unexpected. "I guess Penny's family trusts nobody in the entertainment business. In other words"—and this was much more difficult for him to say—"they don't approve of me. They don't like my background. They are upper class and, I'm afraid, I'm what they would call working class."

"In this day and age? That's the most ridiculous thing I've ever heard." Ruby held out her wine glass, indicating she wished a refill.

"Unfortunately, it's not ridiculous," said Dillon sadly. "They know only one thing—They don't want their daughter to marry me. They have someone already picked out for her."

"Oh," said Ruby, comprehending, "old family connections?"

Dillon nodded.

"What about your girlfriend? What does she think?"

"She's torn up about it. She would chuck it all to come live with me. But I couldn't ask her to do that. I'm hoping one day her parents will accept me because they feel I am equal to their social stature. It's the way I want it."

Ruby could see that Dillon knew what he wanted from life and seemed to know how to go about getting it. He had goals. He was a strong man. His honest nature, which a few weeks before she had snubbed as kiss-ass, now produced positive energy when she thought of him. If only Will had not rebelled so ferociously, he probably would have made a good executive. And Martin . . . She dared not think of the loss she felt about his lack of ambition. Martin wanted everything the easy way, without working for it. Dillon was not that kind of man. He worked hard for everything he had. He believed that working was the only honorable way to obtain what he wanted from life.

His girlfriend's parents are fools, thought Ruby. They are fools if they don't think Dillon is good enough for their daughter.

Halfway through their second bottle of wine, Ruby was digging tender crabmeat from a great orange claw with a two-pronged fork. There was no delicate way to keep her fingers free from the melted butter. She glanced up at Dillon, who was looking on with an amazed smile.

"What is it?" she laughed.

"You seem so . . . so . . . human," he said. Suddenly embarrassed that she might have misinterpreted him, he added, "That's not what I meant . . . I mean . . ."

"I know what you mean," she said. "How's the duck?"

"Very good."

He grinned. He was having a good time. Ruby was in top form. He had told her a lot about his personal life—more than he would have said had he not consumed the wine. But she had asked, and he had let his guard down.

"Dillon," she told him upon finishing her crab, dipping her fingers into the lemoned fingerbowl water and drying them on a linen napkin, "I will have a talk with Graham when he gets back. I would like to have help producing *Motive.* As you saw today, I panicked too easily. If I had gotten on the phone, we might have had to scrap the episode.

"I think you and I make a good team. I had hoped Graham would help me more than he has. But he just doesn't have the time or the inclination. I'm a team-oriented person. I need to work in a team. I want you to produce with me."

Dillon was flattered. His heart began racing. Here was the break he had been waiting for. He had Mrs. Maddox by his side, believing in him. He knew he could become someone with power, with a reputation, with money. His brilliant smile surfaced. "Thank you. Thank you very much," he said.

•

Glory walked five blocks down the street to the gas station. There were no sidewalks, so she crept cautiously along the gutter while cars whisked past exceeding the thirty-mile-per-hour speed limit by at least ten notches. Unfortunately, the gas station was a mini-market and they didn't have a gas can.

She only had three one-dollar bills and the squat, Middle-Eastern man behind the counter told her he didn't take checks or credit cards. She groaned inwardly. The day's tension reached around her brutally taut shoulders and started choking her throat.

She thought of calling Tony but remembered he had curtly informed her he was going out drinking with the guys after work. She knew they all went over to the Golden Time Lounge. Glory had never been in there. A couple of gals she worked with had asked her to go there today, but she had declined, saying she was tired.

Actually, she couldn't face seeing Tony. What if he were with someone else? He might think she was there spying on him. So she had told the gals no, and later, when the Impala ran out of gas and she had to push the hulk by herself to the side of the street, her aloneness became too much for her. Tears splashed onto the unworthy asphalt and she reprimanded herself for being so stupid as to say no to the gals' invite.

Stupid, she thought, was a word she used too often in her life.

She wandered about the mini-market, wondering how she could get gas to her car. She couldn't think of a soul who would come and pick her up. She spied plastic liter bottles of cola stacked in cases with a sign attached that read: "Special $1.50."

A buck-fifty? She could get three bottles for that price at the regular market. The bland, uncaring face of the cashier annoyed her greatly. She bought a dollar-fifty's worth of gas on Pump #2 and a liter of the cola, then went outside the front door where she proceeded to pour the contents out on the oil-spotted concrete. She filled the plastic bottle with gas. It overflowed at fifty-six cents.

"Hell," she said, setting the bottle on the stoop and going back inside for her change.

"Why you pour there?" the cashier demanded about the cola.

"I'm out of gas," she replied.

"Front door. Flies come now," he retorted angrily.

Why couldn't she just call Tony? Or somebody? Her aloneness was excruciating. Los Angeles was too difficult. Why was she even here?

"I'm sorry," she huffed, feigning indignity. "Would you please give me my change?"

"Flies come now," he repeated, slowly counting out her change while customers piled up in the line behind her. They sighed heavily, holding their newspapers and cartons of milk.

She was about to tell him she'd hose down his driveway, when suddenly tears flashed into her eyes and she blurted out, "You are an asshole."

As she walked out the door and stopped to take up the liter bottle, she heard a mild round of applause behind her. It set a grin on her face, until she had to retrace her route next to the sideswiping traffic. With every step, she prayed she wouldn't be hit.

At least, she said to herself, it isn't snowing, it isn't cold, and it isn't windy. It's California. "Where else in the U.S.A. could you find such wonderful weather in the fall?" She heard a comment to that effect every day.

Glory was a veteran at running out of gas. She shoved the neck of the plastic bottle into the gas tank, poured in the fuming liquid, but saved the bottom inch. She didn't even try to start the engine. She opened the hood, removed the air filter, and splashed gas into the carburetor to prime it. Then she got in, pumped the foot pedal, and turned the key. The old engine cranked over once and fired up.

"That a girl," said Glory, her voice sounding so cheery, it surprised her.

Parking under her apartment building, she reluctantly admitted she could have called her manager for help. Shit. Why couldn't she have loads of friends that would be willing to drop whatever they were doing and rush to her rescue? Only popular people had that kind of luck, she thought. Cheerleaders, sorority-types. A category she had never fitted into. But then, *those* kinds of people never ran out of gas.

Oh, she wished she were beyond high school and college stigma. She was an adult now. They were in her past. It haunted her that she might have thoughts about what she *hadn't* been in high school or college for her entire life. She tried to tell herself that she didn't care.

But she did.

The cat knocked itself against her legs, tripping her as she made her way to the kitchen to open a can of cat food. She felt particularly resentful toward the creature tonight. The only time it ever showed affection was when it was hungry. It put its little head into its dish and was totally content. She couldn't even tell it about her running out of gas. *It* just didn't give a damn.

She sat in her armchair and felt like crying. But, now that she was home and nobody could see her and she could cry her heart out, her eyes were dry.

She had been so busy with the trauma of the cola bottle—she had left it on the curb, with the thought it would have made a perfect Molotov cocktail for the mini-market if only she had the incentive and know-how—that she had forgotten to check her answering machine.

Its red light blinked at her. Probably Sondra. Or Richard. Lately, the director had taken to calling her and giving her additional notes over the phone.

She began rewinding the tape. There was a slight whine to its backward motion. She didn't get many messages, so the first couple of feet were all that ever got used. It would get worn out going over and over the same spot, and she'd have to buy a new tape and rerecord her message another twenty times.

It didn't stop but kept on rewinding. Must be broken. Stuck on a dial tone, she thought with despair.

Finally, the playback.

"Hi, darling," the masculine voice said. "I missed you. I had to call to tell you how much I love you. I do. . . ." The message was cut off.

Then she heard her outgoing message again. Then his voice. "I do love you, you know. I'm sitting here in this bar, right here with the boys, and all I can think about is you. They're all making fun of me. . . ."

Her message again. "But I love you. I really think I love you. I haven't been in love for a long time. I wonder where you are? I hope you're having a good time whatever you're doing. I miss you. . . ."

Her message. "Goddamn, this is running me a lot of quarters. I love you. You probably won't even believe me, but I love you. It makes me happy to think about you. It sounds stupid. . . ."

Her message. "Stupid—that's one of your words. But I do, I feel happy. . . ."

She listened to the entire tape. Twenty messages worth. Her heart soared. She even took the worthless cat into her lap and hugged it from the sheer joy of Tony's voice.

Then she rewound the tape. And played it again. And again.

Jeannie had never been to New York. She had booked them into two rooms for two nights at a lavish hotel. The first night, Graham had gone to dinner with friends, assumed that she could amuse herself for the evening, and had not even knocked on her door when he returned around two A.M.

At the end of their second afternoon, Graham said, "Jeannie, I am having cocktails with a business associate, but if you are not busy later, I'd like to take you to dinner. Do you have plans?"

She was tired, having acted as a secretary all day. She had never taken so many notes and didn't know whether to curse or thank her mother for having insisted she learn shorthand in high school. It was the first time since she had started working for Graham that she had had to use it.

His mind was concentrated solely on business. She found him much more intense in New York, like he were afraid of making any mistakes. His usual, superficial ease was gone and replaced by a cool graciousness.

"No, I don't have dinner plans," she replied, pleased that he would finally ask, feeling slightly foolish for having assumed he had brought her to New York for only one reason—to play around with her.

Jeannie wanted to surprise him. She ordered a candlelight dinner in the hotel suite. Room service provided the food, she provided a bottle of very fine single malt Scotch. But when Graham returned, she couldn't tell if he was pleased or not.

"I thought we were going out" was his comment. He didn't like having the plans changed without his knowledge. It threw him off balance for a few minutes.

He stood in his overcoat, surveying the scene. She wore a simple black dress, one that wasn't overtly sexy but still revealed the full, firm lines of her body. Damn, but he'd been looking forward to dinner at his favorite restaurant, one that he dined at on each New York visit.

He noticed Jeannie's disappointed face. His first reaction was anger, but he quickly tempered that. He could keep his cool as long as the first words out of her mouth were not of a sexual nature. She persistently dogged him with her sexual favors. He didn't think she was a nymphomaniac, because she didn't seem to desire anyone but him and the nymphos he had known were incapable of monogamy. He took advantage of her willingness and quelled his lusting appetite, though he also tired of her relentless pursuit. She was a huntress who never set down her bow and quivers.

"Norman called twice," she said, walking to a little table and pouring Graham a glass of the Scotch.

"What did he want?"

"You know Norman. He'll talk to me about *anything* except business. He doesn't consider that any of a secretary's business." She handed him the glass and retreated to an armchair. "Let's go out tonight, if you prefer. My feelings won't be hurt," she said matter-of-factly.

But his mind had switched onto why Norman would have called, since they were flying back to the West Coast the following day. "Did Norman say it was urgent? Do you think I should call him tonight?"

"Norman didn't say *urgent*. He simply said he 'was hoping to catch you in.' " She didn't like Scotch, but since she had forgotten to buy something else, she mixed a small amount of the liquor with a big shot of soda. Being a California girl, she preferred white wine. If Graham decided to stay in, she would order a bottle from room service.

Her instincts told her to act businesslike as long as Graham did. He led, she followed suit. No sense in throwing in the queen of diamonds when he was playing a modest deuce of clubs. She couldn't complain. He was putting her up in one of the finest hotels in the city. She was quickly acquiring a taste for New York, which she knew was not an inexpensive metropolis.

"Norman's probably worried about his wife," said Jeannie.

Graham swallowed a mouthful of Scotch. "Why would he be?"

"Because she's been messing around with her leading man."

"Garrett Gage?"

"Who else? You'd have to be blind not to notice the magnetism between them. I saw them kiss for a scene last week, and when the director said 'cut,' they were the only ones who didn't seem to hear."

Graham didn't want to call Norman. The Scotch was good and he was finally relaxing.

"You know," continued Jeannie, "Garrett and Tanya have been seen leaving the studio together at the end of the day."

"I thought Norman sent a limo for her?"

"I guess she sometimes calls and tells the driver not to come and pick her up."

Graham set down his glass and rubbed his eyes. He felt tired. His body was on California time. Getting up at six A.M. for an early meeting really meant he had arisen at three.

Jeannie moved quietly behind him and started rubbing his shoulders and neck. Beyond them, through the open curtains, New York blazed with lights. She was tempted to kiss his neck but decided to wait until he asked for her affections. He was a difficult man to figure out; she couldn't outguess him.

"Maybe Norman wants you to stop the affair," she said.

"That would be ridiculous," stated Graham. Even if Norman were suspicious of an affair between Tanya and Garrett, what had that to do with Graham? He had already explained that he could not possibly be the keeper for the hundreds of people who worked for him.

"I've never understood Norman's capacity for jealousy," said Graham. "How can he think a woman with looks like Tanya's married him because she loves him? A brilliant business mind like his getting taken in by that gorgeous body."

"She is gorgeous, isn't she?"

"Fabulously so. The ratings have gone up. That proves it."

"I certainly hope that if Norman has the ability to get you to put his wife *on* the show, that he does *not* have the power to get Garrett off." Her words were blunt.

"Do you know something that you're not telling me?" asked Graham. He was vaguely worried. Surely she couldn't have found out about the old secret between Norman and himself?

"I'm only saying I saw the way Norman put pressure on

you to cast Tanya in the role of Janet. How could I have missed it? However, she doesn't make the show. Garrett does. He *is Motive*."

"I would never fire Garrett. *Motive* is making money. Norman would never be that unreasonable. Money is a priority with him."

"Except where his wife is concerned."

He sighed heavily. Who screwed whom did not interest him. He would discuss the matter with Ruby. She was certain to know of the affair between her two leads and would have an opinion about it. Thank God, he could talk these matters over with her. Ruby would know what to do.

Jeannie's neck massage felt good. He took one of her hands and held the palm to his lips.

"Come sit on my lap," he said. "Let's enjoy this last night in New York."

Ruby drove up the coast, along the Pacific Coast Highway. The morning sun sparkled brightly on the sea and she marveled at the clearness of the sky. It was a dark blue. Every detail of the surrounding mountains and coastline was distinct in the morning light.

Motive had a couple of days on location with a story that involved smugglers. It was a very exciting script that she had conceived. Ruby had thought it would be a good way to show Garrett Gage without his shirt, but she had discovered, when the actor was changing costume on the soundstage, that he wore deceptive clothing. His shoulders were not as wide nor his chest as well-defined as it appeared. She realized that she had probably mistaken the strength in Garrett's stunt double when she had seen the raw footage. Will had remarkably supple muscles.

The late fall day was clear and cold. Both actor and double would be glad the script had been rewritten and did not require them to unclothe.

When she had first arrived in California, she could not get enough of the ocean. Landlocked in Texas her entire life, with only a few glimpses of the coast, she would walk along the California sand delighting in the sound of the waves rushing and the gulls crying. They swooped and glided acrobatically in the breeze. The people who walked there also seemed free of restriction. They dressed as they chose and acted as though they were totally alone—kissing walking partners, singing to dogs, skipping in the sand. Sometimes they said hello and sometimes they turned their head to the water when they passed a person. Ruby was never insulted. She had quickly realized how difficult it was to find privacy in a city the size of Los Angeles. If a person walked along the beach and spoke to no one, it was almost as if they were solitary.

Will, on five-year-old legs, would run to the foam, giggling as the cold water chased him with a curling wave. Her first instinct was to rush to the water to pull the child back. But, she told herself, the waves were mild. It was just that she was not used to the ocean . . . and that Will was the most precious thing in her life. She had to resist the impulse to hold him in her arms and stroke the soft brown hair and tell him it wasn't his fault.

He would run back through the deep sand to her, a shell in his hand, pointing at the water, laughing uninhibitedly. The laughs were brought up short when he looked into her sad eyes and remembered the tragedy.

It was here on the beach that she had met Graham. Actually, Will met him first. It was two months after Ruby arrived in the city. She had a split-shift job as a hostess in a restaurant. The manager had promised to move her up to waitress as soon as there was a vacancy. She needed a job, any job, and working at a restaurant fed her and her child. She worked the lunch crowd, left for a few hours, and returned for dinner.

Sometimes she went to the beach during these free hours, and sometimes she went to Beverly Hills and drove along the wide residential avenues, looking at the homes of the wealthy and swearing that one day she would live in one. The day that happened, she believed, no one could hurt her again. She would show Matt Long exactly what kind of superior quality she was made of.

The restaurant was closed on Mondays. This was the day she went to the ocean from early morning to sunset. The flat water was the only openness in the miles and miles of city. Its expanse was almost like that of the Texas prairie.

One day, when a light cloud cover hazily obscured the sun, Will and Ruby played with a large softball. Nearby was their blanket and shopping bag full of picnic goodies. Ruby tossed the ball to Will, who caught it expertly in the well-worn baseball glove the restaurant owner had dug out of his garage for the boy. Will didn't goof around with the ball, but took pride in throwing it back to Ruby with preciseness. They started out close together, but Will would start backing up and the distance would become greater.

Ruby did not consider herself athletic. But she kept throwing the ball to Will to try to appease his insatiable appetite for such sport. At least that was one thing—and probably the only thing—she could thank Matt Long for. He enjoyed playing with the kids.

Of course, Matt had hoped Will would play the Major Leagues one day. That was the way Matt figured things. Always huger than life. Always unrealistically. Always self-centered.

Her arm was getting tired and Will seemed so far back. When she threw the ball, it leaped crookedly, like an explosive kernel of corn escaping from its popper, and rolled toward the surf.

"Ah, Mom," shouted Will, digging bare feet through the sand as the ball rolled right into the wash. The water snatched the white sphere and dragged it out to sea.

The water rolled in again, the wave crashing over Will's knees, the ball tossed about half submerged, just out of his hand's reach. He looked around at his mother, who was trying not to panic as she moved toward the water.

"Here, kid, I'll get your ball," said a young man with black hair, a big T-shirt over his trunks. As the surf receded, the man waded out, but when it came roaring back, he was drenched chest-high. He emerged, dripping, the ball in his hand. He threw it up the beach where it rolled to a stop, coated in sand like a piece of chicken in bread crumbs.

Which was precisely what he was cooking down the beach. Barbecued chicken. He invited the woman and her boy to join him. He even offered to play more catch with the boy, in spite of the mother's protestations that the child didn't need to play more ball and should leave the nice man alone. The man would have rather talked to the boy's mother, anyway, a girl in her mid-twenties, with strawberry blond hair and bangs and terrific legs. There was a quietness about her. Perhaps in her eyes. Something hidden. Haunting.

"You know," the man told Ruby, "you and your son should be careful not to get sunburned."

"Sunburned?" she said, surprised. "Why, it's a cloudy day."

"It'll burn you worse than the sun all by itself. You don't think it's getting you, but you'll be cooked tonight. Guess you're not from California?"

Ruby blushed with slight embarrassment.

"It's your accent," explained the man. "Now, now, let me guess. I know it's Southern-ish."

Ruby raised her eyebrows in mock indignation.

"Sorry," he said with a grin, realizing her origin. "It must be Texas."

Her freckled nose wrinkled slightly with her smile. He seemed to be the most friendly person she had met since arriving in Southern California. He did not seem at all self-conscious. He was cooking twice as much chicken as he could possibly eat himself.

"Are you expecting someone?" she asked.

"No," he said, squirting the charcoals with water and turning over the pieces with a fork.

"What do you do?"

"I'm a screenwriter."

"Oh," she said, impressed.

"I should say, *struggling* screenwriter. My agent's optioned a couple of my scripts to producers. I'm waiting to hear back from them."

She nodded as though she understood the Hollywood game very well. She didn't know what "optioned" meant, but it sounded good. He was a writer, and she had learned that they made almost as much money as producers, directors, and stars. He didn't act rich, though.

"What do you do?" he asked her.

"I'm a hostess at a restaurant," she replied, and told him the name.

"I know where that is. I'll have to come visit you while you're working," he paused at her embarrassment, "—if that's all right?"

She nodded. He hadn't even asked her if she was married. But then, all he had to do was look at her ring finger. The finger still felt forlornly weightless, as though a helium balloon were tied to it.

"What's your name?" she asked.

"Graham," he replied. "Graham Maddox." He extended his hand.

She brushed off her sandy palm on her leg and shook his hand. "I'm Ruby. My son's name is Will."

"He's a cute kid," said Graham. "How does he like L.A.? You taken him to the zoo?"

"No, we haven't been to the zoo. We've only lived here two months."

"Do *you* like it here?" he asked.

"It's all right . . . I guess."

"Why did you move here from Texas?" he asked.

People frequently asked her this question, and every time it took her by surprise. She scolded herself for not having thought up a pat answer. "I needed a change," she said awkwardly.

They ate chicken. They talked. They stayed on the beach until there was almost no light left in the sky. Will had fallen asleep on the blanket and Ruby covered him up.

"I've had a very nice day," she said finally, putting her things into her bag and getting ready to leave. "It was very nice of you to ask us."

"I hope it's not the last time I'm going to see you," said Graham.

When she stood, the cold air made her shiver. "Here," he said, putting his heavy sweater around her shoulders. "I'd like to walk you to your car."

When she was packed and in the driver's seat of the Nash, he leaned in the open window with a gesture to kiss her. She turned her cheek to him and it was met with his warm and soft lips. Her eyes smiled into his.

He realized that it was the first thing approaching a smile that had appeared on her face all day. He kissed her again on the cheek. She put the car in gear, pulled on the lights, and left. He had forgotten to get her phone number. He shrugged, with a cozy, happy feeling in his stomach. No matter. He knew where she worked.

Chapter 8

Penny nestled into the crook of Dillon's arm. Her nakedness was like warm syrup over that side of his body as they lay, their racing hearts returning to restful beats. She had come to his apartment, something they rarely did since he hated the thought of her driving home late at night. Her parents' house was so far away. They both wanted her to spend the night but were continually cognizant of the parental disapproval that filled them with guilt and robbed them of their nights together.

He had offered to pick her up, but she told him it would be better if she gave her parents some excuse instead of the truth. He had suggested a restaurant, yet she had wanted to be alone with him, watching TV and ordering out for pizza.

Then she was late, and he began to worry because the night was rainy. Southern California received so little precipitation that the first rain after a dry spell caused hazardous driving conditions on the freeways. The built-up oil, packed onto the asphalt by thousands and thousands of tires, was treacherously slick. And nobody ever slowed down when the roads were wet. Californians were invincible and they drove to prove it.

Finally, Penny arrived safely, under an umbrella, the wet night falling behind her as she stood at his door.

"I'm sorry I'm late. My parents gave me the grill," she explained. "I made the mistake of telling them I was going to study, and they made a good argument for doing it at home on a rainy night. I'm sure they suspected where I was going."

She slipped out of her coat and Dillon hung it on the oak coatrack near the front door. Her umbrella dripped on the entryway floor and she went into the guest bath to leave it in the shower. He followed her into the small bath and watched while she toweled excess moisture off her short brown hair.

She looked at him in the mirror and said, "Maybe I should have stayed home on a night like this, but I just couldn't stay away." She turned and was in his arms, her mouth giving, giving, her arms behind his neck, pulling his head to hers.

He clutched her tightly to him, his hands under her small buttocks, her petite weight nothing for him as he held her up, her crotch pressed against him. He sank slowly to his knees upon the dark pink carpet, holding her with one arm and unbuttoning her blouse with his free hand. His mouth hungrily pressed between her breasts, devouring their silkiness with pulling lips and tender nips. She moaned and pushed the top of his head down. He kissed her stomach, his downward motion stopped only by the waistband of her wool slacks.

He set her back on the rug and pulled the slacks to her knees. He pushed her thighs apart as far as the bound knees permitted, craving the taste of her center. It was flushed and firm and soft and pushed heavily into his mouth when it met him.

"Dillon, that's good," she murmured, her fingers touching his cheekbones.

He looked at her face and saw her eyes closed as she enjoyed the rapture. His own arousal strained inside his pants—a quick, hard pulse tensing and seeking relief in the velvet he now mouthed.

On his knees, he entered her, his arms under her back, bringing her tight against him. He was lost deep inside her, aware of nothing more than the feeling of wanting to stay there forever, to sustain the physical sensation that was both ironlike and featherlike at the same time. It was a sensation attached to his emotions with indescribable bonds.

For a while, they struggled on the rose-colored carpet, locked between the shower door and the sink. Light filtered in from the living room and he suggested several times they move to the bedroom. She answered with a passionate no, her hands clamped to his rear, pulling him deeper into her as a reply. When they did go into the bedroom, he carried her with her legs wrapped around his waist, his cock buried inside her.

Outside, the rain continued to fall, but they did not hear it until they rested, their sweat drying, setting a chill upon their bodies.

"I like the sound of the rain," said Penny, "when I'm inside and safe and warm. Like this. You make me feel even safer and warmer."

"I want to protect you," he said, drawing the covers up over them, kissing her sweat-dampened head.

"Please tell me I don't have to go home," she said, the words sprinting across his chest and burrowing into the blankets.

"I wish I could," he said. "But you would have hell to pay tomorrow."

"Then don't let me get out of bed until it's time to go," she said. "I've never had anyone like you before. If this is what it feels like to be in love, I've never been in love before." She hugged him and pressed herself as closely into him as she could.

"I have some news," he said quietly.

"Good news or bad news?"

"I think you would call it good. Nothing's definite yet, though."

She raised her head and looked at him, her eyes smiling with expectation. "What is it?"

"Remember the dinner I had with Ruby Maddox? She'd like to promote me to producer if she can get Graham to agree."

"That's wonderful!" cried Penny, kissing him. "When do you start?"

"Nothing's for sure yet."

"But she's the producer on *Motive.* She can hire anyone she wants."

"Yes, I suppose so," said Dillon cautiously.

"This is a fantastic night. I haven't been happier since I've known you."

"It makes me happy, too," he said.

"How can my parents argue with that? And once you're producing one show, there's nothing to stop you from producing others. I love you, Dillon Hughes, I love you."

He didn't mind as much letting her go home after he'd told her. She was buoyant, promising that they would soon be together forever and nobody would raise any objections. Her parents could no longer get away with saying that he wasn't good enough for their daughter.

A peace came over him as he stood watching Penny drive away. The rain had diminished to a light drizzle and he waited until the sound of her tires was gone from his ears. He let out one loud, high-pitched whoop—something he never did, especially not at two A.M.

Jeannie smiled when she heard the message on her home answering machine. Graham Maddox recapped the highlights of their very steamy night together looking out over the lights of Manhattan. He liked her on her stomach with her legs spread. He liked her tea-heated mouth on his cock, followed by ice cubes on his balls. He liked her squatting over him, playing with herself.

Jeannie only needed to listen to the tape one time. She rewound it, ejected it, and stored it in a locked box in her linen closet, under the beach towels. She inserted a fresh tape in the machine.

Then she made her phone call, which had become a nightly ritual. "I told you I am handling everything," she said in a reassuring voice. "You have nothing to worry about. I promise. I promise."

Glory didn't think she had time to try parking her car in her space beneath her apartment building. It was four o'clock and Tony was coming at five, and she had lots of groceries to unpack and dinner to get ready. Getting the

Impala into its allotted stall could take up to fifteen minutes!

Parking a half block from the building and carrying three bulging sacks of groceries was a heck of a lot easier on the nerves. The air was clean and smelled good from the rain that had washed the skies. It made her a little homesick for Minnesota, where all kinds of smells float on an early winter's evening. There was not much daylight left but it didn't matter, anyway, since she kept the curtains in her apartment closed most of the time. It was the only way she felt she got any privacy.

She put the cat out with no reservations. It was Saturday afternoon and that gave the creature until Monday morning to roam free. But it didn't want to go out. She heard its plaintive meow outside her door as she unpacked the groceries, so she let it back in. It sat attentively on the living room carpet, licking its paws and watching her from the corner of its eye.

Even though a meal wasn't the main reason for Tony's visit, Glory had dinner all planned out. She was going to prepare a stuffed flank steak, just like she had seen on a TV cooking show. All she had to do was cut the meat very thin, spread the stuffing over the top, roll it up, tie it, and roast it. She was also fixing brussels sprouts and baked potatoes, and whipping up some pudding for dessert. She'd bought a pint of brandy, which she was going to try putting into the pudding.

On the rickety kitchen table sat the typewriter Tony had purchased. He had been to her apartment a half-dozen times and they had worked on the *Motive* script they intended to submit to Ruby Maddox. This evening, Tony and Glory were going to complete the final draft. She had a couple of ideas about how to augment plot points, though her main concern at the moment was getting dinner ready.

By now, of course, everyone on the *Motive* set knew that Tony and Glory were seeing each other. Tony put up with the crew members' ribbing. She knew he preferred to maintain some independence, so she did not make a fuss if he went off to lunch with the boys. She only wished he would tell her in advance. He always waited until the last minute to make lunch plans and that could leave her hanging, since he was her number–one priority and she never made other plans herself. When he didn't invite her, she rarely went alone to the commissary. She just ducked into one of the unoccupied dressing rooms and read a magazine, hoping no one would notice that she didn't have anyone to go to lunch with.

She felt sure that Tony *liked* her a lot. That was in addition to his declaring his love for her. She knew, because one time he had talked for a couple of hours about how a person could *love* another person and yet not *like* that individual. A case in point, he said, was how Glory felt about her mother.

She protested that she liked her mother, because they did a lot of things together. She just felt her mother was too overprotective. However, she understood her mother, because they had been a team and she was all her mother had in the world.

Glory was wary of Tony's feelings toward her. He didn't want to be crowded. He made quite a point that his sole marriage had lasted only a short time—and that was seventeen years ago—and that no woman had tied him down since. The only thing that made him a little sad was when he said he hoped to have children one day.

She didn't tell him she thought he might be a little old to start having kids. Most of the time, she didn't think about their difference in age, but somehow, with his craggy face and the knowledge that he was the same age as her mother, she could not imagine him holding a very tiny baby—not even his own. Tony lacked a softness that Glory thought all fathers must have.

She wasn't thinking of her own father but rather of how she pictured the ideal father. She adored seeing men in public with their baby strapped onto their backs in a child carrier, or even sometimes holding the child up and baby-talking and kissing it. *That* was the way fathers were supposed to be. She couldn't see Tony's fingers plying a diaper and cootchy-cooing a red, crying face.

But she enjoyed his hoarse laugh and his cynical sense of humor. Things went smoother for her on the show now that she was accepted as his girlfriend. People had a little more respect for her. Maybe her concentration was better. She was conscious of not wanting to make any mistakes that might bring the crew's snickering down upon her—or Tony.

She was also learning a lot. Tony often motioned for her to look through the camera while the director of photography set up a shot.

"That's what we're filming," said Tony as she closed one eye to look through the viewfinder. "It looks different, don't it, from being able to see the whole set?"

"It does," she agreed.

"When you write a script," he said, "it helps to remember what you're going to see through the camera."

They had fun working together on the script. She read Tanya's part, sometimes talking in the breathy way that Tanya had, copying the blonde's sexual swinging of hips and shoulders in an exaggerated movement. Glory thought Tanya was too phony, but it was fun to mimic her.

Tony read Garrett's part, slicking back his own mustache much as the actor always touched his own, a self-conscious, preening gesture that well stated how aware Garrett was of his flagrant good looks. Tony straightened his lips in the look that Garrett thought was the most sexy.

Glory giggled. "Honestly," she remarked, "that Garrett is so damn conceited. I wonder what Tanya sees in him?"

"I'd say the pair of them are conceited," said Tony, reading the next line and again mocking Garrett by pretending to turn his face so its most advantageous angle was to the camera. "Garrett is super-aware of the location of the camera at every moment. He plays to the camera, not to the other actors in the scene. You might not see it in the final edit, because a good editor is splicing all the shots together fluidly."

Glory didn't get the flank steak roast into the oven until five-thirty. Tony was late, but that was okay since she was behind schedule. She checked on the beers she had stacked into the ancient icebox. They were starting to get cold. She wished she had thought to pick up a six-pack that was already cold. Tony usually brought a bottle of whiskey with him when they worked together, which was lucky since she couldn't have afforded more than the dinner and the six-pack. She wasn't earning the extravagant union wages that Tony did.

Fortunately, Richard had gotten her a slight raise. It exactly matched the amount her rent had been increased. "The stove," said the fat old manager, mustache bristling on her upper lip. "We had to fix the stove. You've got a good deal here. You try to find another apartment in this good a neighborhood for this good a price."

At least Glory had a working oven now. The smell of the cooking meat filled the apartment. The flank steak was not filleted perfectly nor rolled into a pretty picture like they had done on TV. Glory didn't realize how sharp a knife had to be to cut a half-inch steak in half. She didn't even know where to go to buy a knife that sharp, but she guessed it wouldn't be a cheap purchase anywhere. With gravy, the meal would look and taste just fine.

By seven-thirty, Glory had called Tony's house three times and not gotten an answer. Where was he? Why hadn't he called? She started typing the final draft of their script but became worried about his whereabouts.

She plopped herself down in the armchair and looked at the bed. She had bought a new piece of material to go over the top, a bright tropical print with parrots. She had also bought a round wicker ball at a cheap import store and, fitting it over a light bulb, hung it over the bed. She thought it looked very atmospheric.

By eight-thirty, the oven, with the roast inside, had cooled. She had almost overcooked it before she had thought to turn it off. Hungry earlier, she had now lost her appetite. Had Tony done this on purpose? Had he stood her up? He was probably drunk somewhere and had forgotten their meeting. It hurt her that he didn't care. She called Information for the number of the Golden Time Lounge, across from the studio. The bartender answered and informed her that Tony had left an hour before.

She sat back in the armchair. She didn't feel like writing. She didn't feel like going out, or calling anyone and talking, or eating dinner, or doing a damn thing. Why hadn't he shown up? If he loved her, how could he do this to her? Was it because he really didn't love her after all? Did he even *like* her? The questions crowded into her furiously whirling brain. She wished they would go away. She wished she had an answer. She wished she hadn't fallen in love.

Her baked potatoes sat on the stove top, wrinkling. They had been perfect—plump, hot, mealy, baked just right—and now they were caving in on themselves. She had even bought sour cream and real butter. Why had she bothered? Why had she fallen in love?

She felt like calling her mother, but her mother would only criticize California men. "They've got their pick of women out there, Glory. They'll hurt you. They're self-centered. Not worth a damn." And her mother didn't even know Tony's age or that he drank too much.

Glory didn't want to face Tony's drinking, but the thought of him sitting at the Golden Time getting shit-faced while she was at home slaving over a special dinner for him made her mad. She wasn't a girl who got mad very quickly, because if anger were involved in the situation, she usually figured she was responsible for causing it. This time she hadn't, and anger bubbled within her.

By ten-thirty, sitting near the phone, she had consumed four of the six beers. She only wished they would make her sleepier. She couldn't even turn on her crummy little black-and-white television.

"Why did I bother believing him?" she asked out loud.

A croak of a meow came from near the door. The cat sat there, waiting for her to put it out. She scooped it up in her arms and buried her face in its fur. But it wouldn't purr and started struggling to be let down. Disgustedly, she opened the door and tossed it out onto the cement walkway.

She remembered her car parked on the street. Why shouldn't she put it in its parking place? She felt stupid for worrying earlier that she might not have enough time to get everything ready for Tony before he showed up. She felt stupid for ever asking him over in the first place and trying to please him with a dinner that she had worked so hard to prepare.

She took her keys and shut the apartment door behind her. She didn't bother turning on the answering machine. She hoped like hell he would call in the next fifteen minutes and that her phone would ring and ring and he would think she had gone out. It would serve him right. It would.

It was raining again. Lucky, she thought. If she met anyone on the sidewalk, no one would know she was crying.

But the street was quite empty.

Every now and then, Graham got into one of his "hiking moods." He always insisted that Ruby go with him. "Hiking" was Ruby's term; "short walk" was Graham's. He enjoyed going to Marina del Rey and walking on the cement pedestrian/bicycle paths that wound around the docks and along the beach.

He and Ruby had owned a sailboat for a while, but Graham discovered he wasn't a sailor. They laughed between themselves at how much they enjoyed the sailing "lifestyle," as long as it didn't involve any actual excursions upon the water. After their walks, they either went to the yacht club, where they were still members, or phoned friends who owned a vessel and visited them on board. Rocking on rippling wakes in the quiet harbor-waters was as seagoing as they wished to be.

On Sunday morning, the clouds had broken enough to let sunlight through, and by ten A.M., Graham had on his walking outfit and shoes and was ready to go. Ruby sat around in her housecoat for another hour, finally changed her clothes, and drove them both down the canyon to the ocean's edge. Graham got out of the Mercedes and stretched, fists jabbing up toward the sky. Ruby locked the doors, put her purse in the trunk, wrapped a scarf over her head, and stashed the car keys in her jacket pocket. She patted Graham's front pocket to make sure he had not forgotten his wallet.

He grinned and said, "Ready?"

"Lead on," she replied.

They walked for a long time without talking. Their shoulders were six inches apart, yet they never touched. Graham was lost in thought. Ruby was watching out for speeding bicyclists who whirred past on thin tires, without giving any warning they were coming. Different from skiing, she thought, where everybody was courteous on a narrow passageway and called out, "On your right!" or "To your left!"

Ruby paid close attention to the people: what they wore, the compatibility of couples, the happiness of parents, the energy of children, the emotions revealed in their faces, sadness, wishfulness, boredom.

"If you had never been to the United States," said Graham, "and you were plunked down right here, you'd sure think we were a race of prosperous, healthy, and active people."

Graham suddenly grabbed Ruby's elbow and pulled her hard off the cement path. Two bicyclists, approaching from opposite directions, narrowly avoided colliding. Wobbling treacherously, the riders exchanged angry words. Ruby's heart beat fast. If Graham hadn't pulled her out of the way, she would have been hurt.

She looked so worried and so cute that Graham leaned over and kissed her on the mouth. It was a kiss of great care. She slipped an arm around his waist and they walked interlocked for a while, following a rocky jetty out to the breakwater where a clean, cold wind edged under their collars and brought up the color in their cheeks. They watched the immense orderly activity of boats filing in and out of the harbor. Beyond, out at sea, a knot of vessels bobbed around, each in its own erratic direction. Gulls screeched down, waiting for tidbits from incoming boats or fishermen sitting along the shore, whose lines ran twenty feet out into the seawater.

The rocks beneath their feet felt very secure. They had only to look at each other to exchange this thought.

Northward from the Marina were the towns of Venice and Santa Monica, then the coastline curved west to Malibu. Ruby thought of her proximate distance to the house where Will lived in Venice, but she did not find it ironic that they couldn't invite him to join them for a drink.

Ruby stopped touching Graham. He pulled away. He knew she was thinking about Will. His eyes iced a little, challenged her, reminded her that once she had had to make a choice between the husband and son. Bitterness set her jaw, and the freedom from the wind that she had experienced moments before became a straight line from her eyes, along the sides of her nose, along the crease of her mouth.

A head of blond hair caught their peripheral vision. A long, beautifully flowing mass swept around the lithe waist of its possessor—a girl of about seventeen, who stood on top of a rock and smiled at her Hispanic boyfriend. Both Ruby and Graham chuckled. The hair had reminded them of Tanya.

"One thing's for sure," said Graham. "If that *were* Tanya, she wouldn't be here with Norman."

"I guess we both know who it would be," replied Ruby, relieved that the tension had shifted off of Will.

"Norman's a very jealous man," said Graham, his eyes still upon the blond hair.

"He should have never married that utter twit." Ruby had not come to like Tanya any better since the actress had joined the show. All Ruby could credit her with is "sort of being able to follow direction."

"Regardless of what Norman should or should not have done, if he gets conclusive evidence that she is having an affair with Garrett, who knows what he'll do."

"What can he do?"

"Pull money out of some of the other deals we're on the verge of making." Graham took another unconscious step away from Ruby.

"You're being paranoid. Norman wouldn't screw up a business deal for personal reasons."

"At lunch, not too far back, he said, 'I know you'll keep an eye on her.' I'm worried about what that means. I didn't think I'd have to be Tanya's babysitter, but why take chances? We're ready to make a three-picture deal. Norman's got lots of money. He could take it anywhere in town."

"*You* could go anywhere in town. I think you're being

unreasonable, but I know you well enough by now. You'll be a nervous wreck unless we do something."

"Thank you."

"What do you suggest?"

"We'll have to talk to Garrett and Tanya."

Ruby stepped across the rocks, past the blond girl, walking back toward the Marina. "Garrett will say it's none of our business."

"We'll make it worthwhile to him," said Graham.

Ruby smiled wryly. "I told you he was a good choice," she said to Graham, who followed behind her. But the wind snatched the words and blew them out to sea.

"What did you say?" Graham asked hurrying to catch up with her.

She waited until he was side by side. "I said he was a good choice. Remember how you said he wouldn't make it?"

Graham tried to catch her elbow, but she stepped from his reach. She didn't seem to do it on purpose, but she also didn't act like she wanted to be touched. They resumed their usual roles of mutual respect.

"I'll talk to them if you like," said Ruby. "Unless you think we should do it together?"

Graham mulled over the situation. "Why don't you try talking to Garrett first. Casually. Tanya would only become uncontrollably emotional."

"I'm glad you see that she has that trait. It comes in handy when she wants her own way," said Ruby. A nasty bite.

"You're right," said Graham. "You talk to Garrett."

Ruby smiled to herself. She wouldn't mind an opportunity to get Garrett alone in her office . . . and talk to him.

Norman was lunching with two Italian investors and he insisted that Tanya join them. He wanted his charming and well-known wife to accompany him. She had two days off from *Motive* because the script required a lot of action on Garrett's part and no participation on hers.

"But I've got an appointment at the spa," she objected. She lay in his bed, the sheet pulled up to her waist. She was really planning to go to the studio during lunch break to find Garrett. It made her indescribably fretful to think of not being able to see him.

Norman, wearing only a shirt and his boxer shorts, sat on the bed next to her. "Reschedule it," he said, putting his hand under the sheet and pushing it below her pubic mound. He slipped his hand between the warm flesh of her firm thighs and roughly felt her.

"Ow," she complained about his ungentle groping.

"But it's what you like, isn't it, Tanya?" said Norman, probing her with his smooth, manicured fingers. "What are you so dry for?"

She wriggled under him, trying to pull back from his grasp, but he had her pinned between his hip and outstretched arms. She felt violated. She had managed to avoid having sex with Norman by satisfying his needs with her hands and mouth, murmuring sexily while he closed his eyes and enjoyed her ministrations. If he had opened his eyes, he would have been dismayed to see her staring off blankly into space, to find that whatever composed her soul did not seem to be in the room at the same time she touched his body.

She could not imagine having sex now with anyone but Garrett. Sweet, warm, vital, hard, alive inside her, the need to touch him and touch him and touch him beginning to take over almost every waking moment. All she could think about was how much she wanted Garrett—and how she couldn't have him. When she did get a few minutes of him, it was never enough. She craved him. Garrett was an addiction she could not satiate; it made her volatile and irrational. Let *him* do anything to her that he wanted; she would allow it. Hurt her—she deserved it—just as long as he didn't leave her.

Her time with Garrett was the only occasion she felt alive, truly alive. She felt vague and unreal when sitting in makeup or rehearsing scenes with other cast members. But when Garrett walked onstage, she suddenly felt plugged in, like a switch had been thrown and reality had substance.

When she was not with Garrett, she worried that she might never see him again. She also worried that he did not feel the same way about her.

He was finally making his career work. He was getting someplace. She was only a recreational drug to him, a little honey he couldn't resist. He never failed to tell her every time he was about to enter her that there was another woman in his life and that that woman took priority. Brenda had his love, his devotion, his support. He would not walk out on Brenda, no matter what. And then he would fuck Tanya hard, vengefully, his lip curling in an animal sneer with total concentration on the physical pleasure that consumed him, satisfied grunts coming from lips that kissed only with dispassion. He let Tanya take from him whatever he could give her on the surface.

Anything was better than nothing. She could not have borne *rien de tout.*

Now, Norman was grubbing between her legs, raping her with his fingers, pressing his face against her chest and sucking her hardened nipples. They had become purplish, like the bruised darkness of a creased flower petal. Her mind would not escape, would not disengage as she was used to it doing. Norman bore down upon her, the terror in her eyes adding to his frenzy.

"This is what you want, isn't it, wife?" he said, taking her wrist and forcing her hand upon his rigid penis. He moved over the top of her, gripping her with both of his knees, placing himself against her lips.

"Take it," he ordered simply.

Tears welled in her eyes and poured down her cheeks. She could not shut her eyes and pretend it was Garrett, for Norman's own smells and noises were above her, unmercifully invading her.

Tears soaked the pillows, but he didn't care. She was his and this was how he wanted her. "Get it good and wet, baby," he told her, enjoying the feel of her teeth edges. He was used to it now. She had never learned how to open her jaw enough or pad the sharp molars with her tongue. So he had learned to love what he got.

He pulled out of her mouth and pushed her up against the headboard, so her neck was bent and she was forced to watch him. He moved his hips between her thighs, pushing on her dryness, ignoring her cries of pain.

"If you won't get wet for me, Tanya, I'll fuck it dry," he said, abrasively putting it into her. "Cry all you want. You are mine, and I intend to have you whenever I want."

If only those words had been Garrett's. But they weren't. It was Norman who grunted and groaned, his massiveness defiling her, his words making her powerless. She was bent almost double, her legs alongside his arms, her ankles against his shoulders.

"You know how many men in America wish they were me?" he asked, taking his time, burning her slowly. "They all think of you as Frank Harrison's girl, maybe even Garrett's girl. But you're not Garrett's girl. You're mine. Frank Harrison is a boy-next-door. He would never fuck you. But Garrett would, wouldn't he?"

She shut her eyes and turned her head from him. He grasped her chin with strong fingers and uprighted her face, squeezing her jawbone hard until she was forced to open her eyes.

"I've found out who Garrett is," he said. "You didn't bother telling me, did you? Do you still want him so much?" He kept moving inside her.

Norman couldn't know for sure. He only suspected. Tanya violently shook her head. "He's in the past, Norman. He's in the past. I've told you that before."

"He better be. That playboy better be. When a woman belongs to me, no one has a right to her but me. Do you understand?" His voice threatened, his body wounded. He began to go faster, working against her, sucking air in through half-clenched teeth. "Do you understand?"

She nodded. She wished her barren body would release a little moisture to ease the burn, but it gave her none; an unyielding desert.

Norman tensed and released, his orgasm momentarily paralyzing him. He started again slowly. "Wish I had time for more. We got a little juice going, didn't we?"

When he pulled out of her and stood up, she involuntarily placed a hand between her legs and shut her knees as tightly together as she could. "Be at the restaurant at one o'clock," he told her, wiping himself with a soft towel and padding into the bathroom.

At one? Tanya could think of only one thing: One o'clock was less than three hours away. How would she be able to see Garrett in that time?

If she took a quick shower and dressed, she could go by the set. All she wanted was to feel Garrett holding her—just for a few minutes—just holding her, temporarily erasing Norman. She counted on having Margi put her hair into an elegant French roll and having Denny do her makeup.

At the studio, she told her limo driver to wait. She might be an hour or longer, but he had to wait. He nodded. He was the third driver that month. Norman had fired the others for protecting their mistress's whereabouts. Now Norman had wised up. He was paying this new driver elegantly to follow only his, not Tanya's, directions.

The set was virtually empty. A technician informed her they had broken early for lunch. Her heart raced. She wore no makeup. Her freshly washed, air-dried hair was a wild mess. And Garrett. Where was he? She had to tell him what she feared. She had to make him promise that he would help her get away from Norman. She had to make him promise that he still loved her. He would. She knew he would.

The technician was moving cable across the stage. "Did Mr. Gage go to lunch as well?" she asked.

The technician shrugged his shoulders. "Try his dressing room, Tanya" was the reply.

The portable dressing rooms were a trailer outside the soundstage. She hurried past her own door, not noticing with any pride her own name. Garrett's door was next, and she knocked with one hand while turning the knob with the other. Laughter was the first sound to hit her and there, upon the short couch, were Garrett with his girlfriend, Brenda, upon his lap, laughing over some hysterical joke.

Though they both looked surprised at the intrusion, mirth glowed in their eyes. Brenda, who had dark, blunt cut hair and was about Tanya's age, gave him a quick kiss on the cheek and slid off his lap. "Hi, Tanya," she said merrily.

Garrett immediately saw the distress on Tanya's face. Emotional strain had pushed her to the edge. "What's up?" he asked her, keeping a protective hand on Brenda's knee.

"Do you need me to leave?" asked Brenda, without an ounce of suspicion.

"Don't leave," he said quickly. "Tanya, come on in and shut the door."

But Tanya couldn't move. It was obvious Garrett cared for Brenda. He had never lied and told Tanya he cared for *her*. She was the other woman, a throwaway. "Could I talk to you a moment alone?" she asked, her voice small and pitiful.

He looked at his girlfriend, who said, "It's all right, sweetie pie," then made her way to the door.

"Wait for me outside," he told her. "We'll walk up to the commissary together."

"Hope everything's all right," Brenda said understandingly to Tanya.

The door shut behind Brenda. They heard her step down to the asphalt. Tanya rushed to Garrett, but he held her at arm's length. "Shhh," he hissed a warning. "I don't want Brenda to hear a word."

"You've got to help me," she said desperately. "I've got to get away from Norman. He's going to make me go crazy if I don't." Her entire head twitched as she spoke.

He pulled her into the hug she had been needing and protected her face against his chest. She trembled there, touching his hand and trying to move it to her breast.

"I can't do that with Brenda outside," he protested.

"You've got to help me. You've got to help me," she said senselessly, her hands gripping him.

"I don't know what I can do, Tanya," he said. "Norman's a powerful guy. A pretty tough one, too. I can't go up against him."

"Don't you want to? Wouldn't you do it for me?" she pleaded, her hand on his stomach, trying to reach under his trousers.

Firmly, he moved her hand and held it tightly in one of his. "I don't know, Tanya. Even if I was uninvolved, I don't know if I would go up against Norman to get you back."

She couldn't believe his words. Not only was he telling her that he wouldn't help her *now* because of a commitment to Brenda, but also that he didn't think he'd help her even if he were unattached.

"Don't you love me?" she cried, backing away from him.

He felt sorry for her, but he couldn't be dishonest. "I don't think so," he said. "I once had all the love for you in the world. I thought I could never stop loving you." He paused. "But it's gone. I don't know where it went, but it's gone."

"But you make love to me!"

"I fuck you," he corrected, "because I can't stay away from you. When you come on to me, I can't say no. You're like poison."

"I'm not poison!" she shrieked.

He moved toward her so fast that she didn't know what happened. His hand was over her mouth, preventing her from screaming again. Oh, God, he thought, why didn't I tell Brenda to go on to the commissary? He pushed Tanya backward so he could lock the door.

"Be quiet," he told her, trying to calm her down. "Be quiet."

And then he was overtaken by that impulse, the magnetic pull to be one with her. He felt himself losing control, his fingers breaking off the soil at the top of the cliff where he clung above the abyss of his desire for Tanya. He slid slowly, going downwards and gaining speed. His hand stayed over her mouth and he had her backed against the wall. She clawed at his pants and loosed him. In another second, he was under her skirt, inside her and driving her against the wall. In a few more seconds, it was over. They came together, shuddering turbulently, their passion wetly spent.

"I've got to go," he said, reaching for a roll of paper towels. He hated her for what she did to him. He left the dressing room after running a brush through his hair and wiping his mouth with the back of his hand.

Tanya made her way to Denny's makeup table and sat before the mirror. She picked up a large powder brush, but only held it and stared at herself. Garrett wouldn't help her. Somehow, she knew he would continue to use her, but he wouldn't help her. And she knew she would let him use her anytime he wanted.

She felt hands on her shoulders and saw Denny's kindly smile. "You look like hell," he said.

"I've got to meet Norman for lunch," she said in a daze.

Denny nodded. "Here, lean back. I'll make you beautiful. Margi will come in a minute and do your hair. Don't worry, Tanya, don't worry."

He reassured her, and she eased under his skillful hands. Could he guess what was wrong? Did he know? Did everyone know about her affair with Garrett? Did everyone see that Garrett didn't really care?

She was Norman's wife. That had been her decision. Garrett was right. She couldn't go back in time and change things. Her heart beat strangely, nervously, like a bird's in a warm breast, a drowning bird who could hear only the strange heartbeat and feel only the icy sluice of water that it was being held under.

The rainy night broke to a very wet morning. In Oregon, the frequent rain made everything green—lush greens backed with grays of barks and dirt and sky and puddles. Los Angeles was just dully gray, having nothing to do with nature. The coastline was socked in with heavy drizzle. The pavement was dull slate; the freeway a haze of mist spit out by tires.

His was practically the only motorcycle driving in the disagreeable weather. The cars were backed up, crawling between zero and five miles per hour. On the motorcycle, he could drive between the lanes of stopped traffic—a common L.A. habit in good weather. But most people were too chickenshit to drive bikes in the rain. They were fair-weather boys. But then, so were most of the people in the Southland, who were used to consistent, "beautiful" weather day in and day out, year after year.

Will found Los Angeles weather as monotonous and trying as weaving the bike in and out of the damn traffic. He hadn't planned on staying more than a week. It was so hard to get away from L.A. What the hell was he doing back here?

It was because of Candy. He couldn't live in the big trees—where the rain brought out every smell of the land and laid a hypnotically soft veil of quiet on the day—because it always reminded him of Candy. And her long, black straight hair. And the way her jeans hung on her hip bones and snugly clothed her thin, delicate thighs. And the way she used to put her arms around his waist and hold on when they rode together on the bike. He'd never taken any risks with her. Never.

It was just one of those things that had happened. And it had happened in Oregon.

So it was better to be away. And be working. He didn't say much to anyone on the set, but he worked real hard. He did his job, doubling for Garrett Gage. Once, the actor had been condescendingly friendly, believing that, although they could not find another actor to play Frank, stuntmen were a dime a dozen.

Will didn't figure the actor's ego was any of his business, so he let it slide. It seemed he had known actors with enormous egos for most of his life. He preferred the company of the camerman, Tony Keene, who enjoyed partying and didn't try to hide that fact. Will appreciated that Tony was not a plastic, Hollywood type. They shared a great sense of humor about most of the other people on the crew and in the cast who took themselves seriously, like they were all so fucking important.

That damned attitude. It reminded him of Graham. That was the way Graham was—important. And everyone that worked for Maddox Productions treated Graham that way, so now he thought he was God.

Will had a hard time respecting anyone who thought he was better than everyone else. So he stayed clear of most of the crew, talking to his mother every now and then, thankful he had not run into Graham. Fortunately, Graham was off doing the important job of running the company and had hired other people to run the actual productions.

Will resented the fact that the main reason he had left

L.A. six years before was to escape Graham's hostility. He remembered one time when his mother had first met Graham, and Graham had mimicked the Texas accents that she and the boy had. "Y'all need to go potty 'fore we leave?" Graham had just been jesting, but Will could still see the embarrassment on his mother's face.

That very night, Will had prayed (because in those days Ruby had taught him to say his prayers) that the unacceptable twang would go away. People from California didn't talk like that. He wanted all the kids in the first grade to think he was from California. And, even more, he wanted Graham to like his mother, because Graham seemed to make some of the stress in her face relax, though sadness still haunted her big eyes.

But nobody can make pain go away inside of another person. It sort of has to leave on its own. One day you realize that the pain's a little less than it was and you know that whoever said "only time can heal" was right.

Will didn't work on a soundstage very often. Usually, they called him out for the flashy location stuff. It was a chore to get his meaty Harley through the guards at the studio gates. Those guys took themselves even more seriously than old Graham. Whenever Will had to come to the lot, he personally told Ms. Sondra to have a drive-on pass ready for him at the gate, 'cause he didn't want to have to fuck with the guards.

The first time he told her that, she looked loftily at him and said, "You've got to be kidding."

"I ain't."

"Ask the second assistant to do it for you, please."

"No dice, lady. I trust you, 'cause you're the one in charge. You think I'm going to trust these other jerks . . . I mean, folks? Come on. And you know those fucking guards. They like to make trouble for a guy like me. They'd all be cops, except they don't have the guts."

She had nodded and agreed, and she and Will had a silent understanding.

On the soundstage, he never quite knew what to do until they needed him. He made his way to the easy-to-find boxes of donuts and the coffeepot, and hung out in that general vicinity. And watched.

Sondra came up and filled a Styrofoam cup. "I can't believe you rode your bike in this rain."

"Keeps ya healthy," said Will, without humor.

"I suspected you were crazy," she said. "Now I know for sure you are."

"Does that bother you?"

"I couldn't care less," she replied, her tone of voice giving nothing away.

He couldn't tell if she cared or not.

He liked the way her face was aging. She was in her mid-thirties and most of the skin was still taut. Only the lines around her eyes and into her cheek, at the corners of her mouth, were pronounced. People call them laugh lines, though it was hard to tell when that girl ever cracked one. He decided to try to make her laugh. Just to see her forget all that anger that was so accessible in her. Her anger was irritating. So visible.

Why should her anger affect him at all? Did it remind him too much of himself?

"You're up next," she said, and walked away from him.

He was doubling for a fight with a man twice his size. They had spent the previous day blocking and rehearsing under the watchful eye of Arnold. The stunt coordinator had them swinging at each other in a set designed as a laboratory. Today, the special effects people were adding a blaze to the glassware, and stages of the fight were to be filmed as different parts of the lab were torched. The edited effect would be an entire lab burning. The reality was that each shot was done separately.

Will did the fighting, and they brought in Garrett for close-ups at different angles while the fire burned behind him. The work was intense and exhausting, and when lunch break came, Will did not have the stomach for food. He found a prop couch off to the side of the set, lay down on it, and shut his eyes. He didn't want to sleep, only rest.

When the crew returned from the commissary, Sondra brought Will a can of pop and a sandwich.

He looked at it and grinned. "Tuna, my favorite. How did you know?"

"Guessed," she said flatly.

As he watched the setup for the afternoon's shoot, he felt a presence near him. A compelling energy that made him turn his head. Graham was standing ten feet away, talking with the director. Graham didn't look as though he'd aged at all since Will had last seen him. Success and money were what kept the man healthy. Will could not look back at the stage, could not turn his eyes from Graham, even though he would have preferred not speaking to him. So far, Graham had not acknowledged him.

But then, the cold, intelligent eyes came up, searching quickly across the faces of the busy crew, halting on the lanky stuntman. Graham left Richard in the middle of a sentence, walked up to Will, and stood his ground.

Will extended a courteous hand. "How are you, Graham?"

Graham ignored the hand and said, "There's just one thing I want you to know, and that is that you wouldn't be on this show if it weren't for your mother."

The bastard, thought Will. Heads had turned and were watching the public humiliation.

"I'll tell you what, Graham," said Will, equally as bold, his hand bravely in front of him. "*I* wouldn't do it if it weren't for Ruby." His voice implied that he was doing Graham a favor. "Sorry you don't feel like being on friendlier terms."

Will knew it would do no good to aggravate himself. He had an afternoon's work ahead of him. He put a lid on his emotions and smiled at Graham. Probably the first smile he could remember giving anyone—except his mother—on purpose in many months. Graham wanted him to flinch, to back down. But Will stood calmly and didn't move his eyes from Graham's.

As Graham turned back to Richard, Will added, "You're looking good, Graham. Really working at it, I see."

Will felt someone tugging his sleeve. It was Sondra. She looked worried. "We need you over here," she said.

She led him to the other side of the set, out of sight of

Graham, where she released his sleeve. She looked at her hand as though it had acted of its own free accord. She summoned a smile for Will. "He's not one of my favorite people, either."

"It goes back a long time," remarked Will, by way of explanation. "A really long time."

"He doesn't like you."

"He hates me."

"Why?"

"He hates me because of my father."

"He's not your father?"

"Stepfather. He's never met my real dad."

"What about you? How long has it been since you've seen your real dad?"

"Not since we left Texas. Nearly thirty years ago."

"How's Bob?" asked Denny.

"He's been working a lot of overtime," Margi replied without much emotion. She was methodically scratching the back of her neck with a bristle brush.

"Miss him?"

"Sure, I guess so."

She had been aloof, bitchier than usual, and more opinionated. Denny thought these were signs that she was not getting enough of "the good stuff," which was what Margi, quoting Bob, called sex.

"Is he making good money?" asked Denny.

"I guess so. Mr. Maddox had Dillon Hughes call a couple of weeks ago and ask Bob to do some consulting on a feature they're building sets for." Margi hung her head upside down and began brushing the underside of her short black hair. It was a soothing thing to do and, with her eyes shut, reminded her of when her mother used to brush her hair as a kid. It calmed her.

"Consulting? That's great. Aren't you excited for him?"

"I guess. It just seems he hasn't been around much."

"I hope I haven't had much to do with that," said Denny, knowing that his presence at the Owenses' house had caused extra tension between Margi and Bob.

"It's not you," insisted Margi. "It's Graham Maddox. He thinks employees should jump every time he wants them to."

"I'd think Bob would be happy to do consulting. He's been in the business for years and knows a lot about how sets are constructed."

"Sure he does. But there is a time and a place for that. He doesn't have to run off on the weekends. He doesn't know how to say, 'No, this is a weekend and I can't make it.' Nobody ever says no to Graham Maddox."

Denny thought it was odd how she found someone else to blame for her problems with Bob. She was so used to everything going right that if there were rough times, it couldn't be her; it had to be an outside influence. She flipped her head upright and her hair stuck out in a fluff. She got a can of stiff spray and applied a heavy dose. She was sure in a peculiar mood.

"Bob's tired a lot," she said.

"Well, I hope it isn't because of me." Denny was wiping off sticks of eyeliner, pencil shadow, and tubes of lipstick with a tissue.

He had one of the cleanest, most organized makeup boxes Margi had ever seen. "It isn't because of you," she said. "Bob can learn to be understanding about my friends. I'm sure understanding about his. You've had your share of hard times lately."

Didn't he know too well? He'd been spending his weekends at mini-golf tournaments on Saturdays and condo hunting on Sundays. It had become a Sunday pastime with him—driving to a new area and going to all the open houses. Sundays were too lonely just hanging around the apartment. He missed reading the paper till noon and fixing a lazy brunch for Jeff and himself.

Weekday evenings he went to the mini-golf course and practiced his putting, but it seemed so futile. He hated sitting in his apartment, because no matter what music he played or how loud the TV set was, he was on edge waiting for the phone to ring. If Jeff actually called, he didn't know what he'd say. Jeff had left two messages when Denny had been at work. They were simply "just-wanted-to-say-hi" types. Denny had not been able to call back.

Now, he prayed that the phone would ring . . . and that it would not.

"That guy is such a jerk," said Margi.

Denny looked around to see whom she was talking about. He saw Martin Maddox, a cute kid with a perfect ass and pretty lips. "Is he?" replied Denny.

"Daddy finally gave him a job 'cause he got tired of the kid asking for money all the time. As successful as Graham is, you'd think his kids would live up to his image." She played with her lighter before putting the flame to the end of her cigarette. "*My* kids certainly don't have everything handed to them."

"Wouldn't Ruby give Martin a job?"

"I think she's disgusted with him," said Margi. "He's his daddy's favorite. She seems to go for Will, that biker-turned-stuntman we see around here sometimes. He's her son by her first marriage."

Margi's gossip amazed Denny. She knew about the lives of everyone on the set. He went over to her, lifted her hair, and peered at her ears.

"What are you doing?" she queried.

"They don't look so big," he joked.

"What's that supposed to mean?" She was reluctant to smile.

"They sure hear everything."

"It's not like a person has to go overboard to catch all this. But you never pay any attention—except to that blonde."

"Tanya? She's a good girl. Married to the wrong guy."

"Shit. She's a princess and a user."

"Actresses are temperamental."

"You can hardly call her an *actress*," said Margi, with a disgusted shiver of her shoulders. "I get so tired of the prima donnas in this business. *You* love them. You *live* for them. I don't know what you find so goddamned attractive about a spoiled princess."

"Actresses need a little understanding, that's all. It's hard to put your emotions on the line every day and reveal them to all the world."

As a response, Margi sighed. He was really too much. Why was it that all the men she knew had become so hard to talk to? Maybe it was just a phase they were going through. The problem with princesses was that they were not very sexy, and she could not imagine a man preferring a virginesque princess to a sexy total woman. Except, maybe, for Denny. He didn't want women, anyway (even though lately he'd been talking as if he wanted to take a few out to dinner.) A sexy woman would be his undoing. Margi knew she was sexy. Sexy was the code she lived by. If she believed in cheating on her husband, she'd probably seduce Denny and give him a run for his money—just to see if she could do it. But she was monogamous. She enjoyed it when other men looked at her, but what really thrilled her was thinking how envious they were of Bob—because he had her and they didn't. She and Bob talked out their fantasies. They were mutually satisfied. Until lately. And Bob with all his goddamned overtime and being so goddamned tired all the time. If he was angry with her about something, why the hell didn't he just come out and say it?

She didn't see the studio guard motion Denny out the door of the soundstage, but when he returned, she saw worry in his face.

"What's wrong?" she asked, sensing danger.

"You've got to come," he said.

Panic seized her throat. "What's wrong?" she repeated, on her feet and following Denny to the door.

Outside, Denny said, "I want you to take it easy. There's been an accident."

"Bob!" she cried. "Where's Bob?!" She grabbed the guard's sleeve. "Where is he? Is he all right?"

"He's had a fall," the guard told her. "He was working high on the scaffolding over soundstage six. He's already left in an ambulance."

"Take me to him," she said, fear numbing her.

"I'll take you," said Denny. "Let me go in and tell Sondra, so she can get someone to take over for us."

"Is he alive?" Margi asked the guard, refusing to yield the

grip on his sleeve.

The guard hesitated. "Yes, ma'am. He was when they loaded him in the ambulance."

Chapter 9

"You know, Denny, in a land where there is no winter, I could forget what frost is. Los Angeles never freezes."

"Believe me, Glory, when you see it again, you'll know what it is."

She laughed, squatted down on the green-felted dogleg, and squinted over the top of her blue golf ball to the hole. It was a move she had learned in pool, though, quite honestly, she couldn't say she was too hot at that game, either. The green surface was what put her in mind of pool, and then, the shade was really more like the frog suit she had worn in a second-grade play.

She hunkered over the ball and tried to push herself upright, but she lost her balance and fell backward. She sat in her blue jeans and sweater, trying not to laugh too hard. She knew how seriously Denny took the game.

He stretched out a hand and helped her to her feet. Behind them, two Oriental couples waited with stoic faces that belied any impatience. It was night and this was the seventeenth hole. The Orientals looked like they wanted to go home, however, they also looked like they would finish the game first. No quitting for them on the second-to-last hole.

"I'm getting serious now," said Glory, not at all serious, but trying to keep a straight face. The course par was 54. Denny had a very respectable 28. Glory had stopped counting when her score topped 100.

"This is a lot of fun," she said, "but do you think we should let them go first?" She indicated the two couples.

"No," said Denny, "just concentrate."

So for the next eight impacts of her club upon the little blue ball, until it rolled its little blue self into never-never land at the end of the course, she did her best to concentrate. What she said was true: This was the most fun she'd had in a long time. With Denny, she could be herself, and she didn't worry about making mistakes or not doing things right.

He had found her sorta hiding out near the set when they were shutting down for the day, sorta caught her kinda looking at Tony, who was joking with the director of photography and the best boy. She was furiously chewing on her nails—her real ones. Her fake ones had disappeared a week before and she had neglected to reglue them on. She hadn't cared. Tony had barely said two words to her since the night he hadn't shown up at her house for dinner. She felt rotten about that, and even more rotten with herself for not having the courage to go up to him and ask him why he had stood her up. It was rotten feeling rotten, having to hide behind a set to watch a man you loved and knew you shouldn't but couldn't stop yourself.

Denny had taken her hand from her mouth and had admonishingly clicked his tongue against his teeth. "Don't do this to yourself," he said. "And don't stand here watching him. You're much too nice a girl to worry yourself sick over him. Why don't you come out to dinner with me tonight?"

She looked into his blue eyes and thin face, which smiled warmly at her. She had a good friend, though she'd never realized it until that minute. She was usually worried that Margi was talking to Denny about "Glory this and Glory that and Glory annoys the hell out of me," and that Denny went along with everything the hairdresser said. Margi was very short-tempered with her, and Glory could be damned if she knew why.

But here was Denny saying no to nail-biting and asking her out to dinner. Her first reaction was to tell him she couldn't go. She gave "going home to feed the cat" as an excuse.

His face lit up. "You have a cat, too?"

"Yes. Why, do you?"

"Big ol' gray mama. But she's got a lot of food in a dish at home. I'll follow you to your place and you can feed the cat."

She couldn't possibly say no again. She admitted to herself she had a few reservations about having dinner with a gay man, mainly because she had never been out with a homosexual before and was panicky because she didn't know what it would be like or what she could talk about. She thought of what she had to eat at home and remembered that she hadn't been eating there much. She hadn't felt like it since Tony had stood her up. She just didn't want to cook. Cooking anything reminded her of that night and the rolled roast that she had worked so hard on. Every time she thought of it, the memory brought tears to her eyes.

She'd sorta gotten out of the habit of eating in the evenings, sorta didn't have an appetite. So when Denny suggested that they shoot a few holes of mini-golf to get their appetites up, she said, "That sorta sounds like fun."

Denny drove with the top down on the blue Alfa. He was delighted to have the blonde sitting there with him, the wind tossing her hair and easing the pain of her broken heart from her face. He didn't dare mention Tony, because he didn't want her to get that look on her face like she had bitten something hard and broken a filling. He also didn't dare mention that he could do a lot with her makeup, because it was always a sensitive subject with women.

Glory was cute, but a little experimentation with her makeup could make her a very chic girl. She needed a new look. Make-overs affect the actions and attitudes of some women, bringing out assertion, grace, and tranquility in their personalities.

He'd give a million bucks if he could pull up at a stop light and see Jeff in the next car. Glory had an innocence to her face that would make any hard-bitten sexual cynic gnaw in contempt. She would make Jeff think twice about what he'd abandoned. Denny only wished he possessed the sexual stirrings for this good-looking chick that an onlooker would assume were there.

"You're very sweet," she told him as he parked the car. "You're being nice to me, and I know you've recently gone through a split-up, too."

"Shhh," he replied. "Let's not talk about that. We're here to cheer you up. And doing that, I guarantee, will cheer me up."

The Orientals might have been crowding them a little on the last two holes, but Denny was not giving them an inch. Let them wait, he thought. A few strong glances in their direction and they backed off. They were a whole lot easier to dissuade than a wrestler-bodied construction worker with four kids and a pregnant wife in tow. On a weekend, a man like that was bound to be short-tempered.

Denny took her to a quiet Frenchified cafe, which had European maps on the wall, accented waitresses who smoked pot out back, and excellent light cuisine.

Glory pulled out her comb. "I've got to do something with my hair. I can never do what Margi told me to. I look a mess."

"You look fine."

"Don't be kind," she smiled.

"I'm not. You look wild and that's good."

She sat across the small table from him, still indecisive about whether or not she felt comfortable with Denny. He was like a brother. He was terribly sensitive. He was almost as old as Tony, but it really didn't matter at all. She ordered a salad with romaine lettuce, chicken breast, avocado, walnuts, sesame seeds, and house dressing.

She held a self-conscious hand to her hair. "Margi would make fun of this you know," she said, indicating the mop of frizz.

"To hell with what Margi would think," he said. "She doesn't know everything."

"She knows everything about what goes on on the set."

He couldn't deny that. "But less since Bob's accident."

"Poor Margi," admitted Glory. "She spends a lot of time at the hospital with him. I don't know how she manages to concentrate when she's at work."

"Margi's a doer," said Denny. "She'd be much more neurotic if she wasn't working. It keeps her mind occupied."

"It sounds like a horrible accident. Painful. Falling right on his groin."

"He still can't walk. They've operated twice to sew up ruptures."

"It would hurt, wouldn't it?" asked Glory, tears filling her eyes. She was sorry she had thought something bad about Margi.

Denny nodded. The thought of Bob's injury—from a freak accident—made Denny shudder. Just hearing about the fall would make any man place his hands over his balls to instinctively protect them.

"Did you go by Margi's house?" asked Glory.

"She asked me not to," said Denny. "She's asked me to help her out at work, help her think things out."

To Glory, Bob's accident was so horrid that it made her own problems seem trivial. But trivial or not, she couldn't get Tony off her mind. She didn't understand why he did the things to her that he did, and she discussed it with Denny.

"Because," Denny told her, "he's an alcoholic. He's used to failure. Just when he's about to get somewhere, he gets to drinking too much and fails again. He's comfortable with failure. A lot of people are that way. He's afraid of taking risks. If he did, he might succeed, so he sabotages himself before he can."

"I wish I could help him," said Glory. "I wish I could make him change."

"He has to want to change himself," said Denny wisely. "You can't do it for him. But meanwhile, don't go running yourself down. Get on to somebody else. You're much too bright and pretty to waste your time waiting for him."

Denny knew she wanted to believe him. When they walked back to his car, she held his hand. He put it to his lips a long moment before he opened her door.

"Thank you for dinner," she said.

"You're welcome."

He pulled up the top, secured it, started the engine, and switched on the heater. The radio played easy-listening sounds of the Beatles' "Yesterday." Glory tilted her head back on the seat and shut her eyes. She was warm. She was fed. She didn't feel alone.

"I don't want to go home," she said.

The drive to Beachwood Canyon was like silent water slipping over very smooth stones—clear, easy, untroubled. It had been many years since Denny had brought a woman home to his bed. But it was all right. She made him feel not so alone.

Ruby awoke early. It was a cold Sunday morning and Graham slept heavily beside her. She vaguely remembered him coming in about three, but had not paid much attention to it and had gone back to sleep. They slept on opposite sides of an extra-firm, king-sized mattress, which relayed so little of a bedmate's movements that they might as well have been in separate rooms.

She slipped on a robe, made a cup of coffee in the kitchen, and went into the living room where she could sit and watch the sunlight creep over the lip of the gulch's shoulders with steady, warming, renewing fluidity.

The gulch was peaceful as she sat, legs drawn under her, in a huge armchair that she had pulled to the window. Sometimes she saw deer early in the morning, browsing contentedly and safely through the undergrowth, so she waited and hoped they would come this morning. Looking down the wild, secluded canyon of sharp-thorned natural growth, it was hard to imagine they were, in reality, situated so close to the miles and miles and miles of houses stretching in every direction over greater Los Angeles.

She didn't feel like reading or working; she just wanted to sit and let her mind go where it would. Most of the time, she mused on or worried about the kids. It did no good to worry about Graham; he did what he pleased and she had given up trying to keep him in line. His infidelities did not hurt her because she would not let them.

She had been hurt once by a cheating man. It would never happen again.

She had been young-young when she had fallen for Matt

Long, fifteen or so when he had first walked into her life. Her older sister, Sally, had brought him home to noon Sunday dinner, after he had helped her fix a flat alongside a dusty Texas road. He was mighty glad to say grace at the family table; it was obvious he hadn't eaten a good meal in days.

He was traveling through in a 1947 Ford pickup, looking for roughneck work. Tall and lanky, about twenty years old, he had a bang of brown hair that fell into his dancing eyes. He had a laughing way about him that made everyone feel at ease. He had plenty of winks for Ruby, and she kept looking to see if he was winking at Sally—'cause he might be a flirt—but he didn't seem to be paying too much attention to the older sister.

Ruby's dad and Matt hit it off right away, with her dad promising to make a few calls to see if anyone was hiring. He suggested that Matt spend a couple of nights with them, till he got a job.

Early every morning, Ruby would tiptoe to the top of the staircase and peer over the bannister at the young man sleeping on the couch. She didn't ever remember seeing anyone so handsome in her life. Just looking at him made her twitch inside and filled her with an unexplainable anguish. She had never before known what it was like to *want* someone—but *want* Matt Long is what she did. She had *liked* boys in school, but they had never done this to her. (She would later describe her reaction to Matt as chemical attraction. Later than that, she forgot she *could* feel that way. Later still, she didn't even care.)

There was Matt—working regular, living at a rooming house, and coming over steady for Sunday dinner. Ruby took such a sudden special interest in cooking that her mother's eyebrows raised and she warned, "He's a rambler. He's charming, but, oh boy, gal, watch out for a man like that!"

However, Ruby was sure Matt felt the same chemistry as she did. They'd go for walks on Sunday afternoon, and he'd tell her how tired he was of being poor and how he was going to make lots of money. He knew people that had made money and it had changed their whole lives. He hardly knew them anymore, but what they had become was exactly what he was striving for.

And, of course, he'd have her out for drives in his old pickup and finally persuaded her to give in. It's hard not to when a handsome two-hundred-pound man that you're madly in love with is cooing over the top of you with his hands on your breasts and his mouth whispering over yours, "I want you, baby. Be my baby. I'll take real good care of you."

He liked her drawings and was real impressed when she won a scholarship to a two-year college sixty miles away. He visited her every weekend for the first month she was gone, then showed up and told her she had to marry him 'cause he couldn't live without her. She hadn't wanted to give up her art schooling, but then she got pregnant and had no choice. He had been a good provider in those days and seemed real content to come home every night to Ruby and the baby, whom he named Will after his great-grandfather, a pioneer Texan.

After a while, it seemed to Ruby that Matt Long did a hell of a lot of talking about how he was going to spend all his money when he got it. Now, a little daydreaming is understandable, but a continuous barrage about money they didn't even have began to drive her crazy. Then, about the time he started saying hurtful, mean things about how she and the kid were holding him back, she got pregnant again with the little girl they ended up calling Belinda.

She'd go home for Sunday dinners with the two kids tow and no Matt. He would kiss her lengthily as she was leaving, and make some excuse she could repeat to her parents, but which she could not remember three days later. She wished like hell she hadn't given up her art scholarship. Matt was running with what he thought was a "fast set," and he told her in plain English, "You can't come. You won't fit in."

She felt like hell about the whole mess, and began to realize that the only thing they shared was their chemical attraction for each other. The way he felt about her seemed to embarrass him. He'd try sleeping on the couch but, in the middle of the night, he would come to bed and pull her into his arms, because he'd been lying out there thinking about her and couldn't keep away. But it didn't hold him.

He'd go away on weekends with his friends. "You can't bring kids along on a deal like this, hon," he'd say.

"Let's get a babysitter," she replied.

"We can't afford one of those."

"But we can afford you running off all the time and spending lots of money on these so-called friends? Who are you trying to impress?" She wanted to shout out her anger, but the words always came quietly, because she loved him so much, it hurt to yell.

So, she would drive out to the prairie with the kids, bringing along an easel, canvas and brushes, and would paint the vast, barren expanse that did not seem nearly as endless as the loneliness within her.

She shouldn't have been surprised when she returned one day to a deserted house. Any furniture of value was gone, and there was a note from Matt explaining that he couldn't live with them anymore and he was filing divorce papers.

Absolute desolation set in. She didn't even know where to find him. A week of searching followed, with the kids in the back seat, a horrible week when she forgot what day it was and forgot to change her dress. She finally found him with a very wealthy young widow in a large house.

"What'd you come here for, Ruby?" he asked.

"You're my husband. You've got kids to feed."

"Look, Ruby. You can't squeeze blood out of a rock. I'm getting nowhere with you. You are a female of no class whatsoever. We live in a dive. I can't stand coming home to it. I wasn't cut out to be a father."

Her voice was bitter. "What the hell's that supposed to mean? I 'got no class'?"

"Exactly that. If I stayed with someone like you, I'd get drug down so fast, I'd never be able to crawl out."

She was standing on the doorstep to that big mansion. She didn't see another face around the place. No one peering out. She wished she had a pistol. She would have pulled the trigger. She was sure of it.

She was sure of it thirty years later, as she looked down the cloistered canyon from a house Matt Long could never have provided for her. She had never heard of him again but guessed he was still around somewhere in Texas, leeching off rich folks for as long as they were amused by him. But the wealthy are wise and spongers do not last long, especially not with Texans.

However, Matt's words still galled her. *He* thought she had had no class, that she wasn't good enough for him. The bastard! She had been able to love once. To care deeply. Now, it seemed as if she'd merely gone through the motions of marriage for the last twenty-six years, her surface affections sufficing, while her heart and all its real pain was back wandering around on a Texas prairie, unable to find its way home to her.

But, oh, she had gained status. She was much *better* now than Matt Long. She was better to start with, but for different reasons. Now she had everything Matt had dreamed of. He had been shallow. She had become shallow to prove she could do it. And she had done it. She was a queen of extraordinary material possessions and social register. But what did it prove . . . finally?

She looked down the canyon, where dew waited in the shadows for sunbeams, and wished the deer would come and feed. Oh, why didn't they come?

Garrett studied Ruby's painting of the Texas prairie and felt he knew the state, even though he'd never been there. He didn't think the painting was all that good; but it was real. He continued watching it because it was the only thing in Mrs. Maddox's office, besides Tanya, that was of any real interest.

The blond actress sat primly in a chair, her back straight, her knees together, her hair in a knot on top of her head. She waited, as did he, for Mrs. Maddox, who had told them she had something important to discuss.

Looking at the painting was the only way Garrett could avoid Tanya's eyes. He felt them boring into him, transfixing him. He was uneasy about the spell she cast over him. And spell it was, for what else could explain the way he was drawn to her against his better judgment, entangling himself in her hair and body until their passion was exhausted?

He didn't trust her; he didn't trust himself around her. She had hurt him once. He wished Mrs. Maddox would come, because being alone with Tanya made him aware of his body urging him to take the blonde in his arms.

Once he touched her, it was impossible to stop. It was the most difficult thing about acting with her. How could the rest of the cast and crew miss their attraction for each other? It was as if he and she were in the same whirlpool, being inseparably sucked down together. How could an audience miss it? Or her husband, for that matter? Garrett wished he could make it go away, that damnable helplessness at being drawn back into a black tunnel swollen with floodwaters.

Yet, when he made love to her, there were dual sensations: the dark tunnel he was whipped through; and a heavenly golden light in which he floated. This dualism was unfair; he didn't know which sensation was the believable one.

Tanya stared at her hands, wishing she could speak to Garrett, but knowing that the walls had ears. She could not get him off her mind. Under her dress, her nipples were erect. The heat between her legs restlessly caressed her groin. Only Garrett's touch could ease the ache.

Tanya was annoyed with Ruby. She and Garrett waited for the lady producer like two children. It was the end of the day. She was tired. Unfortunately, she had a feeling that this meeting was not about the storyline Maddox Productions had planned for *Motive*'s Frank and Janet characters in the upcoming season.

Garrett seemed so resigned that he and Tanya would never be together again. "You're asking the impossible," he had told her the last time they had been together. "You're married to Norman, and he's an *extremely* jealous man. I'm engaged to Brenda. I don't want to hurt her."

Engaged? The word stabbed her. Now some other woman would be getting all the benefits of Garrett's success, after it had been herself, Tanya, that had lived with him through the rough years. He was engaged to a woman and what had they between them? Devotion. That was all. Not love. Not passion. Devotion. He felt he owed Brenda. He couldn't "hurt" her. What about his own feelings? The ones that lusted for Tanya? Wouldn't he have to be true to them? Maybe Brenda wouldn't be so eager to marry Garrett if she knew the truth.

But then, if Tanya told Brenda about the affair, she risked Norman's finding out. That was fearful.

If only the smolder in her groin would go away, it would be so much easier. Getting up, she moved behind Garrett, standing an inch away. He didn't flinch. She took his hand and pressed it against the hard rise of her pubic bone. At his touch, an involuntary moan came from her lips. She imagined if he pressed harder, the moisture she dripped would seep through her dress.

Ruby's heel sounded on the hardwood hallway outside the office for only an instant before she entered the room. The astonished look on Garrett's and Tanya's faces made them look pretty damn guilty. Ruby quickly, politely, dropped her eyes to her desk, scanning the mail and paper upon it, while her lead players found chairs.

What the hell was wrong with them? Had they no couth? Couldn't they keep their hands off each other, even in her office? She had chosen to talk with them because Graham had absolutely no finesse in matters like this. It peeved her that the problem was more out of hand than she had suspected.

"We have to talk about something serious," Ruby began, her voice grave, "that under normal circumstances I believe I should not interfere with. But *Motive* is my conception, my child, and I don't want to see it injured. It is common knowledge around the set that you two are having an affair."

Tanya gasped and shook her head. "That's not true," she said quickly, the denial vocalized before the brain had consciously told her to say it.

Garrett did not respond. Ruby's eyes flickered from actor to actress. "There are a number of complex reasons why your . . . uh . . . romance can not go on. One, of course, is the publicity, which, if mishandled, would ruin Frank's boy-next-door image. Another—as you are probably only too aware—is Tanya's husband."

It was out in the open. Ruby knew that they could not afford to have Tanya the twit withdrawn from the show and risk a drop in *Motive's* high ratings. Though the actress was under contract, her rich—and volatile—husband would not be afraid of any legal repercussions.

"So, on behalf of Maddox Productions, I've got to ask the two of you to cool it," said Ruby, using a professional voice that was the embodiment of a legal pact. "I know Garrett, especially, would have a lot to lose if the ratings went downhill. He's worked hard for what he's got now."

Garrett nodded in agreement. "I trust your judgment, Ruby," he said without reservation. "I'll do whatever is best for the show."

Tanya's jaw dropped. Both anger and tears fought to be the first released. "No!" she screamed, lunging at him with her fists. "You can't let it go like that! You can't! You can't! You don't even care!"

He held her at arm's length. She was wailing, out of her mind, unaware that anyone else was in the room.

"Tanya," said Ruby with well-wrought gentleness, "if *you* really love Garrett, I suggest you begin to make some compromises. And, you'd better watch out for yourself." Ruby debated bringing up the next point, then decided to hit Tanya with it because the blonde was acting like such a spoiled brat. "Norman specifically asked *Graham* to keep an eye on you. Obviously, your husband doesn't trust you. But Graham does not have time to baby-sit a tart who is so self-centered, she can't see the needs of others."

Tanya turned quickly, her eyes flaming in Ruby's direction. Garrett still held her wrists and she struggled, wanting him to let her go.

"You can't talk to me like that!" she screamed.

"Why not?" returned Ruby serenely. "It's true. If you want to *see* Garrett at all, you'd better mind your manners. If your contract suddenly expired and Janet had to go back to that time warp she came from, you'd be off the lot. Back with Norman. I seriously doubt that Garrett would risk coming after you."

Garrett remained motionless and wordless while Tanya wriggled, the tears refusing to pour from her eyes. Ruby certainly didn't mince words. And Tanya didn't like those words. Tough. Both Ruby and Garrett knew Tanya dreaded returning to a world where she was Norman's constant companion.

Ruby's secretary buzzed the intercom and announced the arrival of Tanya's limo. "I'll walk you out," Ruby told the actress. "I'm sure you understand my position. Sleep on it, and let's talk again when you're not so upset. I'm *not* doing this to put a wrench in your life, you know. I'm doing it to save my show."

When Ruby returned to her office, Garrett was thumbing through one of the daily trade papers. "I'm sorry she took it so badly," said Ruby, straightening her desk and getting ready to go home.

"She's a very unstable girl," said Garrett matter-of-factly.

"I don't like being that blunt, but Tanya wouldn't have listened to anything else. I want it clear between us"—and she paused to look directly into his eyes—"that I didn't want to meddle in your business. This was just an unusual case."

"I understand," said Garrett. "It couldn't have gone on anyway. I don't want to butt horns with Norman."

"I've been worried, though," continued Ruby. "Tanya's replaceable, you're not. When I first auditioned you, I knew you were special." She smiled and headed for the door.

"Going home?" asked Garrett, following her.

"Yes," she said, turning off the light.

"How about dinner first?"

His invitation surprised her. She had assumed he needed to go home to his fiancée. "All right," she replied leisurely. "Just let me call Graham and tell him I won't be home till later."

The beer in Will's hand was warm and flat. He wasn't in a

drinking mood, even though he'd agreed to go along with Joe to Spud's. Will had gained a certain respect at that establishment, evoking polite nods from most of the regular customers. The girls that hung out there could make no forays into the unknown land of sleeping with, or even talking with, him. His silence, in fact, was a draw. It created a mystery that made him even more attractive.

But he didn't care. The women of Spud's had absolutely no appeal. Biker chicks never had. They were too dumb and too willing to lay themselves on the line for their "old man." If these women didn't belong to somebody, they were open territory, allowing themselves to be used any way the men saw fit.

Will once again had drinking money and, though he was reluctant to admit it, he was not feeling as depressed as when Joe had dragged him back to L.A. Joe sat happily at Spud's, drinking beer and always finding a woman. Part of the reason that Will accompanied the small fellow to Spud's was that the dive was a place where Joe could invariably get laid if that's what he wanted.

Will stared at the huge plate glass window; it stared back its dim reflection of the contents of Spud's. Outside, the fall night was quite cool, the air not holding the heat like it did in summer. Beyond the window, out in the darkness, Will felt Candy looking in at him. She sat sideways on his bike, waiting, humming low, glancing to see when he was leaving, uncertain if she should enter, take his arm, and lead him out.

Take me for a ride, Will. Tell me how you are. Talk to me. Talk to me.

Will strode to Joe's side, tapped him on the shoulder, and asked, "Can you make it home all right?"

Joe nodded affirmatively, and a minute later the scooter was snaking up the winding pavement in the inky canyon. The sky above was starry. He wore a leather jacket, chaps, and gloves to prevent the cold, rushing air from cutting through. He headed toward the openness of the desert—where the two-lane blacktop dips twenty times per mile across washes and brittle vegetation haunts the black, forsaken landscape. Will's own solitariness was lost in the greater isolated expanse he rode through.

Where are you, Candy? I miss you, darlin'. Can't seem to stop missing you, yet I can't change a goddamned thing.

Candy was so damn pretty the first time he saw her. He'd gone to look at a chain saw for sale. When you're living where he was in Oregon, cutting timber is about the best way to earn a living. So he'd called about this ad in the paper for a saw and drove up to some guy's property. He turned out to be Candy's dad. Of course, Candy's dad didn't like Will at all, coming in there on a big motorcycle and ruffling up the chickens in the yard and stirring up dust.

Not that the yard was anything special. Candy's dad had bought five acres out of town, up in heavy timber, had dozed himself a road, and had cleared out enough trees to put in a trailer house. He'd finished a foundation for a real house, but he was the kind of guy who would probably never complete it. He wasn't very industrious. But God, oh, man, was he tough. Old tough logger. He saw Will as some city punk who didn't know a thing about the woods.

It was true, though. He was right. Candy's dad had seen enough people show up in that part of the country not knowing their ass from a hole in the ground. Pickups were all he cared for. They lived a good mile from the main road. He'd bought Candy's mom a big old American car that she'd had to learn not to get stuck in the muddy drive. That car was never clean. Will thought it must have driven that woman nuts, living out there in the woods and always being surrounded by huge trees and never seeing a view.

When Will first saw Candy, she held a two-year-old baby on her hip. You see a teenage girl like that and you assume that it's her kid. While her dad showed Will the chain saw, she stood in the yard, near a massive stack of uncut wood and a beat-up old shack that he stored stuff in, and watched.

The chain saw was big and heavy, with a thirty-six-inch bar. Will felt real cocky about it until he actually held it. Chain saws look so easy to use until they're running and about vibrating your arms off, and you realize you've got to hang on and cut trees for the next ten hours.

The saw ran okay and Will paid cash for it. But how the hell was he going to get it on his bike? Candy's dad just stood there laughing to himself. At the time, Will didn't know a thing about breaking down a saw, so he just patiently got out a bunch of rope and bungie cords and strapped it onto the back of the bike.

"You ought to put a hat on that damn rider," laughed Candy's dad. Will tried to ignore how ridiculous the whole thing looked. Candy later told him he should have just asked her dad to bring it to town in the truck.

Will lived in an ex-motel, the type that used to be a motel but now is rented as a mini-apartments. Oh, God. If he thought the dirt yard at Candy's dad's place was bad, it was nothing compared to the potholes right outside his own front door. The tenants had tried their damnedest to get the owner to put a load of gravel over the dirt, but the cheap bastard never had. The mud-bath rarely dried out. There was never enough sun between the rain. After a while, Will parked his motorcycle inside his room and bought an old cheap pickup to drive.

One Saturday, he went to the local laundromat to wash all the clothes he owned, which happened to be two weeks' worth, and was tuning in one of the two channels received in the valley on the national fixture of all laundromats, an ancient black-and-white TV, when a little two-year-old girl ran up to him.

He immediately knew who she was, which was weird, because he never paid attention to kids, couldn't have cared less about them. But he looked around because he knew where he had last seen *this* kid.

And there was Candy, with her long black hair reaching almost to her butt, carrying two giant sacks of laundry. She was driving her mom's car and she had three more giant sacks of clothes in it. Will followed her out and helped her carry them in. It turned out her dad had sunk a well up at their place, which gave them drinking and cooking water, but there was no septic system, so they used an outhouse and had to come to town to wash the clothes. Candy didn't seem to mind.

When he told her he thought her daughter was mighty cute, she laughed and told him the child was her sister. He breathed a sigh of relief and she laughed again. He thought later that it had been stupid of him to have then assumed she was single. In a town of that size, there are hardly ever any good-looking women, and when there are, they either get married in a big hurry or leave town.

Candy wanted to leave town. She and Will got to talking and she told him she did artwork. She was jealous, in a real nice way, that he was from L.A., but he reassured her there was nothing wonderful about the place.

Will had never been in love before. He and Candy moved about fifty miles away, where they rented a farmhouse in a flat valley. They were happy. Will finally convinced her to ride behind him on the bike, and on weekends they'd go on long trips. Miles and miles and miles. When she wanted to stop, she had a signal of scratching him behind the left ear. She started doing it so she could get off and pee, but the meaning changed, and she'd give him the signal if she wanted him to stop and make love to her. They were lucky if it wasn't raining. But Candy loved doing it in the rain. Making love was always so easy between them. They didn't have to work hard at it. It was just real natural.

In that part of the country, it seemed like most people got married. Will had never paid too much attention to it until one day Candy said, "Don't you think it's time we were getting married?"

She wanted the wedding in a church and she wanted a big reception outside with a roast pig on a spit and people dancing and lots of beer. Her folks were there and nobody asked Will where his were. They minded their own business. People there respected that a man's business was his own. There were over a hundred people at the reception, what with their friends and Candy's family. And people brought along all kinds of potluck dishes. The band played country and rock, so everyone got to dancing.

Candy was so pretty in her white wedding gown. Will had never thought he'd marry a girl in a white gown. Because he was such a rebel, he figured if he ever did marry, it would be in front of a justice of the peace. But then, when the girl you love really wants to get married in a church in a white gown, you just say, "Sure." Then you're surprised at how absolutely beautiful she is when you turn around to watch her come down the aisle.

As Candy walked down the aisle, she kept her eyes on Will's. Never before, anywhere in the world, had he seen such honesty. There wasn't a single lie in those eyes: her life was his.

People say a relationship changes after you take the vows—usually for the worse. But Candy and Will's got better. Will was still falling in love. More and more every day. He didn't want to stop with the boys to drink on his way home after work. He just wanted to get back to Candy.

She spent most of her days painting. He fixed up a studio for her. Sometimes she'd keep the door shut; sometimes she'd let him come in. She liked showing him what she'd done, but she'd never let him look at the whole thing until it was finished. Once, he told her that his mother used to paint. He remembered from when he was a kid that she painted landscapes. Candy preferred painting people. Will was always comfortable with Candy painting. It made her happy, and when you live with a happy person, you can't help but feel happy yourself.

It sounded corny to say they took it for granted, but damn if they didn't. There's no reason it couldn't have lasted forever. But it didn't. They say it never does. Nothing should have happened to that relationship . . . but it did. He still couldn't believe it, but it did.

And now he was alone.

Candy! Candy! My heart is crying. Where have you gone? Won't you come to me, wherever you are . . .

The breeze off the desert was dry, cold, and smelled of sage. He seemed to feel someone settle in behind him on the bike, warmly wrapping her arms around him, pressing her front against his back, leaning her head between his shoulders and shutting her eyes.

The hospital room was oppressive. Margi was pissed off. "Bob, you didn't land on your mouth, you know. Why won't you talk to me?"

Bob did not open his mouth to speak. It lay inert, hidden under his huge mustache, which made his usually robust face seem even more gaunt. His eyes were dull, unlaughing. His arms lay lifelessly at his sides on top of the bedclothes. He looked like a man who didn't give a shit.

Margi expressed all she felt through restlessness—anxiety, anger, depression, concern, uncertainty. Her heels clicked on the linoleum as she paced the floor between the curtained side of Bob's bed and the window. She resented the patient in the other bed, who must, by now, know many private details of their lives, just as they—who would have preferred not to know—were now acquainted with the relatives, illness, and traumas of the life of the man in the next bed. The wimpy curtain "wall" gave a false sense of seclusion.

Margi turned back to Bob. "Do you hate me? Is that why you won't say a word? Is it my fault?"

But Bob remained silent, his eyes staring straight ahead, his face impassive.

She didn't know what to do. Her insides felt like old plumbing that, after being underground for many years, becomes clogged with roots growing through it. They crisscrossed and knotted like vines through her chest, then headed up for daylight through her throat, strangling and turning back on themselves before they reached her mouth.

She sat on the edge of the bed and took Bob's hand. She didn't dare look at his face. She studied the hand—its massive bulk, the calluses, the cracked nails now growing long after a week away from work, the maze of lines sunken in the palm, the places where it was hard and those where it was soft. Sometimes after they made love, and he pulled her close with her back to him and the two of them locked together, she would study his hand and feel so protected in his arms and so satisfied with his warmth at her back. It was the same hand now, the same man, yet it was she who was now the protector. She had never had to be the ultimate protector of anything. Bob had always been there to lean on.

She might have been feisty, but she had gotten her strength knowing Bob was there to back her up. Now, she was frightened. What if Bob would not be all right?

She pressed the hand against her lips, still afraid to look into Bob's face. She held the hand tightly against her mouth and bent her head, because the tears came so unexpectedly that she was afraid Bob might see them. Their wetness flowed over his hand, but she could not lift her head.

Why had this thing happened to them, this accident? It could have been worse. Sure. Falling from a twenty-foot-high scaffolding could have killed him, and had killed or crippled other stagehands. But Bob had fallen in a freak way, onto the sharp corner of an electrical equipment box. Various gashes had needed stitches and his ankle had been broken. He would be able to walk. She guessed they should be thankful for that. But his groin had been maimed. He'd had two surgeries. Maybe more would be needed, but only time would tell.

Bob was a man whose war injuries were inconsequential in comparison to those of the fall. Shrapnel and bullets were not life threatening; never making love again was.

Margi knew it. Knew that Bob would feel like only *part* of a man. She was grateful that he was alive, but when she had ventured to tell him so, it had sounded so tinny, because if there was one thing they had in their relationship, it was honesty. And the honest question between them—unspoken, inescapable, a thick chunk of lake ice over their heads—was whether Bob would ever be able to make love again.

Bob *was* virility. It was a strong, enviable trait they would never have guessed could be so quickly taken from them. Everyone on the *Motive* set had been very concerned, though she couldn't let them know what the real problem was. She made out that there were head injuries and the doctors were keeping him in the hospital for observation in case of concussion. Fortunately, no one had mentioned it. Denny, her good friend, was the only one she had discussed it with at all, and he would never speak a word to anyone else.

Ruby and Graham Maddox had sent a card. Big deal, she thought. Maddox is loaded. Why doesn't he get Bob a private room, so we don't have to go through this humiliation of everyone in the goddamned hospital knowing our business? I suppose that Bob wouldn't be here now if he hadn't been called in to work overtime on another of Maddox's productions. All the time. Tight schedules. Get those sets up. Who gives a shit if these stagehands have any home life? Just get the set up so they can shoot more and more. And Bob wouldn't say no. He has a sense of duty. He's a boss and he knows the sets, knows where everything's stored, knows how to put it together. They couldn't get anyone near as competent as Bob to come and do the work. And, in the end, all this work really does is fatten Graham Maddox's wallet.

Waiting for her tears to subside, she gripped Bob's hand tightly. It was a motionless thing against her face. If only he would give her a little sign that he loved her, that he cared, that he knew *she* cared. She loved him. He must know that. She wished Bob's fingers would stroke her cheek. But they didn't move. She looked into his face again. He was staring straight ahead.

"Really!" she exclaimed, dropping the hand and getting to her feet, her wrath flowing like hot lava seeking any crack and crevice. "You are the most stubborn man I've ever met! What a pain in the ass! What a waste of time! You might as well talk to me, you know, Bob. We're best friends. I certainly don't like this situation any more than you do, but I can't change the facts. I can only give you all my love and moral support. We can work this thing out together, but for God's sake, don't drive me away from you."

She glanced at his face and thought she saw a spark of reaction. He sighed deeply and shut his eyes, closing out the world again. Margi went to the window and looked out. From six stories up, she viewed a smoggy Los Angeles. There was no way to open the window. The air circulation vent was on the window ledge, emitting a steady stream of air up the surface of the glass.

"Damn, I wish I could have a cigarette," she said out loud, glancing from the window that wouldn't open, to Bob, to the curtain that hid Bob's roommate, then to the door. No nurse had walked in during the last half hour.

"Shit, why not?" Talking out loud made the room seem not as silent. She opened her purse, pulled out a long cigarette and lit it with a match. Releasing her first puff of smoke, she also blew out the match. What satisfaction. She smoked and looked out the window, watching cars below in the crescent-shaped drive loading and unloading patients.

She heard a voice say, "Hey," and turned her head sharply. It was Bob, nodding at the cigarette, his hand outstretched. She smiled, scooted away from the window, and handed him the smoke. He dragged deeply and exhaled. His mouth remained set and serious, but she saw a laugh caper through his eyes.

They heard a sound from the other side of the curtain, and presently the sixtyish face of the patient poked his head around and looked at them. "You aren't supposed to smoke in here," he told them officiously.

Bob didn't say a word, but in his eyes was all the answer the man needed, a look that said, "You gonna stop me?" The man retreated, and Margi lit another cigarette and sat on the edge of the bed to share it with him.

Before the Volvo's nose was the massive gate to the Huntington house, which reminded Dillon of the entrance to an ancient castle. If there had been a moat, he wouldn't have been surprised at crocodiles puncturing his tires with their teeth and stranding him on the fortressed Beverly Hills street, where no one would be kind enough to let him come in to use the phone—that is, provided he could outrun the crocs.

The speaker responded to his pressing the button. "Yes? Who's there?" The voice was that of a professional butler; thin and cold.

"Dillon Hughes," replied the young man.

"I'm sorry, sir. Who?"

"Dillon Hughes to see Penny."

There was a long pause. Finally, the voice said, "Is she expecting you?"

"Yes. She's invited me to a dinner party."

"To the party? Are you sure?"

Why was this already becoming such a frustrating experience? "Quite sure," Dillon replied.

"One moment, please, sir."

The gate, the voice, the humiliation rankled Dillon. He waited an interminable time, during which two other cars pulled up behind him and sat waiting with their lights shining through his rear window. The carriage lamps glowed serenely from the tops of the heavy cement posts supporting the gate. Dillon clicked his teeth together in aggravation.

This won't do, he thought. You'd better be cheerful. After all, you want to outdo them at their own game, don't you? He switched on the radio and a moody jazz piece filled the car.

At last, the big gate opened noncommittally and he drove up to a red-jacketed, blond-headed valet. Dillon smiled. It reminded him of himself ten years before. The kid looked like he was in college, trying to make a few extra bucks. Of course, Penny would not have understood. She had grown up with valets parking her car and she probably didn't even notice them. Furthermore, her parents did not approve of boys who had to work their way through college.

The kid stood at attention when Dillon exited the Volvo, and he had the most surprised look on his face when Dillon asked, "How're you doing, man?"

"Have a nice time, sir," said the kid.

To the Huntingtons, a small dinner party was one of thirty guests. They could all be seated at the same table. Dillon glimpsed the white linen stretching from the front hall as he waited for the arctic-voiced butler to retrieve Miss Penny. Other guests came in behind him and were shown to the edge of the living room, where they were graciously greeted by Mr. and Mrs.

Lord and Lady, thought Dillon. Mr. Huntington wore tails. His shave was so close that it would scare a five o'clock shadow back twenty-five years. The missus had her smooth blond head sleeked back to show off a glittering diamond necklace which was the showpiece over a well-cut, simple black gown.

They both noticed Dillon at the same time, looked at each other, didn't say a word, and looked back at Dillon. At least Penny had warned him to rent a tuxedo. She had apologized for the formality and had tried not to giggle when he said he didn't own one. "*They* don't need to know that," she said. "Get something that makes you handsome."

Penny's idea of a handsome shirt was one with ruffles and a nineteenth-century cut that would make him look like a dashing pirate. Dillon turned down flamboyance in favor of conservatism. He had only worn a tuxedo a dozen times in his life—weddings, banquets, graduations—but, under all circumstances, he wanted Penny's parents to think he had been delivered in one.

Mr. Huntington crossed the foyer with hand extended. "So nice to see you again, Mr. . . . uh . . . young man." He was decorous and had called out a few manners this time, like someone would call out their Dobermans; sometimes they're very handy.

"Dillon Hughes, sir. It's good to see you, too, Mr. Huntington," said Dillon, with clean, clear diction on the man's name, his tongue rolling crisply off the *t*'s.

"You remember my wife?" Mr. Huntington led the way to the petite woman, who extended her neck to its full height as though it were the only way to appreciate her jawline.

"Of course," said Dillon, shaking her limp hand. "I am charmed, exactly as I was the last time." He wasn't lying: he was not charmed before; he was not charmed now.

She looked at him blankly and he told her his name.

"Mr. Hughes . . . motion pictures, was it?" she asked, her hands folded across her front.

"Television, dear," said her husband, as though she had said, "Cadillacs?" and he had replied with "Japanese import."

"Where's Penny?" asked Dillon. Oh, God, this was going to be a long evening.

"I believe she's in the sitting room showing Mallory our family portrait we recently had painted," said Mrs. Huntington.

Before the parents could get in another word, Dillon said,

"I believe I remember where it is. I shall search her . . . them . . . out."

Mallory proved to be formidable—if you happened to be a rare butterfly on an ice floe. He was tall and lean, with narrow shoulders, small hands, short dark hair, and very ruddy cheeks. He had no idea of the effect his smile made on other people, though it appeared frequently on thin, red lips. He seemed to be the kind of guy with a very low libido, but that fact didn't bother him at all. He greeted Dillon with a fraternal friendliness, akin to Dillon being an old school chum from the private circuit. Mallory's accent was Eastern, laced with English affectation.

"Penny was just showing me the new family portrait," said Mallory. "What do you think?" He gave the painting of two parents and four children a regal staring-at.

Penny's eyes glistened with laughter. She went to Dillon's side and squeezed his hand. Dillon gave her a short peck on the lips and anchored a firm hand at the back of her neck, under her hair, which gently massaged her. She wore a dress the color of an apricot stone, which covered most of her calves, and a short, beaded jacket.

Mallory smiled when he looked at them. "Penny is an old family friend. She was telling me how much she likes you. From the smile on her face, I can see it's true."

Penny blushed, averting her eyes from Mallory's and looking at the painting again. With the exception of Penny, Dillon thought the rest of the family looked more real on the canvas than they did in their own living room. Mr. Huntington's eyes were so uncannily depicted that, no matter where you stood in the room, they were staring at you. Mrs. Huntington stared off into her own private world of impassivity. Penny's eyes danced with a secret. Clever painter.

"I understand you are in the family business." Dillon said.

"I'm a junior partner in the firm," said Mallory, with a trace of boredom.

"Mallory's a brilliant lawyer," said Penny. "Finished top of his class. He completed the bar exam hours before anyone else."

"Now, Penny, don't exaggerate," said Mallory modestly.

Dillon liked him—or, maybe, simply liked that fact that Mallory was no competition for Penny's affections. She was obviously fond of poor Mallory, but it was the same fondness she would express for her brothers.

"I wanted to take up entertainment law," Mallory confided to Dillon, "but *they* wouldn't hear of it." He nodded over his narrow shoulder in the direction of the living room, to imply the parental stronghold ensconced there.

"It's never too late," said Penny. "I'd tell them to chuck the whole partnership and just do what *you* want to."

"Penny, dear, dear, Penny, you're a romantic," said Mallory.

Though Mallory and Penny were carved from the same social mold, their likeness extended only so far as to say they both hated it and they both wanted to break free. But Penny needed to break like a dancer pirouetting across a meadow of wildflowers; and Mallory needed to be on hands and knees in the meadow, observing things he had no idea existed.

Dillon thought it ironic that their upper-class background was the one thing he wished he had; yet, if he had it, he would be living in a different world. He would not have to choose his own goals . . . or values.

"Production must be fascinating, Mr. Hughes," said Mallory. "I envy you."

"It's interesting. I'm always learning something new," replied Dillon, flattered that Mallory would be envious. "But don't be fooled that it's so glamorous. I do the accounting and it's quite like other businesses."

"Where did you go to school?" asked Mallory.

"Harvard," replied Dillon.

"So did Mallory!" exclaimed Penny.

"I'm delighted," said Mallory. "A fellow alumnus." He vigorously shook Dillon's hand. "We must have graduated in almost the same year."

Dinner was announced, and Penny hooked one of her arms into Dillon's and the other into Mallory's, so they could escort her to the dining room. Penny smiled from ear to ear. "Dillon's had some good news," she told Mallory.

Mallory asked, "What is it?"

But Dillon crossed his lips with a finger, indicating that it was a secret.

When the threesome entered the dining room, Mr. and Mrs. Huntington did not know whether or not to smile at their daughter, who walked between the man they desired she marry and the man whom she had so obviously fallen in love with. When Mrs. Huntington seated Dillon at the opposite end of the table from Penny, the girl pulled him back for one moment to whisper "I love you" in his ear.

It put a smile on his face and fortified him for dry conversation with a craggy retired stockbroker and the whiny wife of a doctor who had just moved to the West Coast. Fourteen people sat on either side of the table, with Mr. Huntington at one end and his wife at the other. Dillon watched Penny sit near her father's end, with Mallory on her right. Every time she looked the length of the table at Dillon, there was no mistaking the love in her eyes for him. She looked on proudly and didn't care who knew.

A couple of times, Dillon caught Mrs. Huntington looking at him or, rather, felt her disapproving eyes. It was almost discouraging. He tried so hard. He didn't understand why these people did not like him. In his proximity were both of Mallory's parents, the Burtons, to whom he was introduced. They did everything but shake their heads sorrowfully when they said hello, their faces reflecting the sentiment, "The poor Huntingtons."

"Penny has always been such a spirited girl," said Mrs. Burton.

"It's high time she thinks of getting married," Mr. Burton told Mrs. Huntington.

"I know Mallory is thinking of it," said Mrs. Burton confidentially.

This news raised a smile on Mrs. Huntington's lips. "Mallory would be such a good provider."

"Of course," said Mr. Burton, "he comes from good stock."

Dillon did not take part in the conversation. They did not include him, though they wanted to make sure he heard it. He acted like he didn't hear a word, instead getting into a serious discussion on sinus allergies with the doctor's wife, who suffered greatly from them.

Penny was in pain. She didn't know what the topic of conversation was at her mother's end of the table, but she could guess. When the waiter went by with the bottle of wine, she asked for more.

"More?" inquired Mallory.

She flashed angry eyes at him and held up her glass—a breach of manners she had never done before. Mallory sighed heavily and accepted a refill of his glass as well. Penny made him drink the entire glass on a half-dozen toasts she whispered between the two of them.

"To rainy nights . . .", "To *very* rainy nights . . .", "To very *long* rainy nights . . .", "To spring winds . . .", "To . . ." Her voice broke off.

"Love?" offered Mallory weakly.

"Yes," she replied, looking down the table at Dillon.

Food was tonged from silver platters and ladled from crystal bowls onto Dillon's plate. He felt the strain of having to keep up a smile in the face of all this pretentiousness. But smile he did; and that forced *them* to smile back.

Before dessert was served but after the table was cleared, he heard a spoon clinking against an empty wine glass. It was Mallory getting everybody's attention. When the table was silent and all eyes were turned his way, he said, "Penny has something she'd like to announce."

Penny stood up carefully, Mallory moving her chair back out of her way. "I hope you have all had the pleasure of meeting my friend, Dillon Hughes," she said in a sweet, clear voice. "If you haven't, let me introduce you to him now. Mr. Hughes is the new coproducer of the number-one prime-time television show, *Motive*." She was very proud.

Her father was haughty. How dare she get up before so many old family friends and important clients and go on about this Dillon person!

Dillon felt a trickle of dread in his stomach, a movement like the curling of an earthworm in the rain. He kept his eyes steady upon the girl.

"He has been promoted and I'm very proud of him."

It isn't official, thought Dillon. Darn it, be quiet. This is embarrassing. These people don't give a goddamn.

She began walking toward Dillon's end of the table, behind the row of people seated there. "Dillon may be new to our circle of friends, but I trust you will all welcome him." She stood in back of Dillon and put her hands on his shoulders. She felt the ultimate powerful energy of her love for him flow from her hands into him.

"But we have more good news," she went on. Everyone watched. Many of them had known her for her entire life, but they had never seen her like this—so emotional, her voice tremulous, her willpower certain. "Dillon and I are engaged to be married."

The flat clarity of her statement shocked the room. There were simultaneous gasps from Mrs. Huntington and Mrs. Burton. Dillon didn't know which was loudest.

Dillon loved Penny and he wanted to spend the rest of his life with her, but they had never seriously discussed marriage. He had fervently prayed it would be a few years down the line. But she wanted him now. Announced it before God and the world—such as they existed at this dining table.

Then one person began clapping at the opposite end of the table, and Dillon saw a smile on Mallory's face and the young man nodding as if to say, "I guess the best man has won." Gradually, the rest of the guests joined in a light applause.

Penny's arms slid around Dillon's neck and she whispered in his ear, through her brilliant smile, "I love you. I love you more than anything, and I don't care what they think."

Chapter 10

Dillon wished he had a phone in the Volvo, so he could call Penny and say good morning to her. He was still adjusting. Using a vocabulary with words like *fiancée* and *engagement* was new to him. Somehow, he was not like many people his age who, if they hadn't already been married and divorced, at least had been *engaged.* Some people, he guessed, you expected would have had a couple of false starts—preliminary announcements about an impending marriage, initial stirrings about invitations, churches, receptions, and all the stuff that is usually left up to the bride. Those people fell in and out of love easily and felt no remorse at calling off the arrangements.

But Dillon had never before thought seriously of marriage, and in no way could he have made a public announcement if he had not been willing to go through with it. Okay, he reasoned, Penny had jumped the gun in announcing their engagement, but he was not angry with her for it.

He wanted to call her, just to hear her voice say good morning to him. One day soon, he would have a phone in his car. He would be able to afford it with a producer's salary and benefits. He knew Ruby had talked to Graham in the past week, and he suspected that was why Graham had called a meeting for later that morning.

As his mind ran through the imagined conversation with Maddox, he whooped out loud in his car and smacked the palm of his hand against the steering wheel, an ear-to-ear smile on his face. The whoop bounced around the inside of the Volvo. He glanced at the car next to him on the slow-moving freeway and saw the driver grinning. The guy gave Dillon a thumbs-up gesture and Dillon returned it.

Finally, he was going to get what he had been working for all this time. A good promotion. A job with a title everyone respected. He hadn't yet dared to call and tell his parents until the deal was confirmed, but he could see the impact it had made on Penny's parents. The word *producer* meant something to them. As a producer, he would be able to be more creative—proposing and deciding upon story concepts, actors, sets—rather than being a tallying machine whose main job was to keep everyone on budget. As production controller, he was frequently the "bad guy." And he hated anyone thinking of him in those terms.

Graham looked out through the window of the donut shop. "Shit," he said as he blew into a cup of steaming coffee. He had left the de Ville's lights on. He quickly went out and turned them off, then returned to his coffee and opened the paper. He didn't need to think about the workday ahead of him. He had already made his decisions and planned the things he needed to do.

He had left word that he wanted Martin in his office at nine o'clock sharp. Reports from the *Medical Alert* set were that, in general, Martin was arriving on time and staying the entire day. Martin had even hinted that if there were some other, more demanding job he might be interested in taking it. Which was surprising when he considered Martin. Maybe all the kid had needed was for Graham to put his foot down and insist that he work? The kid needed guidance, so had Graham failed by failing to provide any before now?

However, Graham did not think of his parentage in terms of success or failure. He had disassociated himself from his children long ago, leaving it up to Ruby to handle the details of their lives. He was willing to put in a few smiles and lots of dollars on their behalf, but he didn't want to be responsible for how they turned out. He was much too busy for that.

At least this was how he had rationalized it.

Nevertheless, lately, it distressed him to overhear comments about what a worthless waste Martin was. He realized it was a reflection on him. He had thought that with good educations and coming from the "right side of the tracks," all his children would turn out decently. But they hadn't, and it was hard to continue ignoring the results of his progeny.

He decided that no one was going to criticize *him* by criticizing Martin any longer.

Of course, no one could ever say that Graham was responsible for the way Will had turned out. Graham always explained that Will was a stepchild, had always been wild and uncontrollable, and that Ruby had forbidden him from taking any disciplinary action with the boy. Now that Will had grown up and moved out of their lives, he didn't go out of his way to tell friends that his stepson was a biker who did stunts when he needed a few dollars to live on.

People that knew of Will didn't mention the rebel's name in front of Graham. That is, people who knew better. But if they didn't—like that pesky hairdresser, what's-her-name, on *Motive*—they were bound to ask questions and make comments.

"I think that son of yours, the cute one that does the stunts, Will, is fabulous," Margi had said to Graham one day when he was watching the shooting. "You must be real proud of him."

The words galled Graham. He had thanked her as politely as possible and had cursed Ruby for ever letting Will work on the show. Graham didn't want Will around. Will's presence distracted Ruby. She was continually worried about him. Where was he living? Was he eating well? Was he happy? Was he careful not to drink too much? Typical, typical Ruby. Worried like hell over Will.

Did she ever worry like that over Graham? Or over any of her other children? Hell no. Poor Martin probably wouldn't be in the dismal state he was in if she had shown more interest in *him* through his teenage years.

Graham didn't know what had happened to their home life. There was a time—and it didn't seem so long ago—

when he could count on Ruby being there. If he was out of town on business, he would call her and tell her what he was doing. She had always been there for him to talk to.

Now, it seemed, when he needed to talk to her about his ideas, she said she would "later, if I have time." Always later. When she began producing, he didn't think she would stick with it. Most women who have been amply supported for a quarter of a century are not tenacious enough to persevere. Most wives of men he knew "played" at a job for a while, then returned to their homes after a hiatus in the workaday world.

Who would have thought Ruby would love working? The more she worked, the more she loved it. At first, she had needed his advice, had come running to him often. Now, she thought she had the hang of it, telling Graham she "didn't want to bother him." It had driven a wedge between them. He'd let her make a few decisions, and she had gotten power hungry.

And it killed him inside to have lost this contact with her, his control over her.

A few days before, when she had come to him with the idea of hiring Dillon Hughes on as coproducer, she had been seeking his advice. They had been in the kitchen, and while he sat at the table eating a salad, she had been waiting for the microwave to ding so she could serve dinner.

"Graham, I've had an idea"—she was tapping the edge of her wine glass against her bottom teeth—"and wondered what you would think of it."

"What is it?" he asked, his mouth puckering and watering at the same time on a bite of salad in which the vinegar was more potent than the oil.

"I'd like some help producing *Motive,* and I think Dillon Hughes would be perfect for the job. He and I get along very well. He's bright. After the incident with the sponsor, when you were in New York, I'd trust him—"

Graham interrupted. "I don't understand why you need help producing. You're doing fine by yourself."

His tone was brusque. She sighed heavily. It seemed no matter what she said to him anymore, he became angry.

"What I'm saying is that I'd like to work more closely with Dillon. I wish I'd had a son that was as eager as he."

The microwave bell rang and she edged out a dish of cheesy enchiladas. "How many do you want?"

Graham shrugged his shoulders to indicate he didn't care how many. "If you want a son helping you—a real son—let's try Martin out in the spot. He's doing very well on *Medical Alert*."

"He is merely staying out of people's ways," replied Ruby, putting the plates on the table, sitting, and anchoring her strawberry blond hair back behind her ears.

"Do you know what people are saying about us being bad parents?" questioned Graham.

"Hell of a time to start worrying about that now. Martin would drive me crazy and I'd probably get *less* done. No, no, I think Dillon is a much better choice. He's a hard worker."

"Give some thought to Martin," Graham told her. He had already hungrily devoured two of the three enchiladas on his plate.

"You give some thought to Dillon," she had quickly replied, impatience edging her voice.

They had finished the meal in silence.

That morning, Ruby had talked as if the decision were already made, as though Graham had nothing further to do with Dillon's promotion. Of course, Ruby had thought nothing about where Graham would find another production controller. Dillon oversaw five shows, and Graham trusted the young man. Who could replace Dillon? Right off the bat, Graham couldn't think of a soul.

So what right had Ruby to talk as though Dillon's promotion was a *fait accompli?* Ruby had made up her mind that she wanted Dillon by her side. But she had forgotten one little fact: Maddox Productions was still owned and run by *Graham* Maddox.

Dillon ran his hand over his chin. It was still smooth. He had shaved twice before leaving his apartment. He was wearing his three-piece gray pin-striped suit, which Penny had helped him select. (Her comment on seeing him in the outfit had been that he looked like a very important attorney. Dillon had told Penny that he wouldn't hold the remark against her. She had blushed and looked so beautiful that he had kissed her right there in the store, with the salesman and tailor looking on.)

At two minutes before eleven, he left his office to walk to Graham's. That gave him exactly enough time to tell his secretary where he was and when he would be back, and to say hello to the receptionist out front. He always made a point of being pleasant. It was important to him not to be known as a snobby executive.

Dillon felt like jumping up Graham's crème de menthe stairs two at a time, but he forced himself to walk at an even pace. The thick carpet muffled his steps. He became conscious that his heart was beating heavily in expectation. It was like ascending to God's office. But . . . hey . . . he should feel confident talking to one of the big boys.

Jeannie, Graham's secretary, greeted Dillon professionally. She called him Mr. Hughes, buzzed Graham on the intercom, and politely told Dillon to have a seat, that Mr. Maddox would be available in a few minutes. She tossed her head with its fine chestnut mane. Dillon was momentarily transfixed by the wild hair and her green eyes. Her lips were parted slightly, as though she were about to speak.

But she said nothing and he took a seat. "Have you got an extra copy of today's trades?" he asked, referring to the entertainment industry newspapers.

"I'm sorry," she said with some embarrassment. "Mr. Maddox has them."

Eventually, the phone on her desk buzzed two short tones and she said, "You may go in now, Mr. Hughes."

Dillon felt a little offended that Graham had not come out to invite him in personally, since the boss's business manners were usually so much more personable than this. He thanked Jeannie and felt her eyes following him into Graham's office. There was something mysterious about her, something he instinctively felt somebody should be observing. But he didn't know what it was, nor did he know who was in a position to observe her.

Graham was seated behind his walnut desk. The huge surface was clear except for two short stacks of paper, each anchored by crystal paperweights that were the fluid, graceful hands of a dancer. Maddox stood and greeted Dillon with a handshake over the top of the desk.

"How are you today, Dillon?"

"Fine, sir, fine."

This was good. Graham liked being called sir. "Have a seat, won't you? Shall I have Jeannie bring you anything to drink?"

"No, thank you. I don't care for anything." Dillon sat and glanced quickly around the room. He was reminded of Graham's enormous reputation and the many, many television programs he had been associated with. Graham was a genius, a man who successfully guessed and played his TV market better than a seasoned gambler played the horses.

"Let's get right to the point," said Graham. "As you are probably aware, my wife is very impressed with your performance. She enjoys working with you. She thinks you have a great future in television."

"Thank you, sir. I enjoy working with her, as well."

"She has learned a great deal about the practical side of this business, Dillon, and I attribute much of that to you."

"I would say," replied Dillon pleasantly, "that she has probably learned a great deal more from you. I certainly have."

"So you're happy with Maddox Productions?" Graham leaned forward, his gray eyes never leaving Dillon's.

"I've been very happy here. I am lucky to have found such a supportive group of people to work with."

Quit stroking me off, thought Graham. Out loud, he continued, "Ruby has seriously talked to me about offering you a producing job on *Motive.* She feels you would make a capable coproducer."

The conversation was just as Dillon had imagined it would be—Graham direct, yet taking his time about actually making the offer; Dillon remaining composed, trying not to let enthusiasm in his face give him away. He hoped his eyes weren't shining. He believed the best business deals were made when both sides were hard to read. He had been taking his lessons from Graham, a master, and now Dillon could not read his employer at all.

Graham paused (a few beats, it would say in a script.) "However, at this time, I don't feel I can give you a producer's position."

Dillon couldn't believe the words. Why not? Why not? He had earned the right.

"I have a number of reasons," said Graham, watching Dillon's eyes flicker from anxiety to fear to anger to worry. The young exec's mouth did not move. "First of all," said Graham, "I'm not sure you are ready to produce. You do an excellent job as a production controller. You understand the financial side of the business very well. But . . . I'm not sure you are *ready* to make creative decisions."

Dillon died inside. What was there to making *creative* decisions? You didn't have to be a creative person to do that. You just had to know the business.

"Aside from that," said Graham, "I honestly don't know who I could hire that would do such a fine job managing all the finances. I've never known anyone who could bring an entire series in on budget. You do that exceptionally well."

"Surely I could . . . we could . . . train a new person," said Dillon. "I have two assistant managers that would be very good in my job. I feel sure of it."

"Maybe, maybe not," said Graham. "But the timing is not right. Ruby seems to think she needs some help, so—"

"Sir, I don't think Mrs. Maddox *needs* help. I think she wanted to work as a team with someone where they could both feed off each other's energies."

"Maybe so," said Graham, briefly wondering what kind of energies Dillon had in mind. "Ruby is capable, but I think she needs someone who has been exposed to the business longer. As you know, Maddox Productions is a family affair. We are all quite close and are used to working together."

Dillon thought, What is he talking about? Until Ruby had appeared on the scene six months before, Graham was the only Maddox he had ever met.

"I have decided," said Graham, "that I will hire my son

Martin as coproducer. As you no doubt know, he was enrolled in the prestigious USC film school. He has been waiting a long time for an opportunity to open up. And I think mother and son will work together just fine, don't you?"

Blood rushed through Dillon's head, pounding in his ears, flushing his face. Graham was out of his mind. Ruby would never allow Martin to work with her. Too often she had confided that Martin would have to work long and hard to get back into her good graces. Martin had potential? Graham was only fooling himself.

"I'm sorry," Graham said. But his voice didn't sound sorry. "I can see you're disappointed. I'm counting on Martin to work out in this position. Of course, if he does not, I'll reconsider you. At this time, however, I think you should get a raise."

Graham quoted a substantial figure, though it was not as much as a producer makes. It should have taken some of the sting out of their meeting, except that Dillon was blown away. How would he ever explain this to Penny? How would she ever explain it to her parents?

Dillon felt ashamed. Deep inside. A huge humiliation at having jumped the gun, counted his chickens, believed in himself. He thought he had done everything right for Graham and that the executive producer would promote those that deserved it. Dillon had been wrong. Graham supported nepotism, preferring to keep it all in the family. Graham didn't give a shit about Dillon's personal life or career. All Graham cared about was that Dillon did a damn good job handling production funds.

Dillon shook Graham's hand and said, "Okay, you're the boss. I wish Martin the best of luck." And then he excused himself.

All Dillon wanted was to be out of that office, away from Maddox with his insincere face and self-centered interests. He walked past Jeannie and down the stairs without a word. He burst out the front doors and walked in long strides, toward the rows of soundstages, bound nowhere in particular, just needing to move.

He cursed himself for thanking Maddox for the raise, and for not having the guts to stand up to him and tell him what he really thought: that Martin wasn't worth ant's piss as a producer; that Graham was really a lousy father and would *never* save face by promoting Martin; that he, Dillon, would quit Maddox and go out on his own and prove to them all he could be a brilliant producer.

But he hadn't the confidence to quit that abruptly. His insecurities came back. What if Maddox was right and he was not ready for a producer's position? What if he wasn't as creative as he thought he was? What if he should be content to be a glorified accountant? After all, it *was* something he was good at.

He needed to call Penny. Needed to talk to her. Yet he was afraid. She had counted on him. Now he was letting her down. It was quiet among the soundstages. Overhead, the sky seemed very blue in contrast to the tan of the block walls. Very blue and very still. He resented it. Like Graham. Very still, very powerful. Playing his power out on his employees. And Dillon resented that. Very much.

Two feet out from the guard house at the entrance to the studio, a heavy steel post was set into the ground to keep vehicles from hitting the structure. Though Glory slowed as she rounded the corner, she still accidentally clipped the Impala's big chrome bumper against the post. She hit her brakes and the car rocked on its bad shocks, while she shut her eyes and couldn't believe she'd done it again.

The guard had given up trying to be angry with her. "What are you feeling so bad about?" he asked, leaning toward her open window. "That's only the second time this week."

"I'm sorry, I'm so sorry," she told him, catching a glimpse of her self in her side-view mirror and realizing that she had only put on half of her makeup. She'd finished the foundation, powder, and blush, but had forgotten eye shadow and mascara. Her eyes were even more nonexistent than usual, because her blond lashes were dusted with pale powder.

"I know you're sorry," said the guard, with understanding. A car behind her honked. "Better get a move on. You *can* make it to your parking place all right, can't you?"

"Yes," she said. "Thank you." She drove slowly, cautiously following the circuitous route of the yellow line painted on the asphalt. It wound between the soundstages and ended up at the employees' parking lot where, after complaints from other worried owners, she had been given a special parking place—one apart from *all* the other vehicles.

She glanced across the parking lot, quickly scanning the cars and locating Tony's rubbish heap on four tires. She hadn't *wanted* to look for it. Honestly, she hadn't. But she couldn't help herself. Her eyes were drawn like an unwilling puppy on a leash, balking and resisting but finally consenting, to the place where that darned car was. The sight of it made her heart pound harder in her chest. She wished she wouldn't react this way. After all, it was just a car. And, if she had seen Tony in it, her heart would have leapt into her throat and she would have scooted down in her own seat so he wouldn't see her.

With relief, she saw that Denny's blue Alfa Romeo was also parked. They had become fast friends since their first night together. They had ended up in bed, pretty close to naked, with the lights out and Denny's gray mama cat purring around the foot of the bed, and Denny touching Glory like he didn't quite know how, and her touching his bony body and realizing that she preferred a man with bulk on him. Muscles. Tony's muscles, to be exact. She and Denny had kissed, and it had been nice and warm. It had felt good to snuggle with someone. He had pulled her very close. It was almost as if he had to get used to the feeling of soft breasts against his chest.

They had struggled in the dark, under the covers, for close to a half hour. It felt fine, though neither of them had climaxed. After a while, Denny turned on a light and they both lay on their sides looking at each other. Finally, they both laughed softly, each realizing they wished they were there with someone else. But it was not an uncomfortable feeling.

"Come here," Denny had said, extending his hand and motioning for her to turn over.

She did as he asked, and he rubbed her shoulders lightly until she fell asleep. And he held her.

Sometime in the night they had awakened in their dreams, each excited by the sleepy caressing, and had fucked hard. Glory surprised herself by almost climaxing. Denny surprised himself by letting go into the girl. She knew it felt good to him, because he lay exhausted on top of her even after he had caught his breath.

He had an amusing mental picture of his sperm on the way to meet an egg. It came not as a scientific rendition, but rather as a caricature drawing akin to films they show junior high kids where sperms have eyes and eggs look like dime-sized moons.

Denny had been sweet to her in the morning, sweet to her during the day at work. She had been able to talk to him about Tony who, for the life of her, she couldn't figure out.

"He's afraid, Glory," said Denny. "He thought you were going to be another fling, something that got his rocks off, and he started falling in love with you."

"He told me he *was* in love with me."

"See?"

"But . . . I think he only said it when he was drunk," she murmured.

Denny had explained about alcoholics, and Glory had reasoned that maybe Tony really was one. She was so hurt that Tony would not talk to her and had never apologized for the night he hadn't showed up. He hadn't even mentioned one word about their script.

"What script?" asked Denny.

Glory felt embarrassed and she didn't know why. "We were working on one for *Motive.* We were going to give it to Ruby."

"That's wonderful!" exclaimed Denny, truly delighted.

"We were going to polish it that night he stood me up," she explained. "I've been so upset, I haven't looked at it since then. I almost threw it away."

"To hell with Tony," Denny had said supportively. "You get

back to work on it and give it to Ruby anyway. Why do you need Tony? You're a bright girl. You can do it without him."

After parking her car, she wanted to stop by and say hello to Denny, but he was talking to Margi. The hairdresser was smoking a cigarette and looking very gloomy. Glory had hoped to find Denny alone, because lately Margi's usual indifference had turned to great annoyance. Glory suspected it was because of Margi's husband. She didn't know all the details, but she knew Bob's accident had left Margi very unhappy. Glory wasn't very good at finding out gossip; Margi was. However, now the hottest gossip on the set had to do with Margi.

Margi called out rudely when she saw the forever-naive girl walking their way, "Glory be, if it ain't Glory Bell." And she laughed. It was not a nice laugh, but Margi thought it was pretty funny. How this midwestern scatterbrain had lasted almost six months on *Motive* was more than Margi could fathom. Richard must not have the heart to fire the girl.

The girl had even forgotten to put on her makeup. Margi shook her head in disbelief, wondering why the girl didn't have any more sense.

Denny was motioning for Glory to sit in his chair, but she shook her head negatively at his offer. "Thanks," she said, "but I've got to find Sondra and check in with her. You know how mad she gets if she can't give me a bunch of orders first thing in the morning."

Sondra isn't the only one who gets the hell bugged out of her by this absentminded, squeaky-voiced dummy, thought Margi.

"Come back later and I'll finish your makeup," said Denny, an encouraging warmth to his voice.

When Glory was out of earshot, Margi asked, "You think if you did her makeup, it would do any good?"

"She might stop coating her eyelids in that terrible shade of green," he replied.

"She thinks it looks great," said Margi, releasing another not-too-kind laugh.

"I wish you'd be nicer to her," said Denny. "She doesn't

have many friends."

"Look at the way Tony treated her. She doesn't pick them wisely," remarked Margi.

"What about me?" snapped Denny. "You think she didn't pick me wisely?"

Margi regarded him a moment. "I know you two have been to dinner, but just how close is this friendship now?"

Denny blushed before he could stop himself. He had assumed Margi had figured it out and that was why she was being even cooler than usual to Glory. "She needed a shoulder to cry on."

Margi didn't say a word. Was there something going on here that had passed her notice? She couldn't picture Denny in bed with a woman, probably because she had pictured him for all these years with Jeff. The way Jeff had treated Denny was predictable. On the set, everyone else had noticed the way Jeff stared at other men's butts and had almost gotten his own ass beaten by approaching a conservative stagehand. Only Denny had been unaware of Jeff's roving eye—until he caught Jeff in bed with another guy.

Had Jeff's deceitful behavior made Denny seek out the likes of Glory? If he had to choose one woman on the set, why was it Glory? Maybe because the girl was too guileless to damage his ego. It certainly couldn't be because he found her interesting to talk to . . . or sexy.

"Has she been using your shoulder often?" asked Margi, suddenly self-conscious that she, too, had been telling him all her problems.

"She's a sweet girl," evaded Denny.

Nobody's called *me* a sweet girl in a long time, thought Margi. In fact, it was her *lack* of innocence that had attracted Bob. He would buy her all kinds of sexy outfits and liked her to parade around in them. He had an original, inventive imagination when it came to fantasy, and he had enticed Margi into that world. He did nothing violent or weird; he would never hurt or scare her; but, oh, could he excite her! He teased her and lured her and seduced her. And she was nobody's woman but his.

Not only did she need him as a husband—on whom she

could completely rely for support, interdependence, companionship, conversation—but she also needed him for his body and his ability to physically satisfy her. He never went to sleep until she had been taken care of and, sometimes, she had a tremendous appetite. He had created a habit in her she could not live without.

Since his accident, that appetite had risen and fallen erratically. She had become very hungry sexually, because after his release from the hospital, he had not been at all interested in sex. Every time she thought of satisfying herself, she felt guilty. How could she be unfaithful to Bob?

But he would not communicate, and that was so damn frustrating! He spent most of his days sitting or sleeping, lost in a deep depression she could not crack. The groin injury he had sustained was severe: The doctors had already confirmed he would never have more children. Fortunately, he said, he was too old to go through diapering again and, besides, he had teenagers on the hoof—"grocery hounds," he called them.

While still in the hospital, as he and Margi had faced the examining physician, Bob had asked, "I just want to know if I'll be able to get a hard-on again? It ain't so easy to stop those urges from trying to bring life into the old beaver dam and looking down and seeing it ain't even able to move. Why, it's depressing to take a piss and hold that shadow of its former self."

This brief humor had come about because Bob had assumed his condition was only temporary. Margi had cheered him up greatly by giving him head under his covers while the grouch in the next bed had listened for noises behind the curtain. But Bob's good spirits had not lasted long. The doctors said nothing except that Bob needed a lot of rest.

So, he had slumped into depression and Margi could do nothing to rouse him. When she had worn a new negligee of black silk and red lace to bed he had become very angry, and Margi had left the bedroom in fear and gone downstairs to watch late-night TV on the couch, thinking he would ask her back to bed with him. Then she had awakened as the first dim light of dawn competed with the dancing static snow on the television screen, and she realized he had not fetched her back to their bed.

She ground her teeth. "Damn that Graham Maddox," she said loudly.

"Shhh," worried Denny. He didn't want someone hearing her. There were people all around them.

"It's his fault," said Margi. "He knows what a reliable employee Bob is and how Bob wouldn't let him down. So he asks Bob to work on a weekend and doesn't give a shit that Bob's already put in a hard week and is tired out."

Irritation edged Denny's voice. "Why can't you accept that it was an accident? It's nobody's fault."

Margi glared at him. "Look, buster," she said cruelly, "you wouldn't know about climbing around on scaffolding because it's something makeup artists never have to do. It's not a job for chickenshits. It sure ain't a job you do when you're tired. Haven't you ever noticed around here that whatever Graham Maddox wants he gets?"

"Margi," insisted Denny, stepping close to her and putting a hand on her shoulder, "*please* be quiet."

"I don't know why I should? Mr. Maddox probably never gets blamed for anything that's his fault."

She was belligerent, and the more Denny said, the louder she got. So he turned away from her, taking his powder and brush, and headed for the stage, hoping she would keep her voice down. You didn't go around the set criticizing the executive producer, blaming him for accidents. Especially ones that he was not directly responsible for. Nobody would have denied that Bob had been working a lot of overtime hours and that he was tired at the time of his accident. But he hadn't been *forced* into it.

Margi's anger repelled Denny. He hoped she'd cool down and keep her mouth shut. She had been very volatile and it worried him. She'd always had a quick temper, but he had attributed it to her Italian father. However, now she had lost communication with the one person who meant more to her than anyone else in the world—and she raged. Denny didn't know what could be done for Bob. *He* certainly couldn't go by the house to say, "Hi, how are things going?"

Margi was a woman who placed a high value on the sex life in her marriage, and she'd never had to face being without it.

Denny, on the other hand, was the opposite. If he had placed more value on his own sex life, he might still have Jeff. Luckily, Jeff had not called. Hearing Jeff's cocky, confident voice might make Denny come all undone again. He still couldn't stand to be alone. He was taking Glory to a mini-golf tournament the next weekend. She was good company. He only wished it tore him up to know that she was pining for Tony. But it didn't. He wasn't the slightest bit jealous.

Glory was a young girl in the midst of a heartbreak. He cursed Tony for having taken advantage of her willing nature. Denny had spent a lot of time trying to explain to her about alcoholics, but that had only ended with an outburst from Glory: "I *know* alcoholics! My father was an alcoholic! I don't want to hear any more! I don't want to hear any more!" And she had cried bitterly.

His own tears did not seem so important when others needed his comfort. It was fairly easy to put a glowing smile back on Glory's face and to win her over with lighthearted laughter.

But Margi worried him. He knew her well. And he knew her rage would need to find some escape. .

"Hi, I'm home," called Jeannie. There was no cheery response. The only sound she heard came from the never-resting television, as black-and-white voices of an old movie staggered through to the front hall. Jeannie imagined the stillness that always pervaded the house was like centuries-old air inside a pyramid, and each time she visited, she was like the explorer cutting through dusty cobwebs, a participant of the real world returning to a womb that gave such a real sense of false security.

Jeannie made her way to the family room, a large area open to the kitchen, one with a feeling of expanse. Sliding glass doors, which had no drapes, led to the private, secluded backyard, and a low formica-topped counter curved out from the kitchen. There was a dining table, a couple of couches, matching armchairs, and the television. The lighting, as usual, was weak twenty-five-watt.

The back of the familiar head sitting on the couch did not turn from the television spectacle. Jeannie kissed the top of the head and opened the sliding doors, where two small poodle-mixes were wildly scratching at the glass. They bounced at her feet and followed her to the kitchen where she split a can of food into their separate dishes.

"Can I get you anything, Mama?" Jeannie asked, leaning her elbows on the counter and looking at the profile of her mother's face. Every time she saw the face, her heart bleated inside her. It had once been so exquisite, so beautiful. It was the cause of so much that had gone wrong in their lives.

Her mother shook her peroxided head no. An inch of dark roots had grown out, and Jeannie had brought dye to even up the color. It was one of the only things that brought a smile to a face that was a mixture of blankness and sadness.

That the visage resembled a face—with two eyes, a nose, a mouth, a chin—was remarkable. After the accident, the plastic surgery had been extensive. The doctors had had to rebuild the bone structure of the totally crushed cheeks and jaw.

But now, more surgery was needed to take the twist from the mouth (even though they knew the lips would never again be full) to take the scars from the left cheek and her forehead over her right eye, and to lift the sagging muscle below that eye so it would be symmetrical with its mate.

But they didn't have the money. It had run out long ago.

Jeannie's mother did not feel there was much to live for. She had made her living with her extraordinary beauty—men had adored her, women had envied her—and then, it had been taken away.

Jeannie believed the restoration could be much, much better, if only they had more money. So she had gotten herself a good job with benefits. "Mama, what can I get you?" she repeated.

She fixed Bloody Marys, sitting next to her mother on the couch. The two little dogs jumped up with them. Jeannie resigned herself to an evening of television and reached for the program guide. She would make dinner after a while, like she always did.

Sometimes she felt so helpless, like everything she was doing was futile. She visited several times a week, and every time she feared walking into the family room and finding her mother had taken an overdose of sleeping pills. Week after week, things went on the same, and it seemed she was stuck in a rut and that nothing ever changed. Was she any nearer her goals? Once she reached them, could she make her mother happy again?

Something sitting on the TV caught her eye. It was a photo, shadowed in dim light. No photos of any kind had been displayed for years. After the accident, when Jeannie and her mother had moved from San Francisco to Los Angeles, the photos had all been packed up and inaccessibly stored.

Jeannie got off the couch and walked toward the television. She recognized the framed picture and was amazed. It was one of her mother in her prime, wearing the silvery-white bikini-bottomed sequined costume, a sparkling soft boa draped around her neck, hanging over perfect firm breasts and encircling her lean waist, its feathery ends touching the long, black-stockinged thighs. It was the best pose ever taken of her mother, the showgirl with breasts that could only be described as proud and with hips that melted a man's substance.

It was a wonderful photo. Her mother's face was radiant, full of confidence, full of sexuality, full of vulnerability, full of life. This was the last photo Jeannie had ever expected to see again, yet here it was, a shimmering alter ego.

This was the most significant action Jeannie had yet seen. Maybe her mother was finally beginning to believe that there was a solution.

"This is absolutely my favorite picture of you," said Jeannie warmly.

"It is good, isn't it?" said her mother, sipping the Bloody

Mary with a straw.

"Where did you find it?"

She stuck out one thin leg from under her worn housecoat, regarding it as though it were identical to the legs in the photo. "I found it in the drawer . . . the drawer where I keep all the stuff."

"What stuff?" asked Jeannie, surprised.

"The stuff," she replied, continuing to look at the leg. She popped out the other one, pointing both toes like a ballet dancer. "Jeannie, dear, go into that drawer, will you, and bring me the black stockings. I want to see my legs in black stockings. Bring the other things, too."

Jeannie had not known about the drawer. She found the stockings in the back of a dresser drawer, along with the silvery costume. It had been nearly sixteen years since the accident, since her mother had worn the costume.

Her mother dressed with care, sliding hands up silky legs, stroking each breast tenderly, like they were soft, warm prized birds. Her body looked remarkably good, but then, she was barely forty. Jeannie was thankful that the light was so poor, for it heightened the appearance of her mother's body and de-emphasized the misshapen face.

Her mother paraded in front of the glass doors, her reflection flashing touches of glitter through the darkened room. She began dancing lightly, rocking in silver five-inch spike high heels. Jeannie clapped out a soft, rhythmic beat while her mother's arms turned gracefully about her body, first outstretched and then hugging the body, wrists rotating in and then out, fingers beckoning.

There was extraordinary freedom in that moment, a release of the shadow that had been upon her soul.

When her mother finished the dance, Jeannie applauded. Her mother bowed gracefully. Jeannie softly swore to herself that her mother would once again dance like that where people could watch her.

Martin Maddox's strawberry blond bang hung over his eyes. It annoyed him to have to keep flicking it back. He stood near the hairdresser's table and said, "You think you could give me a cut?"

Margi looked at him. His tone of voice surprised her more than anything. He wasn't asking a favor. He *assumed* she would trim his fair locks. There wasn't anything pleasant about his arrogant face, with its freckles and pale green eyes. He had his nerve asking her in the middle of a shoot.

"I don't have time now," she replied.

"You don't look so busy to me," he said, stepping up to her chair.

"Garrett Gage is coming offstage any second and I've got to fix his hair. We're on a time schedule here," she said in her most condescending voice. "Why don't you ask me some time when I'm *really* not busy?"

Martin shrugged his shoulders, choosing not to challenge her. He recognized her as having worked for his father for quite a few years. She looked like she was a real bitch, and he knew better than to start a fight with anyone who was protected by a union.

Within two days, everyone on the *Motive* set knew who Martin Maddox was. Many of them knew of the spoiled youngest son by reputation and disliked him instantly. But he was impervious to their opinions. He didn't care if they liked him or not. If most of the crew preferred not to talk to him and to deal with Ruby, that was fine, it made his job that much easier. He couldn't understand that about his mother. She got worried if she thought somebody on the crew didn't like her. You might never get anywhere in this town if your feelings got damaged too easily.

The only person he detested running into was Will, who now doubled for Garrett Gage at least three days a week. Martin made up his mind that if he could figure out some way to get Will off the show, he would. He was surprised that Will was so well liked. Couldn't all these fools see what the biker was really like? One day Will would beat the shit out of someone, for real, and then they'd see. Will's unsociable glares were the surface of a psychotic, unstable personality. Will was not to be trusted.

Richard, the director, who politely tolerated Ruby, had no

patience with her younger son. Richard was pissed off at Graham for bringing in the kid halfway through the season. It was a disruption to the flow of the entire show. Martin made up his mind to point out to his father how he had heard the director of photography complaining to the cameraman about Richard's lack of ability. Graham would listen to his son's advice about using other directors.

Martin was surprised to find that Sondra, the first assistant director whom everyone called "the dyke," was nice to him. When he asked her about the schedule, she would hand him the day's call sheet and tell him to ask her any questions if he had them. He went over the call sheets, as well as he could understand them, and decided the blonde knew her business. She was organized. She worked hard. She made his job easier by organizing hundreds of details he might let slip through his fingers.

Martin was drawn to what he termed "innocent" women. Most of his friends laughed and flatly told him he liked dumb broads. He didn't like women who thought very much. *They* usually pouted if they were not satisfied in bed. The dumb ones were willing to fuck, fuck him again, and accept the fact that *they* were frigid if they couldn't climax. They were a hell of a lot easier.

Martin thought Glory was about the dumbest thing he'd ever set eyes on. She certainly was uncoordinated, but after you'd watched her drop a half-dozen things, she was endearing. She had a head of blondish curls and wide, shy eyes.

She was off to the side of the set, hurriedly compiling notes for Richard with writing that Martin thought looked like an illegible scribble.

"Do you like me?" Martin asked her.

"What do you mean?"

"I think you're sexy," said Martin directly.

She blushed deeply, the crimson burning her ears bright red. She plainly didn't know what to say, so she mumbled, "Thank you."

"But you kind of like me?" he coaxed.

"Sure," she replied. It would not be smart to tell her boss she wasn't sure—and she assumed he was her boss now that he'd let everyone on the set know he was the new producer.

"Maybe you'd like to show me how much you like me, sometime soon," he said, touching the top of her hair and smiling at her reply of "Sure." He put a finger against her lips and walked off, leaving her puzzled as to exactly what he wanted.

Damn, he thought, but those dumb ones make it all so worthwhile.

Dillon unexpectedly showed up at the Huntington house in the middle of the afternoon and waited for Penny to come home from class. The first thing she saw was Dillon's Volvo in the driveway; the second was the bitter, disappointed look on his face when she climbed into his car and tried to kiss him.

She guessed immediately. "Don't tell me, sweetheart, that you didn't get the promotion?"

He stared straight ahead, unable to look at her beautiful, perky face.

"Dillon," she cried, reaching out her arms and trying to pull him into a hug. She wanted to hold him, to comfort him, but he wouldn't budge in her direction. She stroked his hair, his cheek, her fingers thrilling from the touch of the man she loved, a sense of fear starting within her and running like a frightened rabbit on an open plain, darting about looking for a nonexistent thicket in which to hide.

But Dillon could not come to her, could not bury his head on her chest and lean on her. If he showed one sign of weakness, he would not be able to go through with what he had come to do.

The rabbit was behind her eyes, an animal who has had bullets scattered at its feet and has run from them, not knowing which way to go nor how to escape from the sound of a gun, the most terrifying sound that could ever be imagined.

"Here," said Dillon, reaching into the back seat for a bouquet of yellow roses. "I brought these for you." He put the flowers on her lap. They formed an effective barrier.

"I have something to tell you," he began, "and I think it's going to be the hardest thing I've ever done in my life. You're right. That bastard Graham didn't give me the job. Gave it to his son instead. Made it like Martin deserved it. Made it like I didn't have enough experience. The end result is that I didn't get the promotion and now I can't marry you."

She gasped in disbelief, but he kept on, "I don't want to marry you. It wouldn't work out."

"That's not true," she said excitedly, panic consuming her like sand caving in on itself from the center of a large pit. "Dillon, I love you no matter what your job is. Believe me, my darling, please!" She was crawling over the flowers, trying to grasp him, but he pushed her back into her seat.

"I tell you, Penny, a marriage between us wouldn't work. I'm calling off the wedding. There's nothing else we can do." His voice was mechanical, cold, decisive. "I can't bring any disgrace on you," he said. "I've tried, Penny, honestly, I've tried. I guess I'm a joke. If I were competent, I would go places. Instead, I'm stuck. You don't need to marry a loser. Please try to understand."

She was numb. There was no feeling in her cheeks or lips, no taste in her mouth. "I can't believe you're saying this to me, Dillon."

"Believe it, Penny. You'll be much better off without me."

"I don't understand," she implored. "I love you. That's the only thing that matters. I love you. Don't you love me?"

He looked at her a long time before he answered. "No, I don't," he lied.

The rabbit stood its ground, cowering with no place to run, mortally gut wounded and unable to save itself.

"I've got to go," said Dillon. "I want to get out of here. Away from you!"

He got out of the car and came around to her door. He opened it and pulled her out by the arm. She clung fiercely to the front of his shirt, but he pushed her away. "It wouldn't work, Penny. I don't love you."

She stood on the front step of the house, watching the massive automatic gate close behind the Volvo. The cellophane around the bunch of yellow roses crackled in her hand as she tightly squeezed the stems. Penny turned the flowers up to her face with the intention of smelling them, but she became lost in layer upon layer of their delicate perfection, their intense beauty binding her heart, strangling her until the pain that wrenched her chest shot up, geyserlike, in dry convulsing sobs.

She was in shock.

When she didn't come down for dinner, her mother went upstairs.

"Dear," she told her daughter, "it comes as a relief to your father and me. Thank God, somebody has called it off before you made a dreadful mistake. You should listen to your parents when they tell you that a man like Dillon is not good enough for you."

Chapter 11

"Glory?" called Richard, "Glory, please come here, dear, and take a few notes for me?" The director stood near the camera with Don, the director of photography, while they discussed a shot for the next scene. Tony waited for positioning instructions from the two men.

Glory hesitated when she saw him, then walked calmly over to Richard, holding her notepad and praying she wouldn't trip over a cable. She no longer wore her high heels to the set and, in fact, felt silly for ever having tried them. Long hours on her feet, plus unsure footing, were two strong reasons for not wearing them. The only good thing from the entire experience was the way the stagehands had whistled at her the first day she had worn them.

She stepped nearer to Richard, her eyes on her notebook, sure that Tony was watching her. Tony had started saying hello again, and she wished more than anything that she could walk by him, give him a cold look, and keep going.

But she couldn't. She always replied with a shy hello, her memory overshadowed by the nagging questions, "What did I do wrong? Why did he stop seeing me?" And she hated herself for not being able to go to him and ask him openly. She kept hoping her love for him would fade. Sometimes she even thought it had—until she saw him.

Her eyes were drawn upwards and sideways to his face. However, his glance was following Richard's pointing finger across the set. Her gaze unconsciously locked on Tony as he squinted through the viewfinder, and when he stood upright and looked at her, she didn't know what to expect. But he threw her a handsome, careless smile. And winked.

If only Richard and Don weren't there, she would simply say to Tony, "I think we should go for drinks after work," or "I'd like to get together with you. There are a few things I want to talk about." So why didn't she just go up to him when no one was around and ask him?

If only she could ask him why he'd dumped her. She had finished the script they had concocted for a *Motive* episode. Denny had advised her not to even bother with Tony but to take the script straight to Ruby. However, Ruby seemed so impossibly inaccessible. Though Glory couldn't admit to Denny that Ruby intimidated her, whenever Glory had to ask the producer a question, Ruby looked at the production assistant as if she had never seen her before.

Martin Maddox seemed much easier to approach. Glory figured that since he was new on the job, he would be looking for new material. He was so much easier to start a conversation with. Maybe it was because he was about her age.

When the show broke for lunch, she went up to him and asked if he would look at her script.

Flattered, he replied, "Sure, any time, baby."

"Thanks," she said softly, greatly relieved.

"What are you doing right now?" he asked.

She had planned on picking up a couple of apples and a yogurt from the commissary and eating them outside. Lunch was the only time during the day that she got to be outside in the sunshine, and she really missed it. Life in Los Angeles could be mostly indoors, if that's the kind of job you had, and the only time you got to go outside was walking from a building to your car. Unless, of course, you drove into underground parking and all you had to do was get on an elevator and ride skyward in the guts of the building.

"Nothing," she answered Martin's question.

"Come with me," he said cheerily. "I want to show you something."

He led her out of the soundstage to another building, where there was a hallway of dressing rooms. She followed him inside an empty one, and her warning antennae didn't send a jolt of fear through her until he locked the door.

He looked at her worried face. "Just so I can hear your story uninterrupted like," he smoothly reassured her. "Sit down over there."

"I don't think there's anything in here that you can show me," she said, her squeaky voice barely able to squeeze through her fear-constricted throat. Martin's freckled face and green eyes, which she had always thought so cute and innocent, were now very sinister.

She stood, her back to the wall of the small cubicle, her notepad clutched across her chest. Her knees were weak; she scarcely felt her feet. As Martin slowly stepped closer and closer, the pulse in her neck beat wildly, throbbing heavily under her jaw.

She couldn't move. He stood directly in front of her and took one of her hands from its grip on the notepad. "Here," he said, "feel this." He placed her hand on his hardened crotch.

Her hand shook from fear, but he misconstrued the trembling. "Like it, don't you?" he said, grabbing her behind the neck and forcing his hard lips upon hers.

Her mind raced through a million things she had heard of doing in such a situation. What could she do? Give him a knee in the groin? Scream? Talk her way out of it? Try to run for the door?

But she froze.

She felt like a zombie when he led her to the couch, lay down, and forced her head between the ridges of his opened zipper. He told her what he wanted and she followed his commands, her mind in a fog. She wished there were someone she could call out to, but she could think of no one. Already, disgrace was embedding itself within her with sense of guilt. Nobody cared. Nobody would believe she could do such a thing.

When Martin finished, he pointed to a box of tissues and, as she handed them to him, took a couple herself and spit into the paper. She couldn't even look him in the eye.

He wiped himself with a handful of tissues. "That was

pretty nice, Glory. With a little work, you'll be very good. That made me feel a whole lot better. Now, where is that script you wanted me to look at?"

"I—I don't have it here," she lied, not wanting to hand over any work of artistic integrity under this degrading condition. Oh, she had made a grave mistake not going to Ruby. Or even Richard.

"You'll get me a copy, won't you?" asked Martin. "We can't talk about it until I read it." He stood up and, as he was zipping his trousers, inhaled contentedly. He reached out a hand and touched her cheek. "Nice, real nice."

Glory couldn't look at him, so she stared at the floor. She wished he would leave . . . leave her alone. She wanted to cry, but tears would never come as long as he stood there.

"I'll call you one of the side benefits of my new job," he told her. "We'll have to try it again."

"No!" she cried, the word leaping out as a shield.

"What do you mean, no?"

"You had no right to make me do this."

"Do you want to get somewhere in this business?" asked Martin harshly. "Do you know how easy it is to find a lowly production assistant out there? Someone who could take your job? You know that, don't you?"

She didn't reply, but she looked at his face. He stood by the door with one hand on the knob. She wished she could say, "Fuck you! I don't need your goddamned job!" but the truth was she *did* need the job, she needed to pay her rent.

"You could never get another job doing this, you know," continued Martin. "When anybody called for a reference, we'd have to tell them we fired you for—" he paused, while he thought up his most powerful response, "we fired you because of your extremely lousy attitude."

"I've got a great attitude," she defended herself.

"Who are they going to believe? Some little air-headed blond chick or Graham Maddox's son?"

She hated him instantly, and her eyes glared.

"Don't look at me like that," he said, stepping toward her. "I'll make you do it to me again. Right now."

He gripped her upper arm, pressing his strong fingertips

deeply into it. "I can get a dozen hard-ons in a night," he went on. "There's no reason you can't take care of a few of them during the day." He looked at his watch. "You better get back to the set, Glory. Your lunch break is about over."

He pushed her to the door. She quickly unlocked it and was gone. She headed for the ladies' room, her mind a confused knot of fear, anger, and humiliation. The tears she needed had taken the last bus out of town. Oh, she needed to tell someone—anyone—but there was no one.

Graham lay in bed, fully relaxed, and listened to the sounds outside the hotel window. They were near Los Angeles International Airport, and the constant din of street traffic was broken at one-minute intervals by the screaming noise of incoming planes. Soft yellowish light filtered through the curtains from streetlights, headlights, and advertisement lights.

They were four stories up and anonymous. That was how he wanted it. In Beverly Hills, he would be taking a great risk. Everywhere he went, somebody always emerged saying, "Graham, Graham," and his brain would scramble, like a fat weekend soldier playing war games, to figure out who the person was. But here, near the airport, the nobody clerks in the hotel were used to registering thousands of nobody traveling businessmen, and nobody cared what his business was.

The room was warm and the sheet was around his waist. Jeannie sure had been in the bathroom a long time—at least a long time to pee. Women were funny like that. Give them a bathroom and they can lose themselves for hours. It's almost like a spaceship lands as soon as they go inside and takes them off for a whisk of a ride around the Antarctic Ocean, then brings them back full of icy vim.

He thought about Jeannie's performance in bed—for performance is about all you could call it with its machinelike quality. A rhythmic, rock-steady, well-oiled, non-tiring movement, no matter which way you turned her. The sounds were mechanical, as well. Programmed rather than spontaneous. But it was only now, as he thought back over the past few weeks with the woman, that he realized how emotionally uninvolved she was.

Of course, he had to admit he wasn't terrifically involved, either, but then he had a lot of things on his mind. It made him uneasy to think that she was keeping herself at a distance from him. It would be better if she had slipped off the deep end and had fallen in love with him. He would be more able to control her.

It was always fun to watch the range of emotions in a young woman in love with you—the open desire, the liquid mooning eyes, the favors, the listening, the energy she pours into you until she begins to see you don't feel the same way; then anger and hurt begin to cloud her passions, and she gets going on a real roller-coaster ride, because one day you'll love her madly and she'll be happy, and the next six days you'll ignore her and she'll blame herself.

With these women, he was no ordinary housecat toying with a mouse; he was a lion with a paw on a fragile antelope.

Except when it came to Jeannie. She was more like a wary jackal than an antelope, circling near but keeping her distance, enjoying the spoils of the kill but not getting within a claw's reach.

Jeannie emerged from the bathroom and stood at the foot of the bed. She was dressed, which shocked him because he had been waiting for her to come back, slide in next to him, and tell him, as she did so frequently, that their bodies "were made for each other." It might have been a lie, but it still sounded good.

"Why are you dressed?" he asked.

"Because I want to talk to you," she replied.

He pushed pillows under his back, so he was sitting semi-upright, and rubbed his eyes to dispel sleepy contentment. He reached out a hand to her so she would sit next to him, but she ignored it. "You sound very serious," he said, trying to ply her with a cute smile.

"I am," she said, looking down at him, her massive chestnut mane backlit by light from the bathroom, her shapely curves reduced to a thin, straight silhouette. "Remember all those wonderful and sexy messages I left you?"

Graham felt a baseball land in his stomach.

"And all those delightful and—" she paused, saying the next word in a puff of breath, "*erotic* messages you left me?"

"You told me you erased them," he stated tensely.

"It seems the erase button was broken," she returned smoothly.

He said nothing and waited to hear her out. He didn't like his position, lying naked under a sheet with a woman whom he thought he knew, but obviously didn't, at his feet. She could have a gun in her purse. If this were one of his episodes, she *would* have a gun in her purse and would whistle for her goon boyfriend to enter the room.

She didn't whistle. If her face had been lighted better, he would have seen a touch of a smile on her lips, the cheeks over her cheekbones bunching into smooth hemispheres. "You know, Graham, you have quite an imagination. People would be surprised to know the kinky little things you like discussing. Sick as it may sound, people always want to know what gives other people their hard-ons."

"Do you believe this will finish my marriage?"

"Who's worried about your marriage? That seems to have been merely a working friendship—for years."

"Why are you doing this? Do you think you'll get rich?"

"I just want to be comfortable."

"You're very foolish to try this," he said with bravado.

"I don't think so," she replied. "I don't plan on losing my job. I don't want anyone to know what's going on. I'll let you know how much I want and how often."

"I suppose the tapes are in a safe place?"

"*And* the photos."

"Photos?"

He expected her to move, to look out the window, to shift restlessly so he could see her face. But he wasn't directing this scene. She stood motionless.

"Why pick me? There are men with lots more money. You're good at what you do."

"Why pick you? Because you owe it to me," she hissed.

Her vehemence cloaked him and several knots sprouted on the internal baseball. He was trying to maintain his cool, but he was unnerved because he had not seen this mad-woman behavior coming. She had outperformed many of his Emmy winners. He owed her what? In her sick mind, she was obviously confusing him with a man who had done her a horrible grievance.

"What can I possibly owe you?" he asked. "I never saw you before you interviewed to be my secretary." Why the fuck didn't he just stick with ancient, reliable women that Ruby would never have raised an eyebrow at?

"A sane childhood," she said.

"You're not making any sense."

"I guess not," she conceded. "Let me give you a clue. I'm sure you haven't forgotten the name of a stripper named Odette."

The baseball shifted up toward his heart.

"Of course, you haven't forgotten," she continued, "though you've tried to, haven't you?"

"I don't know anyone named Odette."

"Sure you do. I don't believe you could have forgotten the most beautiful stripper of North Beach—beautiful, that is, until you destroyed her." (At this point, Graham would have written in the acting cue "laughs hysterically," but Jeannie had no inflection.) "She's my mother."

Then she walked to the door and opened it. "I'll see you tomorrow morning at the office, Mr. Maddox," she said, and left.

Will parked the Harley in the driveway and killed the engine. It guttered out in a very sick and dramatic way, the choking sound reminding him that he had not taken proper mechanical care of the machine in many months. Until now, he had hardly noticed, but the rough noise produced a draft of embarrassment, which circled him once before evaporating.

The house was suburban, nice suburban, with a well-landscaped yard and a weekly gardener's flower beds. It surprised him that Sondra would live in a house like this, since he thought of her as more of a societal nonconformist. She hadn't quite smiled when she had asked him over for a Saturday barbecue—"Come mid-afternoon if you'd like"—but her voice had been sincere and warm. Since all the stuntmen and technicians maintained she was a lesbian, he assumed she had invited him out of friendliness. Her body language did not convince him otherwise.

Will glanced up and down the block. All was green and well, the perfect picture of a post-World War II building-boom developer's vision of a "matured" subdivision; the trees were full grown, cultured shrubs hid the flaws in the architectural design, and most of the houses had been remodeled so they no longer had the appearance of tract homes.

The weather was clear, with enough of a wind blowing to chase off the smog. Will rang the doorbell and waited for the muffled sound of approaching footsteps. Maybe he should have said no to her invitation, but he didn't get asked out often; she didn't invite often; he didn't say yes often.

He had been feeling terribly alone. Maybe her company would take some of that loneliness away. She could be personable, even pretty enough, if she'd just smile now and then. On the other hand, he could never be accused of overuse in turning up the corners of his mouth, either.

The door opened and Will found himself face-to-face with a boy of about twelve, who stood leaning on the doorknob, blocking the entrance. The boy had pale, pale hair, an angular face, and icy blue eyes. He was tall for his age and stood on long, thin legs, regarding the visitor with an expression Will would not have termed hospitable. There was no doubt the boy was related to Sondra.

"I've come to see Sondra," said Will, returning the immovable stare.

"I know," said the boy.

There was silence. Will didn't think it necessary to ask, "Where is she?" But the boy didn't move, nor did he speak. He just blocked the doorway.

"Could you tell her I'm here?" asked Will. He did not find the boy aggravating; only annoying.

"She's not home," said the boy.

"Oh," said Will. Then, after another long pause, he said, "She was expecting me. She was going to have a barbecue."

"I know," said the boy.

Will was relieved that Sondra hadn't forgotten the whole deal. He was compelled to smile. Maybe it would soften the kid up. "Any chance I can come in and wait for her?"

"I guess so," said the boy. "But she won't be back for a while." He backed out of the doorway and Will followed him inside to the living room.

Will didn't wait for the kid to offer him a seat. He sat in an armchair covered in tasteful black fabric. The carpet was thick white pile. There was a black padded soft leather couch, an Oriental black-lacquered coffee table, and other furniture to match the black-and-white motif. On one side of the room was a chess board, so unique in beauty that the entire room could have been designed around it.

The boy stood at the entrance to the dining room and didn't say anything.

"Is she going to be back soon?" Will asked.

"I don't think so," replied the boy. He was not being rude or vague on purpose. He just didn't seem too good at communication.

"I'm Will. What's your name?" Good start.

"Scott."

"Tell you what, Scott. I didn't think there was anyone *less* talkative than me in the whole world," Will gently teased, "but after meeting you, I can see I was dead wrong."

A grin passed over Scott's face but vanished as quickly as a drop of water on sand. He continued to watch Will with his peculiar aloofness, but less critically.

"Is Sondra your sister?" asked Will, a finger playing with the end of his long mustache.

The grin gleefully leapt on board the boy's face again. "No! She's my mother!" he exclaimed, as though he could not believe the question. Imagine anyone thinking his *mother* was his sister!

Will swallowed hard. He hadn't known Sondra had a child. "Do you have other brothers and sisters?"

"No," replied Scott, stepping into the room and leaning a leg against the arm of the couch.

"Just you and your mom live here?"

"Yep."

"Where did you say she is?"

"She's shopping. She told me if you came over to make sure you stayed."

That was reassuring. The boy's enigmatic behavior made Will uncomfortable. "I know your mom from work," said Will, trying to make conversation.

"I know," said Scott.

"She never told me she had a kid," said Will, finally feeling he could lean back in the chair and cross his legs.

Scott stared at the heavy black boot that rested on Will's knee. "Is that your motorcycle you rode up on?" he finally asked.

"Yep," said Will.

"Would you show it to me?"

Will nodded and the boy followed him out to the driveway. As wide-eyed Scott gingerly touched the massive machine's handlebars and gas tank, Will flinched inwardly that the bike was not clean. When the boy asked the man to take him for a ride, it never occurred to Will that Sondra might object to her son riding behind a biker who, though he was an excellent and fearless stuntman, had a reputation on the set of being wild.

However, he did make the boy go in and leave his mother a note as to their whereabouts. "It ain't right to let a woman worry," he solemnly told the boy, realizing how hypocritical the statement was. Many women had worried over his ass.

Will drove to the foothills, the bike gobbling the road around the Saturday traffic, the only sounds they could hear being the wind in their ears and the straining motor beneath them. Will left the freeway, followed a four-lane surface street, turned off that, and made his way along a two-lane pavement, which gradually narrowed to a winding road as it began to climb a dry canyon.

They wound way, way up, to the top of a ridge, where Will pulled the bike into a wide dirt turnout. He cut the engine and said, "I gotta take a piss." Scott slid off and Will dismounted, swinging one leg over the top as easily as cowboys do when they ride into town. Will walked over behind the bushes at the edge of the turnout and was surprised that Scott was right behind him.

But he unzipped his pants and began sprinkling. He looked out of the corner of his eye and there was Scott, doing the same thing. No hang-ups or inhibitions. Just two guys taking a long piss together in the middle of nowhere. Dual zippers sounded, and both Will and Scott silently walked back to the bike.

Scott pointed to a sign that stated: "Abandoning animals prohibited. $500 fine."

"What's that mean?" asked the boy.

"Sometimes people want to get rid of their pets," Will explained, "so they bring them up here and dump 'em."

Scott's face showed horror and disbelief. "They just *desert* them?"

"Yeah," said Will. "It's a shitty thing to do."

"Do they ever get caught and have to pay the fine?"

"I doubt it."

"The pets would die, wouldn't they?"

"Yeah. If they didn't starve to death, some wild animal would kill them."

The boy was shaken by this reality. It was an ugly thought on such a beautiful, clear day when he was out having so much fun. They climbed back onto the bike and rode deeper into the mountains.

Will was glad the boy was there. Scott seemed to need the company of a man, and it made Will feel good inside to be able to show the kid something new. Will turned off the road and followed a dirt track a mile down a ridge. Large pines grew sparsely on the stark slopes. To the north, over miles and miles of rough hills, they could see the brown and barren desert way below them. To the south, they could see the San Gabriel Valley east of Los Angeles proper.

"My dad would never bring me up here," said Scott, sharing this painful thought with Will.

"Do you see him often?" asked Will.

"Not too much," said the boy. "I could see him more, but he's remarried and I can't stand his wife. She's got some kids, but she likes them a lot better than she likes me."

"I know what you're talking about," said Will.

Above them, a few wispy clouds were brushed up like a horse's mane flying in the wind. Will pointed to a hawk, its wings outstretched, making slow wide circles. It was high, yet it seemed to be hunting. Will marveled at its eyesight, how acute it was reputed to be. What a wonderful thing to be so refined in a single concentration of one's physicalness. Will shaded his eyes from the sun with a hand and followed the steady, unhurried bird. From underneath, the sun lit the tips of its wings brown-orange, like the color of marmalade made with sage honey.

"Do you know what kind of hawk it is?" asked Scott.

"No," said Will, wishing mightily that he did.

"It's so beautiful, so free," said the boy. "I would like to be a hawk." From other lips, the words would have sounded trite. But Scott was expressing a sudden awareness of Nature—a force he had never before been conscious of—and it burned strongly through him.

When they returned to suburbia, Sondra smiled knowingly. The men stood in the kitchen and told her of their adventure. She had not seen such animation and contentment in her son's face for a long time. It relieved a little of her worry, for Scott had been retreating more and more into himself. She had been unable to bring him out. As he described the sunny day and the wind and the hawk, Sondra leaned close to Will and touched his sleeve as a thank-you gesture.

"Can you guys do me a big favor?" she asked. "Could you please light the barbecue coals?"

She followed them to the patio and handed Will a bottle of cold beer. He smiled, downed half the bottle, and made up his mind not to think of Candy for the rest of the evening.

Once, at the age of sixteen and so angry with Graham that he saw red, Will had tried to look for the motel where it had happened. He wasn't even sure that the motel had been in Hollywood, though he kept remembering his mother's voice saying they were on their way to Hollywood.

So he drove up and down Hollywood streets, looking for an old single-story motel with a curved drive around to all the rooms. It would have been a busy street. At least he remembered it as busy. It must have been busy.

But Will didn't find the motel. It ate at him that he could have so long forgotten it. However, he hadn't forgotten the pain of those first few months in Los Angeles. It was a confused time. It's not easy to understand when you're five and nobody will talk about the details. It was a blur, but he wanted to figure out what had happened.

They had spent days and days on the road, driving from Texas. His mother had said there was nothing wrong, yet she had left the Lone Star State in a bewildering hurry.

The back seat of the old 1948 Nash was unbearably hot. The kids climbed over to the front seat in an effort to escape the furnacelike air that blasted through the car. They were aware of nothing except the endless hours of endless dry land chasing the highway, the dull thirst that came in the heat, and their mother's brooding silence. Little Belinda slipped her three-year-old hand into brother Will's five-year-old one, seeking comfort as they moved through a void of uneasy emotion.

He felt protective of Belinda and would stay awake for hours while her little blond head gently swayed in his lap as she slept. Belinda was too little to know anything was wrong; Will was aware of their flight from his father, Matt Long, but was not old enough to ask questions.

Every time they stopped for gas, his mother would tell him, "Mind your sister, Will. You keep an eye on her." So he would get the restroom key from the station attendant and lead the little girl to the men's room with him, carefully locking the door from the inside so no one could burst in on them.

The best thing was that on each stop Ruby bought them candy bars, something she never did at home. As they got back into the car, she would kiss each child on the cheek, give them both a hug, and tell them she loved them. They believed her, for she was their total world, their entire sense of security.

But she drove and drove without a word to them, her mind rehashing conversations over and over. What could she have said to hold on to Matt? Nothing that she hadn't tried. It burned her up to think he had the nerve to tell her she just wasn't good enough for him. She had suffered a terrible loss—and she had not been prepared for it.

Her only solution was to flee. Take the children and get out of Texas. She had a friend from high school who had gone off to Los Angeles, and as far as Ruby could tell, the friend was the only person from her graduating class who had done well. Ruby's mind fastened onto California with all the optimism of the song words, "Open up your golden gates. . . ."

Matt would be angry she had left Texas. Even angrier that she had taken the children. Belinda was his special pet, with her long blond hair always done in high pigtails and her round, open eyes so full of trust and wonder. Whenever she had been with Matt, she had insisted upon sitting on his lap and hugging his neck. Belinda loved her father very much, and Matt would let her stay on his lap, whispering comforting things in her ear, until she dozed off.

In the car, she would wake with a start and call out, "Daddy, Daddy," in a voice so plaintive, so tender, it broke Ruby's heart to hear it.

If you only knew what kind of rat your father really is, thought Ruby, thankful that Will hugged the little girl and told her to go back to sleep. The kids were beautiful and she was amazed that she had borne such perfection. Sometimes she felt disassociated from the children—like they belonged to someone else—and it was hard to believe that she was a mother. She felt like two people: Will and Belinda's mother; and her own adult self, Ruby.

Ruby put too much responsibility on Will. Her inner voice kept crying, "He's only five. What do you expect?" But her outer shame was much louder. She was preoccupied only with getting back at Matt Long. How could she have loved him so much? How could he have abandoned her?

Will believed his mother when she said, "You're a big boy now. No crying. You're my little man and you've got to help me."

They found this motel in Hollywood which had three tall, waving palm trees clumped near the office entrance and a worn aqua-colored pool in the middle of the semicircle of rooms. It was the layout of thousands of motels across America, motels where a person could drive right up to their own door.

For the first three days after they arrived, they didn't leave the room. In addition to a double bed, a roll-away had been brought in for Will. Ruby lay on the bigger bed, her face to the wall, and alternately cried and slept, cried and slept. She had bought them stuff to make sandwiches in the room—creamy peanut butter and grape jelly on white bread, which they washed down with bottles of Coca-Cola from the vending machine near the motel office. Will was allowed to go out for the Coke, but he had to come straight back.

Will kept the television on, and he and Belinda watched it. Belinda would sometimes climb on the bed with her mommy and try to hug the inert figure from behind. Where were all the kisses and hugs her mommy usually gave her? Where was her daddy? Will would tell the little girl to come to him, and he would give her a big hug and clap her hands together and sometimes tell her stories.

One time when he went to the Coke machine, the motel owner was sweeping the sidewalk and asked, "You the folks staying in number eleven?" But his voice was so rough and unfriendly that Will was frightened to say a word.

"Is everything all right in there?" the man asked. "I haven't seen anyone but you come out in three days."

Will was speechless. He looked at the ground, afraid the man would get angry.

The man squatted down, took a deep breath and said, more gently, "Is your mother all right?"

Will nodded.

"Where are you from?"

"Texas."

"What did you come here for?"

"I don't know," said Will, backing away from the man, wishing he could pass by and go to the Coke machine, but afraid the man would ask more questions. He ran back to Room 11, pausing by the door to look back at the man who leaned against his broom and shook his head.

Will heard laughter from the middle of the courtyard, and saw children playing and splashing in the pool. It looked like fun, and he knew how to swim. But he knew he had to ask his mother first. The children in the water shrieked with laughter. When Will opened the door to the darkened room, he resented the tight, enclosed silence and wished his mother would become herself again.

"What's wrong with you, Mommy?" he asked. "A man outside was asking what's wrong with you."

Ruby rolled over to look at him. "What man? What man was asking?"

"A man out there with a broom. He scared me. I told him we were from Texas." Will put the nickels on top of the dresser.

"You didn't bring us any Cokes?" asked Ruby.

"No . . ." stammered Will. "The man was in the way."

Later that day, Ruby got off the bed and took a shower. She dressed and gave Will specific instructions: "I'm going out for a while. Under no circumstances are you to leave your sister alone. Do you understand me?"

"Yes, ma'am," replied the boy, hating her for leaving them in the room.

"You are not to open the door to anyone, is that clear?"

"Yes, ma'am."

"When I come back, we will go out and get an ice-cream cone." Her voice rang with mock enthusiasm, but Will could see it was an effort for her to promise even a lousy ice cream.

"You hear that, Belinda?" asked Will. "We get ice cream later. Ice cream!" His voice rose with excitement on the words *ice cream,* and Belinda clapped her hands together and giggled.

"Goodie!" she said, her blond pigtails bouncing on the

sides of her head.

"I'll be back in two hours," said Ruby. "All right, darling?" She kissed Will's head and left.

Will heard the Nash's engine start. He didn't know when his mother would be back. They seemed to wait a long time. It was stuffy in the room and Belinda begged him for a Coke.

"Please, Will, I'm very, very t'irsty."

Will opened the door and they both stood looking out at the courtyard, with its palm trees, flowers, and poolful of happy children. The fresh air moving into the airless room felt good.

"You stay right here," said Will. "I'll go get the Cokes."

"Can I come with you?"

"Sure," he said, stuffing the nickels into his pocket, taking her hand, and walking to the Coke machine.

"Are they s'immering?" she asked, pointing to the kids in the pool.

"Yes," replied her brother.

"I want to go simming."

"When Mommy comes back. We have to wait for Mommy."

The pool tempted them and they walked from the Coke machine, holding hands and each carrying a bottle of the brown liquid, to the outside of the chain-link fence that surrounded the cool-looking water. They stood for a half hour, laughing when the children inside laughed.

One little boy came to the fence. "You coming in?" he asked them.

"We wait for our mommy," said Belinda.

Ruby did not return in two hours. Nor by dusk. Every time Will heard a car come into the driveway, he opened the door to see if it was the Nash. He was growing very tired. Belinda had been asleep for two hours, and he was afraid to take his eyes off her. After all, he had promised his mother he would watch the little girl. But he was sleepy, oh, so sleepy.

He awoke with a start. The room was dark except for the light that came from the open door.

"Belinda!" he cried, but there was no answer.

He was positive he had shut the door, but now it was open. Had he locked it? He couldn't remember.

"Belinda!" he shouted again, running out the door and stopping to look in all directions. He didn't see her. The parking lot was full of cars, though very quiet. He ran to the Coke machine. Maybe she had gone to the Coke machine. She knew how to use it. He had shown her how earlier that afternoon.

But she wasn't there.

He looked toward the pool and his panicked heart lodged in his throat. He ran for the fence. He wasn't even sure where the gate was. He had been waiting for his mother to take him into the pool. Where was the gate? Where? Where?

He ran alongside the chain-link fence. Inside, the pool was dark. He was afraid to look. He found the gate and his feet seemed to move in slow motion across the cement. Belinda didn't know how to swim. She had just learned how to float, but she didn't know how to swim.

Why, oh why, hadn't she waited for her mommy to take her "simming"? Why hadn't she waited for her mommy?

On the sidewalk of the Andersons' house, Graham held Ruby's elbow while they waited for the valet service to bring the Mercedes around. She wore a long white dress made of softly clinging material, tucked with rhinestones at all the right places. She was not emaciated or flat-chested. She was a full-bodied woman and she smiled to herself when she thought of the effect her dress—and what it contained—had had on numerous men with whom she had conversed during the course of this party.

The Andersons always held magnificent parties, with a fleet of red-vested parking attendants, a full kitchen staff, a serving staff, and two bartenders. An awning had been set up over the entrance to keep the dew off departing guests. Chinese iron candleholders, shaped like pagodas, stood every two feet up the length of the walk, flickering a magic amber light. From inside the house, they could hear the soft music of a piano, a clarinet, and a drummer, the band playing tunes from the forties on up to the present. Ruby had enjoyed at least three solid hours of dancing with a new man for every song. The champagne had made her light on her feet and made her laughter more bubbly than the sparkling wine.

"I'm driving," announced Graham, pulling a beaded white shawl over Ruby's shoulders.

She clutched the long fringe and wrapped it around her neck, as an East Coaster might do to a scarf in a snowstorm. "I'm not that drunk, darling."

"I don't care," said Graham. "I'm driving."

Ruby didn't like this idea. Graham scared the hell out of her with his driving, and in the past six years she had probably only ridden with him a half-dozen times. "You've been drinking, too," she told him.

"As a matter of fact," he said soberly, "I haven't. I've had two Scotch and waters in the entire six hours we've been here. I haven't touched the champagne."

Ruby's light-headed feeling crashed inside her. Her mouth was a little dry, but other than that, she did not feel drunk. "I'll drive," she insisted.

"No, you won't," said Graham firmly, talking to her out of the side of his mouth while smiling pleasantly at other people who waited for their cars.

"Then I'm calling a cab," said Ruby, pulling her arm from Graham's grasp.

She was stopped, after one step, by his hand reattaching itself to her arm. "*No,* you won't call a cab," he hissed. "And I'll thank you not to make a scene."

She was frightened, genuinely frightened. He was bullying her, exercising his supreme control over her by physically controlling her. He had been controlling her during their entire marriage, and the more she asserted her own independence, the harder he fought to keep her from having it. Professionally, she had made a mark upon the television community. Since *Motive* had done so well in the ratings, they had granted her some credit for its success. They were happy for her, impressed by her.

That is, everyone but Graham, who couldn't stand to lose control over anyone. He enjoyed managing people like they were puppets and he held the strings. And now he was physically demanding that she ride with him. What the heck was wrong with him? She could not think of another time in their marriage when he had used his *physical* strength to force her to do anything.

Her pearly Mercedes rolled to a stop under the awning and Graham guided her toward it. Not waiting for the valet to open the passenger door, Graham pushed Ruby into the seat, where she sat, angry and yet, fearful.

"I don't like this one little bit," she said bitterly, pulling her seat belt across her front and fastening it. "You have no right to make me ride with you."

"You have no right to start saying crap like 'I'm calling a cab,' right there, in front of everyone. Who the hell do you think you are?" he growled.

"What's gotten into you?" she shrieked back at him. "We usually arrive in two cars. Why the hell didn't you drive your own damn car?"

"You're in no shape to drive home," he reminded her.

"I could make it just fine," she cried.

He made a left out of the Andersons' driveway and floored the Mercedes. It lulled for a second before surging forward, the engine unaccustomed to such a brutal attack of lead foot.

"Not so fast," screamed Ruby, her hands gripping the edges of the leather seat, the pliant material choked in her clenched fists.

The residential Beverly Hills street was wide and silent at three A.M. as Graham made for the entrance to the canyon. As the car bounded smoothly through intersections, Graham barely slowed. His eyes were constantly alert for oncoming headlights.

"I don't know what kind of thrill you're getting by scaring the hell out of me!" shuddered Ruby, wishing she could close her eyes but too afraid not to look.

Graham slowed at Sunset Boulevard, where he had the

red light. A pack of cars streaked by on the boulevard and was lost over the next curvy hill. All was very quiet for a moment as they waited for the light to change. Ruby's heart beat insanely beneath her rhinestone-jeweled chest. The glittering stones moved in and out, winking in the red of the traffic light.

"I can't wait all night for this fucking light," said Graham, punching the accelerator. The Mercedes leapt across four lanes of Sunset and began to climb the canyon.

"You are crazy!" yelled Ruby. "You just went through that red light! Let me out! Let me out!"

But Graham ignored her, his mind intent upon the winding road, which was narrow to begin with and made much more hazardous by the cars parked on both sides. They left only one-and-a-half lanes of width through which traffic could flow. The speed limit in the canyon was twenty. Graham was doing his best to double it.

"Stop! Stop!" screamed Ruby, but Graham drove on.

The car had a fine feel. He hadn't driven it very often, maybe only to the little convenience market near their home. He wished Ruby would shut up. It tugged at his concentration. He could stand it as long as she didn't grab hold of him.

"I am praying, Graham," she said. "Right now, I am praying that we will meet no cars coming *down* the hill. Where the hell is a cop when you need one?"

Graham paid her no mind. He was alert. There's a car pulling out ahead. Foot to brake. Mercedes' nose tilts down a little, but really, damn good response. See, Ruby, we're all right.

Ruby made no more noises on the way home, however, the second he stopped for the garage door to open, she was out of the car and heading for the front door. She went straight to her bathroom and took off her clothes and makeup faster than she had ever done before. She took the book she was reading off her nightstand and went inside the guest room, locking the door behind her.

Graham, who was in the kitchen getting a night-cap, heard the door slam and realized it wasn't in the same part of the house as their bedroom.

"What the hell's the matter, Ruby?" he shouted, making his way to the hall outside the guest room. "You're overreacting. We made it home just fine."

"You're certifiably crazy," she yelled through the door.

"There's no reason for you to be angry, darling. I'm not crazy. I'm a very good driver." He pressed his ear against the door and tried to listen to what she was doing.

"You have no right to scare me like that," she said. "We made an agreement years ago that *I* would do the driving. Then, tonight, you *forced* me to get in the car with you." The word *forced* choked her throat with rage. "You are inhumane!"

"No, I'm not. All right, I'm sorry I forced you." His voice was calm and sincere. "But these days, you always seem on the verge of making a scene. I couldn't let you do that in front of all our friends. They'd be wondering what has happened to our marriage."

"They're going to be wondering soon enough" was her retort.

Graham leaned his back against the door. "What do you mean?" he asked softly. When she didn't respond, he asked again, louder, "What do you mean?" He began knocking at the door with his fist.

"I'm not going to live with a man who treats me like you do," said Ruby.

"I treat you pretty damn good," cried Graham. "Look at all the crap you have. You wouldn't have it if I hadn't given it to you. You had nothing when I met you. Nothing!"

Ruby jerked open the door and Graham stumbled into the guest room. "I didn't want to fight with you," she said. "I simply wanted to drive home from the party. But you're pushing it to this. I've put up with your moods for years. When you're not in a 'mood,' you're one of the sweetest guys I know. But when you're like this, you're impossible! You're so damn insecure, you can't stand to see anybody close to you do well on their own.

"I'll tell you one thing," she continued. "You wouldn't be where you are today if you hadn't had me giving you self-confidence every step of the way."

She stood in her pajamas, her hands on her hips, her hair combed out and almost straight upon her shoulders. Without makeup, she looked fifteen years older than she ever did in public. But at the same time, there was a tautness to her cheeks, colored by a beautiful flush, which he never saw when her skin was covered with makeup. She looked angry and understanding; patient and out of patience.

"I've decided to move out for a while," she told him. "I will get a condo and we can see each other on a friendship basis."

His perfectly styled, thick black-gray hair contrasted to his yellowish, disheveled gray face, upon which the creases were deep and unsymmetrical, the skin under his eyes dark, the eyes themselves dull and not fully reacting.

"You can't move out," he said.

"I suppose you're going to beat me up and force me to stay?" she briskly gibed.

"I'm sorry about what happened earlier," he said deploringly. "I don't know why I did it. But you know I can't live without you. I need you here."

"As usual, you're only thinking about what *you* need. *You* need me, because you can't function without me. It has nothing to do with who *I* am or what *I* need. You don't even know who I am."

"That's not true. I care about you, Ruby."

"Well, I don't believe it."

She turned, got into bed, opened the book and pretended she was reading. She had not drawn the curtains, and beyond the large glass door was the night-ridden, wild canyon.

Graham felt exposed, though there were no neighbors to see in. The night was exposing him and there was nowhere to hide. He walked to the window and closed the drapes. Ruby was ignoring him. "Are you mad at me because I didn't hire Dillon?" he asked.

"That's one issue. You want to talk issues? You had no right to hire Martin. He's not qualified. It makes me look like I have absolutely no control on the set for you to go and do a thing like that. Especially after I'd promised the job to

Dillon. So you give the job to Martin, not because he's worthy of it, but because you need to prove that you're still the boss. Nobody ever said you weren't; but you think you have to keep proving it anyways."

"Martin is doing very well."

"So far, the only time that he helps is when he stays out of everybody's way. Martin is a jerk."

"You can talk about your own son like that?"

"Somebody has to. It's both of our faults he's ended up this way. I would never lay all the blame on you, even though Martin is turning out like you. The only thing that's different with him is that he's not waiting until he's fifty to be a jerk. He's doing it in half the time."

"You'd better watch what you say. It won't do to have Graham and Ruby Maddox quibbling on the set."

"I will grant you that, Graham. You've always been able to maintain your public image. Nobody will ever know what kind of monster lurks beneath your facade."

"Public appearance means everything in this town," said Graham.

"That's *all* that matters to you, isn't it? Not what people need. I need things you aren't giving me."

"I give you everything."

"Bullshit. What do you call what you're giving your secretary?"

"She's nothing to me. She's a toy."

"That's supposed to make me feel better? I'll tell you something—it only illustrates my point: You *use* people. You manipulate them. You control them. That seems to be the only thing that gives you pleasure in life anymore."

"Is that so?" he said acidly, sitting in an armchair in the corner of the room and watching his wife. He wished she'd get her nose out of that damn book. "And, I suppose that the only thing that gives *you* any pleasure these days is how much time you can spend with Will, the only child you really think of as *your* child."

Ruby's head jerked up and her gaze was level. "I love all my children."

"You just happen to love one more than the others—the

one you didn't have with me."

"That's ridiculous," said Ruby. "All of my children are important to me."

"And Will is more important. He was fine in Oregon. Why didn't you leave him in Oregon?"

"I didn't ask him to come back here. You know I hadn't seen him in a long time. *You* drove him away. I should have left you then, but I loved you a lot, an awful lot. You made me choose years ago between you and my son. I chose my husband. I should never have had to make that choice, but you can't seem to get over your hate for Will. Which is something I'll never understand."

"It's not Will," said Graham through his teeth, "it's Matt Long—who you secretly wish you could have been sleeping with these long twenty-six years we've been together."

Ruby was tired. She'd heard it all before. Lately, whenever they got into an argument about anything, Graham always ended up blaming Matt Long for their problems. Graham had carried an insane jealousy for years. She didn't understand it; but she could no longer ignore it. She could no longer tell Graham that she really cared for him.

She was out of energy.

"I don't want to discuss it anymore," she told him. "You always deadlock on the issue of Matt. It doesn't matter how many times I tell you I hardly remember him, you don't believe me. Many things are wrong between us. Mainly, we've grown apart. I'm not the woman you married. You're not the man I married. But somehow, I've always loved you, stood by you, and supported everything you've gotten into.

"Obviously, it wasn't enough. Our marriage isn't working anymore. You have no reason to hate Will. He's tried to be a son to you all these years. . . . You never wanted him. Don't try to blame what's gone wrong between us on Will. He's been gone too long. He knew when to get out and he did."

She laid the book down and pulled the covers over her. "I'm going to sleep now," she said, turning out the light.

"Come to bed with me," he pleaded from the chair in the darkness.

"No," she replied, and lay there listening for a long time before he got up and left the room. He touched her shoulder on his way out. Ruby quivered from his touch and felt sad that the quiver was from the past. And the sadness lurked outside the window, in the wild canyon.

Chapter 12

Tony leaned against the bar in the Golden Time and took a deep draw on his mug of beer. Boy, it sure was good going down, the first one he'd had all day.

Next to him, Roy nudged him with an elbow and pointed toward the doorway. "Say, ain't that Bob Owens's old lady?" he asked.

Tony wiped beer from his lips and nodded affirmatively as he saw Margi enter with two other women who worked on *Motive*. "Sure is," he replied, thinking he'd buy her a beer. They were friends, after all, from working together.

"I'm surprised to see her here," said Roy. "I thought she was going home every night to take care of Bob, that poor son of a bitch."

"She usually does," answered Tony, aware that news of Bob Owens's accident had reached all ears on the lot, making all men who heard about the serious groin injury cringe and become extremely sympathetic toward the unfortunate victim.

"What's she doing here?" wondered Roy.

Tony did not know all the details, but he could put two and two together. "Bob's been so depressed, I'll bet she needs to get away from him every now and then. God knows, *you* and *me* don't go rushing home after work, either."

"It's hard to imagine that Bob would let her out of his sight, the way he's so crazy in love with her." Though Roy kept watching and admiring Margi and her two friends, it would never have occurred to him to breach Bob's trust and go and talk to them.

"I'd be depressed, too," said Tony, "if that happened to me. I've heard it said that Bob might never get a hard-on again."

Roy was shocked. "Is that so? That motherfucker didn't deserve all this that's happened to him. He's a great guy. Didn't have any of that bad . . . bad . . . crappo . . . no . . . you know what I'm talking about . . . the bad luck if you do bad things."

"Karma," replied Tony.

"Right, professor, that's it. Karma," said Roy, unwittingly stepping back from the bar and looking at his own crotch.

"Guess that proves you never know when fate will strike you down," said Tony. "I heard they don't do too much talking, don't even sleep in the same room."

"No shit!" exclaimed Roy. "And they were the most in-love and well-sexed couple I'd ever seen—I don't give a damn how old *any*body is. Why don't he see a shrink?"

"He's real stubborn, for one thing," answered Tony. "And, no doubt, it's real embarrassing. He's probably worried they'll say it's all in his head. Who the hell would want to hear a thing like that?"

They drank a toast to Bob's recovery and a second to ward off any evil spirits from throwing the same rotten luck their way. Tony asked the cocktail waitress to take three drinks over to Margi's table.

Margi squinted across the room, through the smoke and hazy light, to see who had sent her the drinks, offended that it might be a come-on. When she saw Tony, her face softened to a smile, and she waved to thank him.

"That was nice of him," she said to her companions, who were the wardrobe and assistant wardrobe ladies from *Motive*. "I need a few drinks. I'm in the mood to get good and drunk."

She couldn't face going home. Every night, she was crying her eyes out before the end of the evening—out of frustration over Bob's condition, Bob's terrible state of mind, her own inability to change the situation or make it any better, and at the thought of what they once had that now seemed to be gone forever. She ranged between being patient and understanding with Bob to being so goddamned angry she couldn't see straight.

Every night, she lay alone in bed, her tears soaking the pillow, knotted Kleenexes surrounding her, before finally drifting off to sleep. If she were lucky, she wouldn't awaken till morning. Her eyes would burn and it would take a couple of minutes for her mind to remember the trauma of the night before. Sometimes she would lie a full five minutes before reality settled upon her. These minutes seemed to be the only bliss she experienced anymore.

The Golden Time was a popular bar, directly across the street from the lot. Other crew members drifted in and said hello. Stagehands from other shows, who knew Bob, stopped to inquire about how he was doing. They were polite and caring, wanting to know details yet unable to ask, because the official story was that Bob had injured his back.

Margi hadn't bothered calling Bob to tell him she'd be late. She figured he didn't give a damn. The kids were used to taking care of themselves and had been quite cooperative about fixing dinner for their dad. But as the liquor settled in and people kept asking her about Bob, a huge sense of guilt began invading her fun. She had needed to get away from her home for one night. It had seemed like such a good idea, but maybe she should have gone to a place where Bob wasn't known.

"Maybe I'd better call him," she finally said, walking back to the phone. One of the kids answered and Margi asked about Bob.

"Dad's not doing much. Just sitting in the family room, reading a magazine or something. He won't let us watch TV. TV reminds him that he isn't working. So now *we* can't watch it because *he* won't watch. I wish you could do something with him, Mom."

There were two drinks waiting for her at her table. "Good," she told her friends. "I'm ready for them." The alcohol made her feel good by removing her from the present.

"You know who's really responsible, don't you?" she said loudly, each word spoken carefully so it wouldn't sound like she was slurring. "Graham Maddox."

"Shhh," said the wardrobe lady. "Don't talk so loud. Especially not about Mr. Maddox. There's lots of people here that would run right to him and snitch on you."

"I don't give a damn," said Margi, raising her voice. "When you come right down to it, Graham Maddox is ultimately responsible for Bob's condition. But do you think I've heard one word from him? No. He thinks that insurance is all it takes to get over illnesses and accidents."

The wardrober leaned forward and said, "I think we'd better go. I'll give you a ride. I don't think you should drive." Margi's friend wanted to get her out of the bar before she said anything else about Mr. Maddox.

"I don't feel like going," replied Margi. "Do you know that Graham Maddox has never once called and talked to Bob. Graham Maddox doesn't give a shit. Think how demoralizing it is for Bob, who's worked for Maddox for over ten years?"

By now, heads were turning to listen.

"Be quiet, will you!" commanded the wardrober.

"Why should I?" cried Margi drunkenly. "I don't give a shit who hears. If you work for Graham Maddox, you'd better be forewarned: He'll not care about you if you're down and out. He'll replace you as soon as he can."

Tony appeared, to help calm down Margi. She was known to have a temper and only Bob was said to be able to control it. They felt it their duty to get Margi out of the bar before she said anything she'd regret in the morning.

"But I don't feel like going," said Margi. "My Bob never did anything to hurt anybody. Now, he's so depressed. It's not fair. . . ." Anger, which had been boiling like milk in a saucepan, began to pour from her in a way nobody had ever seen before.

"I tell you, if anything permanent happens to my Bob, I will hold Graham Maddox responsible! He won't be around long if I get my hands on him."

"Sure, sure," said Tony, trying to calm her.

"Let's get her out of here," said the frantic wardrober, taking Margi's purse.

"Goddamn it," shouted Margi, "I'm not ready to leave."

Tony leaned close to her ear and spoke in a stern voice, "Then shut the fuck up about Graham Maddox. Things will only get worse for Bob if you keep shooting your mouth off like that."

Margi's jaw dropped. "How dare you talk to me like that! I'll say any damn thing about Maddox I want to."

But Tony had Margi on her feet, steering her toward the door and over to his car in the parking lot. "I'll drive her home," he told the costumer. "Do you know her address?"

Margi sat silently as thousands of cars streamed by them on the freeways and orange, milky-green and milky-white streetlights stretched across miles and miles of Los Angeles. Tears burned hot in her eyes and began flowing down her cheeks.

"I don't know what I'm going to do," she murmured. The tears had come again and the night ahead seemed so long. There was no comfort to arriving at her home, opening the front door to silence . . . and another night alone with her pillows.

Jeannie, her mass of chestnut hair pulled back into a great French braid, took four sacks of groceries out of her car and carried them into her mother's house.

"Hi, I'm here," she called out cheerily. This time there was something to be cheery about. The usual tomblike feeling greeted her. It was broken only by the stereo yapping of the two little dogs in the backyard who, upon seeing Jeannie cross the family room with the groceries, tapped their little feet insistently against the glass door.

The television was on, but the sound was so low that it was inaudible. "Why don't you have the sound on so you can hear it?" questioned Jeannie, setting the groceries on the kitchen counter, taking off her coat, and going to kiss her mother's cheek.

Her mother's voice sounded tired. "There's nothing to watch."

It was a remarkable statement for a woman who kept the

television on day and night just to have some noise. The TV blocked out all those creaky little noises that echo through an empty house and make you wonder if someone isn't walking around in the other rooms. It also blocks out all the empty echoes in your head that remind you there is no one to walk around in the other rooms.

"I have a surprise for you, Mother," said Jeannie, reaching into her purse and extracting a piece of paper. "Take a look at this."

Her mother held out her hand like a child about to receive an exciting present. "What is it?" she asked, not comprehending the paper's significance.

"It's the first deposit into our savings account."

"You mean that Graham has paid?" said her mother, staring at the deposit slip.

Jeannie nodded her head yes.

Graham Maddox had first come into their lives, Jeannie guessed, when she was about ten and her mother was billed as "Odette" at a strip joint in San Francisco's North Beach.

Odette was an exotic dancer who packed in quite a crowd of regulars. Her platinum bleached hair was piled on top of her head in a fashion that reminded her young daughter of soft ice cream swirled on a cone. She took exceedingly good care of her body and, likewise, good care of her daughter. Jeannie always spoke enthusiastically of her mother as a dancer, though she did not know the answer to the question: "Where does your mother dance?"

Odette danced in white. Her skin was creamy. She refused to go out in the sun and tan. The other dancers had dark tan lines on their bottoms and no tan lines around their breasts, as they sunbathed topless. But Odette was an even color, holding great long feather fans as she danced, pouting pale pink lips as she saucily stepped down the runway.

When other girls rolled their behinds in the faces of male customers, Odette kept her distance and gave them wide-eyed, innocent looks. Then she'd get down on her hands and knees and crawl slowly forward, her breasts in their scant top hanging low, inviting bills of any denomination to roost against her welcoming chest.

Graham Maddox admitted that he was married. He told Odette he lived in Los Angeles but came frequently to San Francisco on business. His business, he claimed, was insurance. She had no reason to doubt him. He bought her presents and came to see her dance every night that he stayed in the city.

Graham and Odette didn't have sex for four months. The impression he wished to make was that he was not merely desperate to wallow between her legs. She was pleasantly surprised; he was just being tactical. He wanted her to fall for him, to beg him to please, please sleep with her. He enjoyed the easy manipulation of watching her get turned on by him every time she saw him. He found excuses to go to San Francisco.

Odette was thrilled by Graham, though he made it clear he was not going to get a divorce and make her a permanent part of his life. His life in L.A. was private. She didn't even know how to contact him there. So she had to take him as often as she got him. She lived for the days when he came to the Bay Area.

She made one rule, however, and that was to never take him home. She always stayed with him at his hotel suite. Though she told him about her daughter, she didn't want to share this part-time man with anyone. Odette fretted when she knew he was coming to see her. She could think of nothing else all day long.

Graham was never a real, solid person to Jeannie. He existed only through Odette's interpretation. At first, Jeannie was jealous. Then she accepted the fact that Mommy wasn't going to bring this man around and did her best to ignore her mother's neurotic behavior. She also learned to ignore the tears her mother shed for hours after the man returned to Los Angeles.

When Graham sat in her audience, Odette danced majestically, freely, cut loose in a fresh wind where, in her mind, she danced alone for her lover on a distant, sandy beach. Every movement was for him. Enticing. Erotic. Seductive. She always had that look of innocence, as though there were no way she could ever be violated. Dancing like that made her happy. Only rarely did she allow herself daydreams about how much happier she would be if Graham married her.

If Graham was not overwhelmed with business, he always rented a big old convertible Cadillac and took Odette driving around during the day. He made sure he got her to the nightclub in plenty of time for her to dress and do her makeup. Some afternoons, they would go to the club and she would rehearse a new number for him. He always gave her some very useful comments and she would remark that he ought to get into something creative for a living since he was so good at it.

One day, he tore up the Pacific Coast Highway in the Cadillac, his mind intent upon the road while she looked out at the sparkling sea. He liked driving fast. It thrilled her; it never worried her.

"I like being with you," he told her. "You're not at all like my wife. You're full of life. You know how to have fun. You're a beautiful woman. And you aren't stuck up at all. You don't feel you have to be respectable and make a good impression on everyone all the time."

"Are you saying that I'm not respectable?" she asked. It hurt her feelings that she was not as well cared for as his wife.

"That's what I like about you," he said. "You live life the way you want to, and you don't care what anyone says."

She wanted to argue that that wasn't entirely true, but she looked at his face and could see he was content to see her only as he wished. If he were to have a partial relationship with her, perhaps it was best to see her only partially.

The sun shone brightly where they were driving, but to the north, the sky was blackening out over the ocean, rolling fog into the coast.

"Should I put the top up?" he asked.

"No, I'm fine," she answered, retying the knot of her scarf under her chin. "I like the feel of an approaching storm. It makes the air electric." She thrust both hands above her head, the fingers curving with a dancer's grace, reaching into the sky and communing with all the storm-filled energies.

As she danced with the sky, Graham impatiently sped around a large boulder that had fallen in the road. Later, he said he thought he had plenty of time to make it back to his side of the road before meeting the oncoming car. He swerved hard, hitting the brakes, skidding sideways. The dancer was thrown first to the sky, then upon the earth. The other car had somehow avoided collision and had stopped safely. Graham's own grip upon the wheel had saved him.

But the dancer's beautiful face was torn. Only her great love for Graham kept him from getting scalded in a lawsuit. Upon the advice of his dear, wise friend Norman—who thought better of involving insurance companies and wives—Graham quickly and quietly paid off her hospital bills, paid for additional plastic surgery, and put money in a trust account for her.

At the time, it seemed like so much money to her. She signed a paper that ended his financial responsibility to her. She had thought he loved her. Love would carry humans through the worst tragedies in their lives.

But he didn't love her. He couldn't stand to look at her reconstructed face. Her beauty was spoiled. She could no longer dance. She was no longer the escape he needed from his respectable lifestyle. Then he stopped coming to San Francisco. He dropped out of sight.

When the daughter, Jeannie, discovered the truth about the nature of her mother's dancing career, she did not find it shameful. Her mother would never dance again. *That* was shameful. Odette was destroyed because she lost a man whom she thought loved her but who, in reality, had only floundered in her beauty.

Odette used up the trust fund money supporting herself and her daughter. But she needed more plastic surgery. At the time, she believed that if she needed anything further, she had only to ask. Then she realized she could not contact him. Since she had signed the paper, she didn't believe there was any legal way to implicate Graham. And the years passed, and Odette was no more.

Jeannie, who had always mistrusted the man she had

never met, grew to hate him. He owed them.

Odette and Jeannie never bothered reading the credits at the start or finish of a TV program. It was only a fluke that Jeannie ever noticed the name Graham Maddox. Jeannie wondered if it was the same man. A little research and a few phone calls proved that not only was he the same man, but that he had always been a writer and producer. He had never been in the insurance business.

Jeannie made up her mind to move to L.A. and find a job with Maddox Productions. Since her mother, the former exotic dancer Odette, was not able to fend for herself, Jeannie moved her to the area as well.

Jeannie hugged her mother's neck. "Graham has paid, all right," said Jeannie. "His face turned white when I mentioned your name. Kind of like he hadn't thought of you in years."

"Oh" was her mother's reply, a soft sigh that revealed more disappointment than Jeannie could have guessed was there. "He wasn't thinking of me?" The question was timid; she didn't really want an answer.

Jeannie was hard. No use wrapping up emotion with business. "No, I don't think the bastard thinks about much except himself and his immediate needs. He's totally fucked up things with his wife. And I like her. She doesn't like me, but then she's pretty smart and probably intuitively knows that Graham and I have been doing it."

Her mother's peroxided head pivoted in Jeannie's direction, as though a spring had been released and it was snapping back in place. "You've been sleeping with him?"

Jeannie let out a sigh of exasperation. "Of course I did, Mother. It was all part of the plan. When we first talked about it, it was all part of the plan. We needed to get Graham, the bastard, into a position where he would have to pay us off. What better way is there to get to a man besides through his pants?"

Her mother shook her head and looked immeasurably sad. "I didn't know," she said finally. "I just didn't know."

"Who cares!" exclaimed Jeannie. "He's paid five thousand dollars and he owes us a lot more. He promised me he'd have it by Monday. Then we can schedule an appointment with Dr. Reed. Remember? He's the plastic surgeon. I'm so excited, Mother, aren't you?"

But her mother was staring at the deposit slip that had fallen out of her daughter's hand and was lying on the floor.

"Mother," cried Jeannie, "you're going to be beautiful again. We're giving the doctor a copy of that photo"—she pointed to the one of her mother in the silver-spangled costume—"and we're telling him to make you back exactly that way."

She stroked the soft skin under her mother's chin, a gesture of love and encouragement. There was the misshapen face that her mother allowed no one but her daughter to see. "You'll be very thankful when it's all over, Mother," said Jeannie, picturing her mother returning to the robust personality she had been before the accident.

"How can you keep working for him now?" asked her mother.

"I can't quit abruptly," replied the daughter. "I don't want anyone to suspect anything."

Rain streaked the window. It fell from a hard gray cloud that pressed itself against the land. It rattled against her heart like a prisoner's tin cup on the iron bars of a cell. It beat down ceaselessly, pinning her between the bedspread and blankets, where she lay for a little warmth, too weak to get under the covers.

But the rain was only within her.

Outside the window was another clear California day—a replica of the day before, which was modeled from the day before that. Outside the house, California was acting the way it always did, with consistent monotony of good weather.

However, she saw only gray.

Penny's parents were worried about her. Since Dillon had broken the engagement, she had not been out of bed, except to go to the bathroom, had not been downstairs to one meal, and had refused to eat the trays of food sent up to her. The family doctor, making a house call, diagnosed Penny's condition as a minor breakdown and wrote the name of a psychiatrist on a blank prescription slip.

Her parents argued about whether or not they should call the specialist right away. Her mother said yes, she didn't care what their neighbors and friends thought. Her father insisted they give the girl a few more days, believing that Huntingtons could recover from any crisis without the help of psychiatry.

Penny's mother went up to her daughter's bedroom and slowly opened the door to look in. Penny lay on her back. Her eyes, red-rimmed and swollen from crying, were open and staring up at the ceiling. Her mother didn't even know if her daughter were aware of another's presence in the bedroom.

Mrs. Huntington sat on the edge of the bed, smoothing wrinkles in the bedspread within her reach, hesitant about straightening the fabric close to the girl. "Penny," she said, "you are acting very ill. Is it the flu, dear? What can the doctor prescribe for you?"

Penny shook her head, her limp, dirty hair flat on the pillow. Her face was colorless, and her lips were almost as pale as the hollows of her cheeks.

She wished her mother would go away and leave her alone. She wished only to lie and hear the rain drumming against the roof, against the window. It was a comfortless rain, leaving everything wet with no place to dry. But she didn't care. She didn't want dryness. She wanted the rain to dissolve her and wash her downstream.

"Dear," said her mother, "we are very thankful that Dillon is out of your life. He was playing games with you. He didn't want you because he loved you, he wanted you because you gave him prestige he doesn't have on his own. Don't you see that?"

Her voice droned on. It was the same crap she said every time she came into Penny's bedroom. That voice reflected her parents' attitude—the attitude that had driven Dillon away.

"Penny, I hope this teaches you to stay with your own

type. People who are bred and educated like you. Did you see the lovely flowers Mallory Burton sent over? He's very concerned. As soon as you are feeling better, your father and I trust you will start seeing Mallory. He is so reliable. And he is so distinguished-looking—not really *good*-looking, but quite aristocratic."

The voice wouldn't go away. It whittled at Penny in a more brutal way than the rain, hacking, battering, on and on.

Words crept from her mouth, like a bear coming from a cave after hibernation, "Shut up, Mother, shut up!"

"Did you say something, dear?"

"I said shut up! Go away! Leave me alone!" Penny's eyes continued to stare at the ceiling.

"I can't leave you like this."

"Go away!" shrieked Penny. "I don't want you. I want Dillon. Leave me alone."

Yelling made Mrs. Huntington nervous. The petite woman was out the door quickly, hurrying to find her husband and insist that they call the psychiatrist immediately.

Penny felt desolate. If only Dillon would call. If only she could hear his voice, talk to him about it, try to work something out with him. She couldn't believe he didn't love her, she just couldn't. Didn't he know she would stand by him through anything? She couldn't be happy unless she were with him. He had said the same thing to her—that he could never see himself with another woman.

Why had he really dropped her? It was a disappointment not to have gotten the promotion, but there would be other opportunities. She had told him so many times that he was the only thing on earth that mattered to her. . . . He must know, *must* know that she didn't give a damn what he did for a living.

Was there another girl? Imagining Dillon's arms around somebody else slayed her like a bayonet through every vital organ. For the first few days she had tried calling his home, but there had been no answer. She had tried his office, and his secretary had taken messages. But he never called back.

If only she could hear his voice. That's all she wanted. To

hear him and tell him how much she needed him. Instead, all she heard were her parents' voices: "We were right about him. We *told* you so. Thank God he is gone."

But Dillon would never be gone, because she would never love another. Please call, she prayed, please call.

A long way off through the house, she heard the phone ring. Her heart beat strongly as she listened intently for someone to call her. But there was only silence and no cheerful voice beckoning her out of the rain.

Downstairs, Mr. Huntington answered the phone. He listened a moment before replying. "Listen well, young man," he said in a grim, stony tone, "if you know what is good for you. You *cannot* speak to my daughter. She is seriously ill. We will not allow people like you to get your hands on her again. Don't try coming over here, because I will call my security guards as well as the police, and I will slap a lawsuit on you you won't believe. That is, if I don't shoot you first for trespassing. Don't call again. It doesn't matter how many times you call; you are not allowed to speak to her. I hope I have made myself clear. She is seriously ill and it is your fault. You will never get near her again."

Huntington hung up the phone, his eyes narrowed to slits, his teeth clenched at the persistent calls from Dillon Hughes. He had kept his voice low and Penny had not heard a word he had said. Dillon would never get to his daughter again. He would see to that. He would ruin the young accountant.

On the other end of the line, Dillon slammed down the receiver. He was convinced that Penny was thinking about him. All week, everyone who answered the phone at the Huntington house had politely and firmly told him that Penny did not wish to speak to him. At first, he had believed them. After all, look how he had treated the one thing in his life that he loved the most? He had been rash to heedlessly cast her out of his life and he could understand why she hadn't wanted to speak to him.

But this latest conversation with her father shed new light. What the hell was going on? She wasn't even getting the messages that he had returned her calls. What was wrong with her? Twice, her father had mentioned that she was very ill. What could be wrong? No . . . no, she couldn't have tried to take her own life. . . .

If only he had gotten the promotion, none of this snarled mess would have happened. He had put in years of hard work for Graham Maddox. He had counted on the promotion. It had been promised to him. He had promised it to Penny. It was the least she deserved. Penny was seriously ill and there was only one person to blame. Graham Maddox. He played with his employees like they were pawns. Build them up, then shove them off a cliff.

If Penny were sick, Dillon felt he had to tell her he was sorry. Even if she didn't want him anymore, he needed to tell her that he had never loved anyone else in his entire life as he loved her. He had to see her; there *had* to be a way to see her. But her parents would never let him in. And they let no one talk to her on the phone.

"Penny," he cried to the quiet room, "I love you. I love you. Please forgive me for ever having left you."

There was that half a dog tag imbedded in the asphalt of the intersection. Something about it always pulled at Will; the shiny metal with a name stamped on it, cut in half. It was sad, as though an important part of a man's life lay coldly upon the street. Men discharged from military duty usually kept their dog tags around their neck or in a special box. Will had tried to pry it up with his fingernail, but too many tires and too much sun had sunk it into the black tar. It disturbed Will every time he walked past the metal tab shackled in its barren grave.

He and Sondra had gotten into the habit of taking walks in the evening. It went along with their habit of having dinner together a few nights a week at her house. Those evenings were pleasant and gave Will, Sondra, and Scott each a sense of belonging to a family. Will and Sondra never talked much, but it was a comfortable, welcome, easy silence between them. A little smile or eye contact was all it took to let the other know that they had become good friends.

Occasionally, if Will stayed too late, he spent the night on the couch. He had never tried to touch Sondra, but it didn't matter. He refused to talk about Oregon, and had in no way desired physical contact with a woman since his return. Sex had retreated within him. He hadn't craved it, and Sondra seemed as ambiguous as ever when it came to whether she preferred men or women as sexual partners.

They did not say much on their walks. Usually, the predominant sound was Will's boots clomping on the sidewalk. In the dark, streetlights brightened the corners and, after they passed by, sent their elongated shadows shooting out far ahead of them. The shadows made them seem even thinner than they were and made their feet look like they were high-stepping.

Sondra had made a pot roast, an all-day Crockpot affair. The meat had been so tender it had needed almost no chewing, and the taste had been so savory they had eaten very slowly. After the meal, Will and Scott cleared the table and loaded the dishwasher, like they always did. It was mundane, but they both enjoyed it. Then Scott went to his room to do his homework. Nobody had to ask him to do it. He had accepted the routine without questions.

"I've never seen Scotty smiling so much," said Sondra. "I was at the end of my rope because he had gotten so surly and hard to get along with. I really appreciate you coming out and spending this time with him."

Will didn't know how to respond, so they walked in silence, listening to the night sounds around them. Several blocks away they heard the traffic from the larger streets. But closer, except for dogs barking at them from backyards, all was quiet.

"Look at that," he said, pointing up into a tree. "Do you think that's grapefruit up there?"

"Might be," she said. "Why don't you get one?"

After glancing through the lighted windows of the house to make sure the owners didn't see him, he reached into the tree. "It's a grapefruit, all right," he confirmed, pressing the fruit against his nose and breathing the pungent odor.

"I'll bet it's no good," said Sondra, leaning close as Will dug his fingernails into the skin. "It's too late in the year for any good fruit to still be hanging on the tree."

Will split the sphere with his hands and gave her half. They both pulled off a section and put it into their mouths. Simultaneously, their eyes opened wide and expressed immense dislike.

"Oh, God, that's bad!" said Will, spitting his mouthful into the gutter.

Sondra spit hers into her hand and then tossed it under a bush in the yard. She began laughing and said, "Let's get out of here before we get caught."

Impulsively, unaware she had done so, she took his elbow and gently pulled him down the street. They walked and she held onto his arm like it was the most natural thing in the world to do. Her touch was light—perhaps the same way she would have held her son.

Will's first reaction was to tug back his arm, but Sondra was laughing and making sour-grapefruit faces and being so silly, he didn't bring her grip on his arm to her attention. He had fought off physical contact with anyone for so long, there was a pain where Sondra's energy met his, an ache on his arm because it was not Candy touching him. If there were any way that it could be Candy holding his arm, it would be so. But no power on heaven or earth could make it happen. Tears brimmed in his eyes for a moment, and then subsided.

Sondra did not notice the tears, but she did notice her clasp on his arm. Her body became rigid and she tried to turn him loose. Now it was Will's turn to need *her* touch. He gripped her arm fiercely. She looked questioningly into his face, her eyes a mixture of sorrow and mistrust. He looked back at her straightforwardly; not mocking, not faking, not using her. A look of acceptance focused in her eyes, and they walked on.

In a voice that came from one of her hidden places, she said, "You know, it's been a whole lot of years since I've walked with a man and actually held his arm. If anyone passed us right now, they'd think we were a couple. When I first got divorced, I thought I would die because I was all alone and I was so used to depending on another person to give me my identity. I was not Sondra, all by myself; I was Sondra and Jim, half of a couple."

She stopped talking just to see if Will was listening. Sondra didn't like talking, because she figured people rarely paid attention to what she was saying.

Ahead in the street, three or four teenage boys spoke near the curb. Their voices were delightful, a couple of years older than Scotty's, hovering closer to maturity but still young. Having strung an extension cord with a light out to the curb, they peered under the hood of a car—a most socially acceptable activity for sixteen-year-old boys. They lived in an age of cars, and men were the masters. Cars had a lot to do with attaining manhood in the United States.

After they passed the boys, Will said, "So what happened? Where's Jim now? Why'd you split up?"

It was a question that had been a long time coming. Will might have never asked, except that she had brought it up. He did not like intruding too far into her personal space; but he also realized that if he didn't ask, she might think he didn't care.

"Jim was Mr. Achiever, Mr. Macho, Mr. Homebody. He had a fabulous job and got promotions all the time and started making fabulous amounts of money. We had a luxury home, luxury cars, and a baby boy—very important, you know, to carry on the family name. I was part of the apparatus. Part of the show.

"But I wanted more. I wanted to go back to school, to take classes, to learn. Lifelong education is very important to me, but Jim could not understand that. He thought I had everything I needed. Perhaps he was threatened. But to make a long story short, when I couldn't get him to consent to letting me go back to school, and after many vicious arguments, we got divorced. And I was free of him."

"Are you happy now?" asked Will.

"Relatively."

"You don't seem to want a thing to do with a man," Will

said honestly, wondering if she were aware of her reputation as a dyke.

"That's not entirely true. I just don't want to get *involved.* It hurts too much. It's too hard to get out of. No man is ever going to tie me down again. I'm not going to waste any more time massaging tender masculine egos. They can accept me for what I am, or they can go to hell."

"Yeeow, that's brutal!" replied Will. Though she still hung onto his arm, she seemed remote, almost as if she were walking on the other side of the street.

"I don't think so. I don't dislike men. I dislike the way they want to treat me. Why can't I have an equal relationship? Why does it always have to be a power struggle? There is nothing more distasteful to me than to have to use my sexual powers to get what I want. And, believe me, I've used them before. Now, I refuse to."

"Aren't we all essentially sexual beings?" asked Will. "Isn't it part of our human makeup?"

"We are sexual. We need to have sex in our lives or we become bitter—kind of like those damn grapefruits that have been hanging on the tree too long, waiting for someone to pick them off and take them home. But I don't want to manipulate with sex. The thought disgusts me."

"Were those the terms of your marriage?"

"Oh, yes, that I fulfilled his fantasy about what the perfect woman is—how she acts, when she fucks. He used to reward me for a great morning of fucking. How? It put him in a great mood and he'd treat me like a princess all day long. The days I didn't 'put out,' he was a grouch and I had to coax good humor out of him. Is that any way to have a relationship? Hell, no."

"Do you hear from Jim?"

"Sure. He keeps sending child support. Scotty used to go down to visit every other weekend, but Jim's new wife is really mean to him. Always favoring her kids over Scott. Scott doesn't want to have to compete for his father's attention."

"He shouldn't have to."

"Exactly. So Scotty's been pushed out of his father's family nest, and he's tried to take it like an adult. But he's not an adult. He's a twelve-year-old kid and his father hurts him by not stepping in and telling the new wife, 'Hey, you can't treat my son that way.' "

A dryer's worth of a fresh clothing smell drifted through the air. It was a pleasant, well-adjusted scent. As they passed the next house, three tall pine trees broaching the sidewalk left their fragrance in the air. Will plucked a long needle and slid it between his molars, chewing and releasing the taste of evergreen.

"I like Scott," he said. "He kind of reminds me of me. Sometimes I get real angry and I don't know what to do with all those hostile feelings. When I was a kid and Graham got meaner and meaner to me, I used to wish me and Mom could take off and be by ourselves. But she couldn't leave him. She was having his babies, so they were hers, too. A mother can't pack up and leave her kids. But it was my dream, nevertheless."

They both realized they had been *talking* talking, not just babbling about insignificant subjects. Silence stole back between them, but it was not as comfortable as it had been before. The barrier would never again be a complete pristine sea between them. The waves of each had lapped upon the sands of the other. Hopefully, the waters would remain very deep and impassible, because they had unexpectedly become a most beautiful blue.

Ahead, a high hedge bordering a side yard covered the sidewalk in deep shadow. Will stopped in the soft, inky air and turned Sondra toward him. He touched her lips with a fingertip, tracing their surface until they softened. She began kissing his finger, shaking her head as her subconscious kept saying no, no, no, her body responding with a quickening heartbeat.

His finger slid to her chin and caressed her jawline, then he cupped the whole of her face with his palm and pulled it very slowly toward his. He leaned close, breathing in her essence, watching her lips tremble. She closed her eyes to escape the intensity of the moment—she didn't want him to proceed; she didn't want him to stop.

It had been a long time since he had kissed. Was he breaching a trust by wanting to do so now? Inside, he felt cold. The only warmth he could feel was Sondra's breath upon his face. His thoughts whirled through him like ice in a blender, large chunks being broken into smaller and smaller pieces until they became froth.

He lowered his mouth to hers, gently meeting her lips with his, pecking softly until the wetness on the inside of her lip wet the outside of his. A soft, involuntary moan came through her, circling her teeth before flowing into him. He seized both sides of her head with his hands and pulled her to him, laying kiss after kiss upon her mouth.

Her tongue softly explored his lips and she was sure she had never wanted to kiss someone so much in her entire life. She gripped the sinews of his forearms that so delicately held her face, drawing close to him, her mouth unwilling to let go of his for one instant. Fire, ignited upon his lips, slowly devoured her. Her fingers felt his face along his strong jaw and fine cheekbones, stroking the curving mustache. It was a new surface to her, one she had not studied much for fear of liking it.

She wanted to resist him, to push him away, but his kisses were an accelerator flooding her with fever. He was impossible to resist—a potent, overpowering force that willed her to him and clutched at the steaming contents of her gut. It hit her low, somewhere between her ovaries, rocking deeply within her.

He was slow to start, a diesel engine in his own winter. He felt her bony, hard chest against him and slid his hands to her rear end, pulling the small but perfectly formed buttocks into him. He pulled rhythmically, and she gave in more and more. His hands were hot where he touched her, his mouth burned where he kissed her. Her flames were upon him. He began to give in to their melting effect; the solid ice with which he resisted her, dripping slowly, an icicle in the winter sun.

He was amazed at the hard, steady thumping within his chest. His pulse was strong, beating in his arms, behind his knees, on his sides. It was waking his body, waking a frozen man who had been locked into an iceberg.

Headlights from a passing car washed over them, blinding them for an instant before disappearing down the empty street, leaving only its exhaust fumes lingering. Sondra dropped her head against Will's chest, not wishing to break the moment, wanting only to be trapped forever in this space of time. He would hold her—and she would be shielded from the night, from her memories, from his memories.

Suddenly, she wanted to know him, to ask him about himself. It was as if she had been perched on the top of a tall pole, as far away from him as she could possibly get, and now the pole had swung one hundred eighty degrees and she wanted to know everything. It was suddenly horrible not to know anything.

She knew that in the morning, with the sun streaming through the trees outside her bedroom window and spilling over the white sheets of her bed and the white carpet of the room, she would ask. She was no fool. He would not give it all up so easily. But, maybe, a little at a time. She only wanted to lie her head against his chest, listen to his heartbeat, and wait for his answers.

Chapter 13

On Friday morning, Jeannie walked into work wearing a tight-skirted suit that clothed her long upper legs and revealed her perfect rear end. Immediately, Graham had to see her in his office. She went and stood before him, her eyes smiling victoriously, her lips parted in her curious way.

"Shut the door," said Graham from behind his desk.

"Certainly," she said, feeling like an equal before him. Her job was only a charade at this point. "Did you want to talk to me about our little arrangement?" she asked, her back to the closed door.

"Yeah," he replied, the lines deep under his eyes, his lips dry. "I suppose you think you have me worried?" he asked her. "Worried that you will give those tapes to people who could do me damage—personally, professionally—I'm not exactly sure what you had in mind."

"Mr. Maddox," said Jeannie, sitting on one of the white sofas across the room, so that he had to turn his entire body to keep his eyes on her, "as your *personal* secretary, you must remember I know a lot about your *personal* affairs. I know who you do business with and I know what deals you are about to make. I know where you live and I know what's going on in your private life. Surely, what I'm asking is not all that much?"

"Let me tell you something, Ms. Hansen. You're a clever woman who has delectable bedroom skills." He waited for the effect of the compliment and saw she smiled with an "I know it" attitude. "But if you think I'm going to risk jeopardizing everything I've built here because I'm threatened by one secretary-slash-whore, you're very mistaken."

Jeannie's face flushed scarlet, the color moving out from her cheekbones to cloud her forehead, nose, and chin. She was annoyed at not being more in charge. "I wasn't planning on extorting funds from you for *years,* Graham. I asked for one simple bulk payment to help my mother. It's a debt you owe. I know you have the money."

Graham watched the shapely fingernails of her right hand bite into the back of her left as they lay folded in her lap. She was such a pretty thing and had been so sexually satisfying. It was hard to believe she was trying to pull off this tough act. But then, he was unsure of her. What if she were really as tough as he only thought she was pretending to be?

"I've paid you all I'm going to pay you," he said.

"No, you haven't," she came back quickly. "You *must* give me all that I've asked for."

To look at her, he still thought she was a very appealing sexual machine. But she had become so goddamned irritating, always rubbing him in the wrong direction. He had no doubt that she was the stripper's daughter. But so many years had passed since Odette had been thrown from his car. How did he know that Jeannie was telling the entire truth? A woman like Odette, who wasn't very bright and was dependent on men's favors, would always need someone to help her. He had obliged by giving them some money.

"I don't like the way you've gone about this. If you and your mother had come to me up front, without all this sneaking around and blackmail, I might have been encouraged to make some agreement. I haven't even seen your mother in years. How do I know that she is in this present condition? You have given me no proof."

"Proof! Proof? I don't need to give you proof. I have the photos. I have the tapes."

She really was irritating. Irrational. Hard to deal with. He was much too busy to devote any more time to her annoying demands. He had to get her out of his life.

"Who are you going to give them to?" he asked, calling her bluff. If he sounded as tough as she, perhaps she would believe him. "As you know, my wife is no longer living under the same roof as I, so I need not fear her wrath. Norman, my biggest investor, is also my oldest friend. In fact, he helped me set up the trust fund for your mother. I doubt a tabloid would print your ludicrous story. There's too much risk of a lawsuit. Who, just who do you think is going to give a damn about your tapes and your photos?"

Jeannie rose from the white sofa, walking steadily, one shapely leg in front of the other, toward Graham's desk. She was no longer cool. Her eyes flamed. "I think you should know exactly how you destroyed my mother—for destroy her you did. She loved you, and all you did was lie to her and hurt her."

"I was always up front with her," replied Graham to the bitter woman standing before his desk. "I told her I would never marry her. It became obvious to me that she had become too dependent on me. I had to break it off."

"Yes, *after* she became disfigured." Jeannie picked up the crystal paperweights, shaped like a dancer's hands, and balanced one in each hand. "The truth is, all you wanted her for was her beauty. You couldn't bear to look at her after her face had been destroyed in the accident. You didn't have the human decency to ever check up on her after you set up the trust fund. You didn't care what happened to her life.

"After you discarded her, she never regained any self-confidence. How could she? You should see her face. It's scarred. The bones aren't right under it. There is no way in the world that she looks like Odette. She won't go out in public. She can't afford plastic surgery. Why don't I bring her with me one day, down here, so you can get a good look at her?"

"I wouldn't recommend doing that, Jeannie," he replied coolly. "It would be in extremely bad form."

"You're worried, aren't you, Graham, because you know I'd do it? I'll bring her here and show everyone on the lot how you treat your ex-mistresses." She twisted one paperweight up toward the light, looking at the clarity of the glass.

"Jeannie, I think, under the circumstances, I must terminate your employment here immediately. I will instruct payroll to mail you your final paycheck and two weeks severance. I think that's fair," he told her, and looked down at the papers on his desk the way he did when he let someone know they were not of further importance to him.

Jeannie's lips curled back from her teeth. She raised one arm high above her head, then brought it down, loosing the crystal paperweight. On the desk, in front of Graham, the dancer's hand was whole for one instant before shattering, the fingers, in pieces, skidding off the broad wooden surface and flying into the thick carpet.

"I hate you, Graham Maddox. I've hated you for years. You will pay me what you owe me! You will!"

She threw the second crystal hand toward the wall, where it smashed through the glass of a photo framed there.

The exquisite hands of the dancer were no more. Graham felt cold anger boil within him. "You'd better get the hell out of my office and off this lot, before I call security to take you away. And don't ever—ever—come back!"

Tony crushed a toothpick between his molars as he watched Martin Maddox leaning over Glory, talking to her with his cocky California-boy grin smeared all over his face. They were on the opposite side of the set and out of Tony's earshot. Glory Bell was shaking her head and pointing to her notebook.

She had no business liking a guy my age, thought Tony. He's a whole lot younger than me, probably just the kind of guy she likes. She should be going for those surfers.

Even their hair color practically matched; Martin's strawberry blond bleached by the sun, Glory's fluff highlighted in uneven streaks and tufts that looked so home-done it was almost pathetic. She was really a pretty girl—not gorgeous—who, with that warm smile, was comfortable to be around. But she deserved a young guy, she really did.

Tony felt sorry about the night he had stood her up. He didn't remember much about it, because he'd gotten drunk with the guys. At the time, it had seemed so easy not to go and, afterward, so hard not to feel guilty. Though he'd never call his life "happy," going home alone to the peace of his TV, his dogs, and a few drinks seemed a lot less complicated than having to call up some chick and tell her he loved her.

He wouldn't deny that he and Glory had had some good times together. She released something in him that made him feel truly carefree, unlike the temporary escape a few drinks provided. With her, he felt creative. Their ideas got bubbling around together, working up a good head of steam and enough energy to propel them through their hours together.

He shouldn't have told her all those things she had so readily believed—for instance, that he loved her—because she had plunged in with such total commitment. Who would have thought she would have done such a thing? It must be because she's so young, thought Tony. Anybody who had been around the block a time or two would be more cautious about falling in love in general and about falling in love with *him* specifically.

What would a pretty girl want with him? Couldn't she see how much he drank and how he couldn't make anything out of his life? Sure, he used to have potential and he could still talk a good game, but he'd never be anybody important. So why keep fooling the girl into believing he could be?

He would catch her looking at him, with that painful, embarrassed expression on her face. She would always turn her eyes quickly. She ought to hook up with a kid like Martin. A young guy would be better for her. He was on his way to a good career. Look at the way his dad backed him. Not that Martin Maddox was the perfect choice for Glory, but he would be a lot better for her than an old cameraman who was complacent in his job.

Tony watched Glory get up from her chair and follow Martin across the set and out the back doors. She was so shy, always watching the floor. She was so cute.

"But I can't right now," Glory protested.

"Yes, you can," said Martin. "I'm coproducer and I've got some important notes I need you to take. I've got ideas. Lots of ideas. And . . . I've got an appetite . . . for you."

Glory died over and over inside, the centipede sick feeling

squirming in her stomach, crawling up through her throat. What if someone should see her disappearing with Martin and know what she was doing? It was awful. She felt so ashamed. Martin came to her almost daily now, flirting in the public eye, tyrannizing her with that steady stare that let her know she was to follow him.

Each time, he led her to a different dressing room. They all basically looked the same inside: a mirror, a chair, sometimes a couch, a closet. And he'd always lock the door.

"Are you worried I'll escape?"

"No. I know you won't go anywhere. I just don't want any unwelcome visitors interrupting us."

He unzipped and slid his slacks from his narrow hips, the tan line distinct, his erection full. "You're getting much better, Glory." She knelt before him, because he preferred it that way, so he could stand masterfully over her, holding her head steady while he worked himself in and out of her mouth.

The smell, the loathsome smell, was the most unpleasant part. Glory could have shut her eyes and pretended she were somewhere else, except that the smell kept pulling her back to the dressing room and Martin Maddox ejaculating in her mouth. It didn't take him long, and she felt like asking him why he didn't simply masturbate. Thank God, he only demanded oral favors of her.

She spit into a handful of Kleenex. He turned her head up, but her eyes were tightly shut.

"Open your eyes, goddamn it, and look at me," he commanded.

Her gaze slid up his body and rested on his neck. She didn't have the heart to look him in the eyes.

"I mean *look* at me," he repeated, wrenching her chin upwards so her head was completely tilted back.

She had never hated anyone more in her entire life. Part of her couldn't believe she was forced to go through with this; the other part acknowledged that she had no means of escape. The cold eyes set over the freckled cheeks were in some fantasy world. She doubted Martin even knew who she was.

"I want more," he ordered, holding his cock and placing it to her lips.

She averted her head. Her neck was rigid, her teeth clamped together. Wasn't that enough? Hadn't she given him enough?

"If you don't want it in your mouth," he broiled, "maybe you want it another way?" He pushed her over backward on the floor and sprawled himself upon her.

"No, no," she begged, pushing upwards on his shoulders, his weight too great to push away. She should have given in to him wanting her to suck him again. He had never invaded her body. She couldn't tolerate the thought of him ejaculating inside her; there would be no way to spit it out.

"I'll do it," she gasped. "Put it in my mouth. Please!"

He straddled her head and once more thrust himself into her mouth, which was dry. He was gagging her, pushing far too deeply to the back of her throat. He wasn't quite as hard, and she began stroking him with a hand, hoping he would stiffen. Please come, please come, she thought, realizing that a second orgasm might take time. What a horrid position, with this thing in her mouth that she wanted to bite. Just bite hard, she thought. She didn't care if it bled all over her, so long as it excruciated him.

But she didn't bite. Martin grunted and groaned, rising and lowering himself for maximum sensation. She prayed it would soon be over.

Afterward, as he was putting on his pants, he said, "I'm good, aren't I? I've been banging a couple of chicks every night. I'm staying in shape."

Glory's stomach convulsed. His cock was on repeated public performance. She worried he might be carrying any number of sexual diseases. There were so many. Yet she couldn't stop him. She hated herself, but she had no one to tell. She needed the job. He'd even gotten her a token raise.

"I told you I'd take care of you, didn't I?" he stated. "Now, come on. How about a snort of this white stuff. Takes away the appetite and gives you energy when you don't have time for lunch. Like today."

Glory shook her head and spat again into a fresh wad of

Kleenex. She spat warily, so that he wouldn't notice. What was wrong with her? Why should she be worried about offending him?

"I've got to go," she said, sliding out the door. And inside, she died over and over.

Mrs. Huntington knocked twice and entered her daughter's room. Penny lay on her bed, her face turned toward the sunny window. Throughout the room was an unhealthy smell—of unwashed hair, of unwashed body, of confinement.

"Dear," said Mrs. Huntington, "Mallory Burton is downstairs. He has come for a visit. He wondered if you wanted to take a drive with him. It's such a lovely Saturday. . . ."

"I don't want to see Mallory," wailed Penny, shaking her head on the pillow. Why didn't they leave her alone? She was tired. The medication they had given her made her so drowsy.

"But, dear," protested Mrs. Huntington, wishing she could place a hand upon her daughter's brow and soothe the pain which dwelled there, "Mallory is a good friend. He's in such a good mood, so full of life. Maybe he'll make you feel better."

"I *don't* want to see him," stated Penny. "Can't you understand that?"

Three pretty new housecoats were draped over the back of a chair, their price tags still affixed, yet Penny insisted on wearing an old worn pink robe, which she refused to take off. What could possibly cheer up her daughter? Mrs. Huntington fretted. "Could Mallory come up to your room for a visit?"

"No!" said Penny sharply. Her eyes bored into her mother, who stood nervously near the door, smoothing her hair, smoothing her blouse. Penny felt a jolt of guilt when she looked at the woman. Her mother was trying so hard to be sweet and compassionate. Oh, damn, thought Penny, why do I always have these feelings of guilt about Mother? Why can't I just live my life the way I want?

"Mallory asked me to give you this get-well card. If you change your mind, I'm sure he'll be visiting downstairs with us for a while." Mrs. Huntington laid a lavender envelope on the dressing table near the door and left.

Penny didn't want any card from Mallory. She wanted Dillon. But Dillon had said he didn't love her anymore. Poor Mallory, she thought. He was a loyal friend in so many ways.

She kicked off the covers and went toward the dressing table. Sitting on the stool, she turned the envelope in her hand and glanced at herself in the mirror. She did not recognize her visage. Her hair, no longer bouncy and gleaming with reddish highlights, lay flat against her head, mousy drab. Her skin was waxy white and there were dark circles under her eyes. But she didn't care.

She picked at the envelope's seal with unkempt fingernails. She pulled out the card, which pictured a spray of yellow roses. She smiled. So pretty. They were so pretty.

Ten minutes later, Penny came down the staircase, dressed in a blouse, a denim skirt, and tennis shoes. She had rubbed a little rouge into her cheeks, hoping to bring them to life. She found her parents and Mallory on the back porch, which overlooked the deep yard with its pool and tennis courts.

"Penny, dear," said her mother, surprised, rising to her feet. "Come right over here and sit."

"My little girl," said Mr. Huntington, pulling a chair up to the table.

"Hi, Mallory," Denny said, squinting in the daylight.

"Penny," he said cautiously, getting up, taking her hand, and holding it to his lips for a prolonged moment, "it's good to see you." His voice betrayed his dismay at seeing the pretty girl looking so wretched.

"Mallory," she said, "I think I'd like to go for that drive after all."

Penny sat stiffly in the front seat of his BMW. Their parents called them the "BMW twins," an expression they both found annoying and so typical. Penny didn't say a word until the massive automatic gates had closed behind them and they were five blocks away.

"Where is he?" she asked. "Where are we going to meet Dillon?"

Dillon had been unable to get Penny off his mind. He kept seeing her smiling eyes and hearing her giggle. He had to tell her he was sorry, that he had been too impulsive in wanting to spare her embarrassment. He had to tell her he was sorry for telling her he didn't love her anymore. Because he did. Hopelessly.

It sickened him to think her parents wouldn't let him talk to her. She was ill and he knew she needed him. He couldn't have explained how this knowledge came to him, for he was too rational a person to think in terms of psychic connection. Yet, he was absolutely sure her mind was adhering to his with bulldog tenacity.

It had been a risk, but he had placed a phone call to the venerable law firm of Huntington, Burton and Carlson. "Mallory Burton, please," he requested.

Dillon explained his plight to the young attorney. "I've got to see her," he told Mallory.

Mallory was sympathetic. "I see, I see. Of course, you realize this isn't the story they've been telling me?"

"I hate to think what they've been telling you," replied Dillon, "but I will be forever indebted if you will do me this one favor. Penny may not want a thing to do with me after all I've put her through."

"Nonsense," said Mallory, in his jolliest well-bred voice. "True love will find a way."

"Thank you for your confidence," said Dillon. "And your friendship. See you Saturday."

Dillon paced his apartment, unable to sit down. A football game was on the TV, but he couldn't concentrate on it. The thought of holding Penny in his arms made wave after wave of love rise in his chest, made his heart pound.

He heard his front door open, and Penny, with Mallory behind her, entered the apartment. She ran straight into his arms and clung to him as a baby possum clings to its mother. He wrapped his arms around her and kissed the top of her head. She had lost a lot of weight and was so petite and frail compared with the last time he had seen her.

He pressed her face against his chest and looked over the top of her head to Mallory, who stood awkwardly behind them. He mouthed a silent "thank you" to Mallory and gave him a look that conveyed his anguish over Penny's emaciated, unhealthy condition.

Mallory returned the look, equally distressed, shaking his head. He also hadn't thought she would be so debilitated. Politely, he turned his attention from the couple to the football game and sat on the couch to give the pigskin his full attention.

Dillon led Penny into his bedroom, where they could be alone. He turned her so he could see her face. "My love," he said tenderly, bending down to place his lips upon hers. They were soft; they were cold.

"Dillon, Dillon, is it really you?" she whispered.

"Yes, Penny," he said, kissing each of her cheeks softly. Her eyes were dull.

"I've been frantic," she whimpered. "I've wanted you. I've been thinking about you. Why haven't you called me?"

"I have called. I've sent flowers. You haven't gotten any of my messages. At first, I thought you were ignoring me. But the last time I talked with your father, I realized he was keeping us apart. He threatened to shoot me if I came near you. So I called Mallory and asked for his help."

"Good old Mallory," said Penny. "They've put me on medication. I feel drugged all the time. I was so sleepy, I almost didn't read the card that Mallory brought. What if I hadn't opened it? I might have never seen you again."

"You'd have seen me," insisted Dillon, stroking her head. "I love you, Penny. I've always loved you. I can't stop loving you. I want you to marry me. Be mine, Penny, be mine."

"I *am* yours, Dillon," she whispered, her breath hot upon his neck, her lips kissing him over and over on the soft skin of his throat.

He tried to lead Penny to a chair so she could sit, but she said, "No, no, don't move. Just hold me. I thought mv life was over. Over. I couldn't live without you. I just couldn't." Her arms were around him, her fingers kneading his back muscles. "Just hold me, Dillon, hold me."

"How I've wanted you, Penny. How I've needed you." He held her tightly, crushing her in his arms until they hurt. But he didn't care. There was no pain, only the soft, breathing woman against him. He wanted her. He wanted to protect her. She was his. An ache came from deep inside him, and hot tears dropped onto the top of her head.

They stood for a half hour, unmoving, their breaths entwined, the rest of the world nonexistent.

Presently, Dillon became aware of the sound of the football game in the next room. "I've forgotten Mallory," he said. "I'd better get him a beer or something."

"In a minute, darling," said Penny. "I wish you would make love to me."

"I can't. Not with Mallory right there. Besides, he's got to get you home to your parents, so they don't worry."

"I don't want to go," she said fiercely, gripping his shirt. "Don't make me go away. Please, Dillon, don't make me go."

"You've got to go home today, Penny. But we'll meet tomorrow, and we'll fly to Vegas and get married."

"Don't make me go. Don't make me go." Bright tears washed her eyes and fell down her pale cheeks.

"Mallory would get into trouble. He doesn't know we're planning to elope. We'll tell him our plans and trust he can get you out on another 'drive' tomorrow."

Penny hung her head sadly. "I don't want to leave you."

"I know," said Dillon. "But tomorrow we'll be together. Forever."

Her voice was small. "You won't make love to me?"

"Oh, Penny," he said, understanding she was speaking through the tranquilizers. "Tomorrow, baby. Tomorrow we'll be married. I'll make love to you and we'll be happy. Right now, Mallory's got to take you home." Her fingers gripping his shirt were falcon talons sunk into heavy prey. He carefully pried them free and held them, kissing each separately.

"Don't take any more medication," Dillon told her. She followed him back into the living room.

Mallory grinned at them from the couch, three empty beer cans on the coffee table in front of him. "Four touchdowns. Can you believe it? There have been four touchdowns since I started watching." He looked at Penny for a moment, his face revealing his caring for her and her rejection of him.

Penny clung to Dillon's arm, unsmiling, unwilling to go home.

"We'd like to ask you another favor," said Dillon.

"Anything, absolutely anything," replied Mallory with false cheeriness.

"We want to elope," said Penny. "Can you bring me back here tomorrow?"

Mallory swallowed hard. Why should he be surprised at the question? He had expected it. "Of course," he stammered. "But what are we to tell your parents?"

"I'll think of something," said Penny. "I'll write them a note. I'll tell them you aren't to blame. You know, Mallory, you are our only true friend. The only one who believes in us."

The damn red light was taking forever to turn green. While Graham kept his eye on the light, the Coupe de Ville inched forward against the gutter in the far right parking lane. The instant the opposing traffic got the yellow light, he floored the accelerator and shot into the intersection, narrowly missing a candy-apple red Porsche that had the right-of-way through the yellow. Graham didn't bother hitting his brakes. He jerked the wheel to the left as the other car swerved, skidding sideways, its tires screeching.

"Son of a bitch!" muttered Graham, driving on. Within sixty seconds, he saw the Porsche bearing down on his tail. At the next red light the Porsche pulled up beside him, and the driver lowered his window and shouted obscenities at Graham.

Graham flipped him off, holding up the center finger of his left hand, the one that wore the ring with the three diamonds.

The Porsche screamed in front of the Cadillac, stopping diagonally across the street so that Graham was also forced to stop. The driver, a bearded man with lots of white teeth, wearing a suit, strode toward the Coupe de Ville, shaking his fist. Graham's window was closed, but the Porsche owner slugged the glass as hard as he could and kicked the door violently.

"What the fuck are you doing?" Graham shouted at the incensed man.

"Get the fuck out of there so I can knock the shit out of you!" yelled the man. "You almost killed me back there! You almost killed me!" He struck the door again with his foot, this time leaving a small dent.

"You're crazy, absolutely crazy!" shouted Graham, glancing in his rearview mirror and seeing cars piled up behind him. Horns were blaring.

"Get the fuck out of your car," raged the man slugging the window again and, this time, cracking the glass.

Graham could tell that the man had hurt his hand, because he began rubbing it.

"I'm getting your license number, and I'm turning you in and suing your ass!" the man exploded.

Graham put the de Ville into reverse and took his foot off the brake. The car rolled backward ten feet, then Graham cranked the wheel to the left and put the transmission in drive. The Cadillac rolled forward slowly, toward the furious man who didn't want to get out of his way. But Graham was not going to stop. The Porsche owner jumped aside just in time to see the de Ville's bumper nick the back end of the candy-apple German import. The Cadillac left a sizeable dent, but Graham was speeding away before the owner could memorize all seven digits on his license plate.

Graham checked his rearview mirror again and saw the man throwing his arms around wildly while the backed-up traffic flowed evenly around him. The traffic ignored everything that had happened. That was the way Southern California drivers were; they didn't like to slow down for anybody.

A few blocks down the street, Graham made a left, drove

another ten blocks, then cruised very slowly past a fifteen-story building of luxury condominiums. When he passed it, he turned around, came back, and double-parked along the crowded street, where he could see the entire building through his windshield. He counted to the eighth floor and over several windows and balconies. That one in the middle, but more to the south, had to be Ruby's.

How could she have so effectively waltzed out of his life? He hadn't even seen any tears. At the office, she spoke to him like they were the best of friends, using a congenial, superficial tone of voice and refusing to discuss anything except business. Whenever he tried to mention something personal, she would say sweetly, very sweetly, "Not now, Graham."

He picked up his car phone and tried her new number. The line was busy. Who was she talking to? Probably Will, that reincarnation of Matt Long.

Graham had always respected Ruby's privacy. However, when she left—for their "trial separation," as she called it—he went into their garage and rummaged through her boxes of personal belongings, which contained items that had not seen daylight since their marriage. These included photos of Matt Long.

Graham studied the painful pictures: Matt and the two children, Will and Belinda, at a picnic, on horseback, next to a Christmas tree.

It was funny. Will, as an adult, was the spitting image of his father. But all these photos of Will as a child only brought memories of how Graham had first met the boy and Ruby at the beach.

She had been so sad that all he had wanted to do was to take care of her, to give her what she needed. He had fallen deeply in love with her and had relied upon his little family to give him the motivation to work long, hard hours on his projects. By providing the homeless pair a home, he had provided one for himself. The photos of Will reminded him how happy he had been when he had first met Ruby.

But the image of Matt Long brought the bile curling on his tongue. He remembered the long nights of Ruby tossing and turning in a cold sweat and calling out for the Texan who had broken her heart. Only gradually had she come to feel strongly about Graham. She claimed she had always loved him; but he knew she had never fallen *in* love with him, because he had never excited her in the way that Matt Long had.

Ruby had tried to prove Graham wrong by locking away the photos and bearing three children from his seed. Graham felt sure she would have successfully forgotten Matt if only Will had not been around to remind her of him. Why couldn't she have left Will in Texas to be raised by his father? Matt Long, not Graham, deserved the long years of the rebellious youngster. So, finally, at sixteen, Will had moved out. And, during the long silences between his rare phone calls, Ruby had learned to stop worrying about him.

As Will was growing up, much of Ruby's fretting was tied into the guilt she felt about Belinda's death. She shouldn't have left the children alone, especially not a five-year-old to watch out for his three-year-old sister. Will's unintentional irresponsibility was coupled with the unbearable strain of her self-accusation. When the two looked at each other, a memory passed between them and they both believed that the girl would be alive today if *they* hadn't made mistakes.

It was a tragic accident that neither one could overcome. Wasn't it easier to exile the memory? Which they managed to do until they were together. Then, their secret became too heavy.

Why had Will bothered coming back this time? It was amazing that he resembled *Motive*'s Garrett Gage and made such a perfect stunt double for him. But then again, maybe not. As Graham looked at the photos of Matt Long, the answers became clear. It was Ruby who had insisted on hiring Garrett to play the part of Frank Harrison. Obviously her subconscious had chosen the dark-haired, blue-eyed actor because he was the same type as Matt Long.

Graham wished he hadn't found the photos.

He tried dialing Ruby's number again from his car phone. It rang four times before her taped message began to play. At the tone, Graham said, "Look, darling, I know you're there and listening in. I wanted you to know that I'm down here in the street right now, looking up at your apartment. I miss you terribly. I wish you'd pick up the phone, so I can hear your voice. No, no, I didn't mean that. You've got every right to live your life just as you please. I'm beginning to think you like our separation. I guess I'll go find a quiet place to have a drink . . . by myself."

He hung up, but kept watching the condo. He swore he saw the curtains move. "Shit," he said out loud. "None of this would have happened if Will hadn't moved back to L.A. He's the one that probably told her to get her own place."

After two drinks at a quiet club, Graham began wondering what it would take to get Will to leave the city. He was sure Will had a price. Everyone did. Where could he find him? It was the responsibility of the first assistant director to have addresses and phone numbers of all crew members, and on *Motive* the A.D. was that bitchy Sondra Prescott. Graham didn't give a damn that it was ten o'clock on a Saturday night.

Sondra answered the phone and was surprised to hear Graham Maddox on the line. When he told her he was looking for Will, she said, "Just a minute," and clamped her hand over the receiver. Will sat on her couch and she whispered, "How did he know you were here?"

Graham was even more astonished to hear Will's voice.

"What do you want, Graham?" asked the lanky stuntman.

"I want to talk to you. Let's meet for a drink."

"Tonight?" queried Will. "I'm busy tonight. How 'bout tomorrow?"

"Not good enough. I want to talk to you tonight."

His stepfather's voice irked Will to the quick. "I'm busy, Graham. Tomorrow's the soonest I can make it."

But Graham knew which buttons to push. "Listen, kid, it's about your mother. I'm worried about some personal stuff."

Forty-five minutes later, Will arrived at Graham's Mulholland home in Sondra's car. On a chilly November night, with the mists heavy in the sky overhead, a car was much saner than a motorcycle. Having never been to the house, Will was amazed it was not larger. Perhaps the inside would be more commanding. Will knew his mother had never approved of moving out of Beverly Hills, which was strange for a woman who hung a painting of the Texas wilderness on the wall of her office.

Will was not afraid of Graham; he just didn't need the stress that a conversation with the executive producer inevitably brought on. Will, himself, had not felt so much at peace in many months. His few friends attributed it to Sondra's influence. Once, when the two had visited Joe, the small punky guy had even kidded him by saying, "I think I see a smile." Was Joe right? Had there been a long stretch where Will had worn his anger as flashy epaulets? Will was grateful to Sondra for giving him a home whenever he needed one to come to. She made no demands on him, telling him that he could do whatever he wished, because when he had come to her of his own free will, she had not forced him into it.

Graham opened the door, and his hard gray eyes met Will's softer brown ones. He didn't say a word but turned back to the living room. Will followed him, a creepy feeling coming over him in the silent house. It was certainly Graham's domain, with the green and white color scheme, the wall of plate glass looking down the wild canyon, the lack of furniture, the completely uncluttered atmosphere.

"Make yourself a drink," said Graham. It was more of a command than a hospitable offer.

Will poured a shot of vodka over some ice. "What do you want to see me about?" he asked.

"Sit down," said Graham.

"No thanks," returned Will, leaning against a wall and staring at Graham as if he were a complete stranger.

"Did you know your mother has moved out? That she wants a trial separation from me?"

Will was surprised. Ruby had not told him. "No, I haven't spoken to her in some time."

Graham's voice jerked like a body on the end of a hanging

rope. "I don't believe you."

"You've never believed me, Graham—about anything." Will was calm. He could see that Graham was already getting worked up.

"Why should I believe you? You are no good."

Will sighed. "Graham, I didn't come here to listen to you berate me. If you've got something to say, say it. Otherwise, I'm leaving."

Drink in hand, Graham restlessly paced from side to side of the living room, talking to Will. Will stood silently, his mind not quite able to engage itself in Graham's ranting. The older man's irrationality was something from which Will had disconnected himself years before.

"If you had stayed in Oregon, your mother would still be here with me. I'm sure you're the one who influenced her to move out."

Will resisted the anger that had stolen into his jaw and was clenching his molars together. "Graham, I didn't know anything about it. I don't give a shit if you believe me. If she moved out, it's of her own accord. There are more people than I who don't know why she didn't do it long ago. She moved out because she couldn't stand being around you anymore. You're so fucking demanding and self-centered, the pressure must be incredible!"

"I've never made *one* demand on Ruby! Her problem is that she is always torn between you and me."

"Listen to yourself. A woman should not have to choose between her husband and her son. It's absurd. She should have both."

Graham swallowed the liquid in his glass and slammed it down on the bar. "What she really wanted was Matt Long. If she wanted me, she would have changed your last name to Maddox when I asked if I could adopt you."

"She always said it would be my choice," said Will. "Unfortunately, when I got old enough to make that choice, you had forced me to hate you. What you want is control over people. You don't care what happens to them on the inside. That's why Martin is as fucked up as he is. You're still in control of his life because he's never learned to make any decisions for himself."

"You don't come here and talk to me like this, in my house!"

"What? Am I the only person in the world who will tell you the truth? You've been running from the truth for years."

"What truth? That your mother loved Matt Long and that I was only a meal ticket for her, a way for her to do her social climbing?"

"No," said Will definitively. "The truth is that she really loved you and has devoted years to you. It is *you* that has never cared about her. She is only an ornament to you, someone for you to bounce ideas off of, someone to throw wonderful parties. If you'd really cared about her, you wouldn't have been running around with so many women."

"I care about Ruby more than I've ever cared about anyone else."

"Except yourself! But it's pretty hard to get past yourself, isn't it?"

"Fuck you! I called you here because I know I will never have any peace until you are out of my life."

Will was taken aback. He laughed uneasily. What was Graham up to? "Are you telling me that I am the sole cause of all your problems?"

"No, I'm not. But I want your mother to move back here with me, and she'll never do it if you're around to stop her."

"I've never stopped my mother from doing anything. She makes up her own mind. I moved to Oregon because *she* asked *me* to. She said there was never any peace in her house. She said she didn't want to make a choice, but would I understand? Could I please leave? So I left." Will laughed again. "You'd think L.A. would be big enough for the both of us, wouldn't you, Graham?" he added, mockery in his voice.

"How much would it take to persuade you to leave again?"

"What?" asked Will incredulously.

"I want to *pay* you to leave. Leave and, this time, never come back." Graham's voice was heavy, frozen, brittle iron.

"Forget it. I'm not going anywhere," said Will, putting his

glass down. He hadn't drunk a drop. "And I don't think we have anything more to discuss."

Like a pressure cooker that has been shaking under its load of steam, Graham exploded. "You *will* get out of my life!" he shouted. "I've tried to talk reasonably to you, but you've always been pigheaded. You are *off* the show. *Motive* will no longer pay your living. And I'm going to do everything possible to see that you don't get any more stunt work in town. Don't take this as an idle threat. I know *every*one. They won't dare hire you, because they'll never get any more work out of me."

"Don't threaten me, Graham," Will uttered menacingly, clenching his fist around a chunk of Graham's shirt front and drawing the older man to him. "I will beat the shit out of you."

Graham swung low, catching Will in the lower gut with such impact that Will staggered backward, ripping Graham's shirt. Will struck with his fist, punching Graham under the jaw. Graham fell against the plate glass window, cracking his head, making the glass shudder dangerously.

"Get out!" yelled Graham, wiping blood from a split lip with his hand.

Will stepped over him, one heavy-booted foot on each side of Graham's outstretched legs. "If my mother didn't love you so much, I think I'd kill you right here and now. Rid the world of a hateful man. But I could never hurt her like that. You understand me?"

Graham glared at Will, impotently pinned between the younger man's feet.

"Get out," said Graham, "before *I* kill *you*."

Will walked toward the front entrance and then looked back at Graham, who sat on the floor, his face ugly with hate.

"You never gave me a chance," said Will. "And now you're an old man."

Will didn't bother closing the front door. The misty canyon night stole into the house, settling a deathly quiet over the already-dead silence.

Ruby's front hall buzzer woke her. I wonder who that could be, she thought, unsure of the time. She had dozed off during a late night TV movie.

"Yes?" She spoke into the speaker to the doorman below.

"There is a Mr. Gage here," he announced. "A Mr. Garrett Gage. Should I let him up, madam?"

Garrett? What did he want? It must be an emergency. "Please let him in," she said.

Since she assumed it could not possibly be a social visit, she leaned against the jamb of her open door, waiting for the actor to arrive in the elevator. She wore a dark green silk robe. There was no makeup on her moisture-enriched face, and her uncombed hair lay in pillow-frazzled curls on her shoulders.

She appreciated the polite doorman below. She had moved into this security building to get, among other things, security.

She had understood, upon moving into the building, that it was run by superlative managers. Every need was taken care of. It was luxury—and she paid for it. She had not cared about the decorating of her new living quarters. It was spacious and simple, yet did not feel like home. She thought of her new situation as a "trial" separation from Graham. It wasn't final. It wasn't like she was never going to live with him again. She hoped his hostility, which had driven her out, was only temporary.

In trying to analyze his temperament, she could only conclude that he felt she was being too competitive. So much for the award-winning husband-wife producing team.

Before—she presently referred to herself at that time as *Ruby: What She Used to Be*—she had always contributed but had never gotten credit. *Now*—when she called herself *Ruby: What She Became*—her credits were on-screen and Graham had found he did not like it. Surely, he didn't feel emasculated? She was not a ball-buster. What was wrong with wanting a career of her own?

Though she kept telling herself there was nothing wrong with it, at the same time, a little guilty feeling kept saying she'd let her husband down. If only he hadn't treated her with such negativity, she would have stayed with him. But then, who could ever outguess Graham Maddox? She thought he would be proud to be complimented on his wife's work.

Emotionally, he was so immature. He needed immediate gratification of his every need, extravagant praise of his every accomplishment. It had become too much for her and, needless to say, a bore. In many senses, Graham had become the one child left in her life.

And now Garrett Gage was showing up unexpectedly. Why, it must be one-thirty, possibly two A.M.

Garrett, handsome as ever, emerged from the elevator, carrying a brown paper sack. He wore loose white pants, a white shirt, and a royal-blue pullover sweater tied by the sleeves around his neck.

"Hi," he said, smiling.

"Hi," she replied. "What's up? It's pretty late."

"I know," he said, kissing her cheek. There was liquor on his breath.

"Are you drunk?" she asked.

"Maybe . . . just a tad." He followed her inside, cradling the paper sack like it was a baby.

"Something important in there?" She pointed to the bag.

"Yeah," he said, extracting a bottle of expensive champagne.

My God, he's gorgeous, thought Ruby. Though a little glazed, his blue eyes were large and smiling. His hair was black and thick and his features finely drawn.

"I was going to tell the guy downstairs to tell you that Frank Harrison was here, but I didn't know if you'd know who that was."

"Somehow, I think I would know who Frank was," she said, thinking of the detective she had created to be the hero of *Motive*. "What are you doing here at this time of night?"

"My girlfriend kicked me out." He sat down on the couch, tenderly holding the champagne. There was sadness in his face, a boyish look of not quite comprehending what had happened.

Suddenly, Ruby felt self-conscious. It was a social visit, after all. She hadn't even glanced at herself in the mirror, and she fretted because Garrett had never seen her without makeup before. She could take a lot of years off her face when it was carefully applied.

"She says I've been running around on her too much," continued Garrett. "But I haven't been running around—except for Tanya—and I don't think Brenda even knew about that. I haven't seen Tanya since I told you I wouldn't. But there's all these fan letters and presents coming in all the time. I won't say I don't *like* them, 'cause I do. But they don't *mean* anything. They don't mean I'm in love with someone else. Brenda's just jealous. I'm a sex symbol, so she thinks I'm out proving it all the time."

Ruby took the bottle from Garrett, intending to put it in the refrigerator.

"No, open it," he insisted. "I brought it for you and me to drink together. We're in the same boat."

"Oh, what boat is that?" She was irritated with him. She was not good company at two A.M., and he seemed to need her for no other reason than to sit there and gab about himself. She had started the precedent by pushing for friendship with the actor. But a few dinners together was all it had amounted to.

"You and me are single again. I mean . . . you and Graham and all, not living together anymore."

"I didn't realize it was any of your business."

He sat up, closing one eye to better focus on her. "I'm sorry," he told her truthfully. "It's just that everybody knows, and I thought you might be a little lonely. I thought I might do something nice for you. You always listen and listen, and I didn't know if anyone was ever nice to you."

The words were a rainwater-fresh brook, gurgling restfully. They sounded so pleasant, she did not consider that he might not really mean them. He was trying to be nice. Well, okay, if that's what he wanted. She uncorked the champagne over the sink, and returned to the couch with the bottle and two glasses.

"Do you think I'm nice?" Garrett asked after he had drunk

a glass of the sparkling wine.

"Of course I do, Garrett," said Ruby, unconsciously running her tongue around the lip of the glass. It was thin and smooth.

"I can't help it if women think I'm sexy, can I? After all, it was you who made me into what I am."

"I guess I did," she answered. "You were handsome in your composite photo, but there was something special about you when you walked in for the audition. I knew you'd be a star."

He polished off a second glassful in two giant swallows. "Boy, that's good stuff. It's the best I could find. I've got lots of money now. It's unbelievable how easy it is to buy things. I was so used to scrimping and saving. Brenda is the same way. She thinks I'm being too extravagant. New house, new car. But she likes living there. You don't see her complaining about that, do you? She says she doesn't see enough of me. So what? I'm supporting her in style. I promised to do that. So I don't always make it home when I say I'll be there. Does that make me a bad guy?"

Ruby didn't respond to the question. Garrett picked up the champagne bottle and divided the remainder between their two glasses.

"I should have gotten two bottles," he said. "You want me to go out for more?"

She shook her head no. Excusing herself for a minute, she went into the bathroom. How did she look? The mirror couldn't lie. A little voice said: My God, just like somebody's mother. Even somebody's grandmother. Another little voice argued: You don't look over fifty. I'll bet he doesn't think you're over fifty. First voice: What do you care for? He's here because he needed a shoulder to cry on. Second: Don't be too sure. He's awfully handsome. Awfully handsome. He looks like the man of your dreams—if you could dream him up.

Garrett didn't need to do much persuading. Ruby, after all, had the chance to be in the arms of Frank Harrison, *the* national sex symbol. Did men come any sexier? Here was her chance to find out.

She didn't consider that he might be a disappointing lover. After all, being sexy and being a good lover don't always equate.

Mulholland Drive, a drunk weaving along the crest of the Santa Monica Mountains, curved cruelly, then straightened out its act for a couple hundred yards, then staggered ninety degrees to the south, then about-faced to the north. The mists of the night hung heavily in the black ravines. Ridges, protruding riblike along the mountains' breastbone, were dark at the top. However, as they curved lower and lower, sporadic lights appeared like barnacles along their serpentine backs.

Although the eastern part of Mulholland Drive was choked by houses cluttering the hillsides directly above and below the pavement, toward the west, the inhabitation thinned. Only stark, natural desert vegetation lined the ragged edge of the asphalt. Litter—beer cans, broken bottles, Styrofoam cups, soiled diapers, newspaper pages—weathered drearily along the dirt shoulder which, in places, was wide enough for sightseers and lovers to park upon and take in the view.

Frequently, as the road curved around the topmost end of a ravine, this shoulder broke away abruptly and the slope plunged vertically downward several hundred feet to the floor of a gully. At these points, Mulholland Drive balanced precariously—a strip of horizontal pavement with a toehold in a hardened precipice, where the dry earth, having had only fifty percent of the normal rainfall, crumbled brittlely under the motorized surface.

At thirty minutes past "last call," two double-dating nightclubbing couples stared into the full bore of the bar's lights and decided to it was too early to quit for the night.

They drove through the misty lowlands and up a dark canyon to Mulholland Drive where, around two-thirty A.M., they parked on a level stretch of dirt shoulder. At the top of a ridge, it jutted out over deep ravines on either side. Way below, a dense luminous haze obscured both the Los Angeles

Basin and the San Fernando Valley, giving the illusion that the vast city covering both of these plains had vanished. The couples were well fortified by all-night radio and a gram of cocaine. If they sat there long enough, they might even get to see the sun rise.

Giggling, the girls got out to pee. To keep their self-respect, they teetered toward the scraggly bushes on the lip of the hill. Seconds later, they screamed.

The guys ran to their rescue, their hearts thundering when they saw what the girls saw. Below them, in the ravine, were the glowing red taillights of a car that had gone over the edge and was sticking grill-downward in the brush. The headlights, ground into the brutal earth, were burning on a diminishing battery. There was no noise from the engine.

On the far side of the ravine, an eighth of a mile to the east, they heard a car start. Seconds later, bright headlights shot over the black gully and glanced off the two couples. The driver put the car in reverse, backed up, and turned in such a hurry that the tires spun in the dirt and gravel, leaving a choking cloud of dust.

The silence returned as the dust settled. Not knowing for sure if the driver of the car they had seen speeding away would notify the police, the guys instructed the girls to find the nearest phone and report the accident, while they went down to the wreck. The only definite information they could pass along at this point was that the car over the edge was a Cadillac.

"A big one," they said. "Older model. Can't tell for sure in this light, but it could be red. Probably a Coupe de Ville."

Chapter 14

Ruby's doorbell rang and was followed by knocking. It was the second time that night she had been awakened—and it was still dark outside. She sat up and pulled on her robe, while her mind came slowly into focus. The bedside clock digitally read five-thirty. She was not in the house on Fire Gulch, nor was this Graham beside her.

The sleeper breathed heavily and rolled over, dragging the covers with him. "Oh, heavens," she sighed, half regretting, half smiling when she remembered who it was. She was sleepy and the faint odor of sex drifted about her. It smelled raw, but it was a good rawness. It was familiar, yet it seemed a long time since she had last smelled it.

There was the knocking again. Strange, she thought. How did the visitor get past the guard downstairs?

Her doorbell rang. Just a minute, just a minute, she thought. I hope it's not Graham. Please don't be Graham crawling to me after a few drinks, telling me how much he needs me.

As she opened the door, she was trying to sort out what kind of lover Garrett had been. But all thoughts of the actor vanished when she was faced by two uniformed police officers. Her mouth was dry and her head pounded vaguely from the champagne. She squinted against the light of the hallway.

"Mrs. Maddox?" asked one of the officers.

"Yes, I'm Ruby Maddox," she replied seriously, in response to the sober expressions on their faces.

"Wife of Graham Maddox?"

Her heart jumped in a spasm of fear. "Yes, what's wrong?"

"I'm afraid there's been an accident."

Those horrible words were thick smoke circling the tight room of her skull. "A car accident?" she asked.

"Yes. I'm sorry to have to tell you. . . ." The officer reached for Ruby's arm as she stepped unsteadily backward.

"What's wrong? One of the children? Is it one of my children?"

"No. It's Mr. Maddox," said the officer, leading her to the couch.

Garrett, hearing voices in the living room, had pulled on his pants and now stood noiselessly in the doorway to the bedroom.

"What hospital is he in?" she asked. "Will he be all right?"

"Mrs. Maddox," the officer slowly shook his head, "I'm afraid the accident was fatal."

"Oh, no! Not Graham!" screamed Ruby. "Not Graham!" She could only picture his face at the time they had met—his dark hair, his sensitive mouth; she couldn't picture him as he had grown old.

"His car went off Mulholland Drive," said the officer. "We have the body at the morgue, but we need a positive identification. You're his wife. Could you please come with us?"

Ruby nodded slowly. "I need to get dressed. Can you wait for me to get dressed?"

Oh, my God, I don't believe it. My Graham. My Graham. Why did I ever leave you? You weren't able to take care of yourself. I should have been there.

Despite his well-laid plans, Dillon was anxious. Mallory had offered to drive Penny and Dillon to L.A. International in time for them to catch a one-hour flight to Las Vegas, departing at two P.M. Dillon had tickets leaving Las Vegas at eight P.M., destination Acapulco. He figured five hours on the ground in Vegas was all they needed to get married.

His stomach fluttered. Just think, in four, five hours max, you'll be married to her. By the time her parents discover that Mallory isn't bringing her home, we'll be out of the country.

Dillon had decided to tell Ruby he had a family emergency and would be out of town for a few days. But, when he tried phoning her condo, there was no answer. So he wrote her a brief letter, stating that he'd be back on Wednesday and, at the longest, in a week, and arranged for a messenger service to pick it up and hand deliver it to her. He hoped she'd understand.

The messenger grinned, winked, and said, "Must be pretty important . . . delivery on a Sunday."

Dillon was not amused by the nosy messenger. "It's real important. I want you to deliver it directly." He gave the guy a twenty-buck tip to ensure the letter's safe passage.

It was noon. He had an hour to wait until Mallory and Penny would show up. He was nervous. He should have arranged to meet them at the airport. He didn't want Ruby calling and questioning him about his "emergency." Originally, he had planned to tell her the truth—that he was eloping with Penny. Now, he had decided he didn't want *any*one knowing his plans. He wanted to get out of town. He would explain it all later.

What an amazing thing it was—a sensible, upstanding young businessman like himself tortured by his love for an eighteen-year-old girl. He justified his elopement by telling himself he couldn't concentrate properly on his *job* if Penny were not at his side.

He was restless. His suitcase was by the front door, packed and ready to go. He couldn't watch TV, he couldn't read any scripts, he couldn't concentrate at all. He walked down to the street again and paced along the sidewalk. The cloud cover of the night before had burned off. Sunshine glared off of bumpers, windshields, and waxed fenders. He wished he had his sunglasses.

Penny's heart, which had been a wilted flower within her, was now revived—as though a film projector had been thrown into reverse and the flower had lifted its head and come into full radiance again.

She took a shower and washed her hair, looking at herself in the steamed mirror. Her haggard, destitute countenance frightened her. Where had she been all this time? How had she gotten to look like this? She hadn't cared. She hadn't cared about anything. Every day the rain had come and surrounded her, and she had been wet, with no place to hide.

But today there was sunshine. She flung open her windows and breathed in the fresh morning air. The thought of meeting Dillon, sitting in the plane with him and holding hands, brought such a huge grin to her face that it hurt the corners of her mouth.

Now stop it, she told herself. Mom and Dad are going to think something is up if they see you grinning like that. Keep a cool head. It's Sunday morning. Mallory will be here soon.

She packed a small over-the-shoulder bag with a few essentials. She'd have to buy anything else that she needed. She was anxious. What if Mallory were late? They might miss the plane. Oh, why had they brought Mallory in on this?

Dillon was surprised to hear Penny's secret knock on his door. It was an hour early. He let her in, and she put her arms around him and turned her face up to be kissed.

"Where's Mallory?" asked Dillon, looking down the hallway.

"He's not here," she said bluntly. "I decided to leave before he got to my house."

"You what?" snapped Dillon.

"I wanted to see you," she said softly. "It was easy. Daddy was in his study, and Mother was out in the back practicing for her tennis lesson. I just went out the front door, started my BMW, and left."

Dillon put a hand on each of her shoulders. He was angered, but he was trying to be gentle. She was obviously still suffering from effects of her breakdown and the consequent medication. "Baby, I wish you had waited for Mallory. What did you say in your note to your parents?"

She quickly placed a hand over her mouth. "I forgot, Dillon, I forgot all about it."

"Shit."

"I'll call them from the airport. Please, it will be all right. Don't be angry with me."

He looked at her pretty face. Sadness strained her eyes and lips. "I'm sorry, darling," he apologized, kissing her tenderly, lovingly smoothing her hair with his hands.

She put her arms around his neck and drew him into a sweet, long kiss, her warm tongue pressing against his teeth. "Make love to me," she asked. "Please, Dillon, I've got to feel you in me."

He pushed her back. "Baby, we have to make the plane now. We don't have time."

"We'll be all right. If we miss this one, we can catch the next one. There's a plane to Vegas every hour."

"But we're flying to Mexico. I want to marry you today and sleep with you, out of the country, tonight—a long ways away, where your parents can't find us. Where it will be just the two of us. You and me. I thought my career came first in my life, but it doesn't. There is you. Only you."

"And there is only you, Dillon. I love you so much. Please, please, make love to me," she begged, pressing against him, her body yearning to be naked against his.

How could he refuse her when she needed him so? "I want to make love to you, Penny," he whispered.

"For only a few minutes. Please, only a few minutes."

The few minutes gave them a short half hour to catch their flight. Dillon had a cab pick them up; there wouldn't be time to park his car. Penny was clinging to his arm in the back seat, while Dillon leaned forward and told the driver for the fifth time how urgent it was to get to the plane.

Penny smiled brilliantly and then erupted into a giggle.

"What's so funny?" asked Dillon, without humor.

"I'm picturing my parents' faces when they find out. Oh, Dillon, I'm so happy right now. I'm so happy. I've never wanted anything so much in my life. I want to be your wife. I want to stay with you forever and ever. I love you."

"I love you too, Penny, but I'll feel a lot better about it when we're sleeping in Mexico tonight. I don't trust your father."

"I'm of age. There's nothing he can legally do."

"I still don't trust him. He told me over the phone he'd

shoot me."

"He wasn't serious," she said incredulously.

"Want to bet?" Dillon replied crisply.

"He's not like that," she insisted.

"Have you considered what happened when Mallory showed up to take you for another drive and you weren't there? Your father started asking questions, you can count on that."

"How would he have a clue as to where I've gone? He wouldn't know I was with you."

"He would if Mallory clued him in."

With ten minutes to spare, the cab dropped them at the airline door, and Dillon carried their bags to the ticket counter and checked the luggage. Over the P.A., a voice announced the last boarding call for Flight 221 to Las Vegas. Dillon took Penny's hand and they both began running for the gate.

Tickets in hand, Dillon walked up to the attendant at the gate. He felt Penny's grip on his hand tense. She stood rigidly. He glanced at her face. She was frightened. He looked to see what she saw.

At the entrance to the concourse stood Mr. Huntington, an airport security guard, and Mallory Burton.

There was no red Coupe de Ville in the driveway of the house on Fire Gulch. It would never be there again. Ruby hadn't wanted to see it. She didn't want to find out that the facts were worse than anything her imagination could dream up.

Her children had been notified. Martin, along with his sister Sarah, who lived in Brentwood, waited at Ruby's condo until she phoned them. Julia, in London, was flying home. Will insisted on meeting Ruby at the coroner's office.

Sunday afternoon, after she had met with the coroner, Garrett drove her up to the house. Though she was glad he was with her, she could hardly remember that they had spent the previous night together in the same bed making love. That was part of *Ruby: What She Became.*

Now, suddenly, she was thrust back into *Ruby: What She Used to Be.* She was Graham's wife, since they were not legally separated.

His death did not seem real, just as Belinda's had not seemed real. She had seen the bodies—without life—but her mind couldn't focus on *death.* It was like they were sleeping, and yet the energy field that surrounds a sleeping person was gone.

She was in shock about Graham. She walked through the house. Everything she saw belonged to the both of them. Everything had its own little story. She knew the story. Graham knew the story. They had shared; the house and its contents represented a great part of their life together. The material objects were not as important as the stories, but they represented the stories. Millions of forgotten memories pricked at her skin, burning brightly, saying, *You'll never forget . . . never forget.*

Garrett went home for the night, back to Brenda, his girlfriend. He promised to come again first thing the next morning. She thanked him and kissed his cheek. Her children wanted to stay with her, but she insisted they go.

Will had lingered at the door. "We should be together, Mama," he said. "At a time like this, you need family."

"I have to be alone tonight," she said quietly.

"I'll worry about you if you're alone."

"I'll be all right."

"I'm so sorry," he told her.

They weren't empty words. She searched his eyes and saw he really meant them. He saw her grief and it grieved him.

Ruby didn't know what she expected to see, feel, or hear all by herself, but there was nothing unusual. The house felt like it always did when Graham was out of town; he was merely absent. The wild canyon, with its view down to the city lights, was unchanged.

The coroner had tested for the blood alcohol level and found that, though Graham had been drinking, he hadn't been over the legal limit. Perhaps the visibility had been bad or the road damp. Mulholland Drive was a raceway for boys in hot, fast, expensive cars who took chances on the treacherous curves for their own little personal glory. Graham had loved racing, but the de Ville was not built for it. He had been a crazy driver and he had died the way a crazy driver would. He had driven off a precipice because he'd failed to negotiate a turn.

Martin had told her about the letter that had come from Dillon concerning a "family emergency." Thinking it was peculiar that Dillon should leave the state at exactly the same time Graham had been killed, Martin had notified the police of his suspicions that the young accountant might possibly have had a motive and had plotted Graham's death.

Ruby thought Martin had acted outrageously. She immediately called Dillon, meaning to apologize for Martin, but instead she heard the young man explain that the family emergency had been resolved, that he was really sorry about Graham's death, and that if she wanted to find him, he'd be at Maddox Productions.

The one question the police had asked her that kept coming back was: Do you have any idea where Mr. Maddox was going at that time of the morning on Mulholland Drive?

She had not.

She slept in the guest room where she had taken up slumbering before she had moved into her condo. She didn't want to go into their bedroom. She didn't want to know what she might find there—whether it was just Graham's personal effects or whether there was evidence of overnight visitors of the female variety. That night, she didn't want to know. She could face it better in the daytime.

"It's Monday morning and we're all sitting here like bumps on logs," complained Margi, smoking a long, thin cigarette and watching steam curl off her third cup of coffee. "Sure I feel bad about what happened, but they should let us off for a couple of days while they get things straightened out."

A sweet roll sat on a paper plate in Denny's lap, and his hands shook nervously as he tore off a piece.

"You never eat that kind of stuff," observed Margi. "It's got refined sugar. What's wrong with you?"

"I haven't gotten used to the fact that Graham Maddox is dead. It's a shock. Quite a shock. A broken neck from the impact." He chewed on the sweet, golden dough. It didn't have much flavor. It was just sweet.

"The news said that the police have ruled the whole thing an accident," said Margi.

Glory, who was sitting next to Denny, broke a powdered-sugar donut. "The *preliminary* report," she said. "They've got to do an investigation and see if Mr. Maddox's car was tampered with." It was hard to keep the powdered sugar from getting on her clothes and under her long false nails.

"Don't be ridiculous," snapped Margi. "It wasn't tampered with."

"The people that reported the accident said they saw a car parked *exactly* where Graham's Cadillac went off the cliff, and somebody started it and drove away—with screeching tires—like they were in a real hurry to get out of there." Glory brushed her hands together to shake off the powdered sugar.

"Maybe they were hurrying to report the accident," blurted out Margi.

"Well, they didn't report it," commented Denny. "And why didn't they have their emergency flashers on?" The thought made his mouth dry. The chewed-up sweet roll stuck in the back of his throat.

"That doesn't mean a damn thing," said Margi.

"It's creepy to think that someone may be responsible for Mr. Maddox's death," said Glory. She licked the remainder of the powdered sugar from her fingers. She gasped, "What if he was run off the road?"

"I seriously doubt anyone would do that," insisted Margi.

"You know," said Denny, "I heard that yesterday, while Martin Maddox was waiting for his mother to come back from the morgue—she had to go in to identify the body—this messenger brings a letter from Dillon Hughes saying that he's got a family emergency and he'll be back in a week."

Margi sucked in a lungful of air. "It's a coincidence."

"Maybe yes, maybe no," said Denny. "But Martin went ahead and called the police with that information."

"Martin is a little creep," retorted Margi.

The mention of Martin's name made Glory's face hot. She stood up and walked to the end of the table, where she looked into the donut box.

"Donuts'll make you fat," criticized Margi.

"Lay off her," warned Denny in a low voice.

Glory looked at Margi, who seemed even more acerbic than usual. Why was this woman constantly throwing nasty remarks at her? Glory chose a sweet roll filled with peach jam and went back to her seat. "Who would be stupid enough to commit a murder and then tell anyone he was leaving? He'd just disappear," Glory estimated. "Do *you* think Dillon did it?" she asked Denny.

"Why would he?" he asked.

"Well, If *I* was Dillon Hughes, I'd be pissed off seeing that asshole Martin get promoted to coproducer," interjected Margi. "That little jerk is totally unqualified."

"How do you know Dillon was up for that job?" asked Glory.

"Everybody knew that, sweetie," replied Margi.

Every time Martin's name came up, Glory felt ill at ease. She wished somebody suspected Martin, because if he had done it, they would put him in prison and he would leave her alone.

"Don't forget, so far, Graham's death is *only* an accident," said Margi. "Though, if Dillon's pissed off, I can understand why." She yawned and looked around the set, at the rest of the crew who sat and waited. She wished they could all go home.

Denny's eyes flashed at Margi. Damn, why didn't that woman have enough sense to keep her mouth shut? He had heard about the incident at the Golden Time, when she had gotten drunk and had shot her mouth off. Maybe he should have gone with her that night, but hell, he couldn't keep an eye on her all the time. That was what she had married Bob Owens for. Bob made her toe the line and she was used to it. Now, unfortunately, since his accident, Bob had relaxed his hold on the reins.

Glory felt sorry for Denny because he was so nervous. She hadn't really known Graham, so she only felt a distant sorrow, kinda like a sorrow that she was *supposed* to feel when she heard someone had died. An empty sorrow. "It was nice of Richard to say what he did," mentioned Glory.

"A director's supposed to say stuff like that," explained Margi condescendingly. Doesn't that girl know anything? She is so dumb sometimes. Dumb, dumb, dumb. "Graham's death may be a big shock to this production company, but this is still a business and they can't afford to get off schedule. There's too much money wrapped up in it. We've got to finish all the shows we're budgeted for."

Denny wished Margi would treat Glory with a little more respect. Glory, with her high, soft voice and bashful smile, tried over and over to be nice to the hairdresser, and Margi mowed her down with impatience. He had only eaten two bites of his sweet roll and was pulling the rest apart, breaking it into teeny-tiny bits on his plate.

"It's hard to believe he's dead," Denny said. "I just saw Graham on Friday. He came on the set. He said, 'Hi, Denny. How are you?' I hardly ever see him but he still said hi, called me by name."

"Quit moaning," said Margi. "You work for the guy for fifteen years, he'd better know you. Sweetie," she said to Glory, "why don't you go find out from Richard if we're going to do any work today?"

Glory balked at the order. She did enough goferring under Richard's and Sondra's commands. "I'd say it would be difficult to shoot if our two principal actors aren't here, wouldn't you?"

Margi was unfazed. "I'm sure Tanya doesn't find this in the least bit traumatic. Besides, there's nothing emotional that's going to affect her *acting*—or improve it, either, for that matter."

"Tanya's a nice girl," defended Denny. "A little mixed up, but she's sweet."

"About as sweet as fangs on a bitch dog," said Margi. "She's spoiled through and through."

The *Motive* set bored Margi. Frank Harrison's farmhouse. She'd seen it hundreds of times. She was glad the holidays were coming up and she would get a couple of days off. She'd worked on a lot of shows over the years. The sets always bored her after ten weeks. They made her feel her life was standing still.

At lunchtime, Sondra Prescott announced that the crew could go home.

"Good," said Denny. "I couldn't concentrate anyway."

"I think I'll go over to the Golden Time for a few drinks," said Margi. "Anybody want to come with me?"

"No, thank you," declined Glory.

Denny was surprised. "Why are you going drinking at this time of day?"

"Why shouldn't I?" snapped Margi.

"I thought you'd rather go home and spend the time with Bob, that's all."

"Home, hell. I'm in no rush to get there. Besides, you won't find Bob there."

"Why not?" asked Glory.

"Because, sweetie, he left a week ago and hasn't been home since."

On Monday morning, Mr. and Mrs. Garcia, the gardener and housekeeper, arrived early. Ruby, lying awake in bed and watching daylight slowly lighting the curtains and giving shape to the furniture in the room, heard the murmur of voices. She put on her robe and hurried to the front hall.

Mrs. Garcia, a short, stocky woman, reached out her arms to Ruby. "Poor Mrs. Maddox. We are so sorry."

Ruby accepted the hug. "It's very sudden, isn't it, Mrs. Garcia?"

Mr. Garcia patted Ruby's shoulder. "We hear yesterday. On television. Very sorry."

Ruby smiled at the couple and realized how much she had missed their quiet ministrations in the few weeks since she had moved into her condo.

"I fix you toast and coffee, Mrs. Maddox," said the woman, moving toward the kitchen.

"Thank you, that would be very nice, Mrs. Garcia."

Her children, except for Martin, reappeared. Will and Sarah had picked up Julia at LAX from her transatlantic flight. Will rubbed his mother's shoulders.

"Where's Martin?" she asked.

"I believe he's gone into the production office," said Sarah.

"I didn't tell him to do that," said Ruby, annoyed.

"The office can't run itself, Mother."

"Why not?" demanded Ruby. "Martin's presence certainly isn't going to make a grain of difference. Besides, Dillon is there and he's very reliable."

Her daughter burst into tears, and Ruby, sorry she had snapped, went to Sarah and held her in her arms. Ruby was not the only one feeling distraught. After all, the girl had just lost her father.

Before the morning was half over, the house was filled with consoling neighbors and friends. Garrett slipped in and gave Ruby a hug. She thanked him for coming, and his presence curiously relieved some of her aloneness. Flower arrangements poured in and began crowding corners. Lilies. So waxy, so bland, so traditional. She wished there were roses and carnations and daisies. Something cheerful. She also wished people had heeded the "In lieu of flowers . . ." notice that had been printed with the obituary.

A huge limo pushed its way into the driveway, and Norman and Tanya emerged. Ruby greeted them, accepting the cold, childish peck on the cheek from the actress and clinging to Norman's bearlike grasp a long time. When she pulled back to look in his face, there were tears in her eyes—the first tears that had risen, perhaps because Norman was such an old and close friend. The fact that he was there confirmed Graham's death.

"Thank you for coming," she told him, leaning on his arm and letting him support her as they walked back into the house.

Norman had insisted Tanya accompany him to the Maddox house that morning, though she had not felt well and had tried to get out of it. "All right, all right, I'll go," she said, and had to spend the next half hour deciding what to wear and how much makeup to put on. Though Tanya felt sorry about

Graham's death, she didn't think it would have any effect on her role in *Motive*. She was already under contract for the next season. She didn't see what possible good she could do up at the Maddox house, with all the family and reporters crawling around. No one would even notice her.

However, in the driveway, she saw a car she recognized. Only one person in California drove a black Porsche with "FRANK" on the personalized license plate. Her heartbeat speeded up. As she followed Ruby and Norman—"slow old fogies"—her eyes darted about the rooms, searching for Garrett's chiseled face and bright blue eyes.

Garrett sat at the kitchen table with Will, talking motorcycles. He saw Norman, Ruby, and Tanya enter the kitchen. Oh shit, he thought, I hope Tanya doesn't make a scene. Garrett rose, offering Ruby his seat and shaking Norman's hand. Under Norman's scrutinizing eye, he kissed Tanya lightly on the cheek.

She grabbed his hand with both of hers and looked intently into his eyes. "It's so terrible, isn't it, Garrett? I am deeply distressed. Crushed inside. It is so unexpected," gushed Tanya with such sincerity that, for a moment, Garrett believed her.

"Yes, it is, Tanya," he replied, disengaging himself from her grasp, which was difficult to do, kind of like getting your fingers free of fly paper. He leaned against the kitchen counter while Will pulled chairs around for Norman and Tanya to sit in.

"Mrs. Garcia?" called Ruby to the housekeeper. "Would you please bring us more coffee?"

Norman sat next to Ruby, and Tanya sat opposite them. Garrett was aware that the blonde kept looking at him and was trying to catch his eye. But he ignored her. He listened politely as Ruby explained the funeral plans to Norman.

"Whatever you need," said Norman. "Like I told you yesterday, whatever you need. And I want a full investigation."

"The police said it was an accident," said Ruby.

"Not when another car has been seen leaving the scene of the accident." Norman stirred sugar into his coffee and noisily slurped from the cup.

Garrett shifted uneasily against the counter. He could tell

from Tanya's body language that she was in a pout. Probably because she couldn't get his attention. He didn't want any trouble with Norman, who was already so riled that if there were the slightest suspicion his wife was flirting, he might come flying across the room with a fist for Garrett's jaw. Garrett was no fighter and Norman, who might have been old and fat, nevertheless outweighed the actor and might damage a face that had a tight shooting schedule to adhere to.

Waiting until Mrs. Garcia was out of the room, Tanya rose with her cup and went across the kitchen to the coffeepot. She began to pour from the glass decanter, but deliberately miscalculated her aim and sloshed hot liquid onto the counter and floor. "Oh shoot, I've spilled," she said, quickly adding, "Garrett, be a dear and give me a hand."

Garrett glanced at Norman, but the older man had not even looked up from his conversation with Ruby. Garrett grabbed a handful of paper towels and bent down to wipe the floor.

Tanya squatted beside him. "I've got to talk to you," she whispered in a rough hiss. "It's crucial."

Garrett looked at her incredulously. Everything with this broad was "crucial." He shook his head, disinterested.

"We've *got* to meet. I've got something to discuss with you. Something important. *Please.*" There was an urgency in her voice. "*Please,*" she repeated, laying a hand on his shoulder.

If she hadn't touched him, he would have been able to say no. But her touch wounded him, cut a hole in his defense. He nodded. "Soon," he whispered. "We'll get together soon." And then, louder, "That about does it. Maybe a couple more paper towels for that corner."

At the table, Norman was saying, "I'm sorry you and Graham were having your differences, but I know it was only temporary. Graham himself told me the two of you couldn't live apart for more than a couple of months—on the outside."

"Thank you for your concern, Norman," said Ruby. "It helps knowing that you are such a good friend."

"Martin told me about the letter from Dillon Hughes. It sounds fishy to me. Graham told me on the phone this past week that Hughes's attitude has turned very nasty since Martin was moved up in the company."

"Please, Norman, Dillon could not possibly be involved."

"Well, someone's involved. There's no way Graham would have driven himself off a cliff," thundered Norman. "I'm calling an influential friend of mine at the D.A.'s office and having him follow up on this accident!"

With the correct care, California lawns are perennially green. So it was at the cemetery—green climbing over and around headstones—on up the hill where the view was considered pretty, or at least remarkable, on a non-smoggy day.

On Wednesday, Graham Maddox's memorial service and funeral were fit for a king—a Hollywood king. Ruby's one firm request was a closed casket. She let the funeral home take care of the other details. It seemed staged, like a scene they might be filming for an episode. Ruby dressed the part in a somber black suit and waited, with her four children, for the funeral home limo to pick them up.

There were hundreds of cars in the procession. After the memorial service, Ruby thought some of the people might not drive to the cemetery. But the crowd was immense. In addition to noted celebrities, friends, and entertainment industry people of import, nearly every writer, director, actor and technician who had ever worked for him was there. Graham would have loved it, expected it.

Ruby knew them all, shook their hands, thanked them for their sympathy. Most of them didn't know that she and Graham had been separated. She was trying her damnedest to keep that news from leaking out to the press. *Ruby: What She Used to Be* was gracious, bereaved, and family-oriented. The public expected it of her. She expected it of herself.

Martin Maddox thought himself a realist who was "handling his father's death pretty damn well." While all the other members of his family were bogged down with the ceremony, he was the one calm, forward-thinking person who was considering what would happen after the funeral.

On Sunday, the day of his father's death, not knowing she had been fired the previous Friday, he had phoned Jeannie at her home and asked her to stand by the office the following day. He figured she knew most of his father's business and would be able to help with all the details that Martin didn't understand, in addition to tactfully fielding all personal calls to Graham and keeping a thorough record of them. He was delighted when she said she would be there.

Martin's sullen eyes scanned the crowd walking up the lawn to the graveside. Good, there was Norman. Best tell him what was going on, which would be the same thing he had told other family friends wondering about who would be assuming the reins of Maddox Productions.

"Hello, Norman," said Martin, advancing to the older man with an outstretched hand.

"Martin, my dear boy, I'm so sorry. I know how this must upset you," returned Norman. However, looking at the boy's dull green eyes, Norman doubted a single tear had been shed.

"It's quite a jolt, sir," said Martin. "Especially to Mother. You know how she depended on my father and now he won't be able to take care of her any longer. I'm afraid the trauma of his death has immobilized her." Martin's head swung around to look at his mother, leaning on Will's arm.

"I thought she was handling it quite well, my boy," said Norman, watching as Ruby put her arms around the shuddering shoulders of her crying daughter Sarah.

"Mother has a brave face," said Martin, "but I know her deep inside. This has wiped her out. My main concern now is for the future of the company. It needs someone with Maddox insight to guide it through this trying time of despair. Fortunately, I am ready to take that responsibility." He looked Norman squarely in the eye, checking to see if he had an ally in this old family friend, but the man's face was neutral.

Tanya stood a respectful ten feet from Norman, and Martin lowered his voice so she could not hear his next words. "I wouldn't want to see Tanya's career jeopardized just because someone incompetent took over and the high quality of our programs went downhill."

Norman was astounded at Martin's cockiness. "We'll talk soon, boy," he said. "Why don't you see after your mother for now."

Good, thought Martin. Norman was not disapproving. He would back Martin. Why else would he want to get together and talk . . . soon?

Denny and Glory rode in Denny's blue Alfa Romeo. The procession was extraordinarily long and slow.

"Would it be disrespectful to put the top down?" asked Glory, who wore a black silk scarf over her blond hair and green-lensed sunglasses.

Denny thought she looked cute, very 1950's, though he knew she wasn't trying to achieve that look on purpose. "I guess it would be all right," he said. "We need to get a little breeze in here."

She was thankful for his friendship. There was no one else she could have ridden with to the funeral. She got onto her knees and turned in the seat to help guide the top as it arced up and then folded into pleats along the back seat. In the car behind them rode Richard the director, his wife, Sondra Prescott, and several others. Glory waved at them.

"Too bad Margi didn't want to come with us," said Glory.

"At least she made the memorial service," said Denny who, even though he wore sunglasses, had to squint against the flashing glare of sunlight reflecting off the rear windshield ahead of them. "What's got me worried is how she started going on about how she put a curse on Graham with her big mouth and now he's dead because of it."

Clinging to Denny's sleeve as they walked to the grave, Glory balanced on her toes so her high heels didn't sink into the soft, damp earth below the grass. She quickly spotted Martin, with his bland freckles and sullen eyes, and made sure she and Denny stood on the opposite side of the grave, behind some people.

Denny searched each face in the crowd three times. "I'll be darned," he said. "Margi was right about one thing. Who did she say was missing from the memorial service that should have been there?"

"Jeannie."

"Do you see her here, anyplace?"

Glory slipped off her sunglasses and scrutinized the crowd. "Nope," she said.

Sondra rode to the funeral with Richard and his wife. Two days before, the director had given a short, pleasant speech to the cast and crew of *Motive,* stating how they would all miss Graham and how important he had been in all of their careers. Richard went on to say how brilliant Graham had been—setting trends in television shows and creating hundreds of projects. Then Richard had paused, close to tears, and had motioned to Sondra, wanting her to take over. He couldn't bear to continue talking. Graham had been a great friend of his.

At the head of the grave, a minister stood with the family. Sondra felt sorry for Ruby. She'd even gotten to like the producer these past few weeks, because Ruby had shown she could make decisions without running to Graham every few minutes. Ruby respected Sondra's advice and opinions. This was more encouraging than working with even Richard, who always asked for opinions and then went right ahead and did whatever it was he was going to do in the first place.

Will flanked his mother, his face hard and set. It was a defensive look, one that warned he was protecting Ruby. Sondra found it hard to believe that they spent as much time together as they did. From this distance, he looked like a stranger. He looked angry. Did he always look like that? Was it only for her that he smiled? She recalled the first time she had seen Will, in that horrible biker bar, Spud's, when she and Dillon had been scouting locations. Though wildly handsome, he had also looked very bitter, like he was corroding from the inside out.

He still didn't talk about it. Didn't talk much about himself. All the time, it was as if he wanted to forget. She didn't dare question him. Once she had asked him how long he had lived in Oregon and what he'd done for a living there, and he had become so angry that his face didn't even look like his face. It was the face of someone she didn't know, a contorted face brimming with rage. Then the anger had passed, and his eyes had looked at her but not really seen her.

But it had scared her and she'd never asked again. One day, when the time is right, she thought, he will tell me. So he came around to her house, ate supper, talked with Scotty, and made love to her. She tried to keep as distant from him as he kept from her. But it didn't work out that way. Always looking forward to his visits, she was bitterly disappointed when he didn't show up. She didn't want to fall in love with him. She'd sworn to herself she would never fall in love with another man. She couldn't bear it.

But then, there she was, even at work, not concentrating wholly on her job because she was planning on what they were going to do when she next invited him over.

Like now, the minister and three friends had talked for a half hour about Graham Maddox, and she hadn't heard a word of it because she had been thinking about Will. But not once, throughout the service, had he looked around to see if she was there.

After the ceremony, as the crowd was breaking up, Sondra and Richard went to Ruby to give their condolences. Will stood beside his mother and did not acknowledge Sondra. He avoided her eyes.

She decided to wait for Richard by his car, since the director knew many people and was talking to them all. The cemetery was so clean, with not a blade of grass out of place, not an unsightly weed sprouting anywhere.

"Sondra, wait up!" It was Will's voice.

She stopped but didn't turn around.

"What's wrong?" he asked.

"Why wouldn't you say hello back there when I spoke to Ruby?" she asked. "You ignored me."

"I'm sorry," he said. "I didn't mean to hurt your feelings. It's just not a very good time for me right now."

Sondra turned to face him and her ice-blue eyes pierced him. "I can understand your concern for your mother, but don't try to tell me that Graham's death is devastating *you*. I know there's no love lost." She was surprised at her own anger.

"It's not that," he said, starting to put a hand on her shoulder, then deciding not to. He pulled at the ends of his long mustache instead. "It's other things. Other problems. I don't think we should be seeing so much of each other."

"What's that supposed to mean?" her temper lunged. "What other things?"

"I can't keep seeing you."

"Why not?"

"I feel guilty. Guilty all the time."

"Guilty?" Sondra shook her head. She didn't comprehend what he was telling her. "Guilty about what?"

"Candy."

Here was the most unspeakable word in his entire vocabulary. Sondra hadn't even known the woman's name. But Candy and Oregon were all tied up together, and there was no getting Will for herself until Oregon had been resolved.

"It's my fault! Really, it's my fault. I put a curse on him. If I hadn't said I wished he was dead, he wouldn't have driven over the cliff. He'd be alive today."

"Don't be ridiculous, Margi," said Denny. He sat in her living room, holding a glass of Coca Cola in which the ice was melting miserably. He didn't feel like drinking it. His hand trembled and the diminishing cubes rang against the side of the glass.

"I never should have mouthed off," Margi said. "I don't understand why all this bad luck has fallen on top of me. The worst part is Bob. How am I supposed to go on with life if I can't have Bob?"

"He'll be back," reassured Denny. Her mood had been so erratic. She was angry, then she was calm, then she was blaming herself over and over.

"I put a curse on him. I really did. And now look—no more Mr. Maddox." She drank Coke from a bottle. It was her third. She was waiting for it to heal her. It wasn't working very well.

"Graham Maddox is dead from an auto accident," insisted Denny, "and it didn't have anything to do with you."

"How do you know?"

He didn't know for sure. She was crazy sometimes. He knew that. She'd always had Bob to keep her in check. Now

Bob had disappeared. Margi was worried. Then she was angry. Emotion rolled over and over in her, and Denny didn't know a damn thing he could say that would add one ounce of comfort.

Denny felt responsible for her run of bad luck, but he did not have the courage to say so. After Jeff had left him, he had continually gone over to Margi's for her comfort, knowing that Bob disliked him, hated him for being homosexual. He hated Bob in a reciprocal sort of way. Denny had not been welcome and it had driven Bob away.

But Denny couldn't tell her how he felt. As long as Jeff did not call him, he could carry on. He genuinely feared running into Jeff somewhere with a young stud at his side and a smug look on his face. Glory had taken away some of Denny's loneliness, but she could not remove the ache. Logically, that would only lessen with time. He knew he would never let another man hurt him as Jeff had. No man would ever come that close and be able to deceive him again.

Margi played with her pack of cigarettes. "You know, Denny, I used to get horny all the time thinking about Bob. Since he's been gone, I haven't thought about sex once. Isn't that funny? I used to get horny all the time. It's sort of got me worried. That's why he left, you know, because he thought he couldn't satisfy me anymore. He knew what an appetite I have for sex. I never wanted to tell him that. I told him the opposite, in fact. Until the night he left.

"I got so goddamned mad at him that I yelled everything I thought he wanted to hear—that he was impotent, that I didn't want him anymore. It was all lies. But he kept pushing and pushing me into saying it. He believed it and he wanted me to tell him it was so. But it's not so. I just want Bob. I don't know where to find him. Isn't it funny? I haven't been horny at all. I miss sitting with Bob and watching TV, or driving to the market. He used to go with me all the time."

Denny left the house uncertainly. Margi smiled and thanked him for coming. He decided he wouldn't worry, because the kids were around. They didn't seem concerned about their mom's condition, so maybe she wasn't acting as erratically as he kept thinking.

Margi sat in the den with the TV on. If she heard a car in the street, she ran to the window to see if it was Bob coming home. She was filled with immeasurable anger, then with overwhelming remorse. She smashed three china plates on the kitchen floor, then sat crying, holding the pieces. She cried and she dozed, and then she awoke with a start.

"My Bobby," she called softly. "Where are you, my love? I put the curse on you, like I did on Graham Maddox. I killed him and I've killed you."

At four A.M., she put on her warm-up suit and slippers. The car seat was cold but she didn't notice. She pulled up at the police station and walked inside. She addressed the sergeant at the desk.

"I'd like to make a confession, please. Remember that big-time producer that went off Mulholland Drive a few days ago? I did it. I ran him off the road."

Chapter 15

Because of the thing with Martin, a sick feeling settled down in Glory's stomach and never left—an old sponge full of dirty dishwater, and no matter how often you squeezed it, you could never wring it dry. It was gorged with the putrid water all the time.

She always felt dirty. Dirty, and she couldn't get clean. She took long showers, but she never felt clean. Denny was worried about her, because he frequently asked her what was wrong. However, she shook her head and denied everything. It was a shameful thing that Martin made her do. She knew he laughed at her—as much as he enjoyed her. Who said she should date boys her own age? Martin was only two or three years older, and he was a disgusting animal. Every time he looked at her when they were on the set, she felt disgrace. It became her shadow and she knew no happiness at all.

She couldn't concentrate on a thing. She finished her episode script for *Motive,* but she couldn't bring herself to give it to Martin. So she pushed it under the big old armchair in her apartment and forgot about it.

She hated herself for being so poor. She couldn't afford to quit her job. If only, only, only she could borrow some money so she could look for a new job. She hated her mother for being too poor to ask. Glory lived from paycheck to paycheck. If she quit, what else could she do for work? She couldn't even type, and the idea of being a waitress made her heart palpitate. All those dishes to break.

No, she had to stay where she was for now. It was survival.

If Martin were sad about his father's death, he didn't show it. On the surface, it looked like Martin was involved in all the projects. "That's Graham's kid, all right," some people were saying. "The tougher the going gets, the more he's in the middle of it."

But those that knew better simply said, "Right now, we're completing the plans that Graham had laid out. When we're finished with this season, somebody's got to do more planning. And it ain't going to be that backboneless kid Martin."

Glory prayed for the end of the season—so she'd get laid off and collect unemployment. Or maybe Richard would get a job directing another show with another production company, and he'd take her with him. One look at Ruby Maddox's face told everyone she was going through a stressful time. But not Martin. He was more obnoxious, more bossy, more demanding.

"Come on," he whispered. They were on the set and it was the Friday after the funeral. "I haven't had you for a week, and I'm ready."

She shut her eyes. Inside, the black sewer water was sloshing back and forth.

"Come on," he said, smiling that phony smile of his and wrinkling his freckled nose. "I haven't got that much time."

Resigned, she followed him to the cell-like dressing room, where he made her keep silent while she got on her knees before him.

Tony watched Glory. He spat out a chewed-up toothpick. Everybody was taking lunch, but he didn't feel like eating. A hangover sat dully in his head. Thank God they weren't out on location today. Bright sunlight would be a real bitch. In his cooler, a couple of beers waited. It would feel good to find a quiet place, so he could drink them down and feel the hangover ease off.

Tony felt sorry about Graham Maddox's death. He

hoped it didn't mean the end of an era—Maddox Productions. He was always proud to be associated with their series. It provided a good living and gave him plenty of money to party on.

Someone tapped his elbow. It was Sondra Prescott, the first assistant director. "You seen Glory?" she asked.

"Me?" asked Tony, surprised.

"You."

"Come to think of it, she just took off with that Martin fellow . . . thataway." He pointed. "Probably off to lunch."

Sondra snorted. "Or whatever you want to call it. No doubt, trying to work herself into a promotion. She should ask *me* if she can go to lunch. Richard needs her notes and now we're going to have to wait. Shit, is he going to be pissed off. Damn." She went off, cursing under her breath.

Bony ol' bitch, he thought. I'm always working with dykes. If it's not them, then it's the fruitcakes. Or both. No way can you get away from them anymore. Hollywood's crowded with them.

Someone tapped his shoulder. It was Denny. Oh, hell, thought Tony, wouldn't you know it? Both of them in one day.

"You seen Glory?" asked Denny.

Tony was exasperated. It was too much for his hangover. "Everybody is asking me if I've seen Glory! Sondra was just here. Why does everybody think I'm keeping an eye on Glory? What the hell do I care what she does? She split with that Martin dude."

Denny was disappointed. "She and I were supposed to have lunch together. She made a big point of saying, 'Come up and get me for lunch. I want to go with you. Come and get me the very *second* Richard yells "cut." ' Then I get stuck with Tanya's makeup and Glory can't be bothered to wait a few minutes."

Tony didn't know what to say. He didn't want to get involved with the fruitcake's problems. Why would Glory want to go to lunch with him, anyways? Was Denny switching to girls? Glory better be careful, with all the new diseases out and stuff.

"You really hurt her, you know," said Denny. "She'd never say a word to you, but she's still crying about you. All she ever asks me is 'Why did Tony turn his back on me?' I don't know what to tell her, so I make up something. Why the heck *did* you split from her?"

Tony was thinking about his nice cold cans of beers lying in the cooler with the ice cubes melting around them. "Awwww," he grumbled. He didn't owe anybody any explanations, but then there was Denny looking at him with a level gaze, the kind that's hard to back away from. Straight guys don't back down from fags. "Seeing as you're so damned concerned about Miss Glory, I'll tell you why. I'm too old for her."

"You're too old for her, or she's too young for you?"

Tony wanted his beer. "She needs a young guy. She's a sweet kid, but in the end, I'd let her down. She needs a guy like . . . like . . . what's his name . . . Martin."

"No, she doesn't," said Denny. "She's in love with you."

"She's not in *love* with me. I'm like the dad she never had." Tony didn't feel like inviting the fag to join him for one of his beers. He wanted to end the conversation.

"Don't be so sure about that. I think you started falling for her and it scared the shit out of you. You don't want to make a commitment to anyone." Denny paused. "Maybe I shouldn't say anything . . . mind my own business. But I care about Glory, and somebody better tell you the way she feels."

Glory clutched her blouse around her. The more clothes she had on at one time, the better she felt. Without clothes, she felt vulnerable. Martin had had one orgasm. Wasn't that enough? The more sex he got, the more he needed.

"Turn around for me. I want to get you from the back. Something new to turn you on," said Martin, roughly trying to roll her over.

"You *don't* turn me on," she said, the words slapping his face before she could stop them.

"Oh?" he questioned, his voice full of defiance. "Now just turn over!" He was angry.

The saturated sponge began growing and growing, overwhelming her with nausea, filling her up with that sick feeling until her entire insides were full of it. "I'm not turning over," she said between clenched teeth.

"You're going to do what I want you to," he said, grabbing the front of her blouse and ripping it off her shoulder. The material gave way and hung torn, over her torso.

Glory, on her knees, was trying to struggle to her feet. Martin grabbed her at the waist and pulled her down to the matted shag carpet on the floor, then fumbled with her zipper.

"No," she gasped. "Don't! Leave me be! Leave me alone. You've already had enough." She pushed at his hands but could not stop them from tugging at the waist of her slacks.

"Shut up," he commanded.

"No, no. Go away. Leave me alone." She began crying. Wasn't there any way to stop him? He was going to force her no matter what she said. A scream rose in her throat. "Leave me alone!!" The shriek ricocheted around the dressing room, and before he could clamp a hand over her mouth, she loosed another.

The scream, like an animal in pain, came through the open doors of the soundstage.

"What was that?" asked Tony, his ears on edge, acutely listening. The cry came again. "Someone's in trouble!" Tony ran out the open door. Between the soundstages, in the alleys, was a long line of portable dressing rooms.

Denny ran after Tony, his ear as finely tuned, listening for another scream. Ten dressing room doors down, in a trailer that was unused, they heard the sounds of a scuffle.

"No!" cried Glory's voice from inside. "Leave me alone. No more. I won't do it anymore."

Outside, Tony's fists clenched. "Glory, is that you?"

"Tony!" she screamed. "Help!"

Tony was a short, stocky, squarely built man. Everyone

always said he'd make a fine hockey player. He tried the door but found it locked. He backed up and ran into the door with his shoulder. The latch popped and Tony stumbled into the room.

It was small and lit only by the daylight from a skylight overhead and the open door. Glory was on the floor, her slacks below her hips, her blouse a torn remnant across her shoulders. Her eyes were wild and her cheeks streaked with mascara from crying. Martin Maddox was shirtless on the floor next to her. His pants were all the way up but unzipped. He clutched Glory's hair with a hand.

Tony came at him, kicking a foot solidly into Martin's stomach. Martin let go his hold on Glory's hair. She struggled backward, pulling her pants up, trying to get out of the way of the fighting men. Tony knocked the wind out of Martin, and before the surly, freckle-faced kid could catch a breath, the cameraman was all over him, beating the hell out of his face.

"What the fuck you think you're doing?" yelled Tony. "What are you doing to this girl? Big strong man, trying to force her into something she didn't want?"

Martin blubbered between gasps. His lip was split, and he spat blood. "She wanted it, man. She wanted it. She's been doing it for some time now. It's not my fault."

"It's not true," cried Glory, huddled in the corner. "He forced me. He made me come here with him. He f . . . f . . . forced me." She broke into sobs. "I hate him. I hate him!" she screamed.

Tony laid another dozen evenly placed blows into Martin's stomach and stood up, watching the blond kid looking at him with frightened eyes.

"You don't do that to women," said Tony. "Who the fuck do you think you are? Hotshot producer's son taking advantage of this girl? They got laws now to protect women from guys like you, but I ain't waiting around for any law."

Tony's boot flew to Martin's crotch, where the toe landed bluntly and squarely.

Martin yelled in agony.

"I'm going to kick your fucking nuts up to your throat," shouted Tony.

Denny, looking in the door, was dumbfounded by Tony's fury. There was not room for a fourth person in the tiny quarters. Tony squatted down next to Glory.

"You all right, baby?" he asked. He stroked her head and helped pull her blouse around her. "Denny, go find her another blouse, will ya?"

Glory's sobs were relentless—clutching her chest, her gut, squeezing, squeezing out all that hateful stench that saturated the sponge.

"Just let it all out, Glory," said Tony softly, pulling her to him and hiding her face against his chest. "I'm here. I'll protect you from now on. This will never happen again. I love you. I'm so sorry I hurt you. This will never happen again."

"You had no right sneaking out like that!"

"We are your parents. We have a right to know what's going on with our daughter!"

"What did you think you were doing? Going off to get married?"

"And you didn't even leave us a note. Can you imagine how distressed we were to find you had gone?"

"We pleaded with you not to become involved with Dillon Hughes. It was utterly irresponsible of both of you."

Penny was sitting on a chair in the den as both of her parents circled her like Indians attacking the wagon train, aiming their arrows and lances where it would hurt the most.

It was horrid how her father had told airport security that, under a psychiatrist's care, Penny was not fit to travel and that Dillon was practically kidnapping her. Mallory had stood smugly by. He had tried to say something to her, but she wanted nothing to do with him. He had betrayed her.

"I'm not going home, Daddy," she had said as her father

took her elbow and tried to lead her away from the airline gate.

"You are not leaving on that plane with Hughes and that's final," her father sternly told her.

"Daddy, no!" she cried. "You can't make me. I won't go. I won't go! Dillon!"

"I wouldn't even think about trying to stop us, Hughes," warned Mr. Huntington.

She could see Dillon was fuming and wanting to punch her father, but knew better than to tackle him. Mr. Huntington would have him locked up on assault and battery charges.

As Dillon stood alone, Penny kept looking over her shoulder at him, her father escorting her from the airport. If Dillon had tried to interfere, the airport guard would have been all over him. Mr. Huntington had probably shelled out a nice "tip" to get cooperation.

Penny's mind went over and over a scenario she had fabricated about how she and Dillon would be married in Las Vegas and they would kiss right there in front of the Justice of the Peace—for so long, that the JP would finally tap them on the shoulder and tell them to stop. She imagined it would be this way, because when she was with Dillon, it was like the two of them were in their own private world and could not be intruded on by outsiders. And then flying on down to Mexico, the two of them leaning to look out the airplane window and watch the Mexican deserts give way to green jungle, and all the while Dillon would be holding her hand and smiling every time their eyes met. Then they would arrive at their hotel room and be greeted with icy champagne, and they would take off their clothes and lie naked on the sheets, drinking champagne and laughing—laughing at how they'd fooled everybody; laughing at how good it was to be alone together; laughing because they were free from so many weeks of tears and stress.

Penny's parents were two wolves at a kill; bristling, growling, biting off a chunk of meat and chewing it up.

"What happened to your good sense, daughter?"
"I'll tell you what happened. . . . She was entrapped by that Dillon Hughes and he made her think she was in love with him. But you weren't really, were you?"
"I don't care whether she was or wasn't—is or is not," said her father.
"What I want to know," said Penny bitterly, "is exactly what Mallory told you?"
Both of her parents sighed. "He was worried when he came here to pick you up and you had vanished," said her mother. "He seemed to know what had happened to you."
"I asked him," continued Mr. Huntington, "if he had any idea where you had gone. He stammered around, trying to think up something. Let me tell you, Mallory is a poor liar."
"I'd hate to see him in the courtroom," mumbled Penny.
"Mallory's responsibility was to us," said her mother. "He did not know that you are on special medication."
"I'm taking no more medication! Mallory is a god-damned chicken-shit! Tell me . . . tell me why I can't marry Dillon? I'm of age. I'm in love with him. Why do you hate him so?"
"We don't *hate* him, Penny," said her mother. "He isn't the proper sort of man for you. We have much more experience than you."
"In ten years time, you will thank us for saving you from what could have been a disastrous marriage," said her father.
"To hell with your experience!" shouted the daughter.
"Why are you so dead set on disappointing us?" asked her father. "Don't we matter anymore? Or does your whole world revolve around Dillon Hughes now?"
"We love you, Penny," said her mother weakly, "very much."
Penny looked at her parents. There was that nervous, unsettled look about her mother. Of course, she loved them. Why were they so hard to please? Why did she have to feel so guilty about not doing the right thing for them?

"What are we going to do?" asked her mother.

"I want Penny out of the country," replied Mr. Huntington.

"You mean, don't you, dear, that Penny should continue her studies overseas? In Europe?"

"Precisely."

"I'll make travel arrangements immediately."

And they nodded, like they always did when they reached an agreement. Penny gave them a thin smile when they asked her what she thought about sailing.

Her mother said, "A nice long cruise, a year in Paris or Rome, will make you forget Dillon Hughes ever existed."

Tanya was nervous. She needed to talk to Garrett alone, alone in a place where she could tell him what had happened and where they could make plans. During the days following Graham Maddox's death, Norman spent a lot of time either on the phone with Ruby or at her house, and Tanya never knew when he was returning home or when he would make her go with him.

Tanya didn't like Ruby for a number of reasons. First of all, Ruby had always objected to giving Tanya the role of Janet on *Motive*; second, Ruby had an eye for Garrett, and the actor had not been above telling Tanya that for an old broad, Ruby was pretty sexy; and then, of course, Ruby was never, ever friendly to Tanya and always treated her like she didn't have any sense. That was the most infuriating part.

Therefore, Tanya did not feel like going along to Ruby's house and having to act cheerful while Norman held the producer's hand and promised everything would be all right.

Ruby's tall, lanky son—Will, they called him—was always hanging around. He was little more than a filthy biker. They'd had to haul him out of the gutter and give him a job and put clothes on his back. He gave Tanya the creeps every time she went over there. He'd stare and stare and wouldn't say much. He hardly acknowledged Tanya and that drove her crazy. She was one of the most beautiful women in America, and it wasn't asking too much for a man to talk to her and pay her a little compliment.

All men paid her compliments, even that gay makeup artist, Denny. When she was sitting in his chair, he'd back up ten feet and eye the job he'd done. He was responsible for her "look" on the show, so he'd stand there and tell her over and over what a beautiful woman she was.

That was why her photo had appeared on the cover of several magazines. The only thing that bothered her at all about the magazine interviews was her answer to the question, "Who has influenced you most in your career?" She was obliged to say, "My husband, Norman," though she did not really believe it. It wouldn't be proper to give herself all the credit. But who else had been the number one driving force behind her career? Only she. If a journalist had ever gotten around to asking if Norman had used his influence to get her the role on *Motive,* she would have replied that she had made the decision to marry him. Norman had been an opportunity, and she had taken it.

On the set, Garrett avoided her as much as possible. He made sure there was not a single second when she could catch him alone. She needed to talk to him about a very serious matter. She was prepared to leave Norman. It couldn't happen too soon for her. But first, she had to talk it over with Garrett.

It had been a long day under the hot lights, and nobody had been in a cooperative spirit. It was the holdover of mixed emotions about Graham. Tanya believed most of the people were plain worried about their jobs. How much longer would Maddox Productions be functioning? She tried not to lend too much of an ear to the problems of the crew. After all, she was a star and if *Motive* were cancelled next season, she felt certain that countless scripts would come her way. New opportunities.

Arriving home after the day's shoot, she was delighted to find Norman wasn't there. She showered, changed her clothes, and took the keys to her Jaguar. Without much difficulty, she found Garrett's new house in the Studio City hills and parked her car along the narrow street. It was his house, all right. The black Porsche sat in the driveway, right in the middle so there wasn't room for any other cars.

From the street, the house had a cozy feeling. Perhaps in the back, on the downhill side, it was more lavish. Tanya didn't particularly like cozy houses. She had grown accustomed to the sprawl of Norman's money.

She stood on the porch for a moment before ringing the bell. She wasn't wild about the vine curving around the latticework that framed the front door. It went along with small-paned windows and the bluish-gray paint. All cozy. Tanya was not a cozy type of girl.

She rang the bell and Garrett's girlfriend opened the door. "Tanya," she said, surprised.

"Hello," said Tanya. She hadn't remembered his girlfriend would be there. Oh, hell, damn. She groped for the woman's name. "Brenda, isn't it?"

"Yes," replied Brenda. "So nice to see you again. Is Garrett expecting you?" Though her voice sounded hospitable, her body barred the door, saying "get out."

"Yes," lied Tanya. "Didn't he tell you? I guess he may have forgotten. It's been so hectic on the set. It makes me cry to think of poor Graham." Her voice faltered.

"It was sudden," said Brenda, immobile.

Behind her, Garrett came to the door. "Who is it, Brenda?" he asked, poking his head over her shoulder. He saw Tanya and said, with irritation, "Invite her in."

Tanya swept by Brenda, almost running to Garrett. She gripped his elbow and looked at him with pleading eyes. "I need to talk with you."

He shrugged his shoulders and went into the living room, where he sat down on the couch. Tanya, still attached to his arm, sat beside him. She was unable to stop staring at his face. His eyes bypassed her and looked at Brenda who stood, miffed, on the other side of the room.

"Alone, *please,* Garrett," begged Tanya. She daren't look toward Brenda, for she felt the girlfriend's eyes boring into her with sudden hate. Had Garrett said anything? Did Brenda know Tanya and Garrett used to live together and that there was something eternal and binding between them?

"I'm sorry, darling," said Garrett, apologizing. He was on shaky ground. He had been spending too many nights away. Brenda stormed off through the house, and seconds later, they heard a door slam.

Garrett leapt up from the couch, pushing Tanya away. He stood at a distance of six feet and kept his arm outstretched as a gesture to hold her back. "Don't touch me. Let's get this straight. *Don't* touch me."

Tanya, with her hair loose and unruly over her shoulders and back, her great blue eyes moist, put her palm against her mouth to stop the words that had started to come out.

"What the hell are you doing here?" demanded Garrett. "My relationship is about to bust up, and out of all the women in the world to show up, it's you. Brenda's been snooping in my boxes, and do you know what she found? Pictures of you. With darker, shorter hair. But still you. And now she knows and she doesn't want to believe a thing I tell her. I owe that woman a lot. She has supported me. I owe her. But you wouldn't understand that, because the only thing your life amounts to is take, take, take."

"Garrett, hush," said Tanya. She shut her eyes, as if there were a great pain in her chest, and ran her hands over her breasts and rib cage, crossing her arms and hugging her stomach. "I don't know how I can live without you, Garrett. I thought I could. But I don't think I can anymore. Things have changed."

"*What* has changed?" he asked impatiently.

"I'm pregnant," she said, opening her eyes, her arms still hugging her stomach. "I'm pregnant . . . with your baby."

"I don't believe you."

"Look!" she shrieked, tearing open her small leather

purse and throwing papers at him.

He picked them up. They were lab reports stating that she was pregnant. "Does Norman know?"

"No, I'm not going to tell Norman."

"How do I know the baby is mine?"

"Because I said so," she whispered harshly. "Because you're the only man I've had."

He didn't believe her. There was Norman. She had cried too many bitter tears on Garrett's shoulder because she claimed Norman came to her in the middle of the night, and the only way she could live through it was to pretend fat old Norman was Garrett.

Norman was her husband. He had every right to her. He had every right to her baby.

"How do you want me to help you?" asked Garrett coolly.

"What!" she cried. "How do I want you to help me? *Help* me? I want us to move in together so that baby has two loving parents."

"I don't think I can do that," said Garrett. "I can't give up what I have here with Brenda because you *claim* that kid is mine." He pointed to her abdomen.

"It *is* yours!" she screamed at the top of her lungs. "This baby is *yours*!" The words rounded every wall in the house and had certainly found Brenda's ears.

"Calm down," he ejected, "or get out. I don't have to take this from you. I'll call your husband right now and tell him to come and get you." He walked toward the phone.

"No, you won't!" She bolted in front of him, knocking the phone to the floor. The receiver bounced off and buzzed the dial tone.

Brenda had appeared in the doorway to the living room. Her eyes were black with anger, her face composed. "I heard the yelling," she said quietly, "and I wanted to make sure everything was all right."

"It is *not* all right!" screamed Tanya. "Nothing is all right! I'll tell you what your dear boyfriend has been doing behind your back. He's gotten me pregnant." As she spoke, she tapped her sternum in one spot and the skin became very red.

Brenda raised her eyebrows. "I'll tell *you* something, Tanya. Half of America's women are in love with Garrett. And they have all sorts of fantasies about him. You are the fourth woman this month to claim he's caused her pregnancy. I don't know, in your case it *may* be true. But no judge is going to believe it."

Tanya quivered with rage, grabbed her purse, and headed for the front door.

"I'll walk you out," said Garrett, hurrying after her.

"No, you won't," she replied, throwing her fists into his chest and pushing him backward. She ran out of the house and fumbled to get the Jaguar keys in the ignition. She would have blood tests. She would prove the baby was Garrett's.

Whatever happened, there would only be two consequences: one, that she would absolutely not go on living with Norman and, two, that Garrett would not go on living with Brenda.

Graham Maddox's office was a testimonial that the executive producer always did things his way. Contemplating her surroundings as she sat behind his desk, Ruby realized that not a single suggestion she had made for decorating his office had been implemented. She sighed and then smiled slowly. Guess that's Graham. That's the way he is. Was. A brilliant, hardheaded man.

It left an uneasy feeling in her that they had been separated when he died, one in which she felt like apologizing over and over to him.

But there was no guarantee that if she had not moved out he would be alive. Graham had been ruthless—if that's what it took to achieve success. Graham had also been ruthless behind the wheel. It amazed her that the Coupe de Ville had gone over the edge.

Nine days had passed since she buried Graham, nine days of being constantly surrounded by family and friends. They were all so worried about her, treating her as though she were frail. How could she explain to them that she was no longer *Ruby: What She Used to Be?* She was a new person. *Motive* had made her strong, decisive. She told them she would do what Graham would have wished. He would have gritted his teeth and said, "The show must go on."

And so it would. She would personally see to it. They had five prime-time series in production, a half dozen in development, several TV movies-of-the-week on the scheds, and two feature films. They were all under way, budgeted. It was her duty to see that the projects were carried through to a tangible end product, quality product, the type Graham would have approved of.

She buzzed the intercom and asked Jeannie to come into the office. Jeannie entered, wearing a beige suit, her hair in a conservative bun. Her green eyes were somber and alert. Her face was quite neutral.

"Please have a seat, Jeannie," said Ruby. Jeannie sat and crossed her shapely legs. Ruby knew that Graham had been having an affair with this secretary. However, she was determined not to let it affect the business dealings. Since Jeannie, as his personal secretary, knew considerable details about Graham's private matters, it was up to Ruby to befriend her, not to alienate her for petty jealousy.

"I will be open with you, Jeannie," continued Ruby. "I will be relying heavily on you over the next few weeks. You are as well acquainted with Graham's business as several of us within the production company. You know the files. You know what needs to be dealt with immediately. We will work closely together. I realize this is added responsibility for you and may require overtime. You are entitled to compensation, and I want to give you a raise."

Ruby named the figure and saw the pleased response register on Jeannie's face.

"Thank you, Mrs. Maddox. That would be fine."

Good, thought Ruby, the girl can be bribed with money. "Please call me Ruby. I think we can dispense with the formalities."

"That will be fine with me, Ruby," replied Jeannie, relaxing in her chair. She could be at ease now that she was assured of her status.

"I have a question for you, Jeannie, and I hope you will answer me truthfully." Ruby was straightforward, cornering Jeannie in one sentence. "Why weren't you present at any of the services held in Graham's honor?"

Jeannie swallowed hard. Her eyes flitted around the room—over the crème de menthe carpet and white sofas, out the window to the quaking leaves of the sycamore. "I was not on the best of terms with Mr. Maddox. To be honest with you, he fired me the Friday before he died."

"Therefore, you felt no sorrow about his death? No sense of duty to go to his funeral?"

"No," admitted Jeannie. "I was angry. Why should I lie about it?"

"Why did Graham fire you?" Ruby was unsure of receiving an honest answer.

Jeannie's lips were parted in the curious way she had. It made her look so naive. She leveled her eyes upon Ruby, uncertain, for a moment, of her answer. It came slowly. "Mr. Maddox and I had been seeing each other. I wanted to break it off. He didn't. We had a fight."

"I see." Ruby gritted her teeth and fought the urge to walk over to Jeannie and slap the hell out of her smug face. "My husband was prone to such behavior. You weren't the first," stated the widow. "Let me ask you, if you were fired, why are you here now?"

"Martin called me. He asked me to receive phone calls. He seemed quite sure that *he* would be taking over the operation of Maddox Productions." Jeannie recrossed her legs, shifting in her seat.

"Oh, he did, did he?" Ruby had planned to have Martin continue working for the company. She had not paid attention to what he had been doing during the past week since his father's death. "Martin, of course, has a job with Maddox Productions, but Norman, our old family friend, feels that I am the person best qualified to be in charge at this time. I respect Norman's judgment."

"I do, too," said Jeannie, sitting forward in her chair. "But I wish someone would explain the situation to Martin. I didn't want to bother you with this right away, but I have had a number of complaints from writers, directors, line producers, DPs, on down the line, that Martin is coming in, telling them he's in charge, and giving them orders. They don't know what to do."

"How dare he? Find him and tell him I want to see him immediately."

Jeannie stood up. "One other thing, Mrs. Maddox—I mean Ruby. Have you heard about the incident he was involved in?"

"What incident?"

"With that production assistant on *Motive,* Glory?"

"I know Glory. What about her? What has she done?"

"Not her, Ruby. Martin. They found him raping her. Then the whole story came out. Apparently, he's been coercing her into having sex with him for several weeks. Sexual harassment. Nobody's pressed any charges so far."

"Find him this instant!"

Jeannie left the office and Ruby dialed Dillon's extension, asking him to come directly to Graham's office. Minutes later he entered, carrying a stack of reports and flashing Ruby one of his confident smiles. All teeth. All perfect white teeth. He was dressed immaculately in a dark brown suit. His manicured hands set the reports on the corner of Graham's great wide desk.

"Shut the door," said Ruby.

Before he shut the door, Dillon shot a glance at Jeannie sitting outside at the secretary's desk.

"We've got her," confided Ruby. "It was simple. A raise. Now we've got other problems. Have you heard about Martin and his forced sexual advances on Glory, Richard's production assistant?"

"I heard," said Dillon.
"Why didn't anybody tell me?"
"It just happened last Friday."
"I have been in contact with you the entire weekend. You've been down here. You might have told me."
"I'm sorry, Ruby. I didn't think it was a priority at this time."
She was irritated. How could she make decisions vital to running Maddox Productions if her staff was withholding information from her? "In the future, I want to be told about everything. I mean *everything*. Is that clear? It is not up to you to decide what I should or should not hear."
"Yes, Ruby," Dillon replied.
"Jeannie is looking for Martin right now. I have no choice but to fire him."
"Yes, Ruby," replied Dillon.
"That should make you happy," she said. "I know how you've felt about him since Graham promoted him instead of you."
"I was never angry with Martin. I merely thought he was unqualified and had been given the advantage because he was the owner's son."
"I wouldn't let anybody hear you saying that until the police have completed the investigation of the accident."
"I'll be careful. I've worked all weekend to get the production status reports finished, and we can go over them any time you'd like."
His voice was filled with emotion. It was almost the voice of a boy who needs his parents' approval. Ruby softened. She really was fond of Dillon. Her sons could have been as intelligent, sweet, and hardworking as Dillon—yet they hadn't chosen to be.
"What is your status with Miss Penny?" she asked.
He walked to the window and stood with his back to her, his hands pressed against the glass. "I've tried calling her house, but all they ever tell me is that she is 'unavailable.' They know it's me that's calling. I've even had my secretary call and pretend to be a girlfriend of Penny's

from school, but they repeatedly say she's unavailable." He looked at Ruby. "Goddamn, goddamn," he mumbled, his voice wracked with heartache.

Ruby walked behind him and put a hand on his shoulder. He was a hopeless romantic. She had never seen a face so tormented by love. "Do you want to tell me about it? Would it help to talk to me? I have a few years of experience and maybe I can give you my two cents worth?"

"We were going to elope," he explained. "She had had this nervous breakdown and her parents forbade me to visit her. So, I talked one of Penny's old friends into helping us. He was to bring us both to the airport, but on Sunday, she jumped the gun and didn't wait for him. When he got to her house and there was no Penny, her father guessed what had happened—and he cut us off at the airport. He made quite a scene and hauled his daughter away."

"So you've been working all weekend to keep your mind off of Penny?"

Dillon nodded. "They won't let me talk to her."

"I believe, Dillon, that true love will find a way. You must be patient now. Let the rough waters calm down a little, then try contacting her again. You must have faith and believe everything will be all right." Her words were idealistic. She didn't know if she believed them herself. Yet, his wide, haunted eyes looked at her as though she had revealed a great cosmic truth.

He nodded. "Thank you, Ruby, for taking an interest. I haven't known who I could turn to."

The intercom buzzed. "Martin is waiting out here, Mrs. Maddox," said Jeannie. "I'll send him in when you're ready."

Dillon took a deep breath.

"Are you going to be all right?" asked Ruby.

"Yes."

"Why don't you wait outside for me. When I've finished talking things over with Martin, you and I will go over the production status reports. I really appreciate your taking time to complete them."

As Dillon exited, Martin entered the room. He wore loose white trousers and a bright green and blue Hawaiian pattern shirt. His hands were shoved deep in his pockets and his lips were turned down. A thick scab had formed on one side of his mouth. One eye and the cheek below it was black and blue. But his gaze still smoldered with arrogance and surliness. He slammed the door shut and sat down in a chair, facing the huge desk in a sloppy slump. He put his feet on the desk and cocked his head as if to say, "Well, now what?"

"I didn't see you all weekend," said Ruby. "Looking at your face, I can see why. It's disgraceful. Your behavior has been disgraceful. And embarrassing. To think you are my son! Oh, hell. Not only do I find out you've been bossing around your father's trusted friends and employees—people who have years and years of experience in the business—but, to top it off, you've been forcing a girl to have sex with you." She was so angry that her fists were clenched and her fingernails dug into the palms of her hands.

"I didn't force anybody to have sex," fabricated Martin. "She and I were having an affair. It didn't involve anybody else. Just her and me. And this old boyfriend of hers gets a notion to interfere and beat the shit out of me. I'm going to press charges against him. Look at my face! Will you look at my face?"

"From what I understand, she will be pressing charges against you."

"Mom, come on, I don't need to *force* girls into doing it with me. I'm an attractive guy. They come *crawling* to me." He ran a hand through his strawberry blond hair, pushing it off his eyes.

"Martin, I was hoping I wouldn't have to do this, but I'm firing you. I don't think you'll work out anymore."

Martin slammed his hand down on the arm of his chair. "You won't believe me? Your own son? You're siding with all these other people? You can't fire me. I'm heir to Maddox Productions. You can't fire a part-owner. Dad made provisions for me. You can't do this to me."

"Today, I am doing it to you. We will deal with the legalities of inheritance at another time. Even your father would not have stood for sexually coercing a woman. It shows a very sick mind. If your father had listened to me, we would have gotten you into therapy long ago. Now leave my office."

Ruby stared at her defiant son. She didn't know him as her son. He left a raw place on her heart.

"You won't get rid of me this easily," shouted Martin. "I have rights. You watch, you old bitch, I have rights!" He stormed out of the office, a flash of bright blue-green color in the muted world of Graham's suite.

She called Dillon back into her office. The transition would not be easy, but she gained strength from *Ruby: What She Became.*

Will stood in the dirt yard of the Venice canal house, throwing old bread to the ducks. There were eight of them, all white and all arguing mightily in the early morning for possession of the scraps. He had slept well and awoken early. The day was new and fresh; the smell of the ocean was in the air.

Since he hadn't been called to do any stunt work, he could spend some time getting a few things accomplished. He looked at his dirty motorcycle. It was as good a day as any to finally get around to cleaning the black two-wheeler—the chore that had been pressing on the back of his mind for several months.

The ducks squawked and flapped at each other. Will found himself wishing there were someone to laugh with him at the birds' antics. It was impossible to ever have Candy again, and Sondra rested real gentle in that nook. Sondra had not made any demands on him. When he asked for more time alone, she gave it. Funny, he thought, a woman gives you as much room as you ask for, and you find out it's not what you really want. He wanted to spend more time with Sondra.

He got out a bucket, soap, wax, chrome polish, sponges, and rags, turned up the radio, and began cleaning the bike. Gouges were rusted all along the left side of the tank. They served as a brutal reminder of how quickly his life had been turned around.

He had soaped the motorcycle once when he heard a car slow down. Standing and wiping his hands on his jeans, he saw two men emerging from a dark domestic car. They approached him slowly, and Will knew instinctively they were cops.

They went to either side of him and stood at a distance of six feet, introducing themselves as detectives investigating Graham Maddox's accident. One was older, about fifty, with white hair. The other was a short, thirtyish Hispanic who kept his hands clasped in front of him.

"Are you Will Long?" asked the older man.

"Yes, I am," replied Will. He stood stiffly, looking from one face to another. "What do you want?"

"We'd like to ask you a few questions about your stepfather and where you were the night he died. You see, at the site of the wreck, someone had opened the driver's door of his Cadillac and we've found your fingerprints all over that door."

"Are you saying I was there, at the wreck?"

"We're not saying anything. Why don't you tell us how your fingerprints got on the door?"

Will glanced at the investigators, down at his motorcycle, the assorted containers of cleaners, the pile of rags, the soap foam disintegrating in the bucket, and at the ducks who waddled near the front door, squawking at each other.

"Had you seen Maddox that night?" asked the Hispanic.

"Yes," nodded Will.

"Where?"

"He called me. Asked me to come up to his house."

"You saw him at his house." The Hispanic was writing

in a notebook. "Anyplace else?"

"Yeah," sighed Will. "I was there when the Cadillac went off the road. But it was an accident. I went down to see if Graham was all right, but he was dead. I panicked. It was an accident. Honest."

"If that's true," said the older man, "why didn't you report it? What were the two of you doing together on Mulholland Drive at two-thirty in the morning? In separate vehicles? We'd better take you in and you can tell us your story at the station."

Will rode in silence in the back of their car. The Hispanic, who drove, observed him in the rearview mirror, and Will returned the stare, unemotionally. Will hated talking to cops. They were eyeing him with condemnation, because he had gone down to the Coupe de Ville after it went off the cliff and he hadn't reported the accident. That made him look guilty—guilty as hell.

Will had hoped the whole thing would blow over and the police would conclude that Graham had been alone when he had gone over the cliff. But there were witnesses who had seen another car drive away, and there was no way a dead man with a broken neck could have opened his own door.

Will told his story, evenly, matter-of-factly, unafraid. "Graham had called me up to the house that night. It was a misty night, almost a light rain. I'd never been there before, but I followed his directions pretty good. He and I have never gotten along. Since I was a teenager, he's never liked me. I had to finally move out of Los Angeles 'cause I couldn't stand to be within a hundred miles of the man. Big shot producer. The whole family was proud of him. But he wasn't any blood kin of mine.

"At his house, he offered me money—a large sum—to leave Los Angeles and never come back. I told him no way, I'm not interested. All those feelings of hate came back to me again. I'll admit it. We got in a fight at the house. He came at me, and I punched him. Knocked him down. I could have killed him right then and there if I'd wanted to. But I left. Just cut out.

"I was driving west on Mulholland, going to Venice. I had my girlfriend's car, but I was so pissed I couldn't go back to her house for the night. I wasn't in the mood to deal with anybody. All of a sudden, in my rearview mirror, there are these headlights and I recognize a big Coupe de Ville. And I know Graham drives a de Ville. The damn thing is riding my bumper, practically running into the back of me.

"It's then I realize he's trying to run me down, run me off the road. He's trying to kill me. I'm trying to get away from him, but that Cadillac has shitloads of power. It was a heavy car. I outmaneuvered him. He came around a tight corner and he couldn't turn quick enough and off he went.

"Shit, I knew it would be bad, but I didn't think he'd be killed. I thought he'd be knocked out, or maybe cut, or maybe break a couple of bones. I figured that the de Ville was a big car and anybody inside would be a whole lot safer than in any other car. I parked my car and stumbled down to the wreck. Everything was quiet. You know how Mulholland is at that time of night—not a soul in sight.

"I fought my way through all those brambles. Inside, I saw he's slumped over the wheel. I opened the door to help, but he's already dead. I panicked. I admit it. I wasn't thinking clearly. He had just tried to kill me, and it could have been me as easy as him at the bottom of the hill.

"He was an insane driver. Ask people who knew him. His own wife wouldn't ride in the same car with him. The man was insane. But, believe me, I didn't go to his house with any intention of killing him."

However, the cops kept bringing up the same points: Why hadn't Will reported the accident? If he were innocent, why would he be afraid to get involved in the investigation? He was a stunt driver. He certainly knew more about chase scenes and running cars off the road than a respectable executive producer.

And then there was the matter of the investigation held

in Oregon concerning an accident on his motorcycle.

"We're booking you on suspicion of manslaughter," said the older cop. "Read him his rights," he instructed his Hispanic partner.

Chapter 16

Ruby was getting her article in *People* magazine. It was not exactly the one she wanted, since she had envisioned a nice piece, under the "Couples" heading, about how she and her husband had worked as a successful team conceiving and producing television series, one that would prove to the entire nation that she was a person of worth, reputation, and prominence.

However, the reporter had been assigned to write about Maddox Productions and how she had taken over after the untimely death of her husband.

"Was it true," pressed the reporter, "that you and Mr. Maddox were in the process of getting a divorce?"

"Certainly not," declared Ruby.

"But it is true, is it not, that you and he were not living together at the time of his death?"

Ruby answered coldly, "I don't know where you get your information, but it is wrong."

"It must have been difficult to find your son Will had caused his stepfather's death. He's facing a manslaughter charge, isn't he?"

"No comment," replied Ruby. "I'll kindly ask you to omit any reference to my son and his trial in your article."

"The public is entitled to know, don't you think?" asked the reporter, wielding a mini-tape recorder close to Ruby's mouth.

Ruby was playing both sides of the fence. To the

public, she was the loving wife. Yet, as a mother, she had to defend her son. "Would you like your tour of the production facility now? I've arranged for Dillon Hughes to guide you through the soundstages." Jeannie escorted the reporter to Dillon's office.

Thank God Dillon had taken the reporter on the tour! He was closedmouthed and the picture of composure. He could effectively circumvent the reporter's questions. She knew she could not make it through this transition in her life if Dillon were not there to rely on. She liked him. The truth was, she wished any of her children were as competent as he. She wished he were her son.

That night, either Will or Graham had tried to run the other off the road. But which had it been? She was forced to choose between husband and son . . . again.

Guilt was all tied up with confusion. Earlier in the evening, Graham had called her from his car phone in the street in front of her condo. She hadn't answered. Then later, Garrett Gage had come to her door with his champagne. The memory of her heated entanglement with the handsome actor left her blushing. She decided it would be for the best if she just forgot about the affair, pretended that it had never happened.

Will claimed self-defense, that Graham had tried to force him off the road. Why would Graham do that? Will sat angrily in his jail cell and refused to talk to anyone. They had brought him out once so Ruby could talk to him. But he had only spit biting words at her. "He was your husband. You always took his side. Whenever the decision was Graham or me, you always chose him."

What he said was true, and it stung.

"But I wouldn't purposely kill him, Mother, because I love you too much to see you in that much goddamned pain." He had abruptly stood, nodded at the guard, and walked away from her.

And she hadn't known whether or not to post his bail.

Will was angry with her for not knowing if she should

believe he had acted out of self-defense. Graham had been a crazy driver. Impulsive. Prone to anger. There were all those years that she had refused to drive with him. How could she prove that? As a couple, they had not advertised that fact to their friends. How could she prove he was crazy behind the wheel?

She owed it to Will to believe his story. He had no one but her to depend on. Graham was dead. Her allegiances should be with the living. Will could stay with her until after the trial. To hell with the speculations of the press. He was the son who had not betrayed her.

She boiled when she thought of Martin. He was contesting his father's will. He did not feel the ten percent allotted him was a fair share. Each of Graham's three children—Sarah, Julia, and Martin—had received the same amount.

Since Norman had willingly offered any help she needed, she asked him what he suggested she do about Martin's discontent.

"Buy him out," said Norman. "I'll take care of the negotiations, if you wish."

Ruby was thankful. She felt sad about Martin. She had so hoped he would take a positive interest in the company. But he was a spoiled brat. Irresponsible. And she was partially accountable for making him that way. As detestable as he had become, she was nevertheless worried about him. He was hardly capable of taking care of himself. He was prone to overexhausting himself on liquor, drugs, and long nights. He was an adult, yet it was hard for her to admit she could do nothing more for him. She had to learn to let him go.

Motive was nearing the end of its first successful season. She asked Dillon and Jeannie to plan the wrap party. She left it entirely in their hands. She wished she could be more enthusiastic—the cast and crew deserved it—but she had too much to think about.

She needed courage. Though one season on *Motive* had given her valuable production experience, she never would have guessed she would be without Graham to ultimately rely on.

She had wanted her independence. Now she had more than she had bargained for.

Tanya couldn't quite wake up. Sleep was closing her eyelids, pulling her back to her dreams. Morning was beyond the drawn curtains, but she didn't want any part of it. She ignored her wake-up call by packing a pillow on top of her head and burrowing under the covers.

"Darling, darling," called Norman's voice, soft and anxious. He walked into her room wearing leather slippers and a black silk robe, and sat on the edge of her bed. Thinking he was gently waking her, he rubbed her shoulder through the sheet.

"Go away," she mumbled into her pillow, scooting her body away from his touch. "I don't want to get up. I want to sleep."

"You've got a full day of shooting," said Norman.

Tanya groaned. "I don't want to go. I'm too tired."

Norman's hand reached under the covers and pulled out the long blond braid that was the thickness of a mink's body. Stroking it, he marveled at the perfection of its hundreds of shades. "I'm worried about you," he said. "You're so exhausted. It must be the trauma of Graham's death."

Exhaustion attributable to the passing of Graham Maddox from this world had not occurred to her. She hadn't known Graham and so far, it hadn't made any difference to her job. She still showed up and put in a full day's work in front of the camera. The cast and crew of *Motive* had rallied with a "show must go on" attitude. Who gave a damn? She only wanted to sleep.

"I'm calling the doctor," said Norman. "I can't have my wife ill. I hate to see you suffer."

She heard him reaching for the phone. Not the doctor. No, not the doctor. She pulled the pillow off her head, rolled over, and forced her bleary eyes open. "I don't want a doctor," she said, fighting sleep and forcing a smile.

"Are you sure?" asked Norman, concerned.

She yawned and batted her eyelids with effort. She hoped the little life in her was getting his or her rest. Whatever happened, she couldn't let Norman know. She propped herself up on a couple of pillows and pointed to the box of Kleenex. She dabbed her nose with a couple of tissues. "Don't call. I'll be all right."

"What could be causing this? You've been sleeping all the time." The phone sat in his lap. She eyed it with distrust. At this particular moment, it was a forceful weapon.

"People sleep when they're depressed, Norman," she began.

He sighed with irritation. "What are you depressed about, sugar? I thought everything's been going well since your acting career has taken off. What could you possibly be depressed about?"

He was unshaven and the creases around his eyes were very oily. The skin under his neck hung in a soft wattle and he licked his thin lips with a thick tongue. Using the tears she could voluntarily turn on (and which had been the envy of her acting class years ago) she sniffled as the salty droplets flowed silently down her cheeks.

"Our marriage isn't working out, Norman. I'm not happy being married to you. I can't stay with you any longer." There, she had said the words she had so long dreaded.

Norman didn't speak. He rubbed his chin, then rubbed his forehead. He couldn't look at her. He was in love with her. She made him feel like a fool for having this love. He wanted to spend all his spare time with her. He wanted to tell her all his secrets. He wanted her to believe in him absolutely. He felt naked upon a cold marble slab. Vulnerable. Every doubt that every one of his friends had had about the marriage was turning out to be true. He tried to rally his anger, but when he looked at Tanya, his heart melted. She was so beautiful. So damnably beautiful. He felt like the luckiest man alive to have such perfection so close to him, living with him.

But she wanted to leave him. He was positive she didn't have a lover. He had her tailed continuously. His suspicion of a few weeks before was out of the picture. He had thought she and he had resolved their differences and that she was happy—happy with him, her job, the house. Then to find out she was coping with depression all along. She made him so happy, it was hard to admit that she didn't care for him at all. He had no right to keep her if she wanted to go.

There was a knock on the bedroom door, followed by her English maid bringing in a tray of food.

"I asked them to bring up your breakfast," said Norman, placing the tray upon the bed. "I wanted to have a few minutes alone with you." On the tray were orange juice, bacon, poached eggs, toast with butter, coffee—a healthy breakfast by anyone's estimation.

But the smell was too much for Tanya. The bacon grease and butter and toast smells went to the pit of her stomach, and seconds later, she was out of bed and running to the bathroom with her hand clapped over her mouth. She leaned over the toilet with the dry heaves, the retching turning her inside out.

Norman rushed to the bathroom behind her and watched the gasping, red-faced blonde in misery. She was sick with something. There was no doubt about it. The smell of food . . . the smell of food . . . Then suddenly he knew. He remembered his first wife, years ago. The first three months had been the worst and she had apologized daily. Morning sickness. Clearly, Tanya had morning sickness.

"Why didn't you tell me?" he asked coldly.

"Tell you what?" she asked between heavy gasps, bracing herself with one hand on the toilet tank.

"You're pregnant."

She looked up. Her eyes were bloodshot, her hair straggly in her face. "No, I'm not," she lied.

"Yes, you are," he said. "You forget. I've had kids. It was a long time ago, and I should have recognized what the devil was wrong with you. Why do you want to leave me now that you're carrying my child?" He smiled in spite of himself. "I'm going to have another child. At my age!" It was incredible. He was overjoyed.

"I don't want to live with you anymore," she said.

"You can't leave me when you're having my baby."

"It's not your baby," she said, spitting into the bowl and flushing the toilet.

"I don't believe you," he said. "Who else's could it be? I've had you watched. You haven't been with anyone else." He sounded certain.

Nobody wanted to believe her. Not Garrett. Now, not Norman. "Garrett Gage is the father."

"Your co-star?" he asked incredulously.

"Yes. We had an affair."

"I don't believe you," said Norman. "I don't know why you'd want to lie to me. You know I'll give this baby the best of everything."

Tanya swished water around in her mouth. "I can't stay with you and have this baby," she told him. Norman had her trapped. She was cornered. "Why won't you believe me? It *is* Garrett's baby. It *is*."

"Garrett Gage is not that big a fool. If you imagine you were seeing him at one time, let me assure you that you are no longer seeing him. I'm determined this baby will have a good home—with me."

"No." Tanya shook her head. "I want out. You can't force me to stay."

"Tanya, you are my wife. I love you. I will provide for you. Now that I know of your condition, I could never approve of a divorce. I want my child. He or she will be healthy, happy, and will live with both of its parents. That means me . . . *and* you."

Dillon was finally getting what he deserved—his promotion.

"But," Ruby said, "I no longer need a coproducer. I need a vice president, someone I can trust to handle all the financial affairs of Maddox Productions, someone I can depend on to stick with me over the next few months. It will be very difficult for me, but I can't let the company die. I just can't. Graham would want us to keep it going."

Dillon thanked her. "Vice president" would be impressive on a business card when someone asked what he did for a living. It would recapture the respect of Mr. Huntington, who would finally have to accept Dillon.

Penny would be proud. There was no doubt in his mind that she would have gone through with the elopement. At this very moment, Penny could have been his wife and be waiting for him at his apartment.

Damn that little creep Martin Maddox, for running to the police after intercepting Dillon's letter to Ruby. It burned Dillon that *he* had ever been suspected of driving so recklessly as to force another car off the cliff. He was scared as hell of cars. That was why he drove a Volvo, the safest car made. He didn't have the skills to bump Graham's Cadillac into a deep gully. It had never *occurred* to Dillon that killing Graham would be an adequate way to solve his problems at Maddox Productions. It horrified him that anyone had thought he was capable of committing murder. Now Will had come forward with a confession—a solid, unemotional confession, unlike the ludicrous story Margi Owens had told the detectives.

Dillon Hughes, Vice President, Finance Affairs. He couldn't help grinning when he said the title out loud to himself. Looking at himself in the mirror, he was as clean-cut and well-dressed as ever. His eyes couldn't help but gleam with excitement and importance. He was only slightly worried about not being able to live up to everything Ruby expected of him. He knew she would rely heavily on him, would want him to put in long hours, would want access to him twenty-four hours a day, if need be. He felt grateful to Ruby. She was the only one who had ever placed all her faith in him. He was in debt to her. He owed her.

Now, he would finally get his chance to introduce Penny to Ruby. He could picture Penny on his arm as the three of them went out to a very stylish dinner. Penny, with her perky smile, interested in everyone she spoke with. He could see her face, full of love and longing. He needed her so much. None of his new life—his promotion, raise in salary and status—would mean a thing if he couldn't share it with Penny.

He tried to understand her family's position. They had immense wealth and position within the community. But eloping these days could scarcely be called a scandal. It only mattered to him that Penny understand.

"Penny," he said out loud, softly, "you are my wife. My wife in spirit. Whatever decision you make about your family, I will abide by it."

He picked up the phone, determined to talk to Penny. A nasal voice answered with, "Huntington residence."

"Penny, please."

"I am sorry, sir," said the voice with utter control. "Miss Huntington is out of the country."

"What do you mean? Out of the country!!" exclaimed Dillon. His heart pumped dreadfully in his breast.

"Miss Huntington and her mother, Mrs. Huntington, have gone overseas for a few months."

"Where? Where did she go?" asked Dillon desperately.

"To Europe, sir. That is all I know."

"Is Mr. Huntington home?"

"He is taking no phone calls, sir. Please excuse me, I have no further information."

"Wait . . . wait," cried Dillon as the phone went dead in his ear.

He hated Mr. and Mrs. Huntington. They had conspired to take Penny away from him. He was outraged that she could not make her own decisions. He thought bitterly of the psychiatrist who had been brought in when Penny had her breakdown. It would have been easy, at the time, for the parents to have him sign a statement to the effect that Penny was not legally sane.

Where was his beloved Penny? Win one battle and lose another—when he had his Penny, he did not have his career; now that he had been substantially promoted, Penny had been wrung from his life.

There was a knock at his office door. "Mr. Hughes," said his secretary, "I have the mail. I thought you might want to look at it."

Dillon kept his back to her. She put the mail on his desk and hurried out of the room. He stared at the mail with no interest. At that very moment, he did not think he had the strength to continue with his job, with life. None of it mattered if he couldn't have Penny. Where had she gone in Europe? How could he have ever trusted Mallory Burton? It had been extremely poor judgment on his part. He had to fly to Europe and find her, no matter what it took.

His secretary interrupted through the intercom. "Just want to remind you, Mr. Hughes, that you have a meeting at eleven with Mrs. Maddox."

He thought of Ruby. She had placed her faith in him. Would she understand if he told her he was going to Europe for an undetermined amount of time? Ruby had very definitely told him that *she* needed him during this very difficult transitional period at Maddox Productions. Since he had promised to help her, she trusted that he would.

A light blue envelope in the stack of mail caught his eye. His name and address were handwritten. Penny! He knew the writing. The postmark was Los Angeles, two days before.

"Dillon, I have one heart, and it is with you.

"Now they have packed me off to college in Europe, sure

that I will finally forget you. They are wrong. I will never forget you. I will love you forever. The miles are now between us and, as the years come between us, remember me in one corner of your heart . . . I, who was unable to fight my parents and run away. I, who will never know love again. I will always think of you and wish for the things that could have been. My mother has always complained about her pregnancies, but I had looked forward to carrying your child. It would not have been difficult for me. Ever.

"Don't hate me for having so little courage to fight my parents. If I knew how to come to you, I would. But I don't even know my travel plans. My parents have forbidden me to contact you in any way, so do not let them know of this letter. I am mailing it from the airport.

"I don't know what else I can say except I'll love you forever. . . ."

Dillon pressed the letter against his lips. Penny loved him and that was all that was important. But his conscience told him that Ruby needed him as well. He was torn. He wished he could write Penny and tell her that he didn't blame her for a thing and that he would be waiting for her return. But he didn't know where she would be attending college.

An answer began to formulate. He was now vice president of a film company. It was perfectly legitimate that he could scout locations. If he could only wait a month, until things calmed down, perhaps he could push a project with a European location.

His mother having posted bail, Will sat on the deck of the home on Fire Gulch. It was a broad, redwood porch that extended out from the living room at the back of the house and overlooked the wild, vacant canyon. He wore a jean jacket and sat off to the side, where the lights streaming out from the living room wouldn't touch him.

A night wind blew up the canyon. It was unseasonably balmy, more like early summer than winter. It carried the smell of sage, dirt, and dry grass as it galloped silently onto the deck and stood there with its legs quivering.

Will had been drinking tea, but the half that remained in the cup at his side had long since grown cold. He took a sip and then, realizing it was cold, let the liquid rest in his mouth while he decided whether to swallow it or spit it out. Though there was not another house in the canyon, it was not totally cloaked in darkness. It never could be. There was always too much light in the Southern California sky.

Here was Los Angeles, heady whore who, with all her empty promises, pinched out dreams as if they were flames on candle wicks. Here he was, with his back to his mother's house, searching the city below for some answer—as though there were an answer the city would cough up—with no place to call home. No place to go.

He wondered why he had let Joe talk him into coming back to California. Where else could he have gone? He couldn't have stayed in Oregon. They all blamed him for what had happened. Worst of all, he blamed himself. When you've sworn you would never love anyone in your whole life—because everyone you've ever tried to love suffers when you care for them—and then a person comes along who you *do* love, it is certainly the most horrible thing in the world to lose that person.

The wind rocked the canyon's bushes and a bird called out from one of them, a strange, haunting cry that seemed almost human. It was a solitary voice crying out in the night, and he was the only one to hear it. Yet, he could not reply. The bird existed on a different plane than he. *It* would never be atrophied by emotion. What a good thing it would be to be able to bypass emotion.

He looked at the redwood railing and saw Candy leaning against it, gazing up at the few stars and looking down the canyon. The wind swept her long black hair back from her face and ran even fingers along her cheeks and throat. She tilted her head at the calling bird, listening intently, understanding what the bird was saying. Her eyes took on that look of understanding, a flickering smile of contentment. She began to sing, as a reply to the bird. No words, only a sweet melody. She did not look at Will.

He vaguely heard the doorbell, the footsteps, the voices, his mother calling his name. There was a flutter of wings. The bird was gone. Candy had slipped back into the darkness.

At the sliding glass door, Sondra stood with his mother. Sondra's white-blond hair was pulled back into a short ponytail, and it made the bones of her face even more severe. The cheekbones and chin were prominent, while her eyes, with no makeup, receded into two small, glittering points of ice.

"You have company, Will," said Ruby politely, surprised that Sondra would be looking for her son.

"Hi, Sondra," replied Will uncomfortably. He hadn't seen her since Graham's funeral.

"Hi, Will," she said. "I was wondering if we could talk?"

"I don't want to talk," said Will. He looked at her honestly. "I just wish all my memories would go away and never come back."

"You know," said Sondra quietly, "sometimes the best way to get them to leave you alone is for you to talk about them. Once you talk about them out loud and hear yourself talking, they ease off."

Will shook his head. "I don't know about that."

"I have some things I've got to file," said Ruby, turning into the living room.

Will wanted to say, "Mom, don't go. Stay. If I say anything, I want you to hear." But he was silent. That was a continuous problem. He couldn't share. Why was Sondra here? He didn't want her to get too close to him. He could hurt her and he didn't want to. She didn't need to be falling for a loner, for he was liable to bolt if he felt the walls squeezing in on him—that is, if he could beat the manslaughter charge.

Sondra walked past him, going to the part of the railing that was in shadow. She stood where Candy had stood, a sharp contrast to the petite, black-haired waif who had called to the bird. Sondra was tall and skinny. Her strong, thick fingers clutched her heavy sweater at her neck to keep the wind out. She leaned on the rail, but faced in and looked at him.

"You're not getting away from me so easily," she said. "You're not going to break my heart without an explanation." It was the voice she used on the set to boss the crew around.

"I didn't know we were involved enough to bring our hearts into it," he told her.

"I didn't know, either, until you said you didn't want to see me anymore."

"I didn't say I didn't want to see you. I said that it wouldn't be a good idea to keep seeing so *much* of each other." He stood with the light behind him, and his face, pointing toward the canyon, was very black. She couldn't see his eyes. His voice was indifferent.

Sondra spoke. "You said it was because of the guilt you felt—guilt over Candy. You've never told me about her, and I wasn't going to ask. Now it looks as though she's taking you away from me. I won't let her do that. Who is she? Why don't you simply go back to her?"

Will moved into the shadow and sank against the wall where he had been sitting before. The bird cried from a different bush, farther away. "Go ahead, Will," it called. "Tell her about me." Sondra wasn't leaving until she had her answer. But how was he to explain that he had sworn to himself he would never love a living thing after tiny Belinda, his sister, had drowned?

And then Candy had come to him like a soft spring breeze.

He was making pretty good money logging. He'd

bought the chain saw from Candy's dad and was working twelve-hour days out in the timber. All the hard work cut his partying down considerably. He'd go out for a few beers after supper, but he'd try to be in bed by ten. Four-thirty came awful early in the morning.

Of course, after he married Candy, he'd drink his beers at home with her sitting on his lap while they watched TV. She never put any restrictions on him, like when to be home or what friends she didn't like coming over. But he loved her so much that after he was settled in with her, he always came home when he said he would. He preferred her company to that of his rowdy, loudmouthed friends.

She concentrated on her portrait painting and was pretty shy until she got to know people. Then she always preferred to talk to the women and hardly ever to the men. When they went to parties, she'd wander off to the kitchen and chat with the women so that Will could have his time with the men. He'd always roust her out and make her come and sit with him. He just wanted to hold her, touch her, sit next to her. She brought the greatest peace to him he'd ever known. It was as if all his life his soul had been pacing a jail cell with high stone walls, and she had brought him out of that and lain him down under a big shade tree and stroked all the restlessness from his brow. Her fingers on his forehead. Light. Always the right touch.

Life had pretty near been perfect for the two of them. They didn't have all the money they wanted, but they had each other and they were content. They each took the wanting away in the other. They talked about kids and he said, Sure, any time.

On weekends, they'd go for long rides on the motorcycle, sometimes with people, sometimes alone. She'd sit behind him and would always have contact with him by either putting her arms around his waist or her knees against his legs. Because there was a lot of rain in Oregon, they only rode on sunny days, when they could fly down miles of pavement, drinking in the warm, redwood-scented air.

They spent rainy Sundays upstairs in bed in the old farmhouse where there were no curtains on the window and all they could see were the wet leaves of the tree that grew next to the house and the damp sky beyond it. They would snuggle under the quilts, lying quietly, holding each other. That was all they needed. They each felt so complete.

One Sunday, they got a call from friends Wes and Sally, who had moved about fifty miles away, asking them over to the big barbecue housewarming they were having. Wes and Sally had bought property up in the timber, and Will had helped his friend clear ground and cut logs for their cabin. Wes was a mountain man and preferred living in the woods to living in town. It was a long ride through the redwood forests to get to their place.

Though it had rained during the night, the sun came out in the morning and steam rose from fields and roads in its warmth. Will and Candy climbed onto the motorcycle and headed up the highway for Wes and Sally's. The road wound over through the farmland, then climbed a steep grade to a pass. The sunshine held for most of the climb, but by the time they topped the pass and looked down into the long, straight valley, it disappeared behind dark, gray clouds.

"Shit," called out Will to Candy behind him. "You want to turn around, sweetheart?"

"No, I'm all right," insisted his wife.

"You cold?"

"I'll be all right, honest."

The pavement switch-backed down the mountains, leveling out on the floor of the valley. Though it was not raining, the road was wet from a shower that had passed within the hour. Clouds hung low over the redwoods, obliterating the treetops. The air rushing over the riders was clean and cold and the fresh scent of evergreen filled their heads. Clumps of small, yellow daisies grew throughout the bright green grass that covered the roadside ditches. The road was very, very empty. There was no traffic on this rainy Sunday.

Ahead, in the left-hand ditch, Will saw a tawny doe lift its head in surprise. Three other does grazed in the forest on the opposite side of the road. As the motorcycle neared the solitary deer, it panicked and leapt upon the roadway, into the path of the riders.

Will had no time to swerve. The bike hit the doe's rear legs. It fell on its side in the right-hand ditch, thrashing its front feet in the wet grass. The impact threw Candy from the motorcycle, which tipped onto one side and began skidding. Will rode it as it grated across the pavement a hundred feet, slid into the roadside ditch, and ground to a stop in the rain-softened dirt. Under the machine, Will's leg was numb. He managed to crawl free. His leather britches were burned through, and he tried to stand on his leg. It was sore but took his weight.

He looked for Candy. She had fallen on the same side of the road as the doe. She cried out, "Will! Will!" in terror. He saw the deer pulling itself into the redwoods, its back legs unable to coordinate with the forelegs. He ran for Candy. She lay on her stomach, her hands spread before her.

The blood had started. Started from her wrists where she had skidded across the pavement, bracing herself with her hands. Both wrists were snapped and scarlet blood ran freely.

"My hands!" she cried.

Will kneeled in the dirt next to her, taking a tiny wrist in each of his hands and holding tightly. He had to stop the flow of blood or she would be dead within a minute. He clamped hard with his fists over the bones, squeezing, tightening, biting his own lip in his agony. She fainted from shock but was breathing. He glanced over her for other injuries. Her face was badly abraded, but the wrists were the only critical injury. She had obviously taken the entire fall on them. Her hands were mutilated pulp dangling from crunched bone and tendon.

A vast stillness enveloped them. There was not a sound anywhere. No tires sounding on the wet asphalt. The struggling, damaged deer had disappeared into the misty forest. He dared not release his grip on Candy's wrists.

"My Candy, no," he begged. "My baby, no. You can't die. I won't let you."

He knew he had to get her to a hospital and he knew he had to tourniquet her wrists. He remembered the words from first aid: "Only tourniquet a limb to save a life, because you'll lose the limb." He had no choice. Her pulse eased off, and he held both wrists with one hand and pulled the bandana from his neck. He bit hard and tore the rag in half, wrapping each wrist with the cloth and pushing a stick underneath so he could twist the fabric to choke off the flow of blood.

He didn't know if the motorcycle would even start. He prayed for a car to come down the road, but there was only silence and the wet forest all around them. He laid Candy on her back and put his coat over her. He went back to the bike where it had plowed a foot deep into the earth. The light rain started falling again. He reached under the handlebars and pushed up, exerting all his strength, his face streaked with tears.

He righted the motorcycle and brushed the dirt from the engine. He kicked the starter . . . and kicked the starter.

He went back to Candy. Her eyes were open and terrified.

"Save me, Will, save me," she whispered.

"I will, Candy. I love you, darling. I love you." He fought back more tears as he looked at her lying helpless with her blood on the wet grass and dirt. "Someone will come along and give us a ride to town. Someone will come." He took her in his arms and waited.

And the only sign of the doe was the tracks in the wet earth where she had dragged herself into the forest.

And the light rain fell and in the silence of the forest, he could only hear the faint breathing of his love in his arms.

Will paused and looked at Sondra, who sat on the floor on the deck, her lips trembling, her hand outstretched, a line of tears flowing from her eyes. "My God," she said. "Did she live?"

Will shook his head no. "They did a sort of autopsy on her. Blood tests showed she was pregnant. And I was angry. I was so lost. My wife was dead. My unborn child was dead. Both by my hand."

"It was an accident, Will," said Sondra, crawling on her knees to his side.

"Accident or not, it was my fault."

The questions still obsessed him. Why hadn't he seen the doe coming out of the roadside ditch? Why had he ridden the bike on a rainy day? Why did he have to live with the knowledge that Candy had put all her faith in him to protect her . . . always?

Sondra was the first person he had told the story to.

"It was an accident," she repeated.

He wished he could escape from the feeling that Candy's death was his fault, but it haunted him, just as Belinda's death haunted him. His young wife and his young sister—the only two girls he had ever loved in his life—were dead because of his carelessness. He had been helpless to save them. Somehow, he couldn't chalk up their deaths to being mere accidents.

"Thank you for sharing it with me," whispered Sondra. "When you share a tragedy, it becomes lighter to bear. I will lift some of that weight from your shoulders."

He felt a hair's weight lighter—a long, raven-black hair.

"I can't go back to Oregon. They won't have me there. I can't stay here. They may put me in jail for something I didn't do. I belong with Candy. She keeps coming for me, you know. Coming and talking to me. I don't know why I should stay here. Where she is, is the only place left for me."

Sondra took his hand and held it to her face, brushing his fingers against her nose and lips. "Don't talk like that, Will. I love you. I'll help you. I may not be Candy, but I'll love you. I will give you my soul."

When Jeannie walked into her mother's house, she felt something odd. Her heart began to race.

"Mom!" she called, rushing through to the family room in the back. Upon seeing her, the small dogs in the backyard scratched frantically at the plate glass window.

Her mother lay motionless upon the couch, dressed in a worn robe. Her feet were bare, her hair uncombed. Jeannie shook her mother's shoulder and was relieved to hear a deep sigh from the prostrate woman.

"What's wrong, Mom? Are you sick?"

Her mother batted her eyes open and looked at her daughter's face—which seemed to be the same face it had been when Jeannie was a little girl. Yet, Jeannie did not look like a child. How could the face be the same?

Jeannie hugged her mother. "You had me so scared. I came in the door and I didn't hear the TV. You're always watching TV. Are you all right?"

Her mother looked sad—a profound sad—and Jeannie couldn't figure out why. "Tell me why you look like this, Mama. Tell me!"

Her mother continued hugging Jeannie. "You won't understand, daughter," she said, "but Graham's death . . . I can't believe he's dead."

"You're crying over *him?*" Jeannie asked unbelievingly.

"I know it doesn't make any sense to you. But I loved him once."

"Mother, he *hurt* you and we have been suffering for *years* because of it. He destroyed your life!" Jeannie was exasperated. She pulled away from her mother's grasp. The rational side of her brain was telling her that her mother had been emotionally unstable for years, but

Jeannie's mouth couldn't stop. "What is wrong with you? I tried to get a little of what he owed you. And he wouldn't do it. He hated us. How can you cry over a man like that?"

She gritted her teeth when she looked at her mother. So pathetic. So fucking pathetic. Graham Maddox destroys her life years ago, and all she can do when he dies is cry. Jeannie promised herself she would never be like her mother—out of control when it came to loving a man.

Graham Maddox had owed them, and now that he was gone, there was no way she was ever going to get another cent from the Maddoxes. True, she had secured a nice raise and a decent job. Ruby Maddox was even turning out to be a pretty nice person. What had that poor woman been doing with Graham for all those years? Graham had been pulling the wool over his wife's eyes, as well. However, Jeannie saw no way to get the money she was entitled to.

Jeannie let the dogs in and walked to the refrigerator, opened the door, and stared at the metal racks. There wasn't much in there. They had scrimped and saved, and she had so looked forward to getting the chunk of money from Graham. It would have been enough to get the additional operations her mother needed. Maybe those operations would have mended the dancer's spirit.

"Mother, I have an idea," said Jeannie. "Maybe the Maddox family has a conscience. Maybe I can go to Ruby and tell her what happened to you."

"She won't care. She'll be worried about that son of hers, the one that ran Graham off the road. I hope they get him. Nail his ass. How could he have killed Graham? Graham was the sweetest man I ever knew."

"Will is innocent," said Jeannie. "I know he has to be. If I tell them about your accident, it will show them that Graham was a crazy driver. But there's got to be a way to prove it, without a doubt."

"Don't you go to them," said her mother. "Graham

would not want our secret revealed. He made me promise, long, long ago, that I would never tell his wife. I signed papers promising—"

"To hell with your promises, Mama! I want those papers! They are the evidence needed to free Will. It's been sixteen years, but they are solid proof. I will *sell* them to Ruby Maddox for enough money so you can get the surgery you need."

Her mother ignored her.

"Mama, tell me!" shouted Jeannie. "Where are the papers? Do it for *me,* Mama, do it for me!"

For the wrap party, the soundstage was lavishly decorated. The set was resurrected from the most popular special two-hour episode of *Motive* that had aired. Round tables, which seated eight, were ringed by flats painted like the ballroom of an eighteenth-century European palace. At one end, a platform had been set up for the band and in front of it, was a large portable parquet dance floor. Overhead, the lighting was muted pinks, and if one didn't look up to the hangar-high ceiling, the ballroom effect was complete.

The tables were cloaked in white linen tablecloths and on each was a magnificent centerpiece of pink, white, and mint-green flowers. A huge buffet table was spread with every imaginable gourmet delight. The caterers charged a handsome price, but it was well worth it.

About half of the people arrived in European aristocratic costume, as requested on the invitation. These were mostly members of the cast. More modest members of the crew came in suits and ties—which, they felt, was pushing the limit on getting dressed up.

Ruby avoided the dinner but knew she should make an appearance. She was not in costume and did not want to spend much time mingling. She felt too somber and didn't want to bring the guests' mood down. Richard, the director, who was dressed in a hunter-green frock coat and a white wig, stood on the platform, talking into the microphone and glibly recalling some of the funnier moments on the set over the past season.

He was a much better speaker than Ruby had imagined he would be, drawing laugh after laugh from the cast and crew assembled before him. He spotted Ruby and called her up to the stage. There was only a smattering of applause, as though the audience didn't know if they should clap or not. Graham had always evoked a huge applause when called to the stage and, with a huge grin on his face, had moved rapidly to the mike. In a sense, he had been father to them all.

Richard adjusted the microphone so Ruby could talk into it. She brushed her strawberry blond hair back over a shoulder with one hand before she spoke. "I'm very glad that all of you could come here tonight. I'm sure Graham would have been proud. We have completed a very successful season and are in development with over half of next season's episodes.

"As you know, *Motive* is my child, my initial concept for characters and theme. However, I could not have done any of it without the help of my husband, Graham, who believed in me. He gave me the moral and financial backing needed to make *Motive* the smash hit it is today. He believed in me. He believed in the show. But . . . let me tell you that he is not the only one responsible for making *Motive* a success. Each and every one of you have contributed mightily to the effort.

"I did not know everything there is to know about the production business when we first started shooting *Motive*. Today, I know a good deal more. I have all of you to thank. You were patient and helped me. You were my teachers. I can't tell you how much I value your loyalty to me, to *Motive*, to Maddox Productions.

"I propose a toast to the fantastic season we just had, to more success in the upcoming year, and to all of you. Graham would have been very proud. You were all part of a great family to him."

The words choked in the back of her throat, and Richard slipped a glass of champagne into her hand. She nodded and sipped the bubbling liquid. The applause that followed was warm and accompanied by a couple of approving whistles.

Stepping from the stage, she thought of more she could have said and wondered if she had said enough. Richard's wife gave her a big hug. The band got ready to play. Everyone was in a festive mood around her. They glowed. They thanked her. They told her how sorry they were about Graham. They told her how much they had enjoyed working for him. That he had been fair. That he had been brilliant.

Listening to them, she forgot how much of a bastard he had become in the last few months. Standing there in the midst of a crowd at a wrap party, it seemed as though nothing had changed. It could have been a year ago, when Graham had winked at her and officially announced that she would produce a new show called *Motive*.

Someone took her elbow. Garrett Gage, in a flamboyant crimson costume, doffed a plumed hat and bowed very low. "How are you, m'lady?" he asked.

Her eyes flitted around the people who stood near them. None of them seemed to be listening. "I'm well, Garrett. How are you? Enjoying the party?" She had seen a pretty, closely-clinging girl sitting with him.

"Yes," he smiled. "I want to know when I can see you again."

The question surprised her. She hardly remembered their one night together. "I don't think it would be a good idea to see each other again," she told him.

"Please, Ruby," he asked, his voice soft, his lips close to her ear. "I can't stop thinking about you."

They were flattering words, but she didn't believe them. "Garrett, it is not a wise idea at this moment in my life to see anyone. I prefer to keep our relationship solely on a business level."

Her words cut him. She could see the look of rejection on his face. He, the sexiest actor in America, was not used to being turned down.

An instant of pout showed around his mouth. "I need emotional support," he said. "You can't cast me adrift like that. It might affect my performance."

Threats now? She reached her hand behind his head and pulled his ear down to her mouth. "I don't think so, sweetheart," she told him. "You're under contract." And she kissed him very softly on his ear, sniffing the scent of his shampoo, telling herself she had made the right decision—to forget about their one night together.

The band hired to play the *Motive* wrap party was terrific. They played pop, big band, country-western, rock, and just about any request thrown their way. They were having so much fun that they almost forgot to take their break. But not quite.

"We'll be back in a few minutes," announced the leader.

Margi, sitting at her table, was very bored. She and Denny were practically the only ones there without dates. Somehow, she couldn't bring herself to consider the makeup artist, even though he was a good friend, a *date.* Tony and Glory were smooching and holding hands. She was happy for them, but boy, oh boy, with the difference in their ages, it would never last. Two of her hairdressing assistants and their boyfriends were also at her table. Denny had been there, but he had wandered off and was engrossed in a conversation with the art director's date—a too-thin, too-blond young man who too clearly loved all the feathers he was bedecked in.

After the band's break, the leader announced he'd had a request for a member of the crew to sing. "Bobbi, formerly of Bobbi and the Sockettes," he said.

A shriek arose from Margi's throat. All eyes searched her out, and she put her hands over her face in embarrassment. She hadn't sung in front of a crowd in years.

It was one thing to sing at the top of her lungs in the car; it was another to get in front of co-workers who knew the meaning of the word *professional* and make an ass of herself. Who had put her up to it? There was only one person she could think of.

"Come on, come on, Margi," called her friends. "We want to hear you. Come on, Bobbi."

She hesitated, and from nowhere, a big hand enclosed hers and led her toward the stage. It was Bob. He looked back over his shoulder and grinned. She didn't think there was anything funny about it. She balked at the foot of the stage, but his powerful hands circled her petite waist and lifted her up there. The audience clapped and cheered. She glared down at Bob. How dare he humiliate her like this!

But he was smiling toothily. He blew her a kiss and stepped close to her. "I love you," he said gently.

She ignored him and turned her attention to the crowd. "I go back a few years," she explained. "Do any of you remember 'He's So Fine'?" She asked the band if they could back her up. They nodded and she took the microphone in hand. The lights dimmed on the dance floor and brightened on her. She seemed alone for the world to see and she sang her heart out. She looked for Bob as she sang, but he had disappeared into the shadows.

She sang three songs before the audience let her get off the stage. She felt exhilarated for the few minutes it took her to walk through the crowd back to her table. Everyone was saying how great she sang. Margi said "Thank you," over and over.

At her table, only Bob waited for her. Everyone else was dancing or making another sweep along the buffet table. She stopped short and bit her lip.

"Hi, baby," he said.

"Hi," she said, remaining standing and reaching for a cigarette and the lighter. Bob took the lighter from her hand and held a flame up to her cigarette.

"Sit next to me," he said.

"No," she replied, and plunked herself down two chairs over from him.

He immediately moved closer to her.

"I don't think what you did was very funny," she told him.

"You sang beautifully," he reassured her. "Everyone loved you. You haven't lost your touch. We gotta get you in a studio and cut a demo."

"Shut up, shut up," she said. It was hard for her to look at him. She had missed him. She had been worried about him. She was pissed off at him. "How dare you go away and not tell me where you were."

"I'm sorry, baby. I had a lot of things I had to work out."

"I went crazy with worry. With fear. I wasn't myself. Just wasn't myself. You deserted me." She stared at her hands and, for the first time, noticed the signs of age on them. The texture and thickness of her fingers, the wrinkles. They were not the hands of a twenty-year-old. It was depressing.

"I didn't mean to abandon you. It was an awful thing I had to face up to—not being able to have sex anymore. Not being able to satisfy you. How could I keep you if I couldn't take care of you?" he asked earnestly.

"Where did you go, Bob?"

"I went to a special clinic to get help."

She was afraid to ask the next question. "What did they say?"

He took the cigarette from her hand and laid it in the ashtray. He pressed her hand between his two. It was hard to say the words. "I'm a little better, but I'm not one hundred percent."

She reached forward and stroked his head, half balding, half gray-haired. She knew his virility meant a lot to him. It had meant a lot to their marriage. However, she had realized since he had been gone, that wasn't all their marriage consisted of.

"It doesn't matter, Bob. I'd take you no matter what percent you are sexually. That's not as important as all the years we've had together. Just to have you back with me, living with me, will satisfy me one hundred percent." Tears welled in her eyes, and she dabbed the corner of a napkin under each one to blot up the liquifying mascara.

"Are you sure, Margi?" he asked. "I've thought it over. You're a woman with a strong sexual appetite. I couldn't live knowing you gave that up to be with me."

A sly grin came across Margi's face. "Bob, I would never worry that *you* couldn't satisfy *me*. You're the best lover in this whole damn world. Are you sure it will be all right if *you* aren't satisfied every time?"

"Baby, I've got to learn to live with it. I'll get better. The doctors think I'll get better."

He pulled her into his lap and put his great arms around her. She laid her face against his shoulder and shut her eyes. He smelled of man and soap and cigarette smoke.

"Don't ever again put me through what I went through," she said. "I went crazy without you, Bob. Crazy."

"I heard." He patted the top of her head and chuckled.

"Now what's so damn funny?"

"Just thinking of the story you told the cops." He laughed out loud.

"I didn't think it was very funny," she said, stiffening and trying to break out of his hold.

"Baby, baby, come here." He drew her back to his chest. "It's kind of cute, looking back in retrospect. If you're going to fess up to a hit-and-run auto accident, you'd better know what kind of car the other guy was driving. Graham Maddox never drove a Ford and he never drove a white car. His wife drives the white car, but that's a Mercedes. And the part of Mulholland Drive where you claimed the accident took place was only off by five miles." He chuckled again.

"It's not funny," she repeated.

"What a temper you've got. I know you concocted that story just 'cause you were mad and were trying to get my attention. But you forget vital details—like facts—when you're angry." He grinned ear to ear.

"Just don't go taking off again so I can't make mistakes like that."

"That's fine with me. Fine with me. In fact, I don't really want to stick around here anymore, do you? I can think of a nice motel down in San Diego where I'd like to keep you up all night."

"You can?"

"Yep. And I even have reservations."

"You do?"

"Yeah."

She kissed him softly on his mouth, his mustache bristly, his chin unshaven. He ran his tongue over her teeth.

"What if I can't wait till we get to San Diego, Bob?"

Glory edged through the wrap party crowd on her way back from the powder room. She hoped the wet spot on her skirt would dry quickly. During the entire party, if only one piece of three-layered white cake with gooey frosting had to fall off a plate, why did it have to land on her? She hadn't bumped into the guy. She had been carefully negotiating the crowd with a glass of champagne in each hand, and this chunk of cake came flying through the air and hit her dress, which she had rented specially for the occasion, which was extra fancy and had cost extra. The guy hadn't even said he was sorry he'd dropped it. In fact, he hadn't even noticed.

She had put the champagne on the table in front of Tony and hurriedly excused herself. She had forgotten to take her purse, and when she looked in the mirror, she wished she could brush her hair and put on some lipstick. Her mother would think she looked awfully pale.

Finally reaching her table, she found no one sitting

there and all the champagne glasses empty. So, she sat staring at the dancing couples, wishing her glass of champagne hadn't been guzzled because she sure could use a little now. She looked around for Tony but couldn't see him. He had told her he didn't dance unless he was real drunk, and these days, he had promised her he wouldn't drink so much. Maybe she could get him out there on a slow one. She shook out the wet dress and tried to decide how noticeable the spot was.

"May I have this next dance?"

She turned around to see Denny looking over her shoulder in a most perplexed manner. He wore a beautiful costume. The coat was velvet and his favorite #3 medium blue color.

"I'd love to," she said, standing and forgetting the dress came to the floor. She stumbled over the hem. "I'm hopeless," she cried in exasperation. "I've just had it!" She started to sit down again.

"Come on," coaxed Denny, taking her arms. "You're beautiful tonight. Your blusher is perfect like that. Round and low on the cheek. It makes your face look very thin."

She turned and looked at her rear end. "Wish you could do something for that," she grinned.

The song was slow and flowing. Denny was a good dancer. Glory loved to dance and it never occurred to her that she could be clumsy on a dance floor. The music felt like a part of her, and each step, each turn, was pure delight. She wondered if Denny danced with men like this, but she was too embarrassed to ask him.

"I was worried," he confided in her, "that Jeff would be here tonight. I heard he might be coming. He's the agent for the guest star that appeared on the last episode we shot. If Jeff had shown up, I'd have left immediately."

"Don't say that, Denny. You can't mean that. Don't let him run you out of a place." She tried to dance closer to him, to give him a little assurance.

"I couldn't stand it, I just couldn't," said Denny. "I've

been fine, just as long as I haven't had to see him."

"Are you taking a vacation?"

"I'm off to Tahiti on Monday. For a month. Touring through Japan. Maybe even Australia. *Australia*'s very tentative. I plan on returning a new man. And you never know, maybe I'll meet a handsome stranger."

"Wish I could go with you," said Glory enviously. "I've never been to any of those places. I get to stay here and work."

"But you should be happy," said Denny. "Ruby has bought your *Motive* script. It may be rewritten, but you'll get payment for the idea and first draft. It's a step in the door. You'll have a screen credit."

Glory smiled. It was true and she couldn't believe it. Tony had refused when she wanted to share the credit with him. "You've done all the work," he said. "You've written it, revised it. I wasn't any inspiration. It's your project. You take the credit."

She had pleaded with him to take part of the remuneration. "No, doll. You did this one on your own. The next one . . . I'll help you with the next one."

Glory swayed in time with Denny, and he spun her around and around. "I didn't know that Margi was a singer," she said.

"You won't see her doing it very often. I think that's what she wanted to do back when she was in high school."

"Bob really surprised her," said Glory. "He seems nice. He winked at me and he drank a shot with Tony."

"They're a perfect couple in their own way," said Denny. He sounded wistful.

"Are you lonesome, Denny?"

He smiled. "I'd take you home if you weren't already taken."

She blushed. "I thought we've figured we'll just turn out as good friends."

"Even friends get lonely. I hope you'll be happy with Tony."

She hadn't considered being anything but. "Why do you say that?"

"I don't want to see you hurt. You're sweet. You're young. And you'll always trust people—no matter how old you get."

"It isn't wrong to trust people, is it, Denny?" she asked.

He didn't answer. The song ended and he led her back to her table. Tony was waiting, uncomfortable in his suit. He'd already taken off the tie and loosened his collar.

Denny kissed Glory's cheek. "Maybe I can have another dance later," he told her before leaving her alone with Tony.

She sat next to Tony and he handed her a full glass of champagne. "Drink up," he said. "If I get you a little tipsy, maybe I can take advantage of you."

"I don't have to be tipsy for that," she told him, leaning forward and nuzzling his throat with her nose.

"Drink up anyways, girl. Cut loose for once. Have a good time. We're here to party. That's what we work so hard for—so we can enjoy our spare time off." He slugged down the contents of the glass in one gulp and stomped his feet in time to the band.

Glory smiled. He was very manly, and she wanted to feel safe with him. Everyone knew she was his date. They were a couple, an item. His masculinity made her feel soft inside. She wanted him to hold her and hold her.

"I'm in love with you," she told him.

"I love you, too," he replied, tapping on the table, not losing a beat.

She sipped the champagne and looked around the room for Denny. She felt more herself with Denny than with anyone else. Was that important? But she didn't see Denny, and she knew she was going home with Tony.

Sondra sat toward the stage, at Richard's table. She

had no date, but it didn't bother her. She preferred to be there alone. That way, she could speak with whom she wanted and leave when she pleased. It only annoyed her that no one asked her to dance.

They probably all still thought of her as a lesbian. She only wished they could see her with Will. She and Will made a fine couple; both lean and tall, she pale blond, he rich brown, both preferring to keep their eyes open and their mouths shut.

No one asked her to dance, and she stared haughtily at all of them. What did it matter? She was going home soon, anyway. Away from them and all their bullshit and phony camaraderie. They could all be great friends today, then lose touch if someone was fired or laid off, then forget all about their wonderful "friendship" until a few years down the line when they'd bump into each other and talk about how great the old days had been. It was all bullshit. If you didn't feel sincerely friendly toward someone, why fake it? She couldn't stand the thought of wallowing in insincerity. She did her job. She did it well. In the end, that was all that mattered. To hell with them if they didn't want to dance with her.

The wardrobe department had found a lovely dress for her to wear. It was high-waisted, tight-bodiced, and fell in wide cuts of black and white from the waistline. Somehow she had managed to fluff and pile her baby-fine hair on top of her head and spray it rigidly into place. She wore makeup. A choker of rhinestones glittered at her throat. She looked so dramatic and different that a number of people came up to her and told her they didn't even recognize her.

"I didn't know she could look like a real woman" was the comment she overheard from one person who had turned away from her.

There wasn't a damn thing she had to prove to them. She was a woman. She just didn't see the necessity of going around as bouncy femininity, flirting with all the guys to uphold their masculine egos. What a pain they all were.

She was nervous about her hair. To avoid drawing attention to that fact, she would feel the dangling rhinestone earrings, then move her fingertips to lightly tap her hair and make sure it was still in place. She had dressed for Will. Dressed carefully. She had hoped that at the last minute he would call and say he was accompanying her. But he hadn't called.

Will was uncertain about going to the wrap party. Even though Jeannie's testimony and evidence had freed him, many people on the lot were still loyal to Graham and believed Will was to blame. He would not get a warm welcome if he came to the party.

"Do you really care what all those phonies think about you?" questioned Sondra.

He pondered for a moment. "No, but I do care what they think of you, and of my mother, and of Maddox Productions. Just because Graham was, privately, an asshole to me during most of my life, he was brilliant professionally. No one gives a shit if he'd had a longstanding feud with one stepson. Historically, you'll find more stories of hate between stepparents and stepchildren than you will find of love."

"I wish you'd go to the party. They don't blame you for Graham's death. It has officially been declared an accident."

"I wish it were as easy to erase suspicion from peoples' minds. I can't go."

His reasoning made sense and yet she felt uneasy inside. She told him how much she loved him, but she didn't think he wanted her love. He didn't want responsibilities. He didn't want relationships that would tie him up, tie him down. She knew that she would fight with everything she had to keep him. However, she didn't know if it would work. He would have to *want* to stay.

The psychic bond that connected her to Will would not be still. Uneasiness roiled in her gut. She tried to ignore it. She tried not to think about him at all. But the uneasiness kept working inside her, like a boat bumping against the rubber tires in its slip.

A guard tapped her shoulder. "There's a guy out there who says he wants to talk to you." He pointed his thumb toward the side door. "Will you be all right, Miss Prescott?"

"Thank you," she said, rising. "Don't worry about me."

As the soundstage door closed behind her, it shut out the noises of the loud, merry party. She was in an alley between soundstages, and silence surrounded her. It took a few moments for her eyes to adjust to the darkness. Overhead, suspended between the two buildings, was a bridge of stars.

She became aware of Will sitting on his motorcycle—first by the smell of the machine's oil and gas, and then by the man's presence.

"You are beautiful," he said. "I wanted to see you. Just one more time."

Her heart was stricken. "What do you mean, *one more time*?"

"It's not a good time for me to stick around the City of the Angels."

She could smell his leather jacket. "You can't go away," she said simply.

"I've got to," he replied.

"You're running away."

"Maybe so. But I need some breathing room. Thinking room."

She knew his mind was made up. She could hear it in his attitude. "Can I go with you?" she asked.

"What? Fuck up your career for some crummy biker? I wouldn't let you."

"You're not crummy," she protested. Instead of the tears she expected, anger began to foam at her mouth. "I'm sick of hearing that you're not worthy of this or that! That you'll never be a success! Goddamn you!! *I'm* not Graham Maddox. *I* believe in you. You can't go through life thinking you're crummy just because Graham Maddox always said so. You don't have to live the life he always said you'd live. Forget what he said!

"Damn you!" she continued. "*I* was so damn bitter before I met you and now I don't know what the word *bitter* means. Damn you. I was safe. Alone, but safe. I never thought I would love another man in my entire life. Scotty and I would make it alone. That's how I saw things. Then, damn you, you came along."

Will thought, And damn you, Sondra, you came along.

He dismounted, swinging a long leg over his bike, and walked to her. She was one of the hardest women he had ever met. It was difficult to find anything vulnerable about her. She was strong. Very strong. It was ironic to think so, too, as she stood there so physically frail and feminine in the long dress. She stood at her full height, afraid of nothing. If only he had the courage that she had.

They stood on a thin, still strip of reality that was embraced by the soundstage worlds of make-believe. That make-believe encased all she thought of as phoniness; the reality held all he thought of as courage.

"I'm willing to make a sacrifice to have you, Will. I know who you are way beneath all your tough-guy pretense. You know how I know? Because I act just as tough on the outside. And it's more bullshit. It's protection. Against what? Against every asshole in this town they call Hollywood who'll take advantage of you. On one level, my career means everything to me, but on another, it's pure bullshit. I'll walk away from it, Will. I'll walk away and never look back if that's what it takes to prove I love you."

Maybe he didn't want to be loved; because *being* loved asked that you return the love. He was so afraid to do that. If you love, you risk losing that love. He didn't want to dive into that bottomless glacial lake of genuine love and, when he was in the middle, be engulfed by utter blackness, unable to find the shore.

"Will," said Sondra, hands at her sides, shoulders drooping a little, "I can't let you walk out of my life. It might be easier for you, but it's not easier for me."

He knew it would be easier if he could act out of anger; but he could summon none. How can you be angry when all that's offered is love?

"Can I go away for a while?" he asked. "I promise to call. If you want, I'll even promise to come back."

She couldn't bear to let him go. There was no guarantee that he would ever come back. She wanted to fall on her knees, her arms around him, and beg him to stay, beg him not to leave her barren. She had given him her soul, and he would take it with him. She was afraid . . . afraid if she let him go she would never see him again.

The world was immense and it was so easy for a solitary person to disappear. It was the way life seemed to go. People passed through continually. A few stayed around, the rest were gone. Untraceable. Irretrievable. Except through memory. But gone. And there was no way to force them to come back.

As there was no way to force Will to stay.

She looked up into his face. Beyond it were the stars. In that moment, they were the only things that were perfect. Because they were absolute.

She wanted to kiss him. To show that her love was as absolute as the stars. She wanted a memory.

"Go," she told him. "Go."